I0589369

Also by Shireal Renee

Me & My
Man's Wife
A Testimony of Deliverance

SHIREAL RENEE

ByReneeVisions©
publishing house

By Renee Visions, Publishing House
Bloomfield, CT 06002
ByReneeVisions.com

Printed in the United States of America

First Edition: July 2016

Inside Layouts by: FourteenG Marketing Agency.

By Renee Visions, Publishing House is a division of By Renee Visions, LLC, The By Renee Visions Publishing name and logo is a trademark of By Renee Visions, LLC.

By Renee Visions provides its authors for speaking events. To find our more go to www.byreneevisions.com or email info@byreneevisions.com.

The publisher is not responsible for websites (or their content) that are not owned by the publisher.

Library of Congress Cataloging-in-Publication Data
Shireal Renee Lewis, February 2015
    Me & My Man's Wife / Shireal Renee Lewis. – First Edition.
            pages ; cm
ISBN 978-0-9854664-1-1 (hardback) – ISBN 978-0-9854664-2-8 (paperback) –
ISBN 978-0-9854664-3-5 (e-book)

THIS BOOK IS DEDICATED

To my grandmother, Nada, who we lost in 2014. She was one of the strongest women I've ever known. I know it's because of the strength I inherited from her, that I've been able to overcome every obstacle that I've faced in my life. I am so blessed and thankful to God to have known, loved and learned from such a powerful, courageous woman.

ALSO:

To my friend Ajamu,
Thank you for being a light to guide me out of a dark place.
I love you and wish you were here to see what emerged from the darkness.

Me & My Man's Wife

CASEY

Why do people always blame falling in love as a reason to start
a war? I fell in love once. I sat in my bedroom window holding
a letter from my "love," wondering if I should open it or not.
My love story was not sunshine and roses. It was reckless
and full of heartache. I never even saw it coming. I've always
believed God had a plan for my life, but getting involved with
a married man wasn't a part of that plan! Then I heard a word
the other day and it said, "God doesn't promise you that you
won't have to walk through the fire, he promises you that you
won't have to do it alone."

As I sat in the room where I grew up, I thought back
to my childhood and remembered when I first got saved. The
church was as hot as an incinerator. It didn't make it any better
that we were shoved into a hole in the wall. The drummer beat
on the drums, and the four oldest women in the church jumped
around dancing all over the place.

My mom and I were always visiting churches, but that
time it seemed like we would join this one because we were
related to everyone in the church except the preacher and his
family. I liked Christ Tabernacle. I felt like I belonged there. It
wasn't just because my whole family was there; it was because
even at the age of twelve, Pastor Mosley had a way of making
me understand what he was talking about. Being under his
leadership made me want to get closer to God the way that had
the older women dancing around and shouting.

The Sunday I got saved, I found myself wanting to feel
God's presence more than I ever had before. I was missing
my big sister Candice. Since she moved to New Jersey, I only

saw her in the summer. She wasn't going to visit this summer because she was about to have another baby and had been placed on strict bed rest. I was happy I was going to be an aunt again, but it was bittersweet since I was missing her.

As I felt the cloud of sadness rest on my shoulders, I heard Pastor Mosley's voice sing through, interrupting my thoughts. "When you feel like you are all alone and the weights of sorrow are holding you down, all you have to do is call on the name of Jesus, and he will send the Holy Ghost to comfort you." I closed my eyes and followed his instructions. "Just call out: 'Jesus'!"

I whispered, "Jesus, Jesus, Jesus." Keeping my eyes sealed shut, I kept calling out 'Jesus.' I wanted the Holy Ghost, and I wanted him badly. I kept calling, *Jesus, Jesus, Jesus* until I felt the spirit of the Holy Ghost rush over me like a flood, and I jumped up forgetting about the overwhelming heat inside the church and started dancing and shouting along with the older women.

Sitting here today, surrounded by memories of my childhood, I'm reminded of that innocent cry out for Jesus and the gift of the Holy Ghost that saved me. I looked at the letter, in my hand, from my ex and was immediately filled with fear of what it said. I was afraid of the memories that would come rushing back of the love triangle that had taken me so far away from my relationship with God. Knowing that fear was not of God, I decided I had to read the letter. I never would have known that the encounter I had as a child with the Holy Ghost would continue to guide and protect me in the darkest moments of my life. I mustered up all the courage I could find, took a deep breath, and opened the letter.

Chapter One
July

One year earlier…

CASEY

I stepped off the greyhound, grabbed my two huge Louis Vuitton suitcases, and dragged them across the floor of Grand Central Station. As usual I'd stuffed the bags to capacity knowing that my 5'2" frame would struggle the whole way from Connecticut into the city. I pushed the bags onto the escalator, wishing my sister had met me at the terminal gate. Instead, she complained to me about parking in the city and guaranteed she'd be out front when my bus arrived. As I stepped off the escalator, I found myself overwhelmed with excitement knowing that this was the beginning of my claim to fame. However, it was bittersweet having to drop out of college my senior year at Georgetown because my parents ran out of money and I was maxed out on loans. Now twenty-one years old, I, Casey Renee Gardner, had finally gotten my father's permission to move to New York. I would enroll in The New York Academy of Dramatic Arts under the stage name Casey Rea. The timing couldn't have been better, since my sister Candice was separated from her husband. She was now living in Harlem, raising my three nieces on her own, so she was excited to have someone along to help her with the girls.

As I maneuvered over to the automatic doors, I could feel someone's eyes following me. The stranger sized me up. I could feel him looking at my perfectly proportioned frame. He scanned my jet-black hair from the top of my head to the middle of my back, wishing it wasn't covering what my halter-top left exposed. I could feel his eyes burning through the skintight jeans I wore despite the summer heat.

As I lugged my bags across the floor, the staring stranger began to approach me.

"Excuse me, can I help you with that?" the tall, attractive man asked. I almost ignored him, but his bright white smile distracted me. His hair was low-cut and spinning with waves. A man with hair like that and a sparkling smile was my weakness.

"Yes, please—thank you," I answered, mesmerized by his smile. He picked up both of the fifty-pound bags with ease and walked with me outside.

Candice was nowhere in sight.

"I'll take them from here," I said reaching for my bags. "My sister is always late."

He placed the bags down by his side and then extended me his hand. "I'm Tony. But my close friends call me Ty."

I giggled. "Oh really, so I guess I should call you Ty than. I'm Casey," I purred out as he gripped my tiny hand in his.

"First time in the city?" Ty asked.

"Nope, what makes you think that?"

He chuckled. "You have that eager look in your eyes— like a tourist."

"I'm a tourist of the world!" I laughed. "Just in love with life!" I pushed the hair aside that was falling in my face. His eyes followed as my hair swept over my shoulder, exposing my ear and neck. He didn't hide his attraction well.

I heard a loud shrieking come around the corner. Beep, beep! Candice's black Mercedes SUV blared as it turned onto Forty-Second Street, with Candice hanging out the window frantically waving and shouting my name. "Casey! Casey I'm here!" she screamed as she came to an abrupt stop in front of the Station.

She jumped out of the car, with her arms flapping open. "Casey, baby!" she said, throwing her arms around me and smothering my cheeks with kisses. Her excitement was contagious. I embraced her back, planting big kisses on her cheeks. I was shocked as I took my first real look at her. I hadn't seen her in three years, and since then she'd lost so much weight. She grabbed my hips and held me at arms' length.

I raised my eyebrows, admiring her new shape. "You look great!"

"Thank you, girl! I lost sixty-five pounds on Weight Watchers. Where are your bags? I'm double parked," Candice blurted out all in one breath.

Even when she was heavier, Candice always had a great figure. You would never have believed she had three kids. She was almost a foot taller than me, around 5'10" with flawlessly smooth deep cocoa-brown skin. She wore her hair in a perfectly cut bob with Chinese bangs. That paired with her weight loss, she was more stunning than ever before.

Candice spotted my Louis Vuitton luggage and instantly recognized the "off to college" gift she'd surprised me with the summer I got accepted to Georgetown. The truth is, Candice only said *"I love you,"* through very expensive gifts. This was how I ended up in New York: she volunteered to take me in and pay for me to go to Film School. She would have paid for Georgetown if she could've afforded it, but she was living on a smaller budget these days, since she and her husband Bruce were going though a nasty divorce, and he was the primary breadwinner in their family. I was lucky film school was thousands of dollars less than one semester at Georgetown.

Candice rushed towards my bags, snatching them, almost knocking Ty over. He caught his balance and grabbed the bags before Candice could. The Candice Storm came to an abrupt stop as she noticed my fine new acquaintance for the first time.

"I got this, ladies," Ty said smoothly.

Candice stared unimpressed at Ty's handsome self.

She cut her eyes up at him. "Well hurry up and get them in the car. We gotta go," Candice said turning towards the car and motioning for Ty to follow her. I stood there in awe of how my dark, chocolate knight took control of my overbearing sister. Ty easily lifted the luggage into the trunk of the SUV and closed it back. Candice looked him up and down.

"Casey didn't tell me she was bringing a friend," she spat out, defensively throwing her arms across her chest.

"I … I'm not …" Ty began to answer.

I jumped to his rescue. "He's not with me. He saw me struggling with my bags and offered to help."

"Oh, well, thank you," Candice said, waving him off and rushing back towards the car. She jumped into the driver's seat and signaled me to hurry along.

"Thank you for carrying my bags." I started towards the car. "It was nice meeting you."

"Can I call you?" Ty blurted out. My first instinct was to say, *hell yes,* but then he flashed that sinful smile at me again, and I knew, this was not the time in my life to get involved with Ty or anyone like him. I was here to prove to my father I was going to be an Oscar-winning actress, and I couldn't let anyone or anything jeopardize that. So, I took a deep breath, forced my lustful thoughts far into the back of my mind, and slowly shook my head no. "I'm sorry, now is just not a good time. But thanks again." I jumped into the car before he could rebut. As soon as my door was shut, Candice was dashing off down the street into the cluttered midday New York City traffic.

The noise of the city filled the car: beeping horns, yelling cab drivers, and millions of conversations. Everyone had a style, every corner a different culture, every block a different smell, and any restaurant choice you could imagine from all around the world was here! I was in love. The heaven I'd heard described in church had to be something like New York City. The breeze from the open window caressed my face as I closed my eyes and started to become one with all the sounds and smells of the city. In the middle of my private escape, Candice rolled up all the windows in the car and turned on the air conditioner.

"So how you been?" she asked, taking her eyes off of the road to look at me.

"Now, great! I'm so happy to be here." I grinned from ear to ear.

"I'm happy you're here too. I need some adult company around the house. Those kids are getting on my nerves. Tate is fifteen now and has a terrible attitude. I swear one of these days I am gon' knock her clear down all twelve steps of the brownstone."

I just shook my head. I'd heard Candice complain about Tate plenty of times before, and honestly, I usually agreed with Tate. But I couldn't tell her that. The older I got, the more I understood that Candice had a way of manipulating people to feel sorry for her. She acted as if the world owed her something. I never noticed it as a kid, but as I got older, I noticed the disrespect that she had towards my parents' marriage. She never got over our father and her mother's divorce and blamed it on my mom. She always felt that my father left her and her mother high and dry. But my father tells the story completely different. Like they say, there's always three sides of a story, his side, her side and the truth. The facts are, Candice's mom and my dad ended up divorced, he married my mom, I came along, then Candice went to live with her mother.

The summer Candice graduated from Yale, she was supposed to be headed to Harvard Law but instead came home pregnant by someone who wanted nothing to do with her or the baby. She lived with us until Tate was born and by the fall of the next year, just as baby Tate learned to walk, Candice was off to Cambridge—taking half of my college fund with her. Leaving my parents the responsibility of raising Tate, which eventually became another drain of my college fund. This infuriated me.

I was used to being the apple of my parents' eyes, then a new baby was dropped in our home and suddenly everything was all about her. There were plenty of nights when I would pray that Tate would go back to live with Candice so I could have my parents to myself again. When I was in high school, she was a typical little sister, always doing things to annoy me. In the mornings when I was getting ready, she would hide my hairbrush. She was always snooping around my room—she drove me crazy. It wasn't until I went to college that I finally started to appreciate Tate. I missed her. She would write me letters at school and pick out candy she knew I liked for my care packages. I didn't find out that my parents had removed money from my college fund until my sophomore year at Georgetown. I was furious at them all over again! Candice paying for me to go to film school was not only a saving grace, it was retribution in my eyes.

Candice continued on her rant about the girls. "Daisy and Asia drive me crazy too. When did nine become the new nineteen and six the new sixteen? I feel like I'm in a house full of teenagers," she complained.

I let my mind drift away as I watched the numbers go

up on the West Side Highway: 112th Street, 114th, 118th—I could feel Harlem getting closer.

Candice interrupted my daydream. "Casey, now that you're here, you can sit down and talk some sense into Tate. She needs somebody to talk to."

"I talk to Tate everyday," I snapped. I was already getting annoyed of her complaining.

"I know you do, but now that you're here to reinforce what you say, she will really listen."

I rolled my eyes and looked back out the window. I decided it was too early to debate with her.

"Where are the girls at now?" I asked, changing the subject.

"Tate stayed home to wait for Aunt Caroline to drop off Daisy and Asia. She picks them up from camp for me when I have to work."

Aside from the rough patch of getting pregnant sooner than planned, Candice did well for herself. She met her husband Bruce Porter while she was interning at a law firm in Boston.

About a year after they met, Bruce made partner at his firm and was offered an opportunity to run an office in their Hoboken, New Jersey, location. Candice decided to drop out of law school and follow him to New Jersey. Bruce wanted her to stay and finish school, but Candice gave him an ultimatum, stating she may not be around in three years. So, Bruce married her and bought them a beautiful four-bedroom, three-and-a-half bath, two-story penthouse in Hoboken, with a balcony view of the Statue of Liberty. Candice landed a position at a major Investment firm on Wall Street as an accountant. They seemed happily married aside from Candice being spoiled and very hard to please. Bruce could deal with whatever Candice had to dish.

It wasn't until the year I was leaving for Georgetown

that Bruce and Candice got into a really big fight that ended up with the cops being involved, restraining orders, a legal separation and split custody of the girls. After ten years of marriage and two kids together, no one saw it coming.

That's how Tate ended up in Harlem. Candice said she was giving up men and dedicating her life to her girls. So she bought a brownstone for her and the girls in NYC closer to her job. Tate was devastated.

When we pulled onto 122nd, identical brownstone houses lined both sides of the street. Candice stopped in front of a beautiful two-story brownstone just like in the movies, with a brick staircase leading up to historic double doors and floor-to-ceiling windows on either side of the house. My body tingled with excitement. I was finally in New York, a place I'd visited in my dreams over and over again. I'd arrived.

As soon as I stepped out of the car, the double doors of the brownstone flew open and a herd of girls came running at me. Tate, Daisy, and Asia dashed down the stairs, Asia leading the pack with her arms spread wide open.

"Auntie Casey! Auntie Casey!" she squeaked.

Daisy rushed close behind her. When she got to the bottom of the stairs, she lunged at me with all of her nine-year-old body weight, enough to tip us all backwards and fall into the SUV. Tate stopped watching the horrific scene and began laughing hysterically.

"Geeze guys, knock her over, why don't ya!"

Daisy and Asia continued to hug me and shout out my name.

"Auntie Casey!"

Asia was the spitting image of her father, and a dream child: very smart, very articulate, and sweet as can be.

Daisy favored Candice; she was tall and skinny with curves. At nine she already reached my shoulders in height.

"Auntie Casey, I missed you so much," Daisy

announced. "I am so happy you're staying with us now. We are going to have so much fun."

Tate grabbed Asia out of my arms and placed her down on the sidewalk. Then she wrapped her arms around me, and I squeezed her back. We held each other in a long embrace, both of us happy to be together again. We were raised together, and only six years apart, we were sisters at heart. Tate had grown up a lot since I saw her last summer. It seemed like just the other day I was putting ponytails in her hair. She stood about five feet tall, with big brown eyes and an innocent face. Although her hips were just starting to push through, she already had that curvy shape like Candice.

Candice removed the bags from the trunk, setting them on the sidewalk. "Alright, hug in the house. Let's get these bags upstairs."

Daisy and Asia ran over to tackle one of the bags together. "I got it. I'm the oldest," Daisy protested, pushing Asia out her way. As she struggled to pull the heavy bag up the stairs, Tate pulled it out of her grasp.

"*I'm* the oldest," Tate said matter-of-factly. Then she turned to me and cupped her free hand through my arm, smiled and said, "Let me show you to our room."

Candice carried the other bag up, with Daisy and Asia putting their hands on it pretending to assist her.

When I walked through the door, I was excited to see Aunt Caroline sitting in a rocking chair in front the window. She flashed a warm smile at me as I entered the room.

"Come over here baby and give Auntie some suga," she said, opening up her arms and waving me over.

I rushed over to her and gave her a big hug.

"Oh, my baby." She planted a big kiss on my cheek. "Turn around, look at that behind," she belted out, smacking me across my backside.

I jerked away with embarrassment. "Auntie!"

"Girl you know you got your father's genes. All us women got these big behinds back here." She motioned for me to look at her butt, showing off our common family trait.

"I am so happy you're here," she said. "You're going to be a big help to your sister."

"Yes, I know. She's helping me too."

"You are blessed to have a sister who can afford to send you to that school you want to go to. All children are not so lucky to have someone help them out like that."

"I'm very lucky."

"That's why you have to thank God for all his blessings, and help her out as much as you can around here."

"Yes, I will Auntie."

"Especially because I am getting too old to have to keep driving back and fourth from Jersey to Harlem everyday. I get tired quicker now, you know."

"Yes, ma'am, I know."

That night Candice cooked steak, potatoes and corn for dinner. We all sat around the table and Aunt Caroline reminded us to all join hands and say our prayers before eating.

"I know ya'll were raised right. Come on, let's pray," Aunt Caroline instructed as she held out her hands. "Lord grant this blessing for this food we are about to receive nourishing our bodies for Christ sake, amen."

"Amen," we all repeated.

Candice laughed. "Remember Casey would always get in trouble for starting to eat before we prayed? Then Daddy would pop her on the hand as she stuffed a roll in her mouth."

I squinted my eyes at Candice. "Um, no need to bring that up."

"Asia does that all the time." Tate giggled. "She must get it from Casey."

"Oh, don't go there, Tate. You don't want me bringing

up old stories about you, like the time you got your hair caught in the frame of the daybed and we had to cut it out. It took six months for that bald spot to grow in."

Everyone—except Tate—burst out laughing.

"That was just mean, Casey." Tate frowned.

Aunt Caroline couldn't stop laughing. "It was quite funny," she muttered through breaks in her laughter.

We spent hours reminiscing and laughing at all the craziness that went on in our family. Aunt Caroline filled me in on all the drama going on with my family in Jersey, pointing out that she was the sane one that opted to stay out of "all they mess." After dinner, Aunt Caroline gathered her things and headed back home.

Candice put Daisy and Asia to bed while Tate and I cleaned the kitchen. As Tate loaded the dishwasher, I walked over to the window and peered down the street.

"You're going to love Harlem, girl," Tate said, shooting me a wink.

"I know I am."

"And the men, I think they're special grown here." Tate laughed.

"I didn't know you were into gardening now."

"I'm into anything that grows straight up and green."

"I guess your mother was right—I'm going to have to keep my eyes on you."

"Keep up with me if you can," Tate said, letting out a belt of laughter.

"Don't worry, I can, little girl."

"Tomorrow I'll take you down 125th. I hope you have some money because you're gonna want to buy something."

"I already know. That's why I need to stay away from any shopping areas—it's no good for me."

"Sorry to inform you sis, but you have to leave Harlem all together if you want to stay away from shopping, and nothing here is good for you."

It was crazy how much Tate learned in the year she'd been living here. And it was amazing how she knew, before I did, the kind of trouble I'd get into in Harlem.

Chapter Two

August

CASEY

I woke up the next morning feeling stiff. I was not use to sharing a bed with anyone. Since Candice only had a three-bedroom, Daisy and Asia shared a room, and I had to curl up with Tate. Her room was a decent size. She had a full sized canopy bed with sheer blue drapes that hung across the top. I guess blue was her new favorite color because everything in her room was blue: the curtains, bedspread, her stereo, even the lamps.

I crawled out of the bed and stretched out my arms and legs trying to relieve myself of some of the cramps. I woke up hot and sticky. I could feel sweat forming on my forehead. I tiptoed out the door and snuck around the corner towards the bathroom. The door swung open as I reached for the handle. Tate stood wrapped in a towel with a shower cap on her head.

"You finally up?" she said, twisting her neck and rolling her eyes.

"What time is it?"

"Almost one o'clock!"

"One o'clock!"

"Yes, you were knocked out; I was trying to be quiet so I wouldn't wake you."

"Where is everybody?"

"My mother is at work and my sisters are at camp. My mother said that we have to pick them up from camp now so Aunt Caroline won't have to drive out here and get them."

"I don't have a car. How are we going to pick them up?"

"We can walk."

"If it's walking distance, why haven't you been picking them up?"

"Mommy and Auntie didn't want me walking all the way down the boulevard by myself. You know they treat me like a baby." Tate pushed by me headed for the room.

"So where are you going now?" I asked.

"I was just going to walk down the street and get something to eat. Everything in here has to be cooked—unless *you* want to cook."

"Actually, I'm coming with you. Give me ten minutes."

I rushed into the bathroom to get ready. Harlem was calling me.

When I walked down the stairs, Tate's mouth dropped.

"What are you wearing?"

"A dress," I said, spinning around in my hot pink halter dress and flat gladiator sandals.

"For what?"

"I want to make a good first impression."

"You're going to make an impression alright," she joked.

I pranced past Tate in full diva mode. I stopped at the front door and spun around to face her: "Jealousy doesn't look good on you, sweetheart." I smirked then walked out the door. Tate rolled her eyes and followed me outside.

I felt like I was in a dream walking through Harlem.

After five minutes, I'd already decided where I was going to get my hair done, what my favorite shoe store was, who had the best outfits, and where to find my favorite style of Pumas. I was in fashion paradise.

"I have a surprise for you," Tate announced.

"What?"

Tate grabbed my arm and started pulling me down the street. "Come on, you'll see."

After walking about a block, we stopped in front of a barbershop. Cutting hair in the first chair near the window was my cousin Kayden. He was a few years older than me. We used to hang out together every summer when I would visit Aunt Caroline, so we were pretty close.

"I forgot he worked out here," I said, jumping up with excitement. "Tate, let's surprise him. You go in first, and then I'll sneak in."

Tate let out her signature giggle and agreed to the plan. Kayden was finishing up a cut when Tate walked in.

"Hey Kay," she said with a big smile on her face.

"What you doing down here?" he asked.

"I need some money." Tate stuck out her hand.

"The only time you come down here is when you need money."

"I come down here everyday."

"You need money everyday!" Kayden joked.

"Whatever!" Tate stood there, stoic, holding her hand out.

I crept in and snuck up behind Kayden grabbing him by his waist and childishly tickling him. Kayden squirmed around laughing hysterically.

"Who the hell?" Kayden chocked out.

He swung around to find me smiling from ear to ear with my arms stretched out for him to hug me.

"KAYYY!" I screamed.

"CAY!" He returned the excitement grabbing me and picking me up off of my feet. Kayden put me down in front of him, glowing with excitement.

"What you doing here, girl?"

"I'm staying with Candice now, starting film school next month."

"You have to put me in one of your movies."

"You know I will! How you been?"

"I been good, business is good, you know, I'm happy."

"I can't believe it's been a year since the last time I saw you."

"Yes, let's not talk about that …" Kayden burst into laughter.

"What happens in Vegas, stays in Vegas; your secrets are safe with me," I assured him.

"You weren't even supposed to be there. You're always following me around." Kayden protested.

I was known for hanging out with the boys. But what the boys didn't know was that I liked it because I never paid for anything.

Tate apparently knew everyone in the shop because they were all asking her about me.

I should've been prepared for all the attention when I left that house in this dress. I jumped into Diva mode, flashed my winning smile, and gave a small princess wave.

"Hi, I'm Casey," I toyed.

Kayden interjected, "This—my *little* cousin from Connecticut—she just moved out here."

The barber next to him smiled at me with his eyes, and replied to Kayden, "She doesn't look little to me."

With as much bass in his voice as he could muster up, Kayden turned to face his co-worker and said, "She is MY little cousin, no matter how she look to you."

"Chill man. I was just trying to introduce myself."

I put my hand on Kayden's arm, "Relax Kay, he's just being nice."

"Don't get too nice," Kayden warned.

"I'm Chancy," the barber introduced himself.

"Nice to meet you." I smiled.

Chancy smiled back. "Nice to meet you." He chuckled looking over at Kay.

Tate walked over to us with her arms crossed over her chest.

"So are we going to get something to eat or not?" she asked me.

"Where ya'll going?" Kayden asked.

"I want to go over to the grinder shop on Lexington and get one of those hot pastrami grinders with onions and mustard," Tate said as she sucked the tips her fingers, salivating as if the sandwich was already in her hands.

Kayden agreed, "I could go for a grinder too."

"Yo, Kay, get me a triple Italian," one of his clients shouted, handing Kayden a twenty.

Then all at once, all of the barbers joined in and a couple of clients that looked like regulars.

"What do we look like? A delivery service?" Tate snapped.

I backed Tate up. "We don't even have a car."

A raspy voice came from the back of the shop. "I'll take you over there," it said. "I'm on my way out."

I turned around, eager to see who the volunteer was. In the last barber chair in the corner, a client was standing up from his seat.

Tate jerked her head around in surprise, "Really? You're going to take us?"

"Yeah, I'm done now. I was heading over that way so ya'll can ride with me if you want."

Tate crossed her arms across her chest, "Well then,

we'll wait for you outside." She fanned her hand in front of her face. "It's starting to get hot in here," she said, grabbing my arm and pulling me out of the barbershop.

"What's wrong with you?" I asked, snatching my arm out of her grasp.

Tate smiled with her eyes. "August doesn't talk to anybody, and now all of a sudden he wants to offer rides. He likes you!" she said excited.

"I'm not interested for two reasons: one, I am focused on school right now, and two, he is not my type."

"Aw, why—because he's a little chubby?" We both burst into laughter. I was laughing so hard my eyes started to tear up.

When I finally wiped my eyes, August was standing right in front of us.

"What's so funny?" he asked.

Looking at him close up, August was not that chubby at all. He was stocky, and since he was short it made him seem bigger than he actually was. Aside from that he was very well kept; smooth chocolate skin, clean cut with thick, deep waves circling his head like the ocean. His hair hypnotized me.

"You aight?" August asked, snapping me out of my trance.

"Um, what? I … Casey."

"Yeah, I know, I heard you announce it to the shop. You coming or not? I have to get back to work."

"We're coming …" Tate said as she pushed me into the front seat of August's black pimped out BMW 330i, and then jumped into the back sitting behind me.

50 Cent's "Many Men" was blasting out the speakers—I had to catch myself from breaking out and singing along. I was supposed to be leaving secular music behind me since I'd rededicated my life to Christ before moving to Harlem. So, I sat back and enjoyed the black soft leather

seats and the clean linen air freshener. There was another smell, too, that took me no time to identify. Weed. When I was at Georgetown, I used to smoke a lot, but I didn't smoke anymore. I was wild in college, but I knew if I was going to follow my dreams now, I had to be focused and I had to come correct with God.

The grinder shop was only a few blocks away. Once we pulled up, Tate volunteered to go in and get everyone's food, leaving me alone with August. I sat there for a while and debated if I should say something. Maybe ask him if he's from Harlem? The stereo was so loud I would just be competing with the music—so I decided against it. He didn't seem that friendly anyway aside from offering us a ride. He was looking out the window and at his phone ever since we got in the car. I decided to let it go, and wait for Tate to return. As I turned to look back out the window, the volume on the stereo started to go down. I ignored it figuring he must have to actually use the phone instead of stare at it.

"So do you like Harlem?"

I slowly turned to look at him to make sure he was talking to me. "I just got here yesterday, but so far so good," I said, shocked by how nice his smile was.

"As long as you can stay out of trouble, you will like Harlem." He grinned.

"I'm pretty sure I can do that."

"What makes you so sure?"

"'Cause I'm focused on what I came here to accomplish."

"And what's that?"

"I'm going to be an actress."

"Really…"

Tate jumped back into the car cutting August off in mid sentence. When she got in he simply turned the music back up and drove us back to the barbershop. He didn't give us a minute to get out of the car; as soon as the doors were shut he pulled off down the street without even saying goodbye.

As Tate delivered the grinders to their anxious owners, I stopped to talk to Kayden.

"Let's go out in the city tonight," He suggested.

I thought about it for a minute and was inclined to say no, I didn't know how that would fit in with my new salvation, but then I figured why not? School doesn't start for a month. I am in Harlem, I'll be with my cousin…I may as well get a real taste of city life before I'm bogged down with schoolwork. "Sure! Why not?" I'm sure God won't mind, I thought.

"Good, I'll pick you up after we close up, around ten."

"OK, I'll be ready."

Later that night, Kayden pulled up in front of the house. I could see Chancy peering his head out the window. His bulging eyes confirmed I looked good. I had on a low v-neck, slightly fitted white silk spaghetti strap dress that stopped right below my butt with a chunky gold necklace that lay between my cleavage and some sky high nude Aldo peep-toe shoes that I'd been dying to wear. I figured I'd break this outfit out now since I wouldn't be caught dead in it at church. My hair was pinned up into a neat bun and my makeup painted on like I was a professional. Before I could open the door, Chancy jumped out of the passenger seat and opened it for me. "Here you go Miss Lady," he said while motioning for me to hop in the back. As I climbed into Kayden's black Cadillac Escalade, I saw a pretty Spanish girl sitting with her legs crossed looking at me. I scooted my way into the truck flashing her a friendly smile. Kayden turned around to face us. "Casey, this is Brooke; Brooke, my cousin Casey."

"It's nice to finally meet you. I've heard so much about you." Brooke smiled.

I smiled back, hoping it masked my confusion because

Kayden never mentioned Brooke to me, so I figured she was just another one of his girls. Kayden didn't tell me about girls he dated because they weren't around that long.

Brooke's big green eyes lit up her face. Her complexion was flawless. Her Gucci thigh boots and black leather hot pants told me she had style, which meant this was a girl I could be friends with.

Kayden had the music blasting in the car. Outkast's "So Fresh and So Clean," intoxicated the air. I closed my eyes and began to sing along.

I caught a whiff of weed burning. My eyes shot open to Brooke holding the perfectly rolled blunt in front of my face. "You smoke?" Brooke asked, basically pushing the weed into my mouth.

"I quit, but thanks anyway." I pushed the blunt away from me.

Kayden whipped around. "What? You better quit next week. Tonight you with me and we gon' drink, smoke and party till you pass out." He shot a quick look at Brooke. "Give her a shotgun to ease her in."

Brooke smiled at Kayden like he had just given her instructions on how to commit the perfect crime. Brooke quickly put the blunt in her mouth backwards and grabbed me by the back of my neck pulling me in close to her face. Oh God, I thought as I closed my eyes and opened my mouth. The smoke began to fill my lungs. I sucked until I couldn't breathe anymore. Brooke released my head as I swallowed the smoke. I sat back in the seat allowing my head to rest on the headrest.

Kayden glanced back at me and smiled. "That's what I'm talking about!"

Brooke took another puff of the blunt and passed it back up to the front to Chancy. They continued to pass it around until it was finished. I opted out of the cipher because the shotgun had me high enough, and I was sure by the end of the night I'd have plenty more to repent for.

By the time we pulled into the parking lot of the club, my whole body was tingling. When I stepped out of the car, I felt like I was floating. My dress brushed against my skin as I walked, enhancing the sensation from my high. Chancy grabbed my hand and began to guide me in the direction of the club.

We bypassed the line that wrapped around the corner. Kayden knew the bouncer and flirted with the girl taking cash from the patrons. He spoke to everyone as if he'd known them for years. We went straight to the VIP. Behind the red velvet ropes, there were big chairs with plush cushions and glow-in-the-dark tables, each with a bottle of champagne on it. Sheer drapes lined the walls as steam rose up off the floors. Brooke grabbed my hand and led me to one of the couches to sit with her. Kayden and Chancy summoned over the cocktail waitress. R-Kelly and Mase filled the club, singing, "Did you every think that you would be this rich, did you ever think that we would make these hits…" Brooke stood up, swinging her hips back and forth and waving her arms in the air. Kayden and Chancy stood nodding their heads up and down. I couldn't move, I just leaned my head back on the cushion and allowed my high to sink in. I closed my eyes and let the music speak to me like I was the only one in the room.

When I opened them back up, Chancy was standing over me like a predator salivating over his prey.
He slid down next to me and put his hand on my knee, then laid his head on my shoulder and whispered in my ear, "You want a drink?"

I knew I should say no, but my mouth was dry from the weed and I didn't want to get into another debate with Kayden so I just agreed. "Sure," I answered.

He got up and greeted the cocktail waitress that was just on time entering the VIP. She had two bottles of Moet and a tall bottle of Gray Goose sitting on ice. I thought someone else must be joining us with that amount of alcohol. Chancy picked up a bottle of Moet and popped the cork. Champagne sprayed all over the place as Chancy poured everyone a glass. We raised our glasses in the air. I drank it down in one gulp. I was thirsty. No sooner than I put the glass down Chancy was there filling it back up. He kept the alcohol on rotation, popping the next bottle at the finish of the first and then on to the Gray Goose—I guess we weren't expecting anyone else. Coming here tonight was a bad idea.

Just as the room began to spin, Chancy grabbed me, pulling me to my feet, pulling me in close to him. I was too drunk to fight it so I gave in. Suddenly, I was excited to throw my inhibitions out temporarily. I hadn't enjoyed myself like this since college.

Chancy's hands began to explore my inner thighs and lower back; I could feel his breath on my neck, it sent a sensation through my entire body. All I could think of was how long it had been since I'd had sex. I'd never had a one-night-stand before, but maybe tonight I'd be willing to experiment.

The drinks kept flowing, the music kept playing, and the couples on the floor continued grinding until the sun came up. As the club let out, patrons squinted and hid behind their dark shades to ease from the shock of light when we emerged from the dark club. Brooke and I stumbled to the car arm-in-arm, using each other for support. Once in, we collapsed into the back seat, Kayden sped off into the dawn.

Back in Harlem when we pulled up in front of the brownstone, I could barely lift my head off the seat. Chancy jumped out to help me. He opened the door and lifted me over his shoulder. The impact of my stomach hitting his shoulder wasn't good. All of a sudden I threw up all down the back of Chancy's shirt.

Chancy dropped me down on the ground. I almost

smashed my face into the pavement.

"Yo! That's nasty!" he shouted.

Brooke and Kayden jumped out of the car and helped me to my feet. Chancy frantically shook himself off, stripping his shirt off in the middle of the street trying to stop the vomit from sliding down his back. Somehow Kayden and Brooke got me up the steps and into the house. Kayden laid me across the couch and disappeared back out the door.

I was awakened by screaming children dancing around me yelling, "Auntie Casey." My head felt like I'd been hit with a ton of bricks. I was being punished for my sins. I was so embarrassed. I'd only been in Harlem for twenty-four hours, and there were already people I had to avoid. I was beginning to second-guess my ability to stay focused out here. My idea of life in Harlem had changed over night. I needed to regain my focus, because the last thing I wanted to do was disappoint my dad and fall back into my rebellious college ways.

Chapter Three

September

CANDICE

Candice sat in her office, staring at a spreadsheet on her
computer. She'd been looking at the same spreadsheet for the
last hour. She stood up and paced around for a minute, then
walked over to the window, gazing down at the busy city
from her twenty-fifth story view of Wall Street. The phone
rang, snapping her out of her trance. She grabbed the receiver.
"Candice Porter," she answered.

Bruce's angry voice came booming through the phone.
"Why have you been avoiding my calls?"

Without hesitation Candice shouted back: "I haven't
been avoiding you Bruce, I have been busy getting the girls
ready for school. Or did you forget that school started this
week?"

"School starting doesn't have anything to do with you
signing those papers I had my assistant bring over to your
office a month ago."

"Listen Bruce! I said I didn't have time to look at
them. Do you think I'm just going to sign divorce papers that I
haven't had a chance to let my lawyer review?"

"You know the law, Candice! We said we wouldn't get lawyers involved! Everything we agreed to is in those papers!"

"It's easy to say *we won't get lawyers involved* for you, because you are a lawyer, and you work at a law firm where you can have any one of your associates look over them at any time!"

"If you just read the damn papers you can see there have been no adjustments! It's exactly what we discussed!" Bruce barked.

"Listen, I'm at work, and I'm very busy right now. When I get out of work, I have to pick up our daughters from school, help them with their homework, cook dinner, and get them ready for another day. It is not easy being a single parent. But you wouldn't know anything about that because you got to walk away scot-free from your family!"

"WALK AWAY SCOT-FREE..."

"I have work to do, Bruce!" Candice slammed down the phone. Tears fell down her cheeks. Her office door swung open. Terren Mitchell, her company VP, stood in the doorway, staring at Candice with her piercing dark brown eyes that were reminicent of coals. That paired with her pale yellow skin and long straight black hair reminded Candice of Elvira from the Adams Family. Candice wiped her face with the sleeve of her shirt before she looked up at Terren.

"Is everything okay in here?" Terren asked, raising her eyebrows, increasing the amount of wrinkles in her forehead.

"Yes, everything is fine, Terren," Candice said, rolling her eyes annoyed at her boss's superiority complex.

"Great, are those reports ready for the board meeting?"

Candice hesitated. "Almost—I'll have them finished before lunch."

"That's pushing it a little, Candice. We don't need you missing anymore deadlines now, do we?"

"No, ma'am. Don't worry, they will be in your inbox by

noon."

Terren glared at Candice, then turned and walked out of her office leaving the door open. Candice stood up to close the door, but her friend and associate Sarah walked in.

"You alright?" Sarah asked, softly moving her bleached blond hair over her shoulder.

"I'm fine," Candice whispered. "Bruce just called me about the divorce papers, and then Terren came in here riding me about these reports. I just can't get focused."

Sarah looked over her shoulder out the door, and then closed it behind her. She reached into her purse and pulled out a small vial filled with coke. She twisted the cap off and stuck her finger in the top, scooping some out on her nail. Then she put her nail up to her nose and quickly sniffed it.

"Here, take a hit of this"—Sarah handed the vile to Candice—"it'll get you focused."

Candice took the vial from Sarah and stuck her finger inside, then repeated Sarah's actions, snorting the coke up both nostrils. When she was done, she handed the vile back to Sarah, who quickly twisted the cap on and dropped it back into her purse. Candice closed her eyes.

"Now get those reports done so we can get out of here early. I'd like to take a few more hits before I pick the kids up from school," Sarah admitted.

"OK," Candice said, opening her eyes as Sarah closed the door behind her. Then she looked at her computer screen and started speed typing into the spreadsheet.

TERREN

Terren stormed in her office with her assistant Jeanine following behind her.

"Mrs. Mitchell."

"Yes, Jeanine?"

"You have a conference call in five minutes."

"Please call in and take notes for me. I'll be calling in late," Terren informed her while plopping down at her desk.

Jeanine scurried out of Terren's office, shutting the door behind her.

Terren looked at the unfinished slides staring at her from her computer screen and wanted to scream. She hated waiting until the last minute to get things done. She liked to be over-prepared for board meetings, especially since she was the only woman.

She stood up from her desk and began pacing her office. All she needed was frustration at work. Work was her sanctuary, the one part of her life that she had control.

She caught a glance of a picture sitting on top of her bookcase of her husband and two children. Seeing her family immediately filled her with sadness. She and her husband were going through some rough times. After ten years of marriage and two kids, rough times were inevitable. But lately their problems had escalated bigger than ever before because he'd moved out.

She shook her head, trying not to think about their problems because she knew it would make her cry and she'd vowed to never cry at work. Terren was an avid believer in separating work and home life. In her entire career, she'd never let her personal life affect her work. Sometimes she felt she took it too far because she put work in front of everything. She'd missed her son's football games, her daughter's dance recitals. She couldn't even remember the last parent–teacher conference she'd been to. Her husband always took care of that.

But that's why she was able to climb the corporate ladder so quick. She was the youngest VP in her company and the only female board member. She'd worked hard, and because of all her sacrifices she deserved the success she gained.

She wished her family understood that she did it all for them. It wasn't her fault she had to be the provider while her husband chased his many dreams. Having two parents not working was a luxury they could not afford. She had to make sure her children had food, a safe place to live, and the best education New York private schools had to offer.

A knock on the door distracted her.

"Come in."

Jeanine poked her head in. "Some questions have been posed for you," she said pointing at her headset referring to the conference call.

"OK, I'm calling in now," Terren whispered.

Jeanine closed the door, and Terren hurried over to her desk. She took a deep breath in, then exhaled before picking up the phone and dialing into the call. She knew she had to pull it together, because for the first time in her life, her struggles from home were spilling over into her perfectly manufactured career.

CASEY

After throwing up all over Chancy, I decided to stay away from the adventures of Kayden for a while. He called the house a few times looking for me, but I told Tate and Candice I didn't want to talk to him. Candice would make up excuses to explain why I couldn't come to the phone. She never even asked me why I was avoiding him. Maybe she knew he wasn't a good influence on me.

I stayed at home with Tate and the kids for the most part. The only time I left the house was when I had to go to my school for registration. Candice wasn't home much. During the week she went to work before I woke up, and she wouldn't return until late at night. She said she was picking up more hours since she was on a tighter budget without Bruce around.

The weather was changing. The temperature dropped from high 80s to mid 60s in just a few weeks. As the bright colored leaves decorated the ground, Harlem looked like a famous painting that should be hanging on the wall of an art museum.

I sat in the rocking chair in front of the window, snuggled in a blanket, holding my favorite book, *I Know Why the Caged Bird Sings* by Maya Angelou. Just as I opened it up to dive into it for the twentieth time, the doorbell rang.

I jumped up and ran to the door. Kayden stood there with a grin on his face.

"Hey!" I said, shocked to see him. I felt uncomfortable. I started pulling down my tiny Adidas shorts that were digging into my leg.

"What's up with you? You been hiding from me?"

Kayden asked.

"No. Candice has been working a lot, so I've been helping her with the girls. I actually have to pick them up today."

"Well, I've missed you."

"I'm sorry," I pretended.

"Well, you need to find some time for me. We're family."

I slurred out, "I know."

"What are you doin' this weekend?"

I stood there with a blank stare on my face, afraid to admit I had no plans. I knew that question was a setup to be invited somewhere else. "I'm going to get my hair done." I couldn't find anything better to say than that.

"That's it." Kayden laughed. "Good, then you can come to a pool tournament I'm having at the shop. A lot of people will be there. You'll like it," Kayden said, pushing past me and plopping down on the couch.

I couldn't find a way out of this situation. Now Kayden was in the house and cozying up on the couch like he was going to stay a while, and all I could think about was throwing up on Chancy and almost smashing my face into the ground.

"I'm too embarrassed, Kayden."

He looked confused. "What? Why?"

I dropped my head. "Because I threw up all over Chancy."

He burst into laughter. "That's why you've been avoiding me?"

"Yes." I closed my eyes thinking about it. "And poor Chancy." I frowned.

"You shouldn't be embarrassed. We all been there before. I forgot you were a lightweight, church girl," Kayden said, pulling me down to the couch and wrapping his arms around me.

"Let me go," I yelled.

"You're funny," Kayden said, letting me go. "I'm expecting you at the pool tournament tomorrow."

"Fine Kayden!" I said with an attitude, already feeling like it wasn't a good idea. "But I'm not smoking or drinking, so don't even try to pressure me."

Kayden got up and started to walk towards the door. Then stopped and turned towards me. "Whatever prude. I'll see you tomorrow night."

"Yes Kayden," I said rolling my eyes.

Kayden smiled and walked out the door.

Saturday morning I decided to go to the library and get some research done to prepare for my classes before I went to Kayden's pool tournament. I figured I'd be picking up a few books, so I grabbed my large canvas tote bag and threw some notebooks and pens inside. I was looking forward to walking because I used that time to daydream about winning my Oscar. It was in these moments that I was the happiest.

My daydream was interrupted when I heard a man's raspy voice call out to me. "Miss Casey, where you going?"

Hearing my name stopped me in my tracks. I turned around slowly, hoping it wasn't Chancy. I was happy to see it was August.

"To the library," I called out.

"You need a ride?

"It's right up the street. I can see it from here."

"Get in the car," he insisted.

I got in the car and crossed my arms over my chest, a little upset that he'd taken me away from my daydreaming time. I didn't get a lot of time in the house with the kids there, so there were few moments that I got to enjoy my thoughts.

"What you doing at the library?" August asked, ignoring my attitude.

"Getting some books for school," I mumbled.

"You're a good girl."

"Yup, I sure am. Just ask my sister— she practically has me raising my nieces right now."

"How so?" he asked.

"It's a long story," I sighed. "Do you have kids?"

"I'm thirty years old. Most people my age have kids." He laughed.

"Thirty! You don't look thirty."

"Well, I am. I'm a grown man." We both laughed.

When we pulled up in front of the library, I started to jump out of the car, but August grabbed my arm. I turned his way, frowning my face at him, confused.

"You need me to pick you up?"

"No, I don't need a ride. I told Kayden I would go to his pool tournament tonight, so I'm going to go over there after I leave here."

"I will pick you up then. I'm heading over there too." August pulled out a pen from his center console. "You got some paper in that bag?"

I shook my head yes, and pulled out my notebook.

"Write down my number," he said, passing me the pen.

I wrote down August's number and jumped out of the car.

"Call me when you're ready."

I nodded and ran into the library.

Inside the library I was skimming the shelves for books with good monologues. I wanted to be prepared with at least two for my Intro to Drama class. I picked three books. One of them was a writer's guidebook that I wanted to read through to find out about formatting screenplays and copyrights. I sat down at one of the empty tables and opened the first book. As I was turning through the pages, I felt someone standing over me. When I looked up there was an older man with a bald head looking at me.

"Are you a writer?" the man asked.

"Yes, I am."

"I am too. I'm Umaja," the little man said as he extended his hand to me.

I shook his hand, smiled, and returned my eyes to my book, hoping that he would just go away.

"I just finished my first script," Umaja continued, breaking my focus once again. "What are you writing about?"

I looked up at him, now annoyed that this short, middle-aged man was coming on to me. "I'm not writing anything right now. I'm actually looking for a monologue so that I can be prepared for my drama class that I'm starting next week."

"Drama class? So you're an actress and a writer?"

"Yes, I write parts that I want to play."

"Is that right? That's talent." Umaja took a seat across from me at the table. "How long have you been writing?"

I could've screamed. I paused, exhaled and decided to be nice, "All my life. How about you?"

"I started writing after I was in a car accident last year. A drunk driver hit me head on. My car was smashed like a pancake and I was thrown fifty feet into a tree. I was in a coma for six weeks. The doctors said I should've been dead."

"Oh my God!" I gasped.

"Yes, God saved my life. When I woke up I felt different. At the time I was living in Texas, working as an accountant, making a good living for myself, but I wasn't fulfilled. So I quit my job, sold everything in my house except a few articles of clothes, and moved back to Harlem to live with my sister and nephew. I decided I would live a simple life and do what I always wanted to do—write plays."

I was in awe of this complete stranger. I'd misjudged

him. I was so taken by Umaja that I sat there with him talking for hours. We discussed our perspectives on life, the movie industry, our families, and how we saw our futures. He was so easy to talk to. Within that small amount of time I felt like we'd known each other for years. I had an intellectual love affair with this man; I didn't want to stop talking to him. Before I knew it, I looked up at the time and it was five o'clock. Kayden's pool tournament started in an hour, and I wanted to get something to eat before I went. I was dreading having to stop our conversation. As I tried to think of a way to break the news that I had to go to my new friend, he stopped me. "Well honey, it was a pleasure getting to know you, but I have to run. I have to meet up with my writing partner. We have an appointment to work on our script tonight." In our conversation Umaja mentioned to me that he'd been collaborating with another writer on a new script idea that he had. For some reason, I felt a little jealous. I barely knew this man, but I wanted to be the one writing with him.

Umaja got up from his seat and started to pack up his things, I felt a rush of panic run through my veins at the thought of him leaving and me possibly never seeing him again. I didn't know if I should ask him for his number or set up another library date or what; I just knew I couldn't let him leave without a way of contacting him. As I opened my mouth to ask for his information Umaja handed me a business card. "Here, call me sometime. We can do lunch," he said flashing me a warm smile.

I anxiously grabbed the card and tucked it in my purse to keep it safe. "Yes, let's do lunch." I had no idea what was going on with me but I did know I never had an instant connection with anyone in my life the way I just had with Umaja—and I loved it.

"OK, bye honey." Umaja waved. My smile turned into a frown as I watched him walk away. I packed up my things and decided I would walk down to the corner store and grab me something to eat before heading to Kayden's.

The moment I stepped outside, August pulled up. I had completely forgotten about him. I walked over to his car as he rolled down the window. "Are you stalking me?" I teased.

"I thought you might be hungry," August said, picking up a bag off of the seat and handing it to me. "I got you a grinder. Were you about to leave without calling me?" August looked disappointed.

"I didn't want to bother you."

He frowned. "Sure."

I smiled at how cute he looked pretending to be so upset. I got in the car, and August sped off giving me just enough time to get my foot securely inside the door.

"How did you know I was hungry?"

"I figured you were since you been at the library all day."

"Well you were right, thank you."

"You're welcome."

The first bite of the grinder melted in my mouth. Bite after bite seemed like it got better. All my attention was focused on that sandwich. We drove in silence for a while. I watched August, a little intrigued about who he was. He'd been really nice to me, we had decent interactions, he had taken me to the library and brought me lunch without me asking, yet he never came on to me or really showed any romantic interest at all. I wondered what his deal was. I decided to dig a little to see what I could learn about him.

"So how many kids do you have?" I asked.

"Two, a boy and a girl."

"Same mother?" I laughed.

"Yep."

"Oh!"

"You seem surprised?"

"I guess I wasn't expecting you to say yes."

"Well, you should always expect the unexpected with me," he joked.

"So where is your children's mother now?"

"She's in Manhattan."

I cringed knowing she was so close. "Are ya'll still together?"

"Nah, we argued too much."

"Argued about what?"

"Everything. But mostly she didn't like my lifestyle."

"What do you mean?" I pressed on.

"Well, I used to own a nightclub, but now I own restaurants. Those kinds of establishments can have you out all times of night, and around lots of women. She didn't like that."

"I don't blame her. I wouldn't like my man being around women all night either," I admitted.

"Well lucky for you, I got out of that business and now my business is fine dining."

"Lucky for me?" I smiled. I let my curiosity get the best of me: "Is there a chance you will ever get back with her?"

"No! We weren't good for each other, and I can't deal with her mood swings."

August pulled up in front of Kayden's shop. "Come on, let's go. That's enough questions for one day," August said as he got out of the car.

When we opened the door, we were greeted by music blasting out the stereo. The barbershop was packed. We had to push past people to get inside. Kayden was the only one working. There was a mob of men all holding drinks in their hands, focused on the game of pool being played. Kayden greeted me when I entered the shop.

"What's up cuz, you made it," he shouted, looking up from his haircut.

I was going to stop and chat, but the crowd was pushing

me along towards the back. "I'm here, I'll be in the back." I yelled so he could hear me over the music. I grabbed on to August's arm as a guide while he maneuvered through the crowd towards the pool table. We finally found an empty space by the back door of the shop. There was a group of people outside laughing and talking about who they had their bets on. August stepped away from me so he could get closer to the pool table.

I felt out of place. As more people started to pile in, I started to feel claustrophobic, so I decided to go outside in the back. When I stepped outside, Chancy was standing with a group of guys. A smile spread across his face when he saw me. He grabbed a beer out of a cooler that was sitting on the ground near him and walked towards me. I wanted to run away but I knew I had to face him eventually.

"You want a drink?" he asked, bursting into laughter.

I shook my head in disgust. "No thank you."

"Why? Can't hold your liquor?"

I was thoroughly annoyed. I turned around to go back inside, but Chancy grabbed my wrist and pulled me back towards him.

"What's the matter with you?" he barked. "After throwing up all over me the least you could do is apologize."

"Did you forget you dropped me on the ground? I could have scraped my whole face up."

"Do you blame me? That was all I could do when I felt that warm throw up all over my neck. It was nasty!"

I bit my tongue. I did not want to argue with him. Plus he was right, I'm sure it was uncomfortable to have that feeling on his back, so I did the Christian thing and took the high road. "You're right Chancy, I apologize. That was very unladylike of me."

"Damn right it was!"

I rolled my eyes at his response and tried to release my

wrist from his grip, but as I yanked away, he squeezed tighter. "Can you please let me go?"

"Naw, you have to make it up to me. Let me take you out."

I frowned my face in confusion. Why would he want to take me out after he claimed he was so disgusted? I wasn't going to entertain him; he'd obviously been drinking. "No, thank you. I really don't have time."

Chancy's face seemed to morph into another person. "What? So now you're too good?"

Yes, he was drunk. "No, I'm not. I'm just really busy with school and my family right now."

"You weren't too busy the other night!" he said, pulling me closer to him.

"Chancy, please let me go. You're hurting me."

I heard the guys in the back start to laugh. What did they think was funny about this situation? Chancy wrapped his other arm around my waist and dug his fingers into my side. Now, he was violating my space and hurting me.

"Chancy, if you don't let me go I'm gonna scream."

"Scream then!" he said so viciously that spit shot out of his mouth onto my face.

Now I was furious. I ripped my arm out of his grasp and lunged at him, punching him in the face. Chancy stumbled, and fell into the fence. I swung at him again before he could regain his composure, this time jabbing him in his side. I swung again, aiming for his face, but before my last blow could puncture his cheek he caught my arm with one hand and grabbed me around my neck with his other hand before slamming me into the fence.

His grip was so tight around my neck that I started gasping for air. Suddenly, August came running towards us with Kayden right behind him. August grabbed Chancy trying to pull him off of me, "ARE YOU CRAZY?" August roared at

Chancy.

Kayden peeled Chancy's hands from around my neck. Once Kayden released me from Chancy's hold Kayden swung at him, punching him in the mouth so hard that blood squirted out. I ran back over to Chancy and attacked him, punching him in the stomach while Kayden and August had him pinned down. August let go of Chancy, he scooped me up over his shoulder and carried me out of the shop while Kayden and Chancy continued fighting.

When we got to August's car I was still freaking out.

"Calm down!" he yelled. "Let me go check on Kay. I'll be right back. Don't move!" he said dropping me into the car, slamming the door shut and locking me in.

I was so angry I started screaming until I lost my voice. Once my voice went, the silence introduced a blanket of shame. I slapped my hands over my face to hide myself. I knew that Chancy was wrong, but I was too. I shouldn't have hit him. In just one month in Harlem I'd gotten so off track. I'd started smoking weed again and drinking and now I'd gotten into a fight. I'd completely compromised my salvation. If this was what Harlem had to offer, my salvation was the last thing I needed to jeopardize. If anything, I needed to get as close to God as possible because only He would be able to save me from what Harlem had in store.

Chapter Four
October

TERREN

When Terren got home, the house was silent. Her husband picked the kids up and took them to dinner since she was getting home late. She'd been out entertaining board members that were in town. Her contract was coming up for review, and she knew if she played her cards right, she'd be offered a promotion.

She kicked her shoes off and walked over to the window. She loved the view of the city from her Manhattan Penthouse, especially at this time of night when the lights on the buildings looked more like stars.

As much as she appreciated the moment of peace she had before the kids came home, she missed her family. Things weren't the same since her husband left. She didn't know how it got this far. She thought back to their last fight.

He'd come home at six thirty in the morning without so much as a call. When he got home he claimed his phone was dead and he was stuck at work dealing with a crisis that had to be fixed before the next day. She wanted to believe him, but this wasn't the first time he'd stayed out all night at work. She told him time and time again, it's not what you do; it's how you do it. Had he called her or answered any one of her twenty calls, she would have been more forgiving.

His newest career venture, although more lucrative than the last, was also more time consuming. His first business almost ended their marriage, but she fought through it, mainly because she didn't want their kids to have to be the products of divorce. But this time they were older, and it broke her heart more for them to be looking for their daddy to tuck them in at night and he wasnt there.

This time she was also tired of being disrespected. How many times were they going to go through the same things? Maybe it was because she'd gotten older, but her tolerance for nonsense was now at zero, especially because of all the sacrifices she'd made for their marriage and their family.

Terren walked into the kitchen and decided to pour herself a glass of wine. She figured she'd unwind before he brought the kids home. She opened the wine fridge, pulled out her favorite bottle of Riesling, and as she began to pour it into her blue crystal wine glass, she heard the front door open. Her son Jeremiah burst in. She could hear him drop his bag on the floor and run into the kitchen with his dirty cleats on. She put down the bottle and turned to greet him.

"Mommy!" Jeremiah shouted, running into Terren's arms.

At eight years old he was still mommy's baby. Her daughter Kiarra on the other hand worshiped the ground her father walked on.

Terren gave her son a big hug and then quickly ran her hands over her hair and wiped under her eyes. It wasn't much, but she had to try to ensure that she looked good since the only time she saw her husband now was when he dropped the kids off.

She stepped out of the kitchen, and he was standing in

the living room hugging Kiarra, who was putting on her daily "Daddy don't leave me" performance.

"Come on honey, let Daddy go, you'll see him on Monday," Terren said trying to console Kiarra.

"No, please daddy…"

"It's OK baby, you know I'm only a phone call away," he promised her.

"Kiarra, enough!" Terren interjected.

Kiarra snatched her arms from around her father's waist and pushed past Terren, then ran into her room.

"Girl have you lost your mind?" Terren shouted.

"Leave her alone. She's going through a lot right now."

Terren cut her eyes at her husband, "She's twelve. How much could she possibly be going through?"

"She just misses me being in the house."

"Yeah, well instead of you letting her keep blaming me for why you're not home, why don't you sit down and have a conversation with her about the part you played in not being here."

"And what part was that Terren? You put me out."

"I didn't put you out. I told you to go out of frustration. And instead of you trying to get to the bottom of my frustration, you packed up your stuff and left."

"How many times do you think a man can have it thrown in his face that his wife's money bought their home?"

"I didn't even bring that up."

"You didn't have to! The fact that you threaten to throw me out every time you get mad says enough."

"Oh, so it's OK for you to waltz in here at six o'clock in the morning, and I'm supposed to just shut up and say nothing?"

"No, you're supposed to trust I was doing what I said I was and stand by me in our business."

"I stood by you in the last business, and look what

happened with that! You lost all of my father's insurance money and almost gambled us into bankruptcy."

"You're never going to let me live that down, are you Terren?"

"Let you live it down? I pulled us out of that hole you dug. I worked my butt off to get us here, out of my mother's house, and here we go again, you're starting up those same behaviors as last time."

"This is different and you know it. You're just jealous that this time I've made more in three years than you did in seven."

"JEALOUS!" Terren screamed.

Kiarra ran out of her room crying, "Mommy, please don't push my daddy away!"

Terren turned to her daughter. "Go back in the room, Kiarra!"

When Terren turned back around, her husband was half way out the door.

"AUGUST!" she shouted behind him, but he slipped out the house without turning back.

CASEY

I sat in class completely distracted. The drama in my personal life was impacting my ability to focus. School just wasn't my priority at the moment. Candice was having the worst mood swings to the point it was affecting her ability to take care of her children. She was always staying at work late, going in early or not coming home at all. The girls' well being had become my sole responsibility.

On the weekends she would stay at her friend Sarah's house, leaving the girls with Aunt Caroline. She wasn't eating, she never had any money, and when she did show up at home she slept all day. Something really bad was going on with her; I just didn't know what it was.

"Casey!" My instructor called my name, pulling my attention away from my thoughts.

"Uhm, yes," I stuttered.

"It's your turn?"

She had us doing an exercise where we had to say the same sentence in a different emotion each time. This should be easy I thought, I'm very emotional right now. I stood in the front of the class and pictured myself six years ago and how I looked up to my sister. I imagined Candice standing in front of me, looking her in the eyes and saying, "I…don't want this anymore." I delivered the lines like a shy little kid pleading to her big sister that she loved and admired to please stop doing whatever it was she was doing. A blanket of sadness covered my body. I stood in silence while everyone stared at me before delivering the lines seven more times evoking pain, hurt, confusion, mistrust, desperation, anger and fear. Then my teacher said, "That was perfect Casey. Did you feel the difference?"

I took a deep breath, allowing my tears to flow down my cheeks before whispering "yeah," and walking back to my seat.

After class I jumped on the A train to Harlem. When I walked up the stairs of the subway station, August was parked out front waiting for me. He insisted on picking me up because he didn't want me walking home at night alone.

When I got in the car I was still emotional from class, so I wasn't as talkative as I usually was with him. When we pulled up in front of my house, he put the car in park and asked, "You alright?"

"Yea, I'm fine. I'm just thinking of everything I need to do tomorrow," I said half honest.

"What's on your schedule?" He smiled while pulling an already rolled blunt out of the glove compartment.

"I have to walk Daisy and Asia to school, pick them up figure out what I am going to cook for dinner because nine times out of ten Candice is going to have to work late again, then I'll have to get the girls' clothes ready for school, and put them to bed."

"You sound like a single mother," August joked.

"I feel like one too."

August took a pull of his blunt and slowly exhaled the smoke. "Tomorrow I have some time, so let me help you."

"How can you help me?"

"I'll be up early, so I'll pick you and the girls up and drop them off at school, then I'll take you to get your hair done."

"What? Why?"

"Because, you seem stressed and I want to do

something nice for you, is that OK?"

"Thank you, but I can't let you do that."

"I do what I want to do. You deserve it. I've been watching you take care of your family, let me take care of you."

I couldn't contain my smile. I wanted to reject his offer again but I couldn't. He was right, I did deserve something nice, so, I gave in. "Fine, what time will you be here in the morning?"

"I'll be here by seven thirty."

"Seven thirty it is. I'll see you then."

I grabbed my tote bag and hopped out of the car before I changed my mind again. August waited until I got in the house before pulling off.

Inside the house everything was quiet. Upstairs all the lights were off except for a light from the TV in Daisy and Asia's room. I walked in their room and Asia was sprawled across the top bunk passed out and Daisy was sitting up watching SpongeBob—were the girls home alone?

"Where is everyone?"

"Mommy is at work and Tate said she was going to the store," Daisy answered, half paying attention to me and half focused on the TV.

When I heard that Tate left them alone, my confusion turned to annoyance. "Go to the store for what?"

"I don't know. She just said she was going to the store."

I stomped down to the hall to Tate's room, picked my phone up off the bed, and called her.

Tate giggled. "Hahaha, hell...o..."

I had to take a deep breath to avoid screaming. "Where are you?"

"With my friends," she answered nonchalantly.

"Why are you out so late? And why did you leave your little sisters in the house alone?"

"I just went down the street. I will be home in a few." Tate laughed and hung up the phone.

I was furious! I could feel my body temperature rise. I sat down on the edge of the bed and started to take deep breaths. I started praying, "Lord, give me the strength to not punch her in the face."

I woke up to Daisy poking me in the arm. "Auntie can you make us breakfast?"

I jumped up. I must've fallen asleep on the couch waiting for Tate to come in the night before.

"Where is Tate?" I yelled, grabbing Daisy by the arm.

"Ouch Auntie."

I was shocked at my strength. "I'm sorry baby," I said, pulling her close and hugging her.

"Is Tate in her bed?" I asked her.

"No she…"

"No!" I screamed, letting Daisy go and running up the stairs.

I pushed open Tate's room door and was surprised to see the bed was tussled about like someone had slept in it. I looked around the room for evidence that she may have been there. Daisy crept up behind me, "Auntie she's in the shower."

Daisy looked afraid. I picked her up and hugged her. "Honey, I'm so sorry if I scared you. I was just worried about your sister. I didn't hear her come home last night.

She smiled, "It's okay Auntie."

"Is your mommy in her room?"

Daisy squinted her nose up and raised her shoulders, " I think she went to work already."

I grew angry all over again. I hadn't been able to catch up with Candice in two days and now Tate was playing disappearing acts as well.

"OK Dase I'll make breakfast. Go downstairs and wait for me, I'm going to make sure Asia is getting ready," I said pushing her along.

Daisy pranced downstairs, and I ran into the bathroom with Tate letting the door slam behind me.

"What time did you get in the house last night?"

"Oh my God Casey, I'm in the shower," she cried out from behind the shower curtain.

I snatched the shower curtain open; Tate covered herself up with her hands.

"What's your problem?"

"Listen—you do not have permission to go outside at night, especially when Daisy and Asia are here alone!"

"I just went to the store!" she screeched.

"You were at the store for a long time. I got in the house at almost ten and the last time I remember looking at the clock before I passed out it was almost eleven, so when did you find your way home last night?" I asked again.

"Eleven thirty," she stuttered.

"There ain't no corner store in Harlem that takes you a hour to go to, so I don't know who you think you're lying to."

"I'm not ly—"

"Oh stop! Let me tell you something, Tate: you better not leave those girls in this house alone again. You're only fifteen years old. There is no reason for you to be out until eleven thirty at night, period."

"Why are you acting like you're my mother?" she cried.

"Someone around her needs to!" I screamed, stomping out of the bathroom and slamming the door shut.

I fed Daisy and Asia. Tate opted out of breakfast. She had an attitude with me, so she left the house before us. As I was putting on the girls' jackets and book bags my cell phone rang.

Prompt as always, it was August.

I hurried the girls along, "Come on girls."

August helped me buckle the girls in and then he joked with them all the way to school. I ran them both into their classes right on time for the bell.

When I got back to the car, August was fumbling through his center console.

"You lost something?" I asked him.

"Naw," he said unconvincingly. "The salon doesn't open for about a half hour, so let's go get something to eat to kill some time," August suggested.

I was hungry. So, I agreed.

CANDICE

Candice strolled into her job an hour and forty-five minutes late, wearing a casual sundress with big black shades. She slowly crept past the receptionist, trying to avoid her stare, knowing she would be glaring at her since she'd called out for the last three days in a row. She slipped into her office and shut the door, rushed to the window, and stuck her head out.

There was a small knock on the door. Candice lifted her head up and took a seat at her desk.

"Come in," she whispered.

Jeanine, Terren's personal assistant, stuck her head in the door. "Mrs. Mitchell would like to see you in her office." She closed the door behind her before Candice could respond.

Candice knew this was coming, and she already had a story ready. She got up from her desk and proceeded towards her boss's office. She walked in, leaving the door open behind her. Jeanine entered and shut it. Candice stood over Terren's desk keeping her shades on.

"Have a seat," Terren instructed, looking up from the computer for the first time since she entered.

Candice lowered herself down into the chair. Jeanine stood a few steps back like she was there to be a witness.

"Can you please remove your glasses?" Terren asked.

Candice paused for a moment, took a deep breath to prepare herself for the inevitable next question. She put down her head and removed her glasses.

Terren's eyes widened at the sight of Candice's black and blue, swollen-shut eye.

"What happened to you?" Terren gasped.

Candice kept her head down in shame. Yet she said nothing.

"Candice are you OK?" Terren asked, horrified.

Jeanine nearly toppled over as she walked to Terren's desk to see what she was looking at on Candice's face. She let out a small cry then quickly slapped her hand over her mouth to mask the sound. Jeanine looked over at Terren, who was sitting with her mouth open. Jeanine choked out, "Candice, what happened to you?"

Candice sat up in her chair and looked over at Jeanine because she thought she could get the most sympathy out of her.

"I'm going through a really nasty divorce," Candice cried out in the saddest voice she could muster up.

"Bruce did this to you?" Terren blurted out.

"Oh my!" Jeanine sulked out.

"He doesn't want to let me go," Candice cried. "I told him that he can see the kids whenever he wants, but I cannot be with him anymore, and he just snapped."

"How could he?" Jeanine whispered.

Terren sat in disbelief.

"We have to report this to the police," Jeanine insisted.

"NO!" Candice snapped. "I can't bring the police into this. I have my girls to think about."

"But aren't you worried about your girls' safety?" Jeanine asked.

"Bruce would never hurt those girls," Candice said confidently. "He just wants me to hurt."

"What if he does this again? Aren't you afraid of him?" Jeanine asked, shocked that Candice was defending him.

"No, he won't because I'm going to stay away from him. It's my fault that I went over to his house. I will never make that mistake again. Please, don't call the police. I can't bring them into my girls' lives."

Terren pulled her thoughts together. "Candice, because I would rather you and Bruce work this out on your own, I will not call the police this time."

"Oh, thank you so much, Mrs. Mitchell. Thank you."

"But this is the end of this. We cannot continue to conceal incidents like these. This is a very serious matter. Not only for your safety and the safety of your children, but you fell way behind here at work and now this issue is affecting us as a company."

"I understand," Candice sobbed.

"Now go home and pull yourself together. I can't have you here like this. I am going to give you the rest of the week off. When you return I expect the woman I hired back," Terren commanded.

"I will. I promise," Candice said, jumping out of her seat, putting her sunglasses back on and heading towards the door.

"Good luck Candice," Jeanine said waving behind her.

Candice ran to the parking garage. She jumped in her car and locked the door. She dug in her purse, took out her cell phone and called the most recent number.

Sarah answered. "What happened?"

"It worked." Candice laughed.

"I told you it would," Sarah boasted "I've played the damsel in distress role a few times myself, and putting an orange in a sock and swinging it into your eye a few times never fails."

They both laughed.

"Did your husband leave for his business trip yet?" Candice asked.

"Yes he did, and he has no idea I took vacation time, so you can stay here for the week. I'm going to send my kids to my sister's."

"Good. I will call my sister and tell her I have to go away for work. She can stay home with my kids." Candice giggled.

"OK, I'll see you in a few," Sarah said, hanging up the phone.

Candice dropped the phone on the passenger seat and reached into her purse, pulling out a vile of coke. She scooped a little out with her fingernail and snorted it up one nostril, then took some more out and relieved the other nostril. When she was done, she picked up her cell phone and called. Casey.

CASEY

I shot my head up from under the sink and ran to catch my cell phone. The beautician sprayed herself with water in my tirade.

"Hello," I belted out.

"Casey…" Candice shouted in a panic.

"Candice! What's wrong?"

"Oh, girl you won't believe how my boss is slaving me for this Board of Directors meeting coming up next week," Candice said.

"Oh my God Candice, I thought something was wrong. Why do you sound like you're in distress!" I exhaled.

"I am distressed," Candice cried out. "My boss just came into my office and told me I have to fly to Ohio to meet with the corporate accounting team about an audit from last year. I can't believe she just sprung this on me."

"What are you gonna do?" I asked, now nervous that I would be stuck with the kids.

"I need you to watch the girls for me until Monday," Candice said flat out.

"But I have school Candice?"

"Your classes are in the evening. Just have Tate watch them after school until you get home."

I didn't even know how to fit it in the conversation that Tate had stayed out and left the girls in the house by themselves just the night before.

"Candice, I don't know if that's a good idea," I said trying to dance around the real issue.

"What other choice do I have, Casey? I don't know. Call Aunt Caroline if you don't want to leave them alone. I have to go. Call my cell if you need anything."

"Candice…Candice!" I shouted into the phone, but Candice hung up before I could present any more objections. When the beautician finished washing my hair, she put a deep conditioner in it and had me sit with a cap on my head for a while. I sat down near August who had decided to wait for me while I got my hair done. August was looking through his phone. After a few moments he broke the silence.

"So that was your sister on the phone?" He asked.

"Yep," I said, annoyed at the thought of Candice right now.

"What's up with her?"

"She has to go on some trip for her job, so I have to take care of the girls for the rest of the week."

"She's lucky you're here to watch them."

"Yeah, lucky her. Never mind that I have school." I pouted. "I don't mind helping her out, but lately I've been doing everything. I don't know how I'm ever going to be able to get a job. I wanted to get a part-time job so I could have some money in my pocket. So I don't have to have you pay for my hair all the time," I joked.

He smiled. "I don't mind helping you out."

"Thank you, I appreciate that."

"So what do you have to do this week? Bring the kids to school and feed them?" He asked.

"Yeah basically."

"Well, I can pick you up in the morning and afternoon to take them back and forth to school, and food is nothing. Tonight I'll pick up some pizzas. All kids love pizza," August assured me.

"That's really nice, but you don't have to do that."

"I know but everybody needs a little help. You're going to school, helping your family, so I want to help you."

"But—"

"I said don't worry about it. I got you." August flashed me the most sincere smile I'd ever seen. "Now go tell that lady to finish your hair so we aren't late picking your nieces up."

TERREN

Mynanny.com was filled with underqualified college students. Terren looked at what seemed like the twentieth profile of one of the candidates and frowned. She really didn't know what she was looking for as far as qualifications, but she knew she wanted them to have more experience than a high school babysitting job.

She never had to worry about hiring a nanny before; her mom kept the kids when they lived in New Rochelle with her. After they moved to the city, August always made himself available, even with the busy restaurant schedule, because it was more flexible than hers. But ever since he walked out on her after their last fight, he'd not only disappeared from her life, he'd also stopped handling his responsibilities for the children.

The most they'd heard from him lately were phone calls with excuses to why he can't pick them up or spend any time with them. For the first time in her life, Terren was leaving work early to pick up her kids from school and carpooling them back and forth to their activities.

This situation was boggling her mind; it had gotten completely out of control. She was starting to feel like a single mother. To Terren this all came out of left field, because no matter what struggles she and August had before, he'd never neglected their children. Something wasn't right, she just couldn't put her finger on what it is.

The first thing he'd done that threw her for a loop was moving out. She racked her brain on how that came about. What did she do different? What did she say that pushed him to leave? Had she emasculated him by telling him to get out? It's not like she hadn't said that to him before in anger, he'd usually just get out of the room and go sleep on the couch. Never had he ever packed up his things and left before.

She'd noticed he'd changed since the success of the restaurant. He'd gotten cockier, always bragging about how much money it was bringing in. He claimed she didn't support him, but that was not the case. She supported him mentally and by providing a home for him during the times when money was not coming in from the restaurant, during the times they were paying off debts that he'd made.

The support she refused to give was financial support. But he should have understood why. He knew the only reason she didn't invest in the restaurant was because when her father died, she'd taken all of the money he left her and invested it into August's nightclub. When the nightclub got shut down, they were close to filing bankruptcy and had to move in with her mother. Terren had to go back to work and dig them out of that hole because August was either too depressed to work or out gambling. She got them out of that mess, alone.

That's when she landed the job as a Junior Portfolio Manager at the firm she was at now and worked her way up the ladder. The moment she paid off all of their debt and got ready to purchase the penthouse in Manhattan, August had an epiphany to open a restaurant and suddenly he wasn't depressed anymore. He suggested they continue to live with her mother and take the money for the penthouse and invest it into the restaurant. Terren wasn't having it. Not this time. This time she had to think about their children and their future. He'd have to find another investor, but it for sure wasn't going to be her.

He resented her for that decision, and now at any opportunity he would throw it in her face how successful the restaurant has become. Terren wondered if all of this business with the restaurant was finally coming to a head. She wondered if he'd really turn his back on her now the way he feels she'd turned her back on him. She loved August and was definitely not ready for a divorce but if by some chance she found the strength to deal with a divorce, what she couldn't handle was him neglecting his children. His new behaviors showed her that he was capable of it. So she had to figure out a way to work things out between them. They'd already gone too far, and divorce and nannies were not in her life plans.

But between August and her extra workload due to Candice being out, it looked like she had no choice but to get a nanny. Having to leave work early and Candice being out was killing Terren. Candice handled all of the accounting, including reports on the fluctuation in client portfolios, following profit margins and stock trends, all information Terren needed on a regular basis—now Terren had to pick up the slack in Candice's absence.

To make matters worse, Terren's assistant, Jeanine, who happens to be the office gossip, was talking to some of her friends at work and was told Candice was on drugs and probably got her black eye from a drug dealer. Usually Terren wouldn't follow up behind office gossip, however, in this case the situation was directly affecting Candice's performance. If she was on drugs, it was likely to get worse before it got better. So now Terren would have to have the uncomfortable conversation with Candice when she returned, and request for her to take a mandatory drug test. She liked Candice and had a special softness in her heart for her because she understood what it was like to be a black woman in corporate America, but if her drug test came back positive, there would be little she could do to help her.

CANDICE

When Candice opened her eyes, Sarah was lying in the bed next to her. All the shades in the room were drawn, so Candice was oblivious as to whether it was day or night. She was aware however that she'd been at Sarah's house for almost a week. She put her hand over her face to feel the progress on her eye. The swelling had gone down. She couldn't believe the lengths that she had gone to so she could get some time off work. But she was running away from the reality of her life. Depression had its grip on her for a long time. Now the only thing she could depend on to make her feel better was the numbness that her growing drug habit gave her.

She reached over Sarah to look at the clock on the nightstand, it read 9:30 p.m., she gave Sarah a good shake to wake her. Sarah's eyes cracked open.

"Do you know what day it is?" Candice asked.

"I think it's Sunday." Sarah mumbled.

"Sunday!" Candice shouted, jumping out of the bed. "Oh my God! I have to get home," she said, stumbling to her feet and scrambling the floor for her clothes.

Sarah sat up and watched as Candice threw her clothes on. She picked up a mirror that was sitting on the nightstand with lines of coke on it. Then she put her face to the mirror and sniffed a line. She looked up at Candice. "You want a hit before you go?"

Candice stopped in complete stride and hurried over to Sarah. She lowered her face to the mirror and jumped back in shock of her reflection. She quickly shook off her horror, sniffed two lines of the coke and rushed out he door.

She jumped into her car, backing out of Sarah's driveway without looking behind her, hitting the mailbox on her way out and dragging it halfway down the street. She sped through traffic, running through red lights and stop signs, cutting off cars and nearly hitting a group of pedestrians.

Her bare foot smashed against the peddle—she had been in such a rush she didn't realize she wasn't wearing any shoes. She glanced in her rearview mirror and noticed her once swollen eye was now a ring of blue, her hair was matted down on her head, her lips were dry and cracked with a white film outlining them. She didn't recognize herself. She pressed her foot down on the gas pedal and raced back to Harlem. She had to get in the house fast before anyone saw her.

CASEY

August kept his promise. He arrived everyday by 7:30, went with me to take the girls to school, took me to breakfast, then he went to work. At 3:30, he would come pick me up, we would go get the girls from school, pick up something for dinner, get them ready for bed, then he would drop me to class.

It was Sunday night and August dropped off Popeye's for the girls' dinner. Tate loved the biscuits with grape jelly. I fed them and put them to bed early so I could go over my assignment for class. Tate even went to bed early because she was excited about some field trip she was going on the next day. I was sitting on the couch feeling a little claustrophobic from being in the house all day, so I decided I was going to call August to see what he was doing. As soon as I grabbed my cell phone it started to ring. It was August. I answered, "Hello."

"What you doing?"

"Nothing, just sitting on the couch."

"Come take a walk with me."

"Where? I can't go too far, the girls are sleeping."

"We won't go far, we'll just walk around the block."

"OK," I said before slipping on some flip-flops and yelling upstairs to Tate that I was stepping out for a minute.

When I got outside, August was standing at the bottom of the steps waiting for me. My attraction for him was growing. I couldn't allow myself to go down that path with August or anyone else right now. I had to stay focused.

Our conversation started off friendly. He told me about all the crazy things that go on in his restaurants. Then out of nowhere he asked me, "Why don't you have a boyfriend?"

I felt uneasy. I don't know why, but I didn't want to tell him the truth about my past relationships. August saw me as a good girl and I wanted to keep it that way. So, I decided to lie.

I lowered my head and cleared my throat. "My ex broke up with me right before I moved to Harlem. He said he couldn't do the long distance thing."

August shrugged his shoulders. "Well at least he was honest with you."

That wasn't the response I was looking for, so I decided to take my lie a little further. "I thought we would be together forever…you know…because he was my first."

August snapped his head around, looked me straight in the eyes and asked, "He took your virginity?" He was amazed.

"Yes!" I continued to lie.

"How old are you again?"

"Twenty-one."

"Twenty-one and you've only been with one person?"

"Yep." I couldn't believe I was making up such a stupid lie. My pastor would tell me to drop down to my knees and repent.

"Do you still talk to him?" August asked.

"No, it's too hard. He was my one and only."

"He's stupid as hell. He should've married you. There ain't many girls out here like you."

I smiled at how emotional he'd gotten.

As we approached the house, I noticed Candice's car was parked out front. There was a dent in the bumper, and the taillight was broken. I panicked. August picked up on the shift in my mood.

"You alright?" he asked.

I was so antsy to go inside. I ignored his question. "My sister's home!" I said, running up the stairs of the brownstone and leaving him standing on the sidewalk. "I'll see you later." I waved him off without looking back.

When I got in the house, Candice was pacing back in forth in front of the fireplace. She looked as if she'd just broken out of bondage.

"Candice!" I called out to her.

My shout startled her. She turned to me and slapped her hands over her face. I ran over to her, grabbing her hands. She struggled with me to keep her face covered. I let go out of my frustration.

"Candice! What happened to you?"

Candice turned away from me and began pacing back and forth again.

"Are you going to answer me?" I shouted.

She started to mumble something.

"What? I can't understand you," I said, grabbing one of her arms and yanking it away from her face.

"I'm not … well. Not well, I'm sick," Candice mumbled, pulling her arm out of my grasp.

"You're sick? What do you mean? Where were you? Why do you look like that? YOU LOOK HIGH!" I blurted out. I'd only seen behavior like this on TV before, and the actors were always playing someone on drugs.

Candice started slapping her hands on her head.

"Stop that!" I screamed. Suddenly, I heard a noise coming from upstairs. I panicked. I started pushing Candice into the kitchen. The last thing I wanted was for one of the kids to see her.

"Stay right here," I instructed.

I ran to the bottom of the stairs to listen for the girls. I heard someone walking around. One of them had gotten out of bed! I crept up the stairs to see who it was. As soon as I got to the top of the stairs, Daisy exited the room.

"Daisy, what's wrong?"

She looked up at me half asleep and said, "I have to go to the bathroom."

"Oh, OK," I said. "Hurry up because I am about to take a bath." Putting my hand on her shoulder, I hurried her into the bathroom. I stood outside the door until she finished. When she was done, I scooped her up and carried her back to her room. I quickly tucked her into her bed and shut the door behind me.

I ran back downstairs to Candice. She was standing in the kitchen rocking back and forth. "Casey…you're here… you're so beautiful…I love you," she slurred.

I couldn't hold my anger any longer. I whispered at her as loud as I could, "Tell me what is going on with you!"

She opened her mouth to speak but said nothing. She just flashed me a devious smile and kept rocking back and forth.

I was at a loss for words. All I could think to do was pray. I laid my hands on her and started praying, "God please help her! Please, Lord, help my sister. Oh God what is going on with her? Please Father help her get over whatever she is going through. Lord she looks like death right now, please bring my sister back to life."

I heard a small voice in my head that said, *put her in the bathtub*.

I wrapped her arms around my shoulders and started walking her to the stairs. She let all her body weight collapse on me. It was a good thing she did lose weight because she was already taller than me, and if she were any bigger I would have had to drag her up the stairs. Once I got her into the bathroom, I turned on the water as hot as I could bare it, stripped her naked and almost dropped her into the tub, and poured bubble bath, alcohol and Epson salt into the water.

She started to slide down into the water. I went to grab for her then stopped myself. I was upset and truth be told she needed to dunk her whole body under that water. Too bad it wasn't baptism or holy water because Lord knows she needed both. I watched her slide down deeper into the tub, then reached out and caught her before she was fully submerged.

I grabbed a half empty bottle of shampoo on the counter, filled it up with water, and poured it over Candice's head. She began to gasp like she was drowning.

"Shhh, shhh, shhh," I said, quieting her down so she didn't wake the girls.

After a few minutes, she became a little more coherent. She lay in the tub staring at me. I wanted to ask her again what happened, but I was exhausted. I grabbed a clean washcloth, lathered it up with soap and began to wash my sister clean. I washed her body from head to toe, even washed and conditioned her matted hair.

When I was done, I wrapped a big towel around her and walked her to her room. I laid her down in her bed and tucked her in like she was one of the girls, but for some reason I couldn't leave her. So I lay down in the bed with her wrapped my arms around her and rocked her until we both fell asleep.

I woke up around five thirty by instinct. Candice was still sleeping. I snuck out of her room and went downstairs to prepare the girls' breakfast. I didn't want the girls to see the black ring around her eye, so I had to get them out of the house before she woke up.

Everything went according to plan. August and I dropped them off at school. Tate went on her jolly way, and she was extra nice this morning because August had given her money for her field trip. The only thing that was different about this morning was I decided to skip having breakfast with August. I was in a hurry to get back home and confront Candice.

When we pulled up to the house, Candice's car was gone. I ran in the house, shot up the stairs, and burst in her room. I was actually hoping someone had stolen the car or it had gotten towed. But no, she was gone. I sat down on the bed so confused that my head started to hurt. I needed to talk to someone. I couldn't call my dad because he would drive to Harlem to get to the bottom of this. I couldn't call Aunt Caroline because she would surely tell my dad. I didn't want to talk to August about it because it was too embarrassing. There was only one person that came to my mind that I had been able to confide in without feeling like I would be judged: Umaja, the man I met at the library.

TERREN

"Jeremiah! Get your book bag off of my living room floor!" Terren yelled, almost tripping over her son's bag.

She wanted nothing more than to crawl in the bed with some ice cream and cry, but she couldn't because she was on single mommy duty.

Jeremiah came running into the living room still wearing his muddy cleats.

"Boy, how many times do I have to tell you to take those cleats off before coming in my house? Look at my floor!" She pointed to the mud tracking across her freshly polished hardwood floors.

"Sorry mommy," Jeremiah said, kicking his cleats off and tossing then in the corner.

"Is that where they go?"

"No," he whined.

"Then pick them up and get them out of my living room!"

Kiarra stomped into the kitchen and swung open the refrigerator door.

"Mom, I'm hungry! What are you making for dinner?"

"I don't know yet, Kiarra."

"I want tacos."

Jeremiah called out from his bedroom, "No, I want pizza."

"Shut up Jeremiah!" Kiarra shouted. "We're not getting stupid pizza."

"Kiarra, watch your mouth. Don't talk to your brother like that."

"Well, tell him we're having tacos."

Terren sighed. "We'll see. I didn't promise either of you that we were having tacos or pizza."

"Daddy always makes tacos when I ask," Kiarra pouted.

"Well Daddy ain't here," Terren snapped. "So that's an issue you're going to have to take up with him the next time you see him."

Kiarra slammed the refrigerator shut. "I'll probably never see him again because you're a wicked witch and you ran him away!" Kiarra ran into her bedroom, slamming the door behind her.

Terren froze. Usually, she would have given her daughter a good beating for talking to her like that, but right now she was physically, mentally and emotionally drained, and beating Kiarra would only result in one of two things: it would make Terren feel worse, or she would beat her daughter beyond punishment, taking all of her frustrations out on her. She was defeated.

Terren's cell phone rang. She flopped down on the couch and answered it. It was her sister. "Hey Mel," Terren sulked.

"Hey sis. What's wrong with you?" Melissa asked.

"I'm just tired. I need help with my kids."

"You need to call they Daddy!" Melissa blurted out. "August has some nerve playing disappearing acts. You need to call him and tell him it's time to come home."

"I know," Terren whined.

"So why are you still talking to me? Call your husband!"

"OK."

"Right now. Bye!" Melissa hung up the phone.

Terren knew her sister was right. Enough was enough. It was time for August to come home. Her stubbornness was not helping the situation. So she swallowed her pride and dialed his number.

August answered on the first ring. As soon as Terren heard his voice, she burst out crying.

"August," she wept.

"Terren, what's wrong? Are the kids OK?"

"Yes—no. We are not OK."

"What's wrong?"

"They are acting up, August. I can't take Kiarra's attitude, and if she keeps talking to me the ways she does, I might just break her neck!" she cried.

"Terren, calm down."

"I can't, August. I need you to come home. I need you home now. Tonight!"

"OK baby. I'm on my way."

Forty-five minutes later August was walking through the door.

The kids jumped up from the table and ran to him when they saw their father. They almost knocked him over jumping on him to hug him.

Terren peeked out the kitchen and watched as her children greeted their father. Watching how happy August's presence made her kids made her feel better right away.

After several minutes of hugs and questions from the kids, August walked over to Terren, who was putting the kids' cereal bowls in the sink.

"Cereal for dinner?" he asked.

"That's all I had strength for." she frowned.

August put his hands on her shoulders and pulled her in for a hug. Terren melted in his arms.

"I got this," he whispered. "Go take a bath. I'll put the kids to bed."

A tear ran down Terren's face. August wiped her tear away and kissed her on the forehead. She smiled, then disappeared into her room.

When Terren got out of the bathroom, August was sitting on their bed. She didn't know what to do. It had been months since he'd been inside their bedroom, but seeing him there right now, she knew she didn't want him to leave.

She crept over to her dresser and looked in the mirror with her back to him and whispered, "August, where have you been?"

He didn't respond. Terren was afraid to press because she didn't want to start an argument. She was too exhausted to argue. What she needed right now was the opposite of arguing. She turned to face him.

"I don't want to fight anymore. I love you. The kids miss you. We don't work without you." Terren started to cry again. "Please August, come back home."

He stood up and wrapped his arms around her. She lifted her arms to reciprocate his embrace. There was nothing between them but a towel. It had been so long since she was in his arms like this. It felt like home. She needed him on every level.

Terren looked into his eyes. It was a look that said, *I forgive you, please forgive me.* It was a look that gave him permission to consummate their forgiveness, and that's exactly what they did.

August stayed home that night. He woke up, made breakfast, got the kids ready, and took them to school. Terren felt like a new woman. As she got ready for work, she noticed how at peace she was. She hadn't felt this way in a very long time. She was ready to take on whatever the day brought her. Even if Candice failed the drug test, and Terren was forced to take on a double workload, nothing would ruin her mood. She actually welcomed more work. She was ready to get everything in her life back on the right track, and working hard equaled normalcy for her.

CANDICE

Candice sat in her car in the garage of the office building, patting concealer on her eye. She'd woken up when she heard her daughters running around in the hallway getting ready for school. She lay there until she was sure everyone was gone and then quickly found a suit in her closet that didn't need any ironing, ran in the bathroom, freshened herself up, and got out of the house before Casey returned.

She was so high when she got home last night, she knew Casey was going to have a lot of questions that she was not ready to answer. She knew it was a bad idea to take those last two hits before she left Sarah's. She didn't expect it to make her react that way.

After she finished putting on her makeup, she opened up the glove compartment to look for a napkin to blot her lipstick. As soon as she opened it, she saw a vile of coke that she had forgotten was in there. She picked it up and contemplated if she should take a hit or not. *Oh, what the hell,* she thought and decided to just take one snort as a pick-me-up to relax her before walking into the massive amount of catch-up work waiting for her in her office. With her finger she scooped out as much coke as she could and snorted it up her nose. After sucking the remaining coke off her finger, she twisted the cap on the bottle, put it back in the glove compartment, got out the car, and hurried to her office.

When she walked through the door, everything felt like it was in slow motion. She immediately regretted doing the coke before she came in, wondering if they'd gotten a bad batch, because instead of feeling upbeat and focused, she felt paranoid. Maybe that's why she reacted the way she did last night.

Inside the office, it felt like everyone was looking at her. She hurried into her office and shut the door, standing behind the door with her back up against it for a moment. *Calm down,* she said to herself, then took a deep breath and walked to her desk.

When someone knocked on her door, Candice almost jumped out of her skin. She fixed her shirt, turned around, and opened the door. It was Jeanine.

"Hi Jeanine, good morning."

"Good morning Candice, how are you feeling?" Jeanine asked, pretending to be genuine.

"I'm a lot better. New as can be, ready to get back to work, start pounding those books … you know."

Jeanine smiled. "That's wonderful."

"Yes, just wonderful, wonderful."

"Well, before you get settled in, Mrs. Mitchell would like to see you in her office."

Candice felt nauseous. All she wanted was to hide in her office and crank out as much work as possible. She was not prepared to have a conversation with Terren this morning.

"Oh, Jeanine, I have so much work to do. Is there any way I can meet with her later today? I really just want to jump in and see how much I can get done before lunch."

"I'm sorry Candice. She asked to see you as soon as you came in. She's probably really worried about you—she's been asking about you all morning," Jeanine said sarcastically.

Candice pulled at the bottom of her blazer, put down her head and walked past Jeanine without saying another word.

When she entered Terren's office, she was prepared for a long uncomfortable conversation, so she started to close the door behind her. But Terren stopped her.

"No need to close the door, Candice." Terren shouted, "Jeanine please come in here."

Jeanine came running into the office. "Yes?"

"Come here," Terren instructed.

Jeanine walked past Candice over to Terren's desk. Terren handed her a sheet of paper.

"Give this to Candice," she said sternly.

Candice could feel sweat dripping down the back of her neck. Jeanine walked the paper over to Candice and handed it to her. Before Candice could ask what it was, Terren spoke.

"Candice, I need you to take that piece of paper down to Quest Diagnostics and take a drug test," Terren instructed.

"What?" Candice asked, surprised.

"This firm is a drug-free environment, and even any speculation gives us the right to administer drug testing."

Candice let out a loud sigh. She felt like someone punched her in her stomach.

"Ma'am, I just got back. I have so much work to do—"

Terren cut her off. "This is not an option. Go take the test or submit your resignation. After the test is complete, you can go home. If the results come back negative, Jeanine will call you and you can return to work."

Candice felt like she would faint.

"If the test should come back positive, we can offer you a temporary medical leave if you agree to go to rehab."

Candice didn't say a thing.

"Do you understand, Candice?" Terren asked.

"Yes, I understand," she whispered.

"Good. You'll be hearing from Jeanine in a few days." Terren dismissed her by waving her away. Jeanine had to bite her lip to hold back her smirk.

Candice ran back to her car as fast as she could. She slammed open the glove compartment, took out the coke and snorted what was left in the bottle. There was no way she was going to take anyone's drug test. *I don't need this job anyway. I'll get a better one,* she thought.

CASEY

I was on the phone with Umaja for about two hours. After our talk, I felt a little better. At least I had released all my tears. Umaja and I had come to the conclusion that I had to: one, pray and ask God how to handle the situation, and two, confront Candice no matter what. The only way I could help her was for her to be totally honest with me. Then we could figure out from there what to do.

I went into Tate's room and started going through my clothes to pick out an outfit for school that night. I liked to look my best when I went into the city. As I was laying out a few outfits, my phone rang. It was a number with a New York area code. "Hello?"

"Hello, is this Casey?" the voice asked.

"Yes, this is she."

"Hi, this is Patricia Daniels, the secretary at Tatiana's school."

"Yes, is everything OK?" I was getting nervous. No one from Tate's school ever called me before.

"Well, I'm calling to see if everything was OK with Tatiana. She didn't show up to school for the field trip today, and we can't get a hold of her mother. You are listed as her emergency contact—is she sick?"

I felt a knot in my stomach so tight that I had to bend over in pain.

"Excuse me? I saw her leave for school today. She walked out of the house with me."

"Well she didn't show up here. Is there any chance she's with her mother?"

I was stuck, but I didn't want to make the staff at the school anymore suspicious.

"You know that is a possibility. Let me see if I can contact her mother, and I will give you a call right back. What's the number I can reach you at, Patricia?"

Patricia gave me her contact number, and we hung up the phone. Then I called Tate. Her phone went straight to voicemail. I was about to burst. I threw my phone against the wall, and the screen shattered. I lost it. I started tearing all of my clothes out of the closet, and pushing things off the dresser. I'd had it! Between my sister and Tate, I was going to go crazy! I took off out the house, running down the street and screaming Tate's name like a madwoman. I had no idea where she could be, but I knew if I found her alive, she would only be breathing long enough for me to kill her.

Chapter Five

November

CASEY

$\mathbf{P}$eace and quiet was all I wanted, not only on the outside, but also on the inside. I sat on the steps of the brownstone, arms wrapped around my legs, with my head in my lap. Last week flipped my world upside down. After Tate went AWOL from her field trip, she and some of her friends got caught smoking weed and drinking near school property. She got suspended for two weeks and was assigned two hundred hours of community service. Candice was nowhere to be found, so I had the pleasure of having to deal with punishing Tate. I wanted to strangle her, but I opted on punishment for fear that I may have not had the self control to release my hands from her neck in time before breaking it.

The day after that, Candice showed up with a sob story about losing her job. She claimed while she was in Ohio, they'd found some errors in an audit that resulted in the loss of millions of dollars, so they fired her. Then she went on to blame her behavior the night she got home on going out and getting drunk, which resulted in her crashing her car. However, I didn't smell any alcohol on her.

At this point, I didn't care what she said to me. She was

a liar. I mean come on, no fender bender would have that kind of impact on someone's actions, or appearance—she looked like she'd come off a battlefield. She was crazy if she thought I believed her. The only thing I believed about her story was that she got fired. Which meant now she wouldn't be able to pay for me to go to school. As beautiful as Harlem was, it was becoming my own personal nightmare.

I'd been talking to Umaja everyday, and he was helping me look at this situation through a different set of eyes. He came from a Christian upbringing like me, and along with his life experience, he'd helped me put some things into perspective with my sister. He helped me understand that Candice was going through a lot with her divorce, being a single mother and managing a career. He said it's a blessing that I am here to help her out, and that sometimes, God puts us in places for other people, and right now He put me here not only for Candice, but also for my nieces. Once I looked at it like that, it made me more patient to Candice's recent behavior.

I wanted to tell August about Candice, but I felt like he already had a bad impression of her, and I didn't want to make it any worse. Although he had been my knight in shining armor, I didn't want to overwhelm him with my sister's drama. I could depend on him for everything, and most of the time I didn't have to ask because he already knew what needed to be done. As much as I liked him, I knew we could only be friends because my life was too chaotic right now. Plus, I didn't like the fact that he had two kids. I wished I wasn't starting to find him attractive. However, it was difficult not to when he took care of everything. I closed my eyes and smiled at the thought of seeing his face again. When I opened my eyes, August was coming around the corner—he'd read my mind again. I wasn't depressed anymore.

"You're going to live a long time," I said as August

reached the brownstone steps.

"Why you say that?"

"Because I was just thinking about you, and then you showed up."

"Thinking about me." He smiled. "I hope it was good."

"It was," I said, twirling my hair in between my fingers. "Where's your car?"

"It's at the barber shop. I was thinking about you, so after I got my haircut, I took advantage of the nice day and walked over here to see you."

"Aw, you were thinking about me." I slid my hair behind my ear. He took a seat next to me on the steps.

"So how's your sister doing?"

"She's fine, upstairs sleeping. All she does is sleep all day."

"Maybe rest is good for her right now."

"I guess." I shrugged. "It's better than her and Tate arguing all day. That's all they do when she's awake. Tate is walking around with an attitude and Candice is walking around being bipolar. It's a madhouse."

August put his hand on my shoulder. "That's why you sittin' out here looking all depressed?"

"Yep, it's peaceful out here."

"What you doing tomorrow night?"

I took a deep breath. "No plans—besides class." For the first time it really hit me that this could be my last class.

"OK, I'm gonna pick you up from class tomorrow and take you somewhere."

"Where?" I perked up.

August looked me in the eyes. "It's a surprise."

"I don't like surprises."

"You'll like this one," August insisted. "Well, feel better. I gotta get to work."

August stood up and ran his hand over my knee before

walking away.

"See you tomorrow," I said waving goodbye.

When I went back in the house, Candice was in the kitchen. She'd been in the bed all week, so I was happy she was finally out of her room.

I was worried about her. She wasn't her regular loud and over-the-top self.

I went into the kitchen and sat down at the table, watching Candice prepare pancakes. It was as if I wasn't even there. She didn't look my way. I'd been waiting for an opportunity to talk to her, and now that we were finally alone, I couldn't think of anything to say. I didn't want to ask her if she was OK, because that question would have been loaded with a mood swing. I decided to go with something neutral to break the ice.

"Can you make me one?" I asked her, although I wasn't hungry.

She turned towards me; she didn't look well. She'd lost more weight, and she had a scarf tied around her head. She hadn't done anything to her hair since she lost her job.

"You just want one?" she asked in a little above a whisper.

"Yea, one is good."

She continued to prepare the pancakes. Then she looked over at me again.

"I'm sorry that I won't be able to pay for your school now." As the words came out her mouth, I thought she was going to have a breakdown.

"Don't worry about that. I know you're going through a lot right now. You've been with your job for years. For them to fire you because of one mistake is not right. Besides, I'm not giving up on school. I'm going to start looking for jobs so I can pay for it myself. "

Tate walked into the kitchen on the tale end of my statement. She stood at the entrance of the kitchen, eyeing Candice with her arms folded across her chest. Tate had been so disrespectful lately, Candice avoided her glare, knowing it would just lead to another one of their arguments.

Attempting to keep the tension that Tate brought into the kitchen down, I continued telling Candice about my job aspirations. "I am going to apply to some high-end restaurants in the City. I know people at school that waitress, and they bring home good money from their tips."

"That's a good idea," Candice said, pepping up a little.

Tate snickered and walked over to the table where I was and sat down across from me. I shot her an evil glare. Candice ignored her.

I could feel myself getting angry because of Tate's passive-aggressive disrespect. I continued to treat her like the child she was and kept ignoring her.

"Lots of celebrities frequent restaurants in the City."

"That's what I heard. Imagine me catching a big break while waiting tables. That would be a good story I could write about."

"Pleeassse…" Tate blurted out. "Like that would really happen." She laughed.

I turned my head around so fast towards Tate. Candice must have seen my reaction because she responded before I could open my mouth. "You never know what could happen. People get discovered all the time doing stuff like that."

Tate rolled her eyes, dismissing Candice. I could feel my body temperature shoot up. I knew if I kept talking about this I was just going to blow a gasket, so I took a deep breath and changed the subject.

"So Candice, what are you going to do? Do you have any jobs lined up, or are you going to take some time off to clear your head and figure things out?"

Tate let out a loud giggle and blurted out, "I'm gonna guess figure things out, hopefully starting with her hair."

That was it. I couldn't take Tate's behavior, and right about now she was crossing too many lines. I looked over at Candice, who had put her head down. I could tell her feelings were hurt. This made me angrier.

"Don't talk to your mother like that!" I spat out through gritted teeth, allowing my words to seep through while trying to keep my composure.

Tate rolled her eyes. "I'm just saying."

I felt my fist clench together. This girl had no idea how much she had gotten under my skin.

"I don't care what you're saying Tatiana! Don't talk to your mother like that!" Now my words were clear. I couldn't hold my anger back any longer. It seemed like every time she opened her mouth, rolled her eyes, and sucked her teeth, a level of rage was being turned up inside of me.

"Huhhh!" Tate exhaled, sucking her teeth again.

I squinted my eyes at her and lowered myself back into the chair. Candice put the pancakes onto a plate, then turned and looked at us seated at the table.

"Do you want any pancakes?" she asked Tate in a whisper.

"No!" Tate said sharply.

Candice put a pancake on a plate and started to walk towards us with it.

"I said I don't want no pancakes!"

My hands started shaking.

"This is for Casey," Candice responded.

Tate sucked her teeth so loud, I thought one was going to fly out of her mouth. "Whatever!" she snapped.

I lost control. I leapt out of the chair and flew across the table towards Tate. I grabbed Tate by the neck and slammed her on her back while she was still sitting in the chair. Candice jumped back and almost dropped the plate on the floor. I tightened my grip around Tate's neck digging my thumbs into her throat.

"DIDN'T I TELL YOU TO STOP TALKING TO YOUR MOTHER LIKE THAT? "

I was shaking Tate's whole body, slamming her head into the floor. I climbed on top of her, keeping a tight grip on her neck. She gasped out for air, but I didn't care. I was at my wit's end. Tate had pushed me over the cliff; she was disrespectful to me, to her mother and everyone in this house. She thought she was grown now, smoking weed, drinking, getting suspended from school. She had some nerve to walk around the house with an attitude.

Candice stood watching with a blank look on her face. Tate was kicking her legs and pulling at my hands trying to release my grip on her neck, but I wasn't budging. I wasn't letting go until she was about to pass out. I was going to teach her who was boss around here—and it wasn't her.

It wasn't until I could tell that she was losing strength that I let one hand go from around her neck and slapped it into her face. I pinched both cheeks together and said, "NEXT TIME I HEAR YOU TALKING TO YOUR MOTHER OR ANY ADULT LIKE THAT AGAIN I'M GONNA SMOTHER YOU TO DEATH IN YOUR SLEEP. DO YOU UNDERSTAND?"

Tears were rolling out of her eyes. She wasn't fighting back; she was afraid now. I didn't care. She needed to fear someone in this house.

I let go of her. "I ASKED YOU DO YOU UNDERSTAND?"

"Yes," she choked out.

When I stood up, she rolled over onto her side, holding her neck, crying hysterically. Candice continued to look dazed and confused like she wasn't aware of anything.

Watching Candice completely out of touch and Tate curled up on the floor sent a rush of terror through me. I didn't recognize us anymore. I ran out the kitchen, upstairs into the bathroom. I locked myself in and called Umaja.

When Umaja answered the phone I was in tears.

"What's wrong?" He asked in a panic.

"I can't…take it…here any…more!" I said between sobs.

"What happened now?"

"I am going to kill someone, I swear I am!" I cried.

"Casey, you have to calm down."

I wanted to calm down, but I couldn't. Everything had gotten so out of control. Candice, Tate and I were three strangers living in this house together, like a bad MTV reality show.

"We need to pray!" Umaja declared.

"What?" I sobbed out.

"I said, we need to pray."

"What do you mean?"

"I'll pray, you just listen."

"OK?"

Umaja began. "Dear Father up in heaven, we plead the blood of Jesus over Casey and her family. We pray that you bind confusion, anger and frustration and replace it with peace, love and understanding. Help them Lord to be more like you, to call on you and seek your face for answers. Help this family Lord…"

An hour later, Umaja finished praying. His prayer was powerful. He prayed for strength and deliverance, healing and restoration of the relationships in our family. He declared that God's presence fill up our house and that we all come out of the darkness that we are in. He touched on everything that we were going through and he didn't hold back. By the end of the prayer, I had stopped crying and started praying with him and calling on the name of Jesus—in the bathroom, on the phone. With my new unexpected, spiritual friend, Jesus showed up.

The next morning, Tate walked into the bathroom and flipped on the light switch. The lights didn't come on. She flipped them again, and when they didn't come on she stumbled over to the light and removed the bulb. She reached under the sink and got another to replace it. After replacing the bulb, she hit the switch again, but the light still didn't turn on. She screamed and stormed into the hallway.

She reached for the light in the hallway, but again it didn't turn on. She stomped into her room looking around for signs of electricity and noticed that the clock on her stereo was off. She turned the switch on her lamp, but it didn't turn on. She pushed the lamp off of the dresser, and as it crashed onto the floor as she yelled, "OH MY GOD!"

I'd fallen asleep on the couch because I wasn't interested in sharing a bed with Tate last night. I could hear footsteps above me stomping down the hall, then a door being slung open. The next thing I heard was Tate screaming.

"YOU DIDN'T PAY THE LIGHT BILL?"

I jumped off the couch and ran up the stairs. As I approached the top of the stairs, I could hear Candice yelling back, "WHAT ARE YOU TALKING ABOUT?"

When I got around the corner to Candice's room, Asia and Daisy were standing in the hallway and Tate was standing in Candice's doorway.

"WHY IS THE ELECTRICITY OFF?" Tate asked.

Candice looked around, trying to verify Tate's accusations. I did the same. I looked at the clock on Candice's nightstand, and it wasn't on. I looked at the cable box under Candice's TV, and it wasn't on. It was unusually silent in the house, not even the hum from the refrigerator.

Tate's impatience grew as she flipped the light switch

on and off in Candice's room, but nothing happened.

"Maybe it's a fuse," I said, trying to calm her down.

"Yeah, a fuse I'm sure!" Tate turned and stomped out of the room, grunting, "I hate this house!"

There were small streams of dawn light beaming through the gaps in the curtains. I could see Candice's face in the grey room. She looked guilty. I was beginning to get accustomed to seeing this look on her. And without having to ask, I knew she hadn't paid the light bill.

Daisy and Asia crept up behind me.

"Auntie, are we gonna have to live in the dark?" Daisy's innocent voice asked as she grabbed onto my waist for comfort.

"No, we won't have to live in the dark." I put my arm around her shoulders.

Asia ran and got into the bed with Candice, hugging her tight. Candice wrapped her arms around Asia and started to cry out loud. Asia squeezed her back as tight as her little arms could. "Don't cry mommy. Everything is going to be OK."

I couldn't believe this was happening, right after my prayer with Umaja. Just as I thought there was light at the end of the tunnel, we end up in literal, darkness. The reality of how awful our situation was became clear: it was going to take way more than one prayer to get us out of the nightmare that we were in. I grabbed onto Daisy, who'd started crying again. I was defeated, and there was nothing I could do to ease her sorrow.

By late afternoon, Candice had decided to send the girls to stay with Aunt Caroline in New Jersey until she could figure out a way to get the electricity turned on. She told me that her unemployment hadn't come through yet, and that's why she hadn't paid the light bill, and she was too embarrassed to ask anyone for help. I didn't understand where the money from

Daisy and Asia's child support was, but decided not to question her because frankly I couldn't take anymore of her lies.

Candice packed Tate and the girls up and drove them to New Jersey. She told me she would be staying at a friend's house while she figured things out. I decided to stay in Harlem at the brownstone. I wasn't afraid of the dark and couldn't risk going to Aunt Caroline's because I wouldn't be able to keep up Candice's charades. I figured I would finally have some peace and quiet without anyone bothering me.

I exited the building of my school and started to walk towards the train. As I was about to turn the corner, I heard a horn beeping. My face lit up when I saw August poking his head out the window.

"Why you look shocked?" he asked. "I told you I had a surprise for you."

I couldn't hold back my excitement. "I forgot all about that."

"Well, I didn't. Get in."

I threw my book bag in the back seat and jumped in the car.

"How was class?" he asked.

"Good as always." I couldn't stop smiling. "This is a nice surprise."

"Oh, this is not your surprise."

"There's more?" I squealed.

"Of course there's more, why would I brag about picking you up from school?"

"So what is it?"

He smiled. "Relax, all I can tell you is it's something you said you never did before."

I was about to ask him for a hint or something but instead decided to go along with the surprise. He didn't strike me as the type of person who would be very romantic, but I did want to see what he came up with. I sat back and relaxed as he instructed. He turned up the music. This was a nice distraction from of all the craziness going on in my life.

Just as I began to feel more anxious, the sky lit up. Everything around me was glowing. I saw one-hundred-foot billboards and colossal storefront signs, the biggest McDonald's golden arches that I've ever seen, and a million people everywhere.

I rolled down my window and stuck my head out. "Are we in Times Square?"

"Yup! You said you never been here at night, so I wanted to be the first person you experienced this with."

I was elated. "This is amazing!"

August weaved in and out of traffic, until we found ourselves on a side street turning into a parking garage. I jumped out of the car like I was about to explore Disneyland. I had dreamt about this for years, and finally it was happening.

We roamed the streets like tourists. August seemed to be relishing in my excitement. We went in and out of New York novelty shops, and he bought me everything I touched. I got an *I Love NY* tote bag, a long-sleeved T-shirt with a heart in place of the word love, shades and a hat. But my favorite purchase was an NYPD hoodie.

I skipped down the street as if we were the only ones on the sidewalk. I could feel August's eyes following me, and it felt good. I was the star in a movie and he was my leading man. I spun around, lifting my arms up like airplane wings, and almost hit someone. August grabbed me and pulled me close to him, preventing the crash; I froze while he held me in his arms. We were so close I thought he might feel how hard my heart was beating.

"You want to get something to eat?" he asked.

I nodded my head yes.

We walked down the streets of Times Square hand in

hand like a couple in love. We ended up under a huge T.G.I. Friday's sign.

"You want to go in here?"

"Sure!" I agreed.

Dinner was perfect. August told me to order whatever I wanted on the menu. So that's what I did. I fell in love with a drink called the *Rum Runner* and my main course was Jack Daniel's shrimp and steak. The food was intoxicating. I had to stop myself from mauling my steak.

The waitress came back and asked us if we wanted another drink. August asked for another soda, but my third *Rum Runner* was still half full, so I decided against a refill. August wasn't a big drinker plus he was driving. *How responsible of him,* I thought.

After we were finished with our food, the waitress came back and asked if we wanted to look at the dessert menu. I was stuffed. I shook my head no. August told her no and asked for the check. She pulled the black folder out of her apron and handed the check to August. He opened up the folder and looked at the check, and then he reached in his pocket and pulled out a massive roll of cash. All big bills from what I could see. He placed two hundred dollar bills in the folder. I was impressed by his generosity because I know we didn't run up that high of a bill.

"You ready?" he asked as he stood up.

I nodded my head yes. August walked over to my chair and pulled it out for me. I downed the last of my drink, and then we left the restaurant, entering back into the busy Times Square nightlife. For the rest of the night, we continued spending money like there was no end to it.

August parked in front of the brownstone, and I looked up at the dark house, dreading going inside.

"Is anybody home?" he asked.

Not wanting to admit the truth, I figured I'd stick with the where instead of the why. "They are staying at my Aunt's house tonight."

"So you gonna be there all alone?"

"Yup, at least I finally get some peace and quiet," I half joked.

"That's cool," August said opening up the center console and pulling out an already rolled blunt.

I stalled. "I had a really good time tonight."

He smiled and put the blunt in his mouth, lighting it. He took a deep breath in. I watched the fire consume the entire tip. He let his head relax, falling onto the seat's headrest as the smoke entered his lungs.

I watched as August got more relaxed each time he put the blunt to his lips. I wanted to feel like him. I wanted to smoke my troubles away, to forget about everything that has been happening, and forget that I was about to go upstairs and stumble my way around a dark lonely house. I just wanted to relax.

"Can I have some?" I heard myself say faster then my brain could process what was coming out.

August sat up and looked at me with low eyes, then smiled. "I thought you said you don't smoke."

"I don't, but I want to tonight. I'm not ready for the night to end."

"You sure?" he asked, frowning at me.

"Yes, I'm sure." I reached my hand out towards him.

He handed me the half-smoked blunt. First, I waved it back and forth in front of my face. Then I moved it towards my mouth until it landed on the center of my lips.

I took a deep inhale. The smoke slammed against the back of my throat. I coughed so hard my body jerked, almost hitting the dashboard.

August laughed while reaching over and patting my

back.

"I'm fine!" I snapped, pushing his arm away.

"OK," August said, leaning back into his seat.

I was embarrassed. I pulled myself together, repositioned the blunt in my hand then eased it onto my lips. I didn't rush this time. I let the smoke fill my lungs up enough for me to enjoy the taste of the quality marijuana. I closed my eyes and exhaled.

August smiled. "There you go."

I took another pull of the now small blunt, and then handed it back over to August.

He held his hand up at me, "I got more," he said, pulling out another bag of weed from the center console.

I continued to smoke the blunt down while he rolled up another one. We smoked the second blunt together. By the time we were done I'd accomplished my goal; I was relaxed.

We sat for a while in silence. Then, he turned on the radio. I closed my eyes and let the music sing to me.

"You falling asleep?" he asked.

"No," I said keeping my eyes closed.

"It's getting late. You want me to walk you in and check the house to make sure everything is OK?"

I don't know if it was the weed or what, but I wasn't in the mood to dance around the light situation anymore.

"You're gonna need a flashlight to check that house 'cause the lights are off," I said sarcastically.

"Why are the lights off?"

"I don't know? Maybe Candice smoked the money." My brain must have been fried, because I'd never spoke to August about my suspicions of Candice being on drugs before.

August looked surprised. But instead of entertaining it, he went for a more sincere approach.

"You want to stay at my house tonight?" he asked.

All my damning thoughts of Candice left my mind at

the thought of staying over August's house. Before I could respond, August said, "Don't worry, you can sleep in my bed and I will sleep on the couch."

I thought about it for a minute, then decided that probably wasn't a good idea.

"That's really nice of you, but I'm OK. I'm about to go in this house and go to bed anyway."

"I can't let you go in there by yourself, I'll feel bad," he explained.

"Please don't feel bad. I have this thing about sleeping in my own bed. Trust me; you don't want to see me in the morning if I don't get a good night sleep."

"Are you sure?" he asked one final time.

"Yes, I am."

"At least let me come in and check the house first," he negotiated.

In a desperate attempt to get him to drop the sleepover suggestion, I said "yes".

"OK, let's go check the house," I said, grabbing my stuff and jumping out of the car.

I ran up the steps of the brownstone, swinging the door open. "Come on in."

We fumbled around the house using the lights from our cell phones to look around. Once he checked every single room and closet in the house, he was satisfied.

"All clear."

"That's great. I feel safer already," I joked.

He laughed. "I'm happy you're admitting it."

"Well thank you for looking out for me."

"Anytime, I'm here for you whenever you need me."

The smile that spread across my face could be seen very clear in the darkness. I was typically a very cynical person, but I couldn't doubt what he said, because he had already proven to me that he would be there when I needed him. He'd gone above and beyond for my nieces and me, and as much as I didn't want to admit it, I liked it, and that made me attracted to him. I knew I had to be very careful around him now, because although I'm here for school and school alone, August may be one distraction that is worth indulging in.

TERREN

Terren was feeling good. August had been staying home ever since the other night when she had her breakdown over the kids. They were back into their routine, and his presence was not only making her life easier, the kids were also happy again. Even Kiarra was smiling and laughing more, and not getting attitudes with her. Terren loved having her husband back.

The only small issue was, he wasn't officially back. He still had his clothes over at his Aunt Georgia's house, where he'd been staying since he moved out. Terren couldn't stand him being over there because Aunt Georgia never liked her. Even though Terren came from a good family, Georgia never thought anyone was good enough for her precious nephew. Georgia was his mother's twin sister and didn't have children of her own, so she covered August with her bosom and never let him out.

Terren's relationship with Georgia got worse when Terren didn't invest in August's restaurant. Georgia called Terren and cursed her out. Miss Prim and Proper visited the hood that day. Then Georgia graciously decided to become a silent investor in the restaurant with a disclaimer in the contract that if they ever got divorced, Terren had no steak in any of his restaurants' profits.

Terren blew a gasket when she found out about the clause. August talked her into agreeing, stating they'd never get divorced anyway, so what was the big deal? The big deal was that the clause was there in the first place! However, Terren had to sign the agreement because Georgia refused to give him the money if she didn't, and August would have never forgiven her for that—which may have led to divorce anyway.

To add to the disrespect from Georgia and August, once the restaurant went into profit mode, August purchased Aunt Georgia a six-hundred-thousand dollar house in their hometown of New Rochelle, where the first restaurant, Georgia's Pearl was located.

Terren knew that the longer August stayed in the house with Georgia, the worse it would be on their marriage. She knew Georgia was in his ear influencing him to divorce her every opportunity she got. Terren believed that part of the reason that August stayed away this long in the first place was because of Georgia. Terren needed to talk to August about moving his stuff back home. She needed him to get as far away from Georgia as fast as possible.

Terren's plan was to talk to August tonight after work, but he'd dropped the kids off at her sister's house after picking them up because he said he had some business to take care of for the restaurant. Terren figured it was a good idea to have the kids away for the night, so she asked her sister to keep them until the morning. She decided she'd cook August a nice dinner, put on something sexy and get him in a good mood before bringing up the conversation of him moving his clothes home.

After cooking dinner she called August to see how long it would be before he got home—she wanted to have enough time to freshen up—but he didn't answer. She left him a message letting him know she'd cooked and that there was something she wanted to talk about with him, then she took her shower.

When Terren got out of the shower, August still hadn't returned her call, so she called him again. He didn't answer. She looked at the clock and it was still pretty early, only a quarter after nine, and she knew how chaotic the restaurant could be, so she decided to call the restaurant and leave a message with the host to give him.

She dialed the restaurant.

"Thank you for calling Georgia's Pearl, would you like to make a reservation?"

"Hi, no, this is Terren Mitchell, August's wife. Can I leave you a message to give to him whenever he's not busy?"

"Oh, hello Mrs. Mitchell. August took the day off today, so you will probably see him before I will. Did you still want to leave a message?"

Terren took the phone away from her ear and looked at it, confused by what she just heard. She spoke back to the hostess, "I'm sorry, he had some meetings today. I must have confused that with him being at the restaurant. Don't worry about the message. I will just see him tonight when he gets home."

"OK. Have a great night, Mrs. Mitchell," the hostess said cheerfully before hanging up.

Terren ended the call. She didn't want to make too much of the conversation with the hostess. She was sure August didn't share his schedule with her anyway. She chopped it up to him being out of the restaurant, meeting with vendors or looking for new equipment. He'd done that plenty times in the past. She didn't think he'd be that much longer anyway, so she laid across her bed and started watching TV.

She was startled when she heard the front door close. Terren jumped up out of her bed. She'd fallen asleep waiting for August to come home. She fumbled around trying to pull herself together. Her eyes glanced over at the clock, and widened at the time: 3:30 a.m.!

"August," she called out.

August crept into the bedroom. "Hey," he whispered.

"Where were you? It's 3:30 in the morning!"

"I'm sorry babe, we had an emergency at the restaurant that I had to take care of, so I got stuck."

Terren squinted her eyes at him in confusion. "Did you say you were at the restaurant?"

"Yeah."

"What time did this emergency happen? Did you get called in there tonight?"

"No, I've been there all day."

Terren shook her head no. "You've been there all day?" she repeated.

"Yeah."

"You're lying!"

"What? What do you mean I'm lying?"

"I called the restaurant looking for you, and the hostess told me you took the day off."

There was an uncomfortable silence, then August shouted. "What! Who? What hostess? It must've been the new girl. She's stupid, she don't know nothing."

Terren watched his lips moving, but she couldn't hear him because she knew he was telling a lie. She'd known this man most of her life—did he really think she didn't know by now when he was blatantly lying to her? Terren continued to shake her head, no.

"What are you shaking your head for? See this is what I mean about you! You're always finding a way to start a fight. I can't keep doing this. You just don't want me working at the restaurant because it's not yours!"

"Are you dumb?" Terren shouted. "We are married, so no matter what clause your aunt put in that contract, it's mine. And furthermore, don't try to avoid what's really going on, you coming into my house after three in the morning and making up a lie to where you've been.

"I'M NOT LYING!"

Terren took a deep breath. She wanted to try to turn the argument around. This was not in her plan for the night.

"August, OK, let me give you the benefit of the doubt.

If you were handling an emergency at the restaurant, what was the emergency?"

August went pale. He looked like a deer caught in headlights. He was quiet for a minute then he exploded. "WHAT DO YOU MEAN? YOU DON'T KNOW ANYTHING ABOUT RUNNING A RESTAURANT, THERE'S ALWAYS AN EMERGENCY! I was short staffed, the kitchen crew was backed up, some reservations got messed up, then the toilet got stopped up and I had to fix it with my bare hands because it was too late to call a plumber. Go do finances, Terren, because you know nothing about running a restaurant!"

Terren couldn't believe it. Did this man really think she believed a word that came out of his mouth? Did he really think he would bully and insult her into believing him? She was fuming.

"What are you looking at me like that for?" August snapped.

Terren squeezed her lips together to stop herself from saying something she'd regret. She closed her eyes and continued to shake her head.

"You have problems, Terren. I'm going home!" August said as he turned away from her and began to walk out the bedroom door.

The word home coming out of his lips sent fire through Terren's veins. "HOME!" Terren shouted.

Her scream startled August. He flung around to confront her.

"Yeah, home!" he taunted.

"Look at me, August! Look at what I have on. You know why I have this on? Because I was going to talk to you tonight about you coming back HOME! THIS HOME, OUR HOME, WHERE YOUR CHILDREN AND WIFE ARE! HOME!"

"HOME!" August repeated. "It's only my home when

it's convenient for you. When you need help with the kids or something. You don't need me for anything else. You made that clear when you bought this place. I didn't even want to live in Manhattan. I wanted us to buy a house in New Rochelle where our kids could have a yard and fresh air, not in the grimy city."

"We discussed this before. I bought this place because it's closer to my job and better for my commute."

"Convenient for you to get to work because your work is more stable and more important than my pipe dream of owning successful restaurants, right? Well guess what, it's not a dream anymore. My pipe dream now lives and thrives in New Rochelle, Brooklyn, and White Plains."

"I never said it was a pipe dream, August. And all you are doing is proving my point. You travel everyday for work, so it doesn't matter where we live, you still have to commute anyway. You could've opened the restaurants anywhere."

"Of course, anywhere convenient to you. I know, Terren."

Terren stopped herself from responding and realized he succeeded in avoiding the real issue at hand, his tardiness coming home tonight.

"August, I'm not going to have this fight with you again. Just tell me where you were tonight," Terren pleaded.

"Minding my business!" August spat.

Terren picked up a bottle of perfume from her dresser and shot it at his head.

"ARE YOU CRAZY?" he screeched.

"No! But you think I am, so I can show you better than I can tell you what crazy looks like," Terren said, picking up another bottle and throwing it at him.

August dodged the second bottle and started running towards the front door. Terren swooped up as much as she could on her dresser and chased him out of the room, throwing the items in her hands at him, some of the stuff landing on him, others not.

When August got to the front door, he yelled one last insult at Terren before exiting. "This is why my aunt don't like you!" he screamed and dunked out the door.

Terren threw the last bottle of lotion at the door. She screamed as it made contact. She was so upset she wanted to cry, but she couldn't because the only emotion running through her boiling blood was rage.

Chapter Six
December

CASEY

I couldn't believe how fast December had gotten here. I'd only been in Harlem for five months, but because of everything that happened, it felt like a lifetime. Meeting August was the best thing that happened to me since I'd gotten here. He was a saint. The morning after he left me at the house in the dark, he came back and gave me the money to get the lights turned on. He said he didn't feel right knowing that my nieces and I weren't able to stay at home. On top of taking me back and forth to school, he started paying my tuition and giving me pocket money. He just swooped in and was taking care of everything without me even asking.

Once I got the lights on, I couldn't catch up with Candice for two days. I lied to Aunt Caroline, telling her Candice took care of it, and I picked the girls up so she wouldn't have to come back and forth from Jersey everyday to bring them to school. It was fine with me because Thanksgiving was approaching and then they would have a few days off.

When Candice did show up, she wasn't concerned with how the lights had gotten turned back on. She went straight to

104

her room into hibernation and didn't come out until my parents got into town for Thanksgiving.

After all of the craziness that had been going on, Thanksgiving was a breath of fresh air. We celebrated at Aunt Caroline's house. All of my family was there. And to my surprise, Kayden showed up with Brooke. We ate and laughed and drank and at the end of the night August came by to see me. He pretended like he came to hang out with Kayden, but I knew the truth. When he arrived Kayden, Brooke, and I jumped into his car and went to get high.

We drove down to Liberty Park in Jersey City and smoked in the car. When we were done, Brooke and I left the boys to their conversation about football and took a walk around the park. Brooke was a cool girl. She was from Philadelphia but moved to Jersey City when she got a full academic scholarship to Saint Peter's University. After graduating two years ago with a degree in history, she moved to Harlem because she was hired as the Director of Events at The American Museum of African American History. I told her I'd been looking for a job, and she said she'd keep an eye out for me at the museum.

By the end of the night, Brooke and I had shared so much about each other's lives, we were practically best friends. We had a lot in common. We were both into fashion, we were both ambitious and had big goals for our lives, and we were both raised Christian. I felt so comfortable with Brooke, I even opened up to her about what was going on with Candice. She was very compassionate to Candice's situation. She said she'd had family members who suffered from substance abuse, but by the grace of God, they'd all been delivered. She encouraged me to pray as much as I could and promised me that God would do the same for Candice. It was confirmation of not only what I already knew but also of what Umaja had been telling me.

After Thanksgiving, everything went back to normal in the house of chaos. Candice did a great job of fooling my parents into believing everything was OK. While they were there, our father did notice she'd lost some weight, but she blamed it on being stressed from being fired. My dad agreed he would send an extra couple hundred dollars a month to help out. When he questioned me about how I would continue to pay for classes, I lied and told him that Candice had already paid for the whole semester, and I was looking for a job now so I could pay for next semester.

I was getting way too comfortable lying. My pastor used to always reference Proverbs 12:22, "Lying lips are abomination to the Lord: but they that deal truly are his delight." I was sure to be cast out of Heaven for all the lying that I'd been doing.

I was on my way out the house to meet up with August. As soon as I went to reach for the door knob, it swung open, almost knocking me over. I jumped back as Tate stomped into the house with an attitude as always.

"Excuse me," I snapped at her, "you almost hit me in my face."

Tate ignored what I said, stomped up the stairs to her room, and slammed the door.

My first instinct was to run up to her room and drag her back down by her hair. But out the corner of my eye I saw August's car pull up. She was so lucky. I couldn't stand her these days. I didn't even know who she was anymore. Every time I saw her, I just wanted to punch her in the face. I took a deep breath and walked out the house, slamming the door behind me.

I was excited to see August. We hadn't spent any time together this week, besides him picking me up, and bringing me back and forth to school. Between me studying for my finals, meeting with my groups, and class, I hadn't had time to hang out with him. But it was Saturday, and I needed to get out of the house before Tate or Candice ruined my good mood.

When I got in the car, August already had a blunt burning. I'd been smoking weed on a regular basis again. It made me calm in my current stress-filled life.

We smoked while driving around and listening to music. We were driving for a while. I didn't pay it much attention until I noticed we had been riding for over a half hour and it seemed like we were leaving New York. I wondered if this were another one of his surprises.

"Where are we going?" I asked.

"I need to go home real quick."

I was confused. "Home? You don't live in Harlem?"

"No, I live in New Rochelle. I only come to Harlem to get my hair cut, shop and see you."

"What about your restaurants?"

"What about them?"

"Aren't they in Harlem too?"

"No. I have locations in White Plains, Brooklyn, and New Rochelle."

I was stunned and a little embarrassed. In all the time I've spent with August I never thought to ask him about where he lived or even about his restaurants. I just figured he lived in Harlem and his businesses were in Harlem. No wonder I hadn't ever been to his restaurants. They weren't anywhere near me. I guess I'd just been so wrapped up in my own drama—how selfish of me.

Another twenty minutes went by before we pulled into this beautiful gated community. August pulled into one of the driveways and the garage door opened. He pulled his car into the garage, parking beside a white Mercedes Benz truck.

"That's a nice truck," I said, noticing how it sparkled even in the dark garage.

"Yea, that's my aunt's car. That's her baby." He smirked.

"Oh, your aunt's here?" I asked, nervous to meet one of his family members for the first time.

"This is her house. I am just living with her until I buy my new house."

I frowned in disbelief of how much I didn't know about August's life. It made me question what we've been talking about for the last five months. Were we only talking about me?

I was blown away as soon as I walked through the door. The first thing I saw was a wall-to-wall bookcase filled with classic titles, settled behind a big chaise chair overlooking a sunlit patio. My eyes widened. The grand home library excited me. I wanted to stop and admire the books, but August was pulling me along.

When we arrived on the next level, my jaw dropped even more. We entered into an immaculately decorated great room with a marble-encased fireplace that sat directly across from a dining area, adjoined to a breathtaking gourmet chef's kitchen. I couldn't believe I was standing in the middle of my dream house.

August walked me over to the plush designer sofa and motioned for me to sit down.

"I'll be right back. I have to get something out of my room," he explained.

I nodded as he walked away. I couldn't help myself, I had to walk around. I needed to make sure I wasn't dreaming. I walked over to the granite island and ran my hand across it. There was an antique bowl sitting in the middle of the island with nothing in it. I picked up the bowl to admire the design on the inside. As I was rotating the bowl around, delighting in its craftsmanship, I heard delicate footsteps walking up behind me.

"You like that? I got it on a trip to Guam two years ago.

You can have it if you like."

I was so startled I almost dropped the bowl and shattered it all over the granite. I turned around to see a stunning older woman staring back at me. She exuded style. She wore white tailored slacks, a white cotton boat-neck sleeveless shirt and long-sleeved floor-length chiffon cardigan with slits up both sides. Everything about her was flawless, from her perfectly styled short salt-and-pepper hair to her subtle makeup and patent leather red-bottom stilettos. I was in awe of her presence, looking down at my choice of blue jeans, black turtleneck and knee-length stiletto boots. Although I thought my choices were edgy and cute when I left the house, her elegance made me second-guess myself.

"That bowl was handmade by the villagers. It's really a magnificent piece. I have another similar to it, so it's yours if you want," she continued on.

I stood there like a star-struck teenager gawking at her, mouth half open and eyes wide. I couldn't find my words.

"Well, do you like it?" she asked, picking the bowl back up. I nodded yes, and she placed it back in my hands. "Then it's yours." She smiled and walked over to the refrigerator.

"Nuet didn't tell me he was bringing a guest, or I would have prepared something."

Nuet. Who was Nuet? Was she talking about August?

"Are you hungry?" she asked while her tall slender frame stood rummaging through the refrigerator. I knew the answer to that question—yes. I was definitely hungry. I was about to answer her, but August came down the stairs and interrupted us.

"Don't talk to her, Casey, she's a troublemaker," August joked.

His aunt turned towards August, somehow conjuring wind in the house. As she turned around her hair and the bottom of her chiffon sweater blew.

She flashed him an affectionate smile. "I am not the trouble maker in this house."

"So I see you met my aunt Georgia," August said, turning his attention back to me.

"Where are my manners? I didn't even introduce myself." Georgia reached her manicured hand across the island. "Georgia. And you are?"

"Casey," August answered before I could open my mouth.

"I'm sure the young lady can speak for herself, Nuet."

"Yes, I can," I finally said, shooting a glare over at August for answering for me.

"Pretty name for a pretty girl," Georgia said winking at August.

"What did I tell you about calling me Nuet. I'm thirty years old, time to put that name to rest."

Georgia walked over to August and placed her hand on his cheek. "You will always be my little Nuet, baby."

I let out a small giggle.

"See, now you have my girl laughing at me," August said, turning his face away from Georgia and grabbing my hand. "Come on, let's go."

"I thought you were staying for dinner," Georgia called behind us.

"No. I'm taking her out tonight," he shouted back.

"Bye," I squealed just before August pulled me down the stairs and back into the garage.

When we got into the car, August was taking off before I had a chance to buckle up my seatbelt. Once I got myself locked in, I looked over at him and said, "I'm your girl now?"

He smiled at me and nonchalantly replied, "You were my girl since the moment I laid eyes on you." Then he turned his attention back to the road and drove off, as if I should've known where we stood by now.

We ended up downtown, cruising along until he pulled in front of a restaurant called Georgia's Pearl. There was seating outside on the patio, but all the tables were occupied. Looking through the twenty-foot windows, I could see that it was pretty busy inside also.

"There's probably going to be a wait in there," I mentioned, thinking about how hungry I was.

"You don't have to worry about that. I never wait here," August said as the valet attendants opened our car doors.

He tipped them both generously, then August stuck his arm out for me to lock mine with his, and we went into the restaurant.

Inside the restaurant, the notoriety didn't stop. August was greeted by the hostess, the bartenders, waiters, and even many of the guests. I was impressed not only by how much respect everyone had on his name, but also by the appearance of the restaurant.

It was very chic yet sophisticated. Tea candles were lit on each clothed table set with fine silverware and wine glasses. Fairy lights decorated the ceiling, and original scenic framed photography hung on the walls. In the center of the restaurant, there was a winding staircase that led to the upper level and beyond that a balcony filled with additional seating. The hostess escorted August and I up to the balcony, past all the other guests to a corner table that overlooked all of downtown New Rochelle.

"Will you be having your regular tonight, Mr. Mitchell?"

"Yes."

"And shall I give your guest a menu, or will you be making suggestions for her?"

"Bring out one of each appetizer, and for her dinner, the Sunday seafood platter," he instructed.

When the hostess walked away, I couldn't wait another minute to confirm what I had been thinking since the moment we pulled up. "Is this your restaurant?"

"Yes. How did you guess?"

"It wasn't hard to figure out. Everyone here treats you like the president," I joked. "It's beautiful."

"Thank you. Aunt Georgia actually did all the interior decorating."

"She did a great job! Did you name it Georgia's after her?"

"Yes, her and my mother. They're twins; my mother's name is Pearl. It's also a play off of an oyster's pearl, since we have an oyster bar on the main floor."

"So what is this Sunday seafood platter you ordered me?"

"Oh, you're going to love it. It has baked stuffed shrimp, bacon-wrapped scallops, a lobster tail, crab claws and a piece of hickory-smoked salmon."

"Oh my God. That sounds amazing!"

"Trust me, it won't disappoint you either."

August had me smiling all night. As promised, the food was outstanding. I ate everything on my plate and tasted all of the appetizers—even the oysters. We had a very expensive bottle of wine that I drank most of. But the best part of the night was watching the sun go down. It was breathtaking. I was on top of the world with August by my side. Even though I wasn't totally sure about him calling me his girl, if this was what life was going to be like as his girl, I was willing to give it a shot.

When I got home, I was on cloud nine. I floated into the house, twirling around in circles, reflecting on the night. I pranced up the stairs, heading towards Tate's room. As I approached the door, I overheard Tate yelling at someone. I was about to walk away because I didn't want whatever she was going through to affect my mood. But then I heard her say something that sent a chill through my body.

"I wish I never had sex with him!"

I couldn't move. Did she just say she had sex? The thought of Tate having sex made me sick. I pushed the door open so hard, it banged into the wall. I ran over to her, and snatched the phone out of her hand.

"YOU'RE HAVING SEX?"

"CASEY WHY WOULD YOU BE LISTENING TO MY CONVERSATION."

"SO YOU'RE GROWN NOW? YOU'RE HAVING SEX? WHY, TATE?"

Tate didn't answer me, she just dropped her head in shame.

I asked again. "Why Tate?"

When she looked up at me, her face told me she was hurting, and anytime Tate hurt, I could feel her pain. I sat down on the bed and wrapped my arms around her. She fell into my arms and started sobbing. I rocked her, and we cried together until she fell asleep. I didn't sleep at all. Every time I closed my eyes, all I could picture was Tate having sex. I thought I would explode. I felt like that a lot lately.

I sat on the steps of the brownstone sulking. I was overwhelmed. I needed to get away. I wished I could escape to a private island where I didn't have to deal with anymore of my family's drama.

I exhaled, and inhaled and exhaled again, and then the tears started, again. I was so sick of crying. I lifted my head, wiping my eyes with my sleeve. When I moved my sleeve across my face, August's car was pulling onto my street. He pulled in front of the brownstone and rolled down the window.

"Why you not answering your phone?" he yelled up to me.

I forgot about my phone. "It's dead."

August got out of the car and walked over to me.

"You've been crying?" he asked.

"I'm alright," I said, not wanting to go into detail about Tate.

"What can I do?"

I laughed, knowing there was nothing he could do. So I joked. "Take me to peaceful."

"To peaceful? You want go to somewhere peaceful?"

"Yep."

"I know what you mean. I've been having issues with my kids' mother, and the restaurants have been killing me. I could use some peaceful in my life too."

I frowned. That was the first time August had mentioned his baby mother. I'd forgot all about her.

"You know what? I'm gonna take you to peaceful," August announced, cutting off my train of thought.

"What?"

"No!" he said. "No questions asked. You want to go to peaceful, then that's where I'm taking you. Pack a bag. I'll be back in a few hours."

I was confused. I watched as August started walking back to his car.

"Are you serious?"

"Hurry up," he shouted as he got in his car and drove off.

I wasn't sure what happened or what I'd agreed to, but just the thought of getting out of the house for the night was enough incentive for me.

About an hour later August was back. I grabbed my bag and raced down the stairs.

He frowned at my small duffle. "You pack light for a girl."

I thought I'd packed too much. "Really?" How much

did he expect me to pack for an overnight trip?

"Don't worry, I'll take you shopping when we get there."

"Shopping? Where are we going?" I asked, not really caring now that shopping was involved.

He winked at me. "To peaceful." Then we drove off, leaving the nightmare that was Harlem behind us.

Welcome to Maine. That is what the highway sign said when I opened my eyes. I'd passed out when we hit Massachusetts after smoking our third blunt. August would not tell me where we were going, but the further we got away from home, the more nervous I became. The weed made me paranoid about this rash decision. In the light of day, down from my high, all my insecurities came rushing in. I couldn't believe I didn't get any details of this trip. What was I thinking? On top of that, I was in such a hurry before I left the house, I took my cell phone not my charger. So now, I didn't even have a way to call home and check in. What were the kids going to do without me? Would Candice be home? Would Tate be OK dealing with her virginity issue on her own? Would they be worried about me?

As my internal freak out multiplied, I looked out the window and we were in a real life *Green Acres* episode. As we drove along, there were large stretches of open fields, some with cows grazing on them, some with tall stalks of vegetation sprouting out of the ground. Every few miles a house would appear. The sky looked bigger. There were no buildings obstructing the view of its beauty, just miles and miles of endless sky.

We turned onto a secluded winding driveway that stretched what seemed like a mile from the street to the house. The closer we got to the house, the bigger it got. The enormous yellow house was set up on a hill with at least ten acres of land surrounding it. On the side of the house, there was a wall of stone separating the land from a lake.

"Where are we?"

"Peaceful," August giggled.

I shot him an evil look.

"OK we're at my mother's house," he admitted.

"What?" I screeched. "Your mother's house!"

"Don't worry," he said getting out of the car, "she's cool."

I sat in the car stiff as a board. I could not believe he brought me all the way to Maine to meet his mother. I wasn't prepared to meet his mother. I didn't even know if I wanted to meet his mother.

August hopped out of the car and disappeared inside the house, leaving me sitting in the driveway alone with my anxiety attack. A few minutes into my breakdown, he reappeared sticking his head out of the screen door and waving for me to come in. I closed my eyes and braced myself. There was nothing I could do. I was literally stuck there, with no money, no cell phone, and no way of leaving without him. I took a deep breath, climbed out of the car, and made my way across the lawn to the front door.

I stepped on to the wraparound porch and took my time before entering the house. August came running to the door and hurried me inside. The house was unbelievable! It was nicer than his aunt's house. I took off my shoes in fear that they would leave marks on the cherry wood floors. I looked around at the high ceilings and oversized windows and could see the resemblance in style of Georgia and Pearl, and I hadn't even met Pearl yet.

"My mom's not here. She's on vacation with her boyfriend," he said sarcastically.

"Come on, let's sit on the porch. I'll show you around later," August said, walking towards me with two freshly rolled blunts.

I followed him to the screened-in porch. It was nice out for December. The sun was shining bright, the temperature was in the low 60s, I didn't even need a coat. August handed the blunt to me.

"Here, I want you to spark it," he said, handing me a lighter.

I put the blunt to my mouth and lit it up. I took a few puffs and handed it to August.

He held his hand up, refusing to take it from me. "No, I want you to smoke that alone." he said before picking up the other one and lighting it.

We sat there both smoking our individual pieces. After I was done, I rested my head against the back of the cozy patio chair and closed my eyes. We sat in silence until I heard a familiar sound that I hadn't heard since I left Connecticut— birds were chirping. I could smell the freshness in the air. I didn't remember the last time I'd felt this calm. There was no noise coming from outside, no one moving about the house, no talking, no music, no TVs, no phones ringing, just quiet, and birds singing. After basking in this unfamiliar calmness, it hit me: August had done it. He took me to peaceful.

It was peaceful for the rest of the day. After relaxing on the porch, August showed me to the bathroom with heated floors, double sinks, a vanity, and a walk-in shower, overlooking a large soaker tub. I ran a steaming hot bath and let myself sink under the water, covering my whole body from the top of my head to the tip of my toes. I stayed under long enough to not lose consciousness. I sat back and let the hot water soothe my muscles. I started humming to clear my mind. I didn't allow myself to worry about anything that was going on in Harlem.

August left to get dinner while I was in the tub, so I took my time getting ready. I massaged lotion into every part of my body, brushed my hair into a neat bun, and laid across the plush king-sized bed in the guest room before heading downstairs.

August came back with a large spread of food. He had fried chicken, barbeque ribs, macaroni and cheese, collard greens, dirty rice, corn on the cob, and dinner rolls with a large sweet tea and a bottle of Merlot on the side. Everything was so delicious, and I ate it all.

After dinner we went out back and sat on the patio overlooking the lake. I looked over at August and thought about how good he'd been to me. He was so kind, and he had a great spirit. He'd been taking care of me form the moment we met, and he did it without wanting anything in return. He had the ability to read my mind, and he was a man of his word. He was amazing.

I was at a crossroads. I knew that I said I wasn't going to get into any relationships, but being with August was effortless, and he hadn't distracted me at all since we met. He was the one supporting me and making sure I was still able to go to school.

I was exhausted so I told August I needed some sleep. And I did. My head was hurting from the weed mixed with the Merlot. Plus, if I didn't go to bed, I would be sleeping with August tonight, and I wasn't sure I was ready for that just yet. I was extra excited because August told me I could sleep in; he assured me his mother was out of town and we'd have the house to ourselves for the entire weekend.

The next morning I woke up to the smell of coffee and bacon. I went into the kitchen, and August had all six burners running on the oversized chef's stove. He was standing over one of the pans, scrambling eggs. The table was set and our plates already had bacon and sausages on them. I watched August cook the eggs and thought, *Why is he doing this to me?* He was making it so hard for me not to love him.

"Good morning," I said as August finished up the eggs.

"You hungry?" he asked, flashing his big smile at me.

"I am." I smiled back.

We sat down at the table and ate breakfast together.

I looked up from my food and said, "If I haven't said so already, thank you for a nice, peaceful weekend."

He smiled. "You're welcome."

No sooner than the words came out of his mouth, I heard cars pulling onto his mother's lawn and people started pouring out of the vehicles. August jumped up from the table, leaving me to go see who it was.

I heard August say, "What are you doing here? I thought you were going on vacation?"

Then I heard a woman say, "This is my house. What are you doing here? Why wouldn't you tell me you were coming?"

The door swung open, and Aunt Georgia's identical twin walked in.

"Who are you?" she asked me, then shot a hard glare at August.

"She's…my…friend," he blurted out. "I'll tell you later. What happened to your vacation?"

"Your sister called and said she needed to get away, so she and the girls are coming here for a week, so I shortened my trip to spend time with my girls."

"Margaret is coming too?" August said in a panic.

"Yes. She's on her way now. Now, who is this?"

"Casey," I said, standing up to greet her.

August cut in. "This is Casey. She needed to get out of town; she's been going through a lot. Casey, this is my mother, Pearl."

I frowned my face at his introduction.

"Casey. *Uhm hum*." Pearl said poking her lips out. "Georgia told me all about Casey—"

"OK, mom," August interjected.

"Don't worry. We'll talk about this later, son," Pearl said rolling her eyes at him. "Hello Casey, well since you already here, make yourself at home. My son doesn't bring company to my house, so excuse me if I seem unwelcoming. I'm just caught off guard."

"It's no problem, I understand," I said, reaching out my hand towards her.

She shook my hand. Then she sat down at the table. "Well looks like I came just in time. Boy, fix me one of them plates. Momma's gotta eat too," she said waving August along.

August's family was warm and welcoming. His sister Margaret was nice and laid back.

She had three adorable kids, a son and two younger daughters. Her daughters took to me right away. They kept talking to me and showing me their dolls and wanting me to play with them. August's mother was just as gorgeous as her twin Georgia—and she called him Nuet too.

The morning after his family arrived, I took a shower before everyone got up and went to sit on the porch. His youngest niece Jasmine was on the porch, coloring.

"Good morning Auntie," she said looking up from her coloring book and smiling at me.

Hearing her calling me Auntie warmed my heart. She made me miss Daisy and Asia. I hadn't checked in on them since I left. What kind of aunt was I? I needed to call home.

"Do you want to color with me?" Jasmine asked, smiling at me with her big brown eyes.

"Sure honey."

About twenty minutes later, a minivan pulled into the driveway and August and Margaret got out, unloading grocery bags. I ran out to help them. "I thought you were still sleeping."

"Naw, I been up. Me and my sister went to the store.

My mother is about to cook breakfast. "You hungry?" he asked me.

"Yes!" Jasmine said excited.

I laughed, "Yes, I am."

"Good because we bought a lot of food."

And he was right. The spread was unbelievable. There was bacon, eggs, ham, sausages, grits, pudding, gravy, home fries, fried fish, pancakes, Belgian waffles, a fruit platter, muffins, homemade maple syrup, and biscuits that she'd made from scratch.

Before we dug in, everyone joined hands and August's mother prayed over the food. I didn't know what to eat first, everything looked so good. August passed me the platter of her homemade biscuits. I decided not to take a biscuit since I'd already taken a waffle. As I was passing the biscuits along August stopped me.

"You have to try my mother's biscuits!" he said placing one on my plate.

"OK, if I have to," I said smiling at his enthusiasm over his mother's biscuits.

The first bite into the biscuit changed my life. I never tasted a biscuit like that. It stimulated every taste bud in my mouth. Its buttery, warm fluffiness hypnotized me. I ate three more.

I overate. I wasn't by myself either. Everyone looked like they were ready for a nap. But instead of napping, we stuck around and cleaned up the kitchen together. When we were done, we all walked down to the lake. We brought blankets and wine and laid out relaxing until we all fell asleep.

I woke up to August staring at me. "Can I help you?" I said playfully.

"Take a walk with me," he said, standing up and reaching his hand out to help me up.

He took my hand, and we walked down this long

gravel path along the lake.

"You make me happy," August confessed.

I wasn't expecting him to say that. I stopped walking. I wanted to say it back, but I felt like if I told August how happy he'd made me over the last few days, there would be no coming back from it. I'd been holding back my feelings this entire time. One false move and I would be exposed.

"Are *you* happy?" he asked, lifting my head up and looking me in the eyes.

I wanted to say yes. I wanted to scream it. I wanted to tell him I've never been more attracted to anyone in my life. I wanted to tell him that he'd been my savior since I moved to Harlem and I didn't know what I'd do there without him. I wanted to pour my heart out to him, but I couldn't. I was too afraid of what that would mean. I still wasn't ready. But he'd been too good for me to just leave him hanging, so I whispered, "Yes."

August grabbed me by the waist and pulled me close to him. And then he kissed me. A chill shot through me. His thick soft lips caressed mine. His tongue danced with my tongue like they'd been rehearsing for this dance their whole lives. He started to move his hands up the back of my shirt, his caress made the hairs on my neck stand up. I kissed him harder, grabbing his head and pulling him closer to me. He pulled back, then placed his lips on my neck. It felt so good I let out a loud moan.

"I love you Casey," he whispered.

I jumped back and pushed him away.

He looked confused. "What's wrong?"

What was wrong was I wanted August now more than I wanted air. By the look in his eyes, I knew he felt the same. I panicked. I had to turn this perfect moment around, because if I didn't, I knew I was about to break a very important vow I made with God and as far as I've already strayed from my rededication to Him, this would take me all the way over the cliff. I did the only thing I could think of to turn him off—I shut him down.

"I can't love you," I blurted out.

August looked as if I'd just slapped him in the face. I immediately regretted it.

"What? Why would you say that?"

"Because I feel like you're going to be a distraction, and I won't be as focused on my career if I fall in love with you."

He was disappointed. "So you're saying you'd rather have a career than love me?"

When he said it like that, it sounded so bad. I wanted to take the words back. "I don't mean it that way, but yes, my career is very important to me."

"So why have you been leading me on? Why didn't you correct me when I called you my girl? I thought we were building something all this time. But instead you were what? Using me?"

"I...I..." I was at a loss for words. August stared at me waiting for an answer, but I had nothing to say. After a long uncomfortable pause, August turned and walked away from me.

"August, where are you going? Don't just walk away from me," I pleaded.

August stopped, turned around, looked me in the eyes and said in the coldest voice I'd ever heard come out of his mouth, "There's no future for us!" Then he turned back around and walked away.

His words knocked the wind out of me. I felt horrible. I never wanted to hurt him. I've only been concerned about me and what's been going on in my life. I never even considered how August was feeling.

As I walked back towards the house, I contemplated

what I was going to do. I had to be honest with myself first. Did I want to be with August and risk losing focus? As I approached the house, I saw August sitting in the passenger seat of his sister's car smoking by himself. I opened the driver's door and got in. He didn't say anything, he just took a pull from the blunt and passed it to me, never looking my way.

I smoked with him. As I was about to deliver another apology, the song "Milkshake" by Kelis came on. He and I had made fun of it a couple times, but ultimately we decided we liked it. We looked at each other and started smiling. I turned up the radio and got out of the car. I stood in front of the car and started dancing to the song. He was laughing.

I danced around imitating Kelis in the video. When I saw him bite his bottom lip, I knew I had him. I got in the car and climbed on top of him. We mauled each other. Our kiss was so hot, the windows got foggy. I could feel his manhood pressing into me.

He pulled my shirt over my head and started kissing my bare chest. I was in ecstasy wanting more than his kisses. When we both couldn't take anymore teasing, somehow we got our pants off. Before his pants hit the floor he pulled a condom from out of his wallet. I took it from him and did the honors.

We started off slow. For a moment I thought in my head, *yeah, I got this*. Then he took over. He grabbed my waist with his big hands, and holding me tight, he yanked my body down onto him. I screamed. My eyes rolled into the back of my head. He kept pulling me closer and closer, until I exploded. I screamed again! All my muscles tensed up, but he didn't stop. All my screams and cries didn't make him stop. He kept on until my whole body went weak, and I peed on him. And that's when he decided he was done. He squeezed me tighter than he did all night, and in unison we howled at the moon.

I lay on top of him unable to move except for the occasional uncontrollable tremor. When we finally separated,

I had to crawl over to the passenger seat. I pulled my jeans on as gently as I could. My skin was extra sensitive; as my jeans were rubbing against my legs, they were sending my body into Tourrette's-like shocks.

August got out of the car and went into the house. He came back with a towel and started wiping the seat. I couldn't believe I peed. Oh my God! I peed in his sister's car! How in the world were we ever going to explain that? How was I going to get in the house? I couldn't walk.

After August was done wiping up the seat, he opened the driver's door and grabbed my hand. He led me to the guest room.

"You still can't love me?" He smirked.

I submitted, "Yes, I can!"

He grabbed my hair and wrapped it around his hand until he had a good grip, then he pulled my face close to his and said, "You belong to me! You understand?"

"Yes."

That night was the first time I'd ever experienced multiple orgasms. I didn't even know my body was capable of doing that. I was ruined. I went from being a little girl to a woman that night. Everything that people said about orgasms was true. They were absolutely fantastic!

We ended up staying in Maine for an entire week. I missed my exam, and I didn't care. Every time that I would try to care, August would sweep me away into a quiet room and remind me he was in charge. I didn't have a clue what I'd gotten myself into.

TERREN

Terren was going through the motions. She'd drop the kids off at school, go to work, taking on way more than she was mentally capable of handling at the time, leave work early to transport the kids to their after-school programs, go back to work, then finally pick the kids up, go home, help with homework, cook, sleep, and wake up to do it all over again. Being a single mother was the toughest job she ever had to do.

She hadn't spoken to August in a week, and she wasn't planning on calling him. She didn't have the strength to deal with any of his nonsense. He was clearly going through an early mid-life crisis, and she wasn't going to allow him to drag her along. They'd never gotten that irate with each other, and she was in no rush to go there again. And since he never answered her question of where he'd been that night, there was sure to be a reoccurrence.

She sat at her desk, looking over data while waiting for her meeting to start. She'd been making some huge strides on this account they were grooming. Landing this client was the one thing she had to look forward to in her life right now. Not to mention that it would solidify her promotion. The only problem was she would have to find a nanny quick, because once they signed with her firm, she would be working a lot more hours.

Terren picked up her purse and took out her phone. She wanted to see if she'd gotten any responses back from the inquiries she'd sent out for nannies. As she picked up the phone, her alarm went off with a description stating, *last day of period, pick up new birth control*. Terren frowned at the message. Her period wasn't on. She opened up the alert and looked at the date on the calendar—she was late. Her period was six days late. Terren's heart started to race. She was never late, especially while on the pill, because it regulated her cycle. How was she late? The only time she'd ever been late was when she was pregnant.

"Oh my God!" Terren blurted out.

She couldn't be pregnant. The pill was supposed to protect her from being pregnant. Terren started to hyperventilate. She felt like someone punched her in her gut. She picked up the phone and called her sister. As soon as she heard Melissa's voice she shouted, "I'M PREGNANT!"

"What?" Melissa chocked.

"I mean, I think, I am. I'm late—"

"—and you're never late," Melissa finished Terren's sentence.

"What am I going to do?" Terren cried.

"First go get a test from the pharmacy. If it's positive, then panic."

"I can't have another baby right now!"

"I told you to burn your tubes girl! You were the one like, *what if I want another baby one day*?" Melissa mocked.

"Shut up, Mel. I don't want to hear that right now."

"I'm just saying, I tied, burned, ripped out and buried my tubes, girl."

Jeanine walked into Terren's office. "The meeting is starting."

Terren waved Jeanine away.

"Bye Mel," Terren said, hanging up on her sister and rushing out of her office to the meeting.

Later that night Terren sat frozen on her bed. All she could hear in her head was her doctor's voice on repeat saying, "Congratulations, you're eight weeks pregnant."

She'd called and begged for him to squeeze her in today due to an emergency. She left work right after her meeting. She didn't want the added stress of questioning the home pregnancy test, but she couldn't deny the heartbeat blasting through the ultrasound machine.

Terren was mortified. She hadn't spoken to August in a week, and after their last encounter, announcing a pregnancy wasn't exactly the way she pictured their next meeting to go. This was a terrible time to have a baby. *But maybe, just maybe this baby would bring the family back together,* she thought. As much as she didn't want to be the one to call first, she knew she couldn't hold a secret like this from her husband, so she picked up the phone and called him.

"Hey Terren," a women's voice came blaring through the phone.

"Who is this?" Terren barked.

"It's me, Margaret," August's sister announced.

"Hey…Margaret…where are you? Why are you answering August's phone?"

"I'm in Maine at my mom's house. August and I are visiting her. We've been here all week."

"Maine! Oh, he didn't tell me he was going to Maine."

"He surprised us. We weren't expecting him but he showed up."

"Oh…that's…nice," Terren said sarcastically. "Can you tell him I'm on the phone? I need to speak to him."

"He's not here. He went to gas up the car, he's heading back home tonight. He left his phone here on the charger, and when I saw it was you calling, I picked it up."

"OK…well can you please have him call me when he get's in? It's very important."

"I sure will. But how are you, girl?"

"I'm…OK…I guess."

"I can't believe what's going on between you and

August. I've been meaning to call you."

"Uhm…Yeah," Terren mumbled. "He told you?"

"Yeah, he did. It's crazy because I thought you two would be together forever."

Terren was getting annoyed. "Well, every couple goes through hard times, Margaret."

"That's what I said, but divorce? I never thought you two would get divorced. How are the kids taking it?"

"EXCUSE ME? August told you we were getting a divorce?"

"Well…he didn't…use those, words."

"Then why would *you* use *those words*?"

"Uhm…" Margaret stumbled. "It's…his…actions, that made me… assume."

"WHAT IS HE ACTING LIKE? HOW DOES A MAN WHOSE GETTING A DIVORCE ACT?"

"He's…acting…single. Or at least, not married…to… you."

"WHAT IS THAT SUPPOSED TO MEAN?"

"Terren, I don't know, I'm sorry. I shouldn't have mentioned it. I know this is a difficult time, and I should've kept my mouth shut. I was just concerned about you and my niece and nephew."

"Well you know what, Margaret? I don't need your concern or anyone else's. But while your brother is in MAINE, ACTING SINGLE, let him know HIS WIFE IS AT HOME PREGNANT WITH HIS THIRD CHILD!"

"Oh, my God! Terren," Margaret sighed. "You're pregnant."

"YES! Eight wonderful weeks pregnant by your SINGLE-ACTING BROTHER!" Terren snapped. "And what a joy it is to know my husband is planning on making our unborn child a bastard!

"Terren—" Margaret gasped.

Terren cut her off. "No, Margaret, thank you for the update. That's all I needed to hear!" Terren cried out before ending the call.

CASEY

Our drive back to Harlem was uncomfortable. August was acting really weird after a conversation he had with his sister before we left. Something was off. We pulled up in front of the brownstone, and it looked dark. We brought my bags up the stairs into Tate's room. As August put the bags down, I closed the door behind him.

"What's up?" he asked.

"Nothing," I said as I pushed him up against the bed and kissed him.

He pulled away from me. "I have to go," he said, moving me to the side.

I grabbed him and stuck my hand in his pants. "You still want to leave?" I asked planting my lips on his neck.

"Chill out." he snapped, pushing me away.

"I gotta go," he said coldly, then slid out the room.

I was confused. He hadn't turned down sex from me since we started having it. But he just left, walked down the stairs and didn't even say goodbye.

Later, I called August to see if he wanted to come over, but I got his voicemail. I had a really bad feeling in my gut, I just didn't know what it was. That night I found myself in the house alone. I finally charged my phone and there were voicemails from my father, my mother, and Aunt Caroline. I figured this was a good time to return these phone calls.

I started with my parents. They were disappointed and told me how irresponsible it was to leave without my charger, or without letting anyone know where I was. Aunt Caroline let me know that the girls were over her house. She said Candice had been gone for a couple of days and left them in the house alone. I wasn't surprised at all.

I called August again and the phone went straight to voicemail. Since I'd known him, that never happened before. I'd been complaining about how much I wanted peace and quiet, but now that it was being forced on me, it was terrifying. I lay in the bed, holding the phone, waiting for August to call back. But he never did. I woke up in the morning in the same position, with the phone in my hand waiting for it to ring.

I called August a few times, but he never answered. I was beginning to feel like I'd been played. Around nine o'clock that night my phone finally rang, it was August.

"Come outside," he instructed.

I wanted to tell him to no, but I couldn't. I was yearning for him. So I put on some sexy boy shorts, a half tank, and covered it up with a peacoat and went outside to see him.

I got into the car, trying as hard as I could to be angry, but August just ignored me. We both sat in silence while he drove to New Rochelle. When we pulled up to his aunt's house, instead of parking in the garage, he stayed in the driveway.

He turned the car off, pulled a blunt out of the console and lit it.

"Why are we in the driveway?" I asked.

"Because I don't smoke in my aunt's house, not even the garage," he snapped. Then he looked down at my bare legs. "Isn't it a little cold for shorts?"

"No!" I said rolling my eyes. He passed me the blunt, and I smoked it without passing it back until I felt high.

After I was done, I unbuttoned my coat.

August's eyes popped out of his head.

He put his hand on my leg and started to massage it. I started getting worked up. I missed him too much. I couldn't wait anymore. I jumped over the seat and straddled him. I unzipped his pants, pulled off my shorts, lifted the shirt over my head and sat my naked body down on him - not concerned about a condom.

We went at it. I threw my head back, basking in our bliss. I wrapped my arms around his neck and opened my eyes. A black Lexus truck pulled up behind us and a woman jumped out. I stopped moving.

"August, there is a woman coming towards the car!" I said, expecting him to be just as confused as I was.

"Terren!" he whispered.

"Who's Terren?" I shrieked.

Before he could answer, Terren was at the driver's seat window, banging her fist into the glass.

"August! Who is she?" I asked as my bare naked body straddled him.

Terren was banging on the window so hard I was sure that the glass was going to shatter all over me. August picked me up off him and threw me into the back seat of the car. I grabbed a hoodie that was on the backseat and wrapped it around my naked body. August zipped up his pants and jumped out of the car. As soon as he opened the door, Terren attacked him.

"HOW COULD YOU DO THIS TO ME AUGUST?" Terren screamed as she and August tussled about. She kept punching him, he was trying to block her blows. But she was relentless. She slapped him and he held her, she broke loose and he pinned her against the car, she fought back screaming the whole time.

"I AM HIS WIFE! WE HAVE BEEN MARRIED FOR TEN YEARS! WE HAVE TWO KIDS TOGETHER! I AM PREGNANT RIGHT NOW!"

Her screams echoed through the car. I was shaking and crying and stuck in the back seat.

They kept fighting until she started trying to get into the

car to me. I am a fighter, but I've never been afraid of anyone the way I was afraid of Terren. I don't know if it was because I was naked or because she caught me off guard, but all I knew is I didn't want to fight her.

August pinned her down on the car so she couldn't move. I could hear her crying.

"How could you do this to me August? How could you do this to our family? Why, why, why?"

I wanted it all to stop. I was stuck in this car with no escape. Then, God sent me a sign. I heard a jingling inside the pocket of the hoodie. I stuck my hand in the pocket and there were August's keys. I examined them to see if any of them looked like a house key. When I pin pointed the two potentials I decided to make a run for it. I opened the door on the opposite side of the car that they were fighting and I sprinted to the house. I put the first key into the door and it worked. I ran in the house and locked the door behind me.

For the next two hours I sat in August aunt's library, rocking myself and crying while August argued with Terren. Then there was quiet. A moment later, there was knocking at the back door. I peeked out the window to see who it was. It was August.

I opened the door, and he fell into the house. He grabbed me to catch his balance. I caught him in my arms and hugged him tight. He returned my affection, squeezing me into his chest. Then I broke down.

We sat on the chaise in front of the bookshelf, and he held me while I rested my head on his chest.

"I am so sorry, Casey. Tell me how to fix this. I know you probably want to go home, but she threw the car keys somewhere, and I don't know where they are. Do you want me to call you a cab?"

I didn't know what to say. What did he mean *how could he fix it?* He's married. She's pregnant. There were so many questions running through my mind. I couldn't process them all. If I were in a sane mind, it would've made sense for me to go home. *I should run away from him, but then what?* I didn't want to be home by myself crying all night. I needed him to console me. *If I went home, would he go console her?* Hell no! He wasn't leaving me tonight, and furthermore, I never got my orgasm. She interrupted us before I could. At the very least I needed some angry sex. I wiped the tears from my face and looked at him. "I'm not going anywhere. I am staying with you."

He kissed me on my forehead, then led me upstairs to his room, where for the first time we didn't have sex. Instead we made slow passionate love all night long.

Chapter Seven

His Wife

TERREN

Terren paced back and forth around her living room. The living room was a shrine of her life with August. There were pictures everywhere; on the walls, on the tables, the TV stand, and above the fireplace. She looked at all of their happy memories, confused about how her husband of ten years—who'd never been knowingly unfaithful before—could turn into someone who she didn't recognize.

She'd been up all night crying. She walked past a mirror and caught a glimpse of her tear-stained face. Her tears made her angry. Out of frustration, she slammed her hand down on the fireplace mantel and slid it from one side to the other, sending all the photos crashing to the floor. She looked down at the broken glass and thought of her children getting cut, so she bent down to clean up the mess. The first broken picture she picked up was of her and August standing on top of the Gros Piton Mountain at Jade Mountain Resort in St. Lucia on their honeymoon. She stared at the photo. She looked at their faces and remembered how happy they were. She sat down on the sofa, holding the picture to her chest, and thought

136

back on their life together.

She remembered the day they met like it was yesterday. She was so excited because it was her first year as captain of the volleyball team, and they made it to the state championship. They were competing against their rival high school. August and some of his teammates from the football team were in the gym watching her game. Her team took home the big victory. August approached her as she was celebrating with her teammates and told her she had the best spike he'd ever seen. He went on to say, she was going to be his girl because he needed a winner to compliment him. She was unimpressed. She remembered thinking how cocky he was. But August was persistent and wasn't taking no for an answer. He followed her to the bus and wouldn't let her get on until she gave him her phone number.

For the first year of their relationship, all they did was talk on the phone. Terren's father had a rule that his daughters could not date before the age of sixteen. But August was adamant. He found ways to spend time with her. He went to all of her games, and he would meet her after school to walk her home. Other than that, the extent of their relationship was phone calls. On her sixteenth birthday, August showed up to her house with roses and asked her father if he could take her to dinner, and her dad reluctantly agreed. They'd been together ever since.

Fifteen years, a marriage, and two kids later, she and August had been through their fair share of ups and downs. They both lost their fathers just six months apart. She had two miscarriages before having their son. They went broke and had to move in with her mother after August invested all of their money in a nightclub. When the nightclub got shut down because of an issue with the liquor license, he almost went to jail. If that wasn't enough, he started gambling and spent all her father's life insurance money in Atlantic City, all in an attempt to get money to reopen his club. He was very depressed during that time, but through it all, she stuck with him.

Terren didn't have a problem stepping up and taking care of the family while he got himself together. The change in him didn't come until the restaurant took off. They made so much money the first year in business, he opened a second location, and before year three, they were opening a third. Aunt Georgia, who's a prominent interior decorator, utilized her extensive network to promote the restaurants, and in no time they'd made millions in profits.

Aunt Georgia kept August busy. She wanted to ensure that she could cash in on her investment. She had August everywhere. He was always out networking and meeting all of her rich friends, and he ate up the attention and notoriety he was getting.

When he went out and bought Georgia that house, he didn't even consult with Terren. She was so hurt when she found out. He didn't even respect her enough to tell her—she found out from his mother.

The night she confronted him he came in high—a habit of his that she hated, but with his new lifestyle he did more often. He flipped out on her, telling her how she had no right to question what he did with *his* money and that she should be happy that he could repay Aunt Georgia for all she's done.

The last four months had been absolute hell. August had gotten worse, and now Terren knew it was because of this other woman. *Who is she? Where did she come from? How long has he been seeing her? Has he been cheating on me our entire marriage?* She'd never thought he would ever cheat on her. Who was he? Was this the man she married?

Terren got nauseous. The nausea reminded her of her unborn baby. She thought about the night he came back from Maine and all the lies he told her. He was so excited that she was pregnant. He said he was moving back home and that he was sorry and they were going to be like they use to be. He even stayed over and made love to her that night. What he failed to mention was that he was sleeping with another woman!

She questioned him about Margaret's observation of him "acting single." He said she made that comment because he hadn't brought Terren with him. Now Terren believed what Margaret said. August probably did say they were getting divorced. Terren started to cry. She put her hand on her stomach. What was she going to do now? How could he do this to her? Had things really gotten that bad between them that he had to go be with someone else? It's not like Terren ever turned down sex with him. No matter how mad she was or what they were going through, she always let him share a bed with her. *This is insane,* she thought. *He can't leave me. Not after everything we've been through. We have children together. What am I supposed to tell my children?* She'd joked about being a single mother, but she never thought that could be her reality.

Terren jumped up off the couch. "He's out of his mind!" she shouted. "If he thinks he's leaving me alone with two kids and one on the way, he's got another thing coming. He's my husband, and ain't no woman in hell going to come between us."

I hope they've had their fun, Terren thought, *because game over. I'm getting my husband back! My family will be together again. When we said until death do us part, I meant it, so if that chick knows what's best for her, she better stay out of my way because the only way she can have my husband is in a casket.*

CASEY

I'M HIS WIFE…I'M HIS WIFE…I'M PREGNANT!!! I woke up in a panic. Terren's screams were pounding in my head. The sun was shining in my face; I could hardly open my eyes. I rolled over to escape the sun's rays and there he was, the married man I was sleeping with.

In the light of day, everything seemed so surreal. I sat up in the bed and covered my face with my hands. Now sober, I couldn't wrap my head around the fact that he was married! *How—when—where has she been all these months?*

Married?

Was this some sick joke his baby momma was playing on me to scare me away from him? He couldn't be married. It was impossible. *If he's married, why is he living here with his Aunt? If he's married, why has he been at my beck and call … why did he take me to meet his family … and why wasn't there any mention of her from any of them … if he's married then why did he stay with me last night and not with her … and why did he make love to me like that last night? Why, why, why? She's a liar! He's not married!*

I wanted to scream! I looked over at August sleeping so peacefully, and I wanted to knock him over the head. He needed to get up. I needed the truth, and now! I started pushing against his back, each push turning into more of a pound. His eyes shot open.

"Hey! Why you hittin' me?" he asked, bracing himself.

"You're married?" I shouted, more like an acquisition then a question.

August sat up in the bed.

"She's pregnant?" I asked.

He put his head down. His silence answered my questions. I knew in my heart that Terren wasn't lying. I'd slept with a married man, and I loved it, I loved him.

"Why August?" I cried.

He was guilty.

I raised my voice. "Are you going to say anything?"

August lifted his head up.

"We're separated," he whispered.

"Separated means you're married."

"She kicked me out, and now that I moved on, she wants me back."

I just stared at him wondering if he thought that anything he was saying equaled *not married* because to me everything sounded like *blah…blah…blah.*

I got out of the bed and started picking up pieces of my clothes off the floor. I thought, *Why didn't I go home last night?* August jumped out of the bed and grabbed me.

"Where you going?"

"I need to go home, August. I need to process this."

"You can't leave like this, we need to talk about…"

"Talk about what? There is nothing you can say to me to change the fact that YOU'RE MARRIED AND YOUR WIFE IS PREGNANT!"

"I don't love her!" August shouted, grabbing my face. "I'm in love with you."

My knees buckled.

"She knows I love you and that's why she's going crazy."

I sat down on the edge of the bed. "Love is a dangerous word, August. You can't just go throwing that word around all over the place."

August held my hands in his.

"Do you think I tell everyone I love them? If so, you

don't know me at all. I've never loved any woman besides my wife. I didn't set out to fall in love with you. You made it hard for me not to love you, Casey."

"What am I supposed to do with that August? You're still married," I reminded him.

"I know, but we're not together. We're getting a divorce."

A divorce? She didn't seem like a woman preparing for a divorce, and besides that I couldn't erase his infidelity out of my head. "August, you're not divorced yet. And she's pregnant. I can't compete with that."

"You don't have to compete. I don't love her anymore, I love you."

"This is too much for me, August. All this time I've been pouring my heart out to you, and you never thought to mention to me you were married. How have you been able to hide that? At the very least, I thought we were friends, but friends don't keep secrets like this from each other."

"I wanted to tell you about her before, but there was never a good time. You were going through all that stuff with your sister and we *were* just friends, I didn't know we would ever take our relationship this far, so there was no need to worry you with my issues."

I thought about what August was saying, and he was right because I definitely didn't ever expect for us to be together. I knew why he didn't tell me about Terren, it was the same reason I lied to him about only being with one person— we didn't want to ruin each other's image of one another.

August put his arms around me, pulling me close to him, and then he kissed my forehead.

"I would never do anything to hurt you," he whispered.

I could hear his heartbeat, feel him breathing, and I knew that I wasn't ready to let him go. I just didn't know how to keep him. We loved each other, but could our new love handle this? I didn't know if I was strong enough to wait it out until they got divorced. I didn't know if I was OK with being the reason they got divorced. My parents are married. I believe in what marriage stands for. I know how sacred marriage is to God. What would that make me if I were the cause of breaking God's union? I'm sure Pastor Mosley would have lots to say about this.

August and I parked in front of his restaurant. He needed to check on something before he drove me back to Harlem. Even though it was only one in the afternoon, I needed a drink. I deserved it after everything that happened. So I sat at the bar while August did what he had to do.

The bartender placed a napkin in front of me. "Will you be ordering lunch?"

"No, just a drink. I think I want something sweet. What do you recommend?"

"I know what you need." He smiled and started pouring different liquors and juices into a shaker. When he was done he poured the contents into a chilled glass and garnished it with cherries and orange slices. "This is my special mix," he said, pushing the glass towards me.

I picked it up with much anticipation, hoping that it would take away some of my anxiety. As I put the glass to my lips to take my first sip, I was jerked out of my temporary bliss by a familiar voice.

"You've got to be kidding me!" Terren shouted.

Terren charged towards me. August raced from the back. jumping in between us right before she got in my face.

"What are you doing here?" she yelled to me.

I jumped up, feeling braver today now that I had clothes on. "August, you need to handle your business!" I shouted.

"Why are you here?" Terren asked again.

Using sarcasm I replied, "I *was* having a drink!"

"You need to leave!" she insisted.

"No, Casey you don't have to leave. Terren, you need to leave!" August barked.

"What? *I* need to leave?" She pushed August.

"August, take me home!" I said, trying to push past him, but he wouldn't let me by.

"I said you ain't going nowhere." He pushed me back towards the chair.

"Why do you keep telling her to stay?" Terren cried. "WHY ARE YOU DOING THIS?"

"You need to leave, Terren. I will talk to you later."

"No! I can't take this, August. If I leave, I'm done," Terren cried out.

"Terren, just go!"

Terren posed her ultimatum. "No! You need to choose right now, August. It's either going to be me or her."

Without any hesitation August answered, "Her!"

Time froze. I could tell Terren felt it too. The restaurant went silent. Even though I was happy that he chose me, I was taken aback to hear him say it to her face. Terren looked like someone just punched her in the stomach. I felt bad for her, but couldn't hide the vindication on my face.

"Her?" Terren choked out.

"Yes, now leave." August's words were cold-blooded.

For a moment we all just stood there looking at each other. Then I began to feel uncomfortable. I didn't belong there.

I pushed past August. "Listen, I'm gonna go." Not really knowing where I was going, I walked towards the door. Before I could get my foot out the door, I heard Terren calling after me.

"Excuse me, can I talk to you? Can I talk to you?"

I turned around and Terren was right behind me.

"What do you want?" I asked, crossing my arms over

my chest.

She walked up closer to me. "I want to talk to you, woman to woman."

It was the first time I got a good look at her. She was a very pretty woman. We were the same complexion, had the same long black hair. The only significant differences were she was a little taller than me and she had big intense brown eyes.

"Talk!" I said, moving my neck from side to side, annoyed at how pretty she was.

"Listen, my problem is not with you," she said. "I don't even know how much he's told you about me."

"Nothing," I admitted.

"He didn't tell you he was married?"

"Nope," I said, assuming she meant before his confession this morning.

"Did he tell you he had kids?" she asked, pointing to her car, where two kids were peeking out the back window.

"Yes, he told me he had kids," I said, feeling my defenses break down.

"Well if he didn't tell you he was married, I guess he also didn't tell you I was pregnant?"

I turned my head away from her in shame. "No."

"Well I am. I see he's been lying to you, so just in case he said we were getting a divorce, we're not. He's not going to leave our family. We were just together the night he came home from Maine."

"What?" I couldn't believe it.

"Sweetheart, he's my husband. We've been together since we were kids. We will get over you."

I started to cry. Everything she was saying made sense. The reason I couldn't get in touch with him the night we got back was because he was with her. He made me trust him, and as soon as I let my guard down, he ran home to his wife. I was a fool.

Terren went to her car, opened the glove compartment, and pulled out some tissue. She handed some to me. "I know you're hurt. Here, wipe your eyes," she said sincerely. "How old are you?"

I wiped my eyes. "Twenty-one."

"Honey, you have a lot to learn and a lot more life to live. You have to walk away from this."

"I love him," I cried.

"Listen, I know he's charming," she said, wiping my face. "But our family comes first, and no matter what, I will always be in his life. I'm asking you to please leave him alone, not only for me and my family, but for yourself. You deserve better than what he can offer you."

I could not believe what I was hearing. August's wife was telling me that I deserved better.

On cue, August rushed out of the restaurant. "Let's go, Casey," he said, grabbing my arm and pulling me towards his car.

"Are you going to say anything to your children, August?" Terren snapped.

August shot Terren a death stare when he saw his kids in the car staring out the window. He shoved me inside his car, and then ran to Terren's car to see his kids. He said something to them that I couldn't make out. Terren was yelling at him. He ignored her and hurried back to the car. We drove off while she continued yelling behind us.

We didn't say one word to each other the entire ride back to Harlem.

When we pulled up in front of the brownstone, I reached for the door handle and August grabbed my arm.

"I'm sorry, Casey."

"I know," I said. I got out of the car, walked up the steps, closed my eyes, and stood at the top of the brownstone steps with my back to him until I heard his car pull off.

When he finally left, it felt like a weight lifted off of my shoulders. I did love August, but not as much as Terren did. What I couldn't understand was why she was so nice to me. Regardless of her reasoning, she was right; I had to leave August alone. There was no way I could justify staying with him after that conversation with her, and adding adultery to my already long list of sins was not on my things to do list.

TERREN

Terren slammed her fist down on her sister's dining room table. "She's a damn child!" she blurted out.

"Was she at least cute?" Melissa asked, shifting her daughter from one arm to the other.

"That's beside the point!" Terren sighed. "But yes, she's cute."

Melissa shook her head. "Wow…"

"I talked to her. The poor thing started crying."

"What? What did you say to her?" Melissa frowned.

"The truth! I told her I was pregnant, I wasn't leaving my husband, and she needs to leave my family alone."

"What did August say?"

Terren closed her eyes as to relive the moment. "He has his head in the clouds over this young girl. He says he wants to be with her."

Melissa gasped. "Get outta here!"

"Yes girl, he's lost his mind."

She sat down at the table across from Melissa, who was rocking her sleeping daughter.

Terren paused before whispering, "He loves her."

"Oh, Terren," Melissa said, reaching out and grabbing her sister's hand.

"He loves her," Terren repeated. "How can he love her? After everything we've been through! How could he love someone else?"

Tears started to run down Terren's face. "What am I going to do, Mel?"

The front door swung open. Melissa's husband Josiah

walked in the house. Terren snatched her hand away and started wiping her face before Josiah saw her tears.

"Hey babe. How was work?" Melissa asked.

"Same ol', same ol'." Josiah said as he took off his jacket, which revealed a gun sitting in a holster hanging over his shoulders. "Just another day in the life of an NYPD detective." he said as he removed the holster and put it inside a locked cabinet by the door. "Hey Terren."

"Hey Jo," Terren said, forcing a smile on her face. She wasn't ready to let Josiah in on all of her drama.

He walked over to Melissa and gave her a kiss. "I'll let you ladies talk." he said as he took their daughter out of Melissa's arms and headed towards the bedroom.

Melissa took Terren's hand again and squeezed it. "Don't you worry about August. He's going to come back to you. He may say he loves this girl right now, but he married you, and that means a lot. However, if he wants to run around like a child chasing little girls, you should let him, but you have to be strong. You have to cut him off. You can't give him any access to you or your house. Make him suffer."

"I don't know if I can do that," Terren admitted.

"You have to try. Then watch, once he feels like he's losing you, he'll be crawling back in no time. You're going to have to beat him at his own game. Show him what it feels like to lose you, then he will come crawling back."

"Mel, I don't have time for games. I just want him to come home," Terren said placing her head down on Melissa's shoulder.

Melissa rubbed her head. "I know, Terren, I know."

CASEY

When I got in the house, I was surprised to see that Candice was home. She was dressed, her hair was done, and she'd cleaned up.

"Hey little sister," she said cheerfully.

"What's going on?"

"Nothing much." She smiled.

I asked the million-dollar question. "Where have you been?"

"I've been looking for jobs. Getting together with old friends who have business connections. I've even been thinking about going back to school. I've wanted to do that for a long time, and I think now would be perfect."

"Really?" I asked, wondering how much of what she was saying I could take serious. She'd just stopped paying for my classes and couldn't even keep the lights on, how was she going to afford to go back to school?

"Yep, and you watch, I am going to start my own law practice. Bruce thinks he is so smart, but I'll show him."

"Bruce? What does Bruce have to do with this?" I asked.

"Everything!" she shouted.

Tate walked through the door from school, looked at Candice and I, and walked upstairs to her room without saying a word.

"Well, hi to you too, Tatiana!" Candice shouted behind her.

Tate ignored her.

"I am so sick of her. I swear she is really going to make

me hurt her one of these days," Candice mumbled through gritting teeth.

"Where are Daisy and Asia, Candice?"

"They're at Aunt Caroline's for the night. I just needed her to keep them for one more day. I want to get this house together. I am going to pull out the Christmas decorations soon so we can put them up as a family."

BANG, BANG, BANG, BANG, BANG. Candice and I jumped at the pounding on the door.

"Who is it?" I called out.

"It's Bruce," Candice whispered.

"Bruce?" I repeated.

Candice hurried to the door and opened it. Bruce bust through the door, pushing Candice out of the way and charging into the house like a maniac.

"WHERE ARE MY KIDS?" Bruce hollered.

"Don't come in my house acting crazy!" Candice shouted back at Bruce.

Bruce got up in Candice's face and shouted again, "TELL ME WHERE THE HELL MY KIDS ARE?"

"They're at Aunt Caroline's house for the night!" Candice said, backing away from Bruce.

"FOR THE NIGHT CANDICE? YOU'RE A LIAR! THEY HAVE BEEN OVER THERE FOR OVER A WEEK! YOU THINK I DON'T KNOW WHAT GOES ON WITH MY CHILDREN? I'M NOT A GOOD FOR NOTHING DRUG ADDICT LIKE YOU."

I gasped at Bruce's words. I couldn't believe he called Candice out.

"DON'T CALL ME THAT, BRUCE!" Candice screamed back at him.

"YOU ARE! YOU'RE SO STUPID YOU GOT FIRED FROM YOUR JOB, YOU HAVEN'T BEEN PAYING THE BILLS. WHAT ARE YOU DOING WITH MY DAUGHTERS'

CHILD SUPPORT MONEY? ARE YOU SPENDING THAT ON DRUGS TOO?" Every word coming out of Bruce's mouth was like fireballs being thrown. And each ball of fire hit Candice and burned all the lies she'd been telling down to the ground.

"I told you when I left that if I found out you were using again I would take my daughters. Did you think I was playing?" Bruce's words penetrated through me.

"You can't take my kids, Bruce!" Candice cried.

"Don't cry now! Those tears can't save you, you're finished! I am so tired of your lies and your games. You're a sorry excuse for a mother, and I will not have my daughters being raised by you. What kind of example are you setting for them? If I were a different man, I would beat your head in!" Bruce said as he raised his fist to Candice.

"STOP BRUCE!" Tate screamed from the top of the stairs.

Bruce, Candice and I looked up, for the first time noticing Tate standing there watching this live horror movie.

Tate ran back into her room, slamming her door behind her. Candice was shaking. Bruce turned his focus back to Candice.

"You are poison to everyone around you. I'm taking my kids, and I dare you to try and stop me. Don't worry about seeing them again. I am going to pick them up from Caroline's house, and you can go rot in that crack house you crawled out of."

Bruce turned around and stormed out of the house.

Candice dropped down to her knees and started screaming at the top of her lungs. Her aching screams made me cry. I ran to her and wrapped my arms around her. I didn't know what else to do. All my suspicions were confirmed. Candice was on drugs and spending the girls money on it too. I was furious with her, but as she sat there curled up on that floor crying like a baby, my heart hurt for her. I wanted to take all her pain away, but there was nothing I could do or say to erase the fact that Bruce was taking the girls.

Later that night the house was silent. Tate had run out and went to God knows where, and Candice locked herself in her room. I lay on the couch with the covers over my head thinking about my life. I couldn't believe Candice was really on drugs, Tate was having sex, and I was sleeping with a married man.

I hated that I had mixed emotions about August. Even after everything that happened, it didn't change the fact that I loved him. And now that we'd been intimate, my body was yearning for him. When I thought about his touch my body shook. I loved everything about him, his voice, his smile, his kiss, and his eyes. I was crushed that I couldn't be with him.

Just when I felt I was going to jump out of my skin, my phone rang. It was a New York number I didn't recognize.

"Hello Casey?" The voice of an older woman came from the other end.

Confused, I answered back. "Yes."

"This is Georgia, August's aunt."

"Oh… Hi."

"I wanted to talk to you about Terren, August's wife."

I took the phone away from my ear and looked at it to make sure this was really happening. "Uhm…OK," I answered.

"Terren is crazy, Casey. She put my nephew out of his house and now that she found out that my nephew has moved on, she wants him back. You can't believe anything that woman says."

Was she for real? Terren didn't seem like she was lying to me. Or did she? She was a little bit over confident with her story, and why was I the only one crying out there? It was her husband, but she didn't shed a tear.

Then Georgia dropped a bomb of information on me. "I

don't even believe that's his baby!"

I was stunned. "Why would you say that?" I was desperate to know.

"Because he hasn't been there. When would he have time to get her pregnant?"

"Why are you telling me this?" I asked. Even though I was happy to be receiving this unexpected information.

"Because she's had her claws in my nephew for years, and I'm sick of it!" she yelled. "August loves you. He told me what happened, and I don't think it's fair for her to lie to you and ruin things between you guys before you even get started. I haven't seen him this happy in a long time, and he deserves to be happy."

I sat quiet. The hope that I had for August was being restored.

"Are you there?"

"I'm here," I said softly.

"Listen, don't let Terren come between you two. OK?"

Without second guessing it, I let the word escape my lips. "OK."

"OK now. I hope to see you soon. I owe you a nice dinner," Georgia said and hung up the phone.

This had to be the most insane thing that ever happened to me. One thing I will say about the women in August's life is that they love him. Aunt Georgia made some serious accusations about Terren, and I was confused because what she was saying didn't match the woman that I'd met. I needed to speak to August myself. I picked up the phone and dialed his number.

August picked up on the first ring.

"I didn't think I was going to hear from you again," he said pitifully.

I got right to the point. "I need to talk to you."

"OK?"

"In person," I demanded.

"OK, I can be there in about an hour."

"Alright. I'll get ready. See you in a few." I hung up the phone and ran upstairs to take a shower.

When I saw August pull up, my heart skipped a beat. I didn't want him to know how excited I was, so I took a deep breath to calm myself before I got in the car.

"Can we go back to your house?" I asked.

"Whatever you want," he agreed. "Open the dashboard."

I opened the dash and there was a freshly rolled blunt in it.

"That's for you. I know you had a stressful day," he said.

I smiled and lit it right up. After taking a few puffs, I was ready to talk. "Your aunt called me."

"I know."

"She said she doesn't know if Terren's baby is yours?"

"Did she?"

"Yes, but your wife says you were with her the night we got back from Maine."

"She's a liar. I haven't touched her since before I moved out."

"This is a lot for me to process, August. One minute you're just this sweet, non-complicated guy, the next you're married with a pregnant, crazy wife, whose baby may or may not be yours. I don't know what I'm supposed to do with that."

"You don't have to do anything with it. The reason I never brought it up to you in the first place is because I didn't want to add any more stress to your life than you already had to deal with. I will be divorced soon. You will never have to deal with her. Put her out of your head. I'll take care of it."

"Are you sure?"

"I'm positive. Please just trust me and let me handle it."

Even though I had so many more questions, I decided they weren't all going to get answered tonight. "OK, I'll trust you August. Until you give me a reason not too."

"I respect that." He smiled.

The rest of the way back to New Rochelle, I confided in him about what happened earlier with Bruce, and as always I felt better once I got it all off my chest.

When we got to his room we cuddled on his bed. The room was dark aside from the light from the TV.

"I'm happy you're here, Casey."

"I'm happy I am too."

He kissed the back of my neck while he entered me and whispered in my ear, "I love you."

I smiled.

Then he said, "I missed you."

I moaned out in ecstasy.

"You ready?"

I opened my mouth to answer him and exploded from his touch, "Yesssssssssssssssss!" August hit my G-Spot like he had a personal invitation to it.

I was a goner! It didn't matter what had happened in the last couple days, August was mine. Even though Terren told me she wasn't going to leave him, August kept drawing me in. *And why should I give him up? He keeps chasing me. She shouldn't have put him out if she wanted him.* I'd made up my mind. I wasn't letting him go. Maybe I would have to put up with her, but she was going to have to put up with me too, and she had a rude awakening coming because I was a handful.

Chapter Eight
January

CASEY

Christmas came and went. Nothing was the same since Bruce
took the girls. Candice couldn't even gather the strength
to decorate. Tate went home to my parents, and I stayed in
Harlem to be with August, although I should've gone home
because I didn't spend much time with August during the
holidays. Now that the truth about Terren was out, he was
comfortable with using her and his kids as an excuse to be
absent. On Christmas Day I didn't see him until late at night
since he was with his *kids* all day. Candice and I stayed in the
house, and Brooke came over, we cooked some food, had some
drinks and turned Christmas into a dance party. When August
showed up late that night, he handed me five hundred dollars
and said Merry Christmas. I was grateful, but putting money in
my hand wasn't the romantic gesture I was expecting. My gift
to him was thoughtful. I framed a poem that I wrote and gave
him a picture of us. A week later I found the picture stuffed into
the pocket behind the driver's seat in his car. I was furious. He
said he'd forgot to bring it in the house.

Terren got my number out of August's phone. She

started calling me everyday to check in. I'm convinced she's bipolar. I never knew what mood she'd be in when she called. One day it's all about how much of a whore I am because I broke up her family, the next day she'd call me to complain to me about how hard it is being a single mother. She would walk me through her daily routine of what I now called the *thanks to me*: thanks to me, she had to explain to her kids why daddy isn't coming home; thanks to me, she had to bring her son to basketball practice; thanks to me, she had to play mommy and daddy. I figured she needed a friend. Brooke and I started playing jokes on her. Brooke would answer the phone and pretend to be me. It was hilarious to watch. Brooke was my new best friend. We were always together. When I wasn't with August, I was with her. I was happy I had her in my life because I needed a sounding board for all my drama.

I pretended the situation with Terren wasn't bothering me; the truth is it was tearing me up. Every night I'd lay in bed thinking about her. I wondered if she was OK and how far along she was in her pregnancy. I wondered if she was going to those doctor's appointments that you would want your husband at, alone. I prayed for her. She'd become a part of me, a sad part that I wished would disappear, but she wouldn't. She made sure I didn't forget about her.

Kayden's birthday was coming up, and he was having a big party to celebrate. August was excited about the party because his birthday was only a few days apart from Kayden's. I was excited because I hadn't been out in a long time, and August hadn't been the guy who used to show up and wisp me away to Maine or take me out for a night in the city anymore. Everything had changed since I found out about Terren. I'd noticed a lot of things about him now that I hadn't before. For one, he smoked a lot of weed. He woke up smoking, he smoked all throughout the day and before we went to bed. He was fine as long as we were smoking, but if for some reason he weren't able to smoke, he'd become a jerk. He'd zone out for long periods of time and not want to be bothered.

The day of the party, Brooke and I started drinking in the morning. We'd bought our outfits a week in advance and had our hair done the day before, so we decided to kill time with a bottle of Remy and a couple bags of weed. August must have been excited too, because he went all out and he gave me a really big allowance to do the same. I bought this short skintight gold metallic dress with a low V-neck that almost reached my belly button, and my back was completely exposed. To finish my look off, I found these magnificent light gold Jimmy Choo stilettos that made my legs look long and sexy.

Around nine p.m., Kayden came to pick up Brooke, and they left for the party. I stayed and waited for August. He took so long, I finished off the bottle of Remy and smoked a whole blunt to myself. Nowadays I could go through two blunts alone—anything to keep my mind off my current relationship status. August hadn't mentioned his divorce, and if I brought it up he would get upset and say he was handling it. It didn't matter because I couldn't leave him anyway. At some point I'd sold my soul. I knew what I was doing was wrong, but besides August's moodiness from weed withdrawals and now having to deal with him having a family, he was still the person I relied on. He took care of me, I could talk to him about anything, he made me laugh. And our sex was magical, there was no denying that.

It was ten forty-five when August called me letting me know he was about to pull up. I went into the bathroom and freshened up my makeup before he arrived. While I was looking out the window waiting on his BMW to come around the corner, I saw a shiny black Cadillac Escalade parked in front of the house. The driver's side door opened and August stepped out looking real good in a white linen outfit. I opened the door as soon as he reached the top step.

August eyes widened when he saw me. "Baby you look sexy as hell!"

"You look good yourself." I smiled.

He licked his lips. "I'm scared to bring you out looking like that."

I couldn't stop blushing. I cupped my arm in his, and we walked to the car. He opened my door like a gentleman and helped me up into the truck.

When we pulled up to the club, there was a crowd of people lined up to get in. Of course we walked straight to the front of the line and were escorted in by one of the bouncers. Inside was crazier than outside. I couldn't believe Kayden knew so many people. We walked into the VIP, and Kayden and Brooke were standing in the middle. Kayden was holding up two bottles of Belvedere in each hand. Brooke ran up to me practically falling into my arms.

"Case, you got to try this," she slurred, opening her clutch and handing me a piece of tissue.

"What is this?"

"It's an E pill!" she shouted over the music.

I handed it back to her. "Oh no, I don't do that."

"Trust me, you haven't had sex until you had sex on E."

"I said no!"

She stuck it back in her bag and tapped her hand against it. "OK, well I have it right here if you change your mind."

August brought over a tray full of shots just in time. Brooke and I took three back to back. From there, the drinks didn't stop coming. Before I could get one down, another one was being pushed in my face. I was drunk and we hadn't been in the club for an hour. Brooke grabbed my arm.

"I have to pee, come to the bathroom with me," she said dragging me along.

When we got in the bathroom, my body must've known I was near a toilet, because I had to go. I shut myself into a stall, pulled down my g-string, and squatted over the toilet to pee, keeping my arm pressed against the wall of the stall so I wouldn't fall and touch the toilet. When I stood up, my panties hit the floor. I was disgusted. I stepped out of them and threw them in the toilet and flushed them. I wasn't drunk enough to wear panties that touched a public bathroom floor.

I stumbled out of the stall towards the sink. Brooke was still locked in a stall. I wanted to throw some water over my face, but I didn't want to mess up my makeup.

"What is taking you so long?" I yelled.

She opened the stall and waved for me to come in. "I have a surprise for you."

I went into the stall with her and she had a blunt rolled up.

"Surprise!"

I was happy. I needed something other then liquor right now. One more drink and I would have been done for the night.

We lit the blunt and I smoked first. I took a deep pull—I wanted to get high fast. I pulled it a couple times and the blunt started crackling and popping.

"Why is it popping like that?" I asked.

"Girl, I probably left a stem or a seed in it trying to roll it up quick in this bathroom."

I twisted up my face. "You got me smoking cheap weed?" I complained. August only bought quality weed, and it never had stems or seeds in it.

"It shouldn't be. I paid good money for this," she explained.

I passed her the blunt and as she was smoking, I noticed it wasn't burning like normal weed, and it had a funny smell.

"Girl I don't know where you got this trashy weed from, but don't buy it again," I said waving the smoke out of my face.

"I won't," Brooke said passing the blunt back to me.

I complained about it, but I still helped her smoke it, hoping it would level out my drunkenness.

When we left the bathroom, I was super high. As soon as we walked into the VIP August pulled me close to him and whispered in my ear, "Where were you?"

"I went to the bathroom with Brooke."

He started running his hands over my body. I was being turned on with every touch. All my senses felt as if they were heightened. The lights, the music, the smells, and any touch may as well have been orgasm injections. August handed me a glass of champagne. As I drank it, a little bit escaped my lip and dripped down my chin to my neck. I grabbed August by the head and shoved his face onto my neck. "Lick it off," I moaned.

August dragged his tongue from my neck to my earlobe, and I went crazy. I started jumping up and down, dancing and waving my arms in the air. I was singing out loud, then I jumped up on a table. I was winding my body so fast, I stumbled and would have fell smack on the floor if August hadn't caught me. The near fall didn't stop my dancing. I swayed over to Brooke and started dancing with her. We were grinding on each other and feeling each other up and down. Her touch felt so good against my skin, I wanted more. She rubbed my bare back until I felt her hands start to go up my skirt. It was so bad people started throwing money at us.

August snatched me away from Brooke and pushed me into a corner.

He was furious. "What the hell is wrong wit' you?"

"Nothing. What's wrong wit' you?" I laughed in his face.

He pushed me into the wall. "Why the hell you dancing on her like that?"

"I'm just having fun. What, I'm not allowed to have fun?" I rolled my eyes. "You want me cooped up in the house waiting for you like Terren?"

August backed up, taking his hands off me for the first time. I almost toppled over. As I tried to catch my balance, he grabbed me by my shoulders and slammed me back into the wall so hard, my head bounced off of it, sending me into a daze.

"DON'T YOU EVER MENTION MY WIFE AGAIN!"

As I came out of the daze, he pushed me into the wall again. Then he turned to walk away. I blinked my eyes trying to adjust my vision from the daze and felt a rage come over me. I ran up behind him and smacked him in the back of the head. "I HATE YOU AND YOUR WIFE!"

August turned around and charged me. I stared swinging at him wildly. He scooped me up, threw me over his shoulder, and carried me out of the club kicking and screaming and punching him.

He tossed me into the passenger seat and sped off down the road. I started laughing hysterically.

"What's the matter Daddy?"

"Shut up Casey!" he yelled.

"Let Mommy make you feel better," I said crawling over to his seat and trying to straddle my legs over him as he was driving. August strong-armed me pushing me back down into the passenger seat.

"Come on Daddy, let me make you feel better," I said, trying to grab at his pants.

"Move!" he said, pushing me away again.

"Let me make you feel better, I owe you one." I laughed.

Suddenly, I felt a dizzy spell come over me. I lost muscle control in my neck, my head dropped down in his lap like a dead weight, and I blacked out.

When I came to I was being thrown down on August's bed. He had the light on in the room and it was blinding me. I covered my face with my hands.

"Where your panties at?" August screamed.

"I flushed them down the toilet. Why? Does that turn you on?"

"You're drunk!" he snapped.

I bounced up off the bed, grabbed onto August and started kissing him all over his neck. He tried to resist, but I kept pulling him towards me, unbuckling his pants. He finally gave in. He took all of his aggression and pushed me down on the bed, ripped my dress off and pinned down my arms. "This is what you want?" he barked.

The moment he entered me he hit my G-spot. August wrapped my hair around his hands, pulling my neck back so hard, I thought my head was going to pop off. I was stimulated by his every touch. It was like a bomb went off in me. I screamed, totally out of control. August put his hands over my mouth to quiet me down until I passed out.

When I woke up the next morning, I couldn't lift my head up off the pillow. I couldn't even open my eyes. I stretched my arm out to wake August, but he wasn't there. I forced my eyes open and looked around the room, he was gone. I pulled the covers over my head, and when I looked down at my naked body under the covers, I saw that I still had my shoes on. I started to reach down to try to take them off, but my whole body cramped up. I was in so much pain. I didn't remember how much I had to drink. My memories of last night were very foggy.

I heard the door swing open. August entered the room and pulled the covers from over my head.

"Get up!" he shouted.

It was like someone had hit a Chinese bong on my

head.

"Why are you yelling?" I whispered.

"Oh, you have a hangover now? What happened to all that mouth you had last night?"

"What are you talking about?" I asked, clueless.

"Yeah, I bet you don't remember." He pushed a coffee in my face. "Here, drink this."

I inched my way up in the bed.

"You're a piece of work, you know that." He frowned.

"August, I don't remember what happened last night, but can we talk about it later, please?"

"We don't have to talk about it at all. Put this on so I can take you home." He threw an oversized sweatshirt at me and some of his old sweatpants and walked out of the room.

I was confused by his anger. I didn't think whatever happened could have been that bad since we clearly had sex.

It took me about twenty minutes to pull myself out of the bed and get those clothes on. I looked a hot mess with his clothes on wearing my fabulous Jimmy Choo stilettos. My curls were completely flat on one side and stuck to my head on the other. I tried to pull my hair into a ponytail, but it hurt too much, so I left the bird's nest alone.

August was sitting in the Escalade waiting for me. That truck was even more beautiful in the light of day. We drove to my house in complete silence. He'd never been so angry with me. I wished he would just tell me what happened last night.

We pulled up in front of the brownstone, and he didn't even put the car in park. I looked over at him but he didn't look back at me. "Are you just going to give me the silent treatment?"

August continued to look away from me.

"That's real mature of you, just ignore me," I said, staring at him.

August turned to me, stared in my eyes and said, "I hate

drunk bitches!" Then he turned away from me and looked back out the window.

His words stabbed through me so hard I let out a gasp. I couldn't think of one of my usual witty comebacks or something equally rude to say to him. I was at a loss for words. I opened the door and slid out of the truck. Before I could close the door, he sped off. I stood there watching the smoke from the tires blow in my face. I had this pain in my chest, suffocating me. I knew it was my heart—

Broken.

TERREN

Terren sat on her bed debating if she was going to do something for August's birthday. Over the years she'd done everything from throwing parties to going on vacations. This year was different since she was dealing with him being with another woman.

She'd developed this sick obsession with Casey. She'd gone through August's phone one day when he came over to see the kids and found Casey's number. She'd been calling her ever since. She called Casey every day, partially because she wanted to be a constant reminder to her that August had a family. The other reason was she needed to know more about Casey. What was it about her that August was so drawn to? Yes, Casey was a pretty girl, but she wasn't a supermodel. From what Terren understood, the girl didn't even have a job. She was completely opposite of Terren. Terren was ambitious and driven. Maybe August didn't want that anymore, maybe he wanted someone who 'needed him,' who had to depend on him. He'd mentioned that Terren worked too much, and he didn't really like when she was the breadwinner. Maybe he wanted someone less ambitious.

Terren just didn't know how to be less … anything. Furthermore, she didn't completely trust August to be the sole source of income. Yes, the restaurants were doing well now, but what happens in ten or twenty years? There is no retirement plan, no stock options in the restaurant business. Her job was their security.

She had gotten them established and was making smart financial investments for their children's futures and for their retirement. She was also a rising star in her company. The way she'd handled all the changes at work had secured her a promotion. She would be given bigger accounts and a significantly bigger salary. She didn't care how much August was attracted to Casey's neediness; she wasn't going to stoop down to her level to satisfy him. The reality was she couldn't afford to. And looking at how things were going, it wouldn't be in her best interest to give up her job right now anyway. August running around spending money on his new toy and taking money out of their household wasn't helping to convince her that she should leave her job. What if he really divorced her, then what?

She couldn't believe she was even thinking about a divorce. At first she thought August's relationship with Casey was just a phase, but it'd been months and he still hadn't come home. She wished she didn't miss him, but she did. Being pregnant wasn't helping; her emotions were all over the place. Some days she wanted August around and some days she hated him.

During Christmas, August really threw her off. They have a tradition with the kids that they can open two gifts and unload their stockings on Christmas Eve, and he showed up to be with them. It felt like old times again. He stayed all night, and on Christmas morning while the kids played with their toys, he snuck into her room and made love to her the way that he used too. It was the first time he touched her in months. It was also the first time since she'd been pregnant he acknowledged their baby. After they made love, he laid his head on her now-showing belly and said, "Hey little man." It wasn't much, but to her, he'd had a whole conversation. He even stayed for dinner; they sat down at the table like a real family. It gave her hope that they'd be able to work it out soon.

But after Christmas, he went right back to Casey. Terren couldn't stand it. She wanted his touch again, and she was willing to do anything she could to get it. She thought of using the kids, have them plan something to get him over to the house again. He would never disappoint them. But that wasn't sexy enough. She needed to do something that would make him remember why he married her. She needed advice. So she picked up the phone and called her sister.

Melissa answered the phone half asleep. "Hello," she slurred.

"Mel, wake up I need your help."

"What, what's wrong, is it the baby?" Melissa panicked.

"No. I need your help coming up with something I can do for August's birthday."

"Oh, I have an idea," Melissa perked up. "Not a damn thing!" she spat.

"Mel, I'm serious."

"I'm serious too. You should get him some divorce papers. Maybe he will like that."

"That's not funny, Mel. Come on, I need your support."

"I'm trying to be supportive, but my patience is running thin. I'm tired of you crying all the time and allowing him to come in and out of your life when he feels like it."

"What am I supposed to do? He's my husband!" Terren cried.

"I know you're emotional right now, especially because you're pregnant, but I can't support you making a fool of yourself."

"Just help me out with this one thing," Terren pleaded. "When you were pregnant, did you do any freaky pregnant tricks in the bedroom?"

"Yes, but my husband wasn't sleeping with another woman."

"I know but ..."

"There is no but. This is pathetic Terren, you need to leave him alone!" Melissa shouted.

"Forget it, Mel. I didn't call you to make me feel bad."

"I'm not trying to make you feel bad, I'm trying to help you be strong and to stick up for yourself. You need to treat August how you treat your employees at work. When they are not doing their job, you hand them a pink slip. August is not doing his job, time for the pink slip."

Terren was frustrated. "OK whatever. Thanks for the advice. Talk to you later." She hung up the phone before Melissa could respond.

Terren thought she had to do something to show August that she was still the sexy, spirited girl that he fell in love with. She also needed to show him she was willing to do whatever it took to save their marriage. It needed to be spontaneous, exciting and sultry. She could figure it out, she knew him like no one else. Casey may have him now, but she didn't know August inside and out—Terren did.

CASEY

I pulled my head out of the toilet long enough to catch my breath while Brooke patted a wet towel on my forehead. I'd been throwing up all day. I couldn't believe how drunk I'd got. I know I drank a lot, but I'd never blacked out before. Brooke filled me in on what she could remember, but it wasn't much. Besides, nothing she said justified August calling me out of my name.

Brooke helped me back to Daisy and Asia's room. I'd been staying in there since Bruce took them. I lay on the bottom bunk in the girls' room curled up in a ball. Any sudden movement would send me back to the toilet. I hadn't talked to Terren today. I'm guessing she wasn't very happy about that because she wouldn't stop calling.

"Hand me my phone," I said to Brooke, limply dropping my arm down on the bed.

I answered the phone prepared to hear the foolishness. "Terren," I said her name as patiently as I could.

"Casey, you've been avoiding me today?" she sneered.

"How could I possibly avoid you, Terren?"

"Have you seen my husband today?"

"Not since this morning," I answered honestly.

"I hear there was a party last night that I wasn't invited to. Do you think it's because I'm pregnant? Or maybe the party wasn't for the wives, it was for the whores?"

"I'm not sure Terren, maybe the party was for people he actually liked."

"That's really cute and that may have even hurt my feelings if he didn't marry me so it is likely that I am one of his favorite people in the world."

"Well, if that's how he treats his favorite people then I hope he hates me," I snapped. I was too sick to deal with this chick. I was over this conversation. "Terren as much as I love our little chats, I'm not feeling well so I'm gonna have to catch you on the next go around." I fully intended to hang up in her face, but my reflexes were so slow at the moment, I heard her next plea.

"Wait Casey, don't hang up. Believe it or not I wanted you to…help me with something."

"What? You want me to *help you with something*? Please don't mistake your harassment calls as a sign of us being friends, Terren."

"Sweetheart please, I make all the decisions around here, and I've decided to give my husband a gift for his birthday that he's never had before. Something that he and I discussed a long time ago, but never got around to."

Now I was annoyed. This chick really called me to help her get *my* man something for his birthday. I know he was her husband, but not for long. Soon he would be all mine. I couldn't believe the nerve of her to call me with this nonsense. "Terren, I'm hanging up."

"Don't you at least want to know what it is?" She asked.

"Not really." I didn't know what upset me more, the fact that she was getting him something for his birthday or that I was so broke that I couldn't afford to get him anything.

"It will make him really happy if you help me with this, I promise."

I could tell that she wasn't going to give up. At this point I wanted her to just get it out so I could say no and hang up the phone.

"Fine, what is it?"

"I want us to have a threesome."

My mouth dropped. "Are you out of your mind?" I shouted.

"What did she say?" Brooke eavesdropped.

"No, I'm not. I know my husband, and I know this will make him happy. I figured you should be happy that I am including you; it can be your last hurrah because he's going to leave you and come back home to his family soon, so you may as well go out with a bang. You will be helping fulfill one of his fantasies, and you won't go down in our family history as just another harlot."

"You're crazy, and I feel sorry for you."

"Maybe, but you'll do it if you know what's best for you, because either way I will be giving him this present with or without you, and he will accept it. So I will let you sleep on it and hopefully you will make the right decision." She giggled. "I really don't want to bring another woman into my husband's life if I don't have to."

"Whatever!" I was so furious I hung up the phone. Terren had officially lost it. It was all making sense to me why August was leaving her now.

A week after my drunken spell, I still hadn't recovered. I don't know what I drank, but it did some serious damage to my body. I was weak and exhausted. I barely got out of the bed unless it was to run to the bathroom and throw up. However, it didn't kill my appetite, because I was still able to eat like normal if not more.

August still hadn't spoke to me. Whenever I called his cell I got his voicemail. Terren however continued to check in everyday and according to her he was not over there either. I thought maybe he was sick of both of us. I was about at my wit's end with this trio. This sick little twisted nightmare was getting worse by the second. Maybe it was a blessing in disguise that he wasn't talking to me, then I wouldn't have to be the strong one to break up with him. Even though I did miss him.

Brooke had been tiptoeing around me like I was going to break. For some reason I felt like she knew something about August and she was afraid to tell me. She walked into the room with a pizza in her hand, looking all timid like she had for the last couple days. She took a slice of pizza out of the box, put it on a plate and handed it to me. Then she sat down next to me on the bunkbed.

She was aggravating me. "Brooke spit it out. What's on your mind?"

"I laced that blunt we smoked at the party with E." She spoke so fast I couldn't understand her.

"You did what?"

"I laced the blunt," she confessed. "I just wanted you to have a good time and some good sex. I didn't think it would make you sick, it never made me sick."

I jumped out of the bed with more energy than I had in days. "Why would you do that?"

"I wanted you to see what sex felt like on Ex."

"Me and August have great sex without Ex!" I screamed. "You drugged me!"

She dropped her head. "I'm sorry."

"I don't care if you're sorry. You let me lay around here all week like this and you haven't said anything. I could be having some kind of reaction from that drug, Brooke!"

"I know, but Casey, it shouldn't have made you sick." Brooke protested. "It never made me sick."

"Everyone's bodies react different … duh. I smoke enough weed! I don't need to add any other drugs to my list. You see what drugs did to Candice."

"Candice is doing a lot more then Ex," Brooke joked.

"I don't care! Don't ever do that to me again."

"I won't, I'm so sorry."

I rolled my eyes. I was upset, but I couldn't be too mad at her. I know Brooke wasn't trying to hurt me, but it was still wrong. I'm lucky it wasn't a stronger drug.

"Are you going to call August and tell him that it was my fault how you acted?" she asked.

"No, why should I? I've been sick all week and he hasn't called to check on me once, I owe him no explanations. Besides why would I put the blame on you? Us drunk bitches have to stick together."

We burst into laughter.

I woke up to the phone ringing. The TV was still on, and Brooke was asleep at the foot of the bed. I looked over at the clock: it was 1:30 in the morning. I answered half asleep. It was August.

"What's up baby? You miss me?"

I wanted to pretend that I didn't miss him, but my heart skipped a beat as soon as I heard his voice. "I guess," I mumbled.

"Come outside, I want to take you somewhere."

I thought about the fact that I hadn't taken a shower in two days because I have been laying up in the bed sick, and I knew I had to pull it together before I went outside to see him for the first time since the party.

"I was sleeping. You have to give me a few minutes."

"I'll wait."

"Fine," I snapped.

"Put on something sexy," he added.

"Seriously?" He had to be joking. I hadn't talked to him all week and now he calls me for sex.

"Yes, I miss you. I'm sorry. Let me make it up to you," he insisted.

"Fine August!"

I jumped out the bed and ran to the bathroom. I took the fastest shower I could. I pinned my hair up in a bun, then drowned my body in Victoria Secret lotion. I put on a red lace panty set that August bought me, then threw on this long black v-neck halter dress that cut so low it exposed my pretty bra. I bundled myself up in my coat and ran out of the house, excited to see August, knowing he was going to make up for not calling me.

When I got outside, I tried to tone down my excitement so that I could interrogate him about his whereabouts.

I saw August lick his lips as I slid in the car. "I missed you," he said, throwing me off guard.

"Why … am I … just … hearing … from you?" I stuttered.

"I was upset—I didn't like seein' you like that. I'm sorry." He apologized like he knew that would be enough for me to let it go—and it was. More so because I didn't want to go into detail about that horrible night again.

"I missed you too," I purred.

August reached over, put his hand on my thigh and started to massage it. My body began to respond to him. It didn't take much. He had me trained.

"It's past twelve. It's officially my birthday," he announced.

"I have something for you," I alluded to what was under my dress.

"Ask me what I want," he whispered.

"I'm sorry baby. What do you want Mommy to get you for your birthday?" I played along.

"It's not something I want you to get me, it's something I want you to do for me."

"Oh, yeah," I said opening up my coat thinking we were about to get it on in the car.

"It's a surprise." He smirked.

"You want to surprise me with your surprise?" I asked, stopping before revealing my dress.

His eyes molested me. "Yep!"

"O…K…" I said, now intrigued about what he was up too.

He picked up a blunt that was laying in the center console and lit it, passed it to me, then turned up the music.

I zoned out while we drove and admired the New York City nightlife. It was so different from Connecticut, where everything pretty much shut down after eleven.

Once in Manhattan, we pulled into a parking garage of a tall apartment building.

"Where are we?" I asked, very excited at the possibility that he got us a place together.

"It's a surprise. Close your eyes."

"Are you serious?" I said anxiously.

He placed his hands over my eyes. "Yes."

He escorted me inside the building into an elevator. When the elevator opened, we took a few more steps and we stopped. I heard a door open. We walked through the door. It smelled like lavender and apples. I usually liked those scents, but for some reason tonight they were making me nauseous. There was low music playing, something old school I couldn't make out.

"Open your eyes," August said, removing his hand from my face.

When I opened my eyes I could not believe who was in front of me. It was Terren. She sat on a cream leather couch with her legs crossed in a silk black lace nighty with her very pregnant belly poking out.

Her house was immaculate. It looked like she paid someone to decorate it for her. I didn't know if I should admire her place or freak out because I was actually in it.

"Surprise!" Terren said, smiling at me.

The look on her face made me want to choke her. I looked over at August, who looked like a kid in a candy store.

"What is going on?" I asked, acting oblivious to the threesome proposition Terren had made to me a few days before.

Terren stood up and walked towards me. "Oh stop it, Casey. You know we talked about this."

I couldn't believe this was happening. Were these two nutbags really going to force me into having a threesome with them?

Terren rubbed her hand across my arm. I flinched, shaking her off of me.

"Don't be scared. I won't bite…yet." Terren giggled.

August grabbed me by the waist. "Cay, this is what I wanted for my birthday."

I looked in his eyes to see if he was playing a joke on me, but when I saw how they were bulging out of his head, I knew this was no game. Terren had set me up, and she knew exactly how to play me into her trap—through August.

My mind was racing in so many different directions. I didn't know how I was going to get myself out of this. *Maybe I should just do it. Was I crazy to even be considering this? Why would August put me in this situation? If he didn't want to be with his wife, then why were we here with her now? If this is a couple getting a divorce, then I wonder what kind of freaky stuff they did when they were happily married.*

Terren unzipped my coat, peeled it off and laid it down on her beautiful blue, green, and cream accent chair. She stood admiring me.

"You are beautiful," she said, running her hand across my cheek.

I felt a cold chill shoot through me.

She took both her hands and ran them down my arms

until she got to my hands, she held them up and looked at them.

"Looks like you haven't worked a day in your life," she said, taking my right hand and kissing it. My body shuttered.

"Relax," I heard August say as he approached me from behind.

He untied my halter, and the top of my dress dropped down, exposing my full breast in my red lace bra. He wrapped his arms around me, pulling me close to him, and kissed the back of my neck. I could feel him rise. Terren wrapped her arms around me, and August brought all three of us together like an erotic human sandwich, and I was the meat. Her belly pressed up against me so tight I thought I felt the baby kick. She kissed my shoulder, moved down to the top of my breast to my stomach. I felt her start to pull the bottom half of my dress down while her cold wet tongue licked my side. I grabbed my dress, not ready for it to come off yet. She stood up, pulling me close to her again, this time grabbing August by the neck, moving his lips off of me, and she started to kiss him with me right there in the middle of them, and he kissed her back.

I couldn't take it. I wasn't ready for this kind of crazy. I had enough crazy in my life already, but this was taking it to another level. I felt vomit start to come up in my mouth. I pushed my way out of their uncomfortable embrace.

"I need to go to the bathroom," I choked out, trying to hold back the throw up that started to gush in my mouth.

"You OK?" August asked.

"It's the second door on the right," Terren instructed, pointing me in the direction of the bathroom.

I ran to the bathroom. I couldn't have made it there any sooner, because as soon as I got the toilet seat up, vomit poured out of my mouth. August poked his head in the bathroom.

"What's going on?" he asked, catching a glimpse of me bent over the toilet. "You OK?"

"No, I'm not OK." My words escaped my lips in just

enough time before I threw up again.

August came into the bathroom and closed the door. He grabbed a washcloth off one of the towel racks, wet it, and handed it to me. I wiped my face, flushed the toilet and stood up.

"Get me outta here right now!" I demanded.

"Casey …"

"Don't say anything to me. I don't even know who you are. You two are meant for each other!"

"She told me she talked to you about everything and you were down."

"And you just believed her without even running it by me? I haven't talked to you in days, then the first thing you do when you see me is take me to have some freaky ménage à trois with your pregnant wife. Are you stupid? In what universe does that make sense?"

August tried to wrap his arms around me.

"Get off of me!" I said exiting the bathroom. "I want to go home!"

Terren was sitting on the couch still smiling.

"You all better now?" she asked, rolling her eyes at me.

I snatched my coat off the chair and started to walk towards the door. August followed behind me. She jumped off the couch.

"August, where are you going?" she yelled.

"Shut up, Terren," he grunted following me out the door.

Terren ran to the door. "Fine, follow her August. She's not a real woman! She can't even please you! She won't be around for long, AND YOU'LL BE CRAWLING BACK TO ME!"

When we pulled up in front of the brownstone, I jumped out of the car. August chased me up the steps, grabbing my arm before I could get the door open.

"Talk to me Casey," he pleaded.

"August, you just stopped talking to me for almost a week over getting drunk at a party, *which is what people actually do*. Now you want me to forgive you in two minutes for putting me in *the most uncomfortable position I've ever been in*, in my life? No! I need a couple days to figure out what I'm going to do!" I snatched my arm away from him, went in the house and slammed the door in his face.

Brooke couldn't believe it when I told her what happened to me. She thought it was the funniest thing she'd ever heard. She kept trying to imagine Terren trying to be sexy while pregnant. The most disgusting part was the baby kicking me. It was like the baby was telling me, *don't have sex with my mommy*. I would've had nightmares for the rest of my life.

A week later, I still wasn't ready to talk to August. He continued to call me and stop by, but I had Brooke send him away. I wasn't sure what I would say to him if I did see him, so I decided until I figured out what that conversation would sound like, I wouldn't have it.

I still wasn't feeling well; my nausea had now included dizzy spells. I couldn't get out of the bed too fast in the morning, or the room would start spinning. One of the reasons it was so easy to avoid August was because I was sleeping most of the day away.

Brooke's guilt for drugging me had her at my beck and call. She was doing anything I asked of her and I was hungry, so I called her to bring me some Spanish food after she got off work. She stopped by with my bag of goodies. I opened it up, and sitting on top of my food was a pregnancy test.

"What is this for?" I asked, pulling the test out of the bag.

"I think you should take it."

"Why? We both know why I'm sick! Remember you drugged me!"

Brooke rolled her eyes. "Oh please Casey, there is no way you're still reacting to that little bit of Ex."

"How would you know? Everybody…"

"Everybody reacts different, blah, blah, blah," she mocked.

"I'm not pregnant!"

"OK, if you believe that, just prove me wrong and take the test."

I stared at the horrifying test while Brooke kept her eyes locked on me. I knew she wouldn't let it go, and I loved proving her wrong so I figured why not kill two birds with one stone.

"Fine! Just so you can leave me alone, I'll take it," I said, laughing my way to the bathroom.

"Fine with me," she yelled behind me.

I went in the bathroom and closed the door. I opened the test. Lay the wrapper flat on the counter. I looked at the test once more before going through the uncomfortable process of aiming at the stick.

When I was done, I lifted the test up to lay it on the wrapper, but before I could lay it down, a little plus sign was glowing in my face. I squinted my eyes at it. There was no way this test was reading positive so quickly.

I picked up the box to read how long it was supposed to take for a result and it said, *quick response within two minutes, minus sign is negative, plus sign for positive.* Why did it take only seconds for me? I dropped the box down and picked the test back up to make sure I wasn't seeing things. And there it was, bright as day, a big pink plus sign. I thought I felt the bathroom floor shift under my feet. I'd never felt as sick as I did in that moment.

Brooke was right. I was pregnant.

Chapter Nine
February

CASEY

Pregnant! Baby! Abortion! Mommy! Bastard! This is what was going through my head! Pregnant, mommy with a bastard baby, on her way to get an abortion! That is who I was. When I was a little girl I had this dream of who I was supposed to be. In this dream I was successful, an actress with a couple best-selling novels, a few hundred red carpet appearances, best dressed on Joan Rivers' fashion police, a role model, a mentor that all young women looked up to and aspired to be—but that's not who I was. I was a pregnant, mommy with a bastard baby, on her way to get an abortion.

It had been two weeks since I found out I was pregnant. I took five more tests, all different kinds to confirm, and they all came back positive. I didn't tell August because I didn't want the drama. I wasn't sure how he would react, but I knew nothing he could say would make me feel better. If he wanted it I would be upset, and if he didn't want it I would be upset, so I just spared him and myself the trouble of that conversation. Besides, it had taken me all of ten seconds to decide I was aborting this child. When I saw that little plus sign staring up at me, I went brain dead for nine seconds, and after the quick blackout, the first thought in my mind was: abortion.

My only problem was abortions were expensive. I knew people that got them before, and they were over three hundred dollars. At this time in my life that was a fortune. I couldn't really ask August for the money without him wanting to know what I needed it for. I needed a job and fast. I know there was a time limit on this abortion, and the further along I got the more expensive the procedure was. I sat on the toilet wishing that the baby would just fall out and I could flush it instead of having to go lay on a table and have it sucked out of me with a vacuum cleaner. I needed to figure out how far along I was. I didn't have any health insurance, and didn't really want to go to the clinic, so I decided I would search pregnancy online and diagnose myself.

I snuck out the house, bundling myself up until I was almost unrecognizable, and walked to the library. When I got there, I found myself a computer in a corner where no one could walk behind me and see what I was researching.

I went to Google and typed in *stages of pregnancy.* I clicked on the first link: Pregnancy week-by-week body changes baby development. I clicked around the links reading about how pregnancy is broken down into trimesters. The first trimester was weeks one to twelve. I was definitely under twelve weeks. August and I first had sex without a condom after we got back from Maine in the car that night I met Terren, and we haven't used one since. That was the week before Christmas, and it was now the second week of February so I guessed I couldn't be more than eight weeks at the max. I found out I was pregnant two weeks ago. The e.p.t. said it could detect pregnancy as early as five days, so I am two and a half weeks at the earliest.

The article said in the first weeks of my pregnancy some clear symptoms would be my period stopping. I tried to

think back to the last time I saw my period. I didn't remember
having a period since before I went to Maine with August.
If I was judging by that, then I probably got pregnant the
first couple times we had sex without a condom, because I
didn't get a period in January, so that puts me at around eight
weeks. It also said other symptoms would be tiredness, tender
swollen breast—I put my hand on my breast and realized they
were kind of tender. I'd been sleeping a lot, and there was no
question about the throwing up that had become a part of my
daily routine. I was also experiencing sensitivity to smells. I
noticed that when I went to Terren's house, that lavender smell
drove me crazy.

I clicked another link: How will my baby develop week
by week? It said at four weeks, the baby's brain spinal cord and
heart started forming. At eight weeks the baby's heart beats to
a regular rhythm; the arms legs, fingers and toes begin to form;
and the baby has eyelids. It said it starts to look like a human
and even the sex organs begin to form. The article said the
umbilical cord is also visible. I touched my stomach, trying to
see if I could feel a heartbeat. I couldn't.

There was so much information; I stayed in the library
for three hours reading about baby development and pregnancy.
I was intrigued; I wanted to know as much as I could about this
strange change my body was going through.

When I got back to the house, Tate told me that August had
stopped by. I really didn't feel like dealing with August. I still
wasn't over the attempted ménage à trois with Terren, and I
had too much baby stuff on the brain to be around him. I didn't
want to slip up and say something I would regret.

Brooke thought I should tell him. She said I shouldn't
be going through this alone and that he should be dealing
with some of the stress. I didn't feel like I was going through
anything really. I wasn't stressed—if anything I was exhausted.

I hadn't realized how much of a toll all this stuff with August and his wife had taken on me. All the little mind games that Terren was playing and always trying to figure out if August was lying or telling the truth. It was exhausting. One good thing was Terren's calls stopped since the night at her house.

I ran a hot bath, eased my way into the water, and relaxed. I needed to clear my head. I decided not to think about August, Terren, Candice, Tate, or anyone and just clear my mind. But there was one thing that I couldn't ignore, and that was the baby that was growing inside of me. I closed my eyes and imagined it inside me blinking its little eyes. The article said the sex organs would be forming by now. I wondered if it was a boy or a girl. I didn't know which one I would want if I kept it.

If I kept it … that was the first time I'd thought about keeping it. I started running my hands over my stomach and remembered that it had a heartbeat. I had this sudden urge to protect its heartbeat. The water in the tub was warm. I wondered if the baby could feel it. I thought about that ecstasy that Brooke slipped into the weed we smoked, I wondered if that made the baby sick because that is when I really started throwing up. I wondered if I'd hurt it, then I felt this overwhelming sadness just thinking I made my baby sick, and I burst out crying.

I wrapped my arms around my stomach. I cried for my baby. And for the first time, I didn't want anything to happen to it. I didn't want to abort it. I couldn't abort it. I cried more just thinking about killing it. I apologized to the baby over and over again. I knew then I was keeping it, and I would figure out whatever I had to do to take care of it, with or without August.

That night I called August and he didn't answer the phone. I didn't want to sleep alone, so I snuck into Tate's room while she was sleep and curled up with her. We used to curl up together all the time. I missed her. I thought about how she would react when she found out I was pregnant. I knew she would be a great aunt to my baby. She was rude to me, but she loved kids, and I knew she would love mine. Thinking of how she would react made me think of how my parents would react. I pushed that thought out of my mind. I wasn't ready to deal with that. I fell asleep thinking about what boy and girl names I loved. I knew for a boy the name Justin was my favorite name in the world, and if it were a girl I think I would name her Savannah. That name reminded me of the sun. And she would be the sunshine in my life.

TERREN

Terren stood in the doorway to her bedroom watching August sleep. She didn't know why she continued to let him come in and out as he pleased. She rubbed her stomach over her almost seven-month baby bump and thought about how much she loved her husband. She loved him so much that she was willing to go through her pregnancy alone. She loved him enough to invite his whore into her house to offer him sex with both of them. She loved him enough to let him go through this apparent mid-life crisis, then come back in her home at any given moment and sleep with her with no protection. She loved him so much she was foolish.

Terren held on to the belief that once this crisis was over, he would come back home to her and look at her the same way he did when they were kids. She knew he loved her, and she knew he would never really leave her. She just had to be patient and let him get this crisis out of his system, and she was willing to wait until death did them part.

She hated Casey though. She was disrespectful. She was sleeping with her husband, but refused the gift she'd planned for him? Did she think she was innocent? She was sleeping with a married man! *These young girls are so dumb,* Terren thought. Terren warned Casey that she was going to give August his gift with or without her, and that is what she did.

After Casey ran out, Terren called in her plan B, a girl she went to college with that went both ways. She always used to flirt with Terren, and if Terren weren't straight, she would have given her a chance because she was beautiful. She called up her old friend, told her about the gift she wanted to give her husband, and the girl jumped at the opportunity. The next day Terren's plan was carried out.

August was very pleased. That girl did all kinds of freaky stuff with them. She even taught Terren a few things. Terren couldn't remember the last time they had that much fun together. She felt like she'd brought the excitement back into their marriage. It worked out in her favor that Casey didn't do it, because it was an experience that she would be able to share with her husband that wasn't tainted by his affair. As an added takeaway from their delightful night, August moved back home.

Terren was surprised because she didn't have to bring it up. August showed up to her office with flowers and lunch and told her he was ready to come back home. She couldn't believe it. She wanted to have a conversation about everything that occurred and how they should go to marriage counseling, but she couldn't risk ruining the moment, so she agreed without any hesitation, just, "Yes, you can come home."

August jumped right back into their routine; he was picking the kids up again, helping around the house, coming straight home from work, even checking in on her throughout the day. She was loving the new improved him. The only thing was every once in a while her mind would drift off to Casey. She'd think about her when the house was quiet, or when August was watching TV and not paying her any attention, or when she was cleaning. She wondered what happened between them. Did he finally wise up, or was it Casey who came to her senses? Was her husband home because his mistress didn't want him anymore? Or did he really want to be with his family? How was Casey handling it? Was she OK? Terren didn't know why she cared about Casey's well-being but something about her made Terren sad. Maybe it was the mutual understanding they had of being helplessly in love. Casey had become the only person Terren could talk to. Melissa didn't understand, but Casey did, she was right there in the trenches with her.

The only difference between Terren and Casey is Terren couldn't let Casey win this battle. Terren's family meant everything to her. All Terren wanted was her family back. She wanted August to be the man she knew he was: a loving father and faithful husband. She wanted him by her side for the rest of her pregnancy. She didn't want to spend any more nights alone. She loved having him there. She missed him.

Terren crawled in the bed. August turned over and wrapped his arms around her belly, then laid his head on her breast. She didn't even care that they were swollen and tender, she loved when he did this. She kissed him on his forehead and rubbed her hand across his back. He snuggled up closer to her and woke up out of his sleep long enough to whisper *I love you* in her ear. Then he fell sound asleep while she stayed awake enjoying every second of this intimate moment with the man she loved, and periodically thinking about the pink elephant in the room—Casey, the other woman he loved.

CASEY

I almost jumped out of my skin when Tate's alarm went off. I hadn't been up that early in a long time. She got right up and started getting ready for school. I got out of her bed and went into the girls' room and crawled into the bottom bunk. I thought that maybe I would've changed my mind about keeping my baby once I got a good night's sleep and cleared my head, but I wanted it more then ever.

I looked at my cell phone to see if August had called back while I was asleep, but still nothing. Now I was getting annoyed. Why was he not available? I decided to call him again. I didn't care if he picked up or not, I just wanted to call just in case he was with someone right now so they could see that he is being checked on at six o'clock in the morning. The phone rang until it went to voicemail. I hung up.

Now that I decided to have my baby, I had to find a way to tell him. Him playing these disappearing acts was not making me feel secure in what his role would be. Would he deny my baby? *I wish he would! I'll get a DNA test so quick it will make his head spin.* No matter what his reaction I had to be prepared. I needed to get a job and start saving some money because one thing I'd realized about August is he was not as dependable as I thought he was.

I also needed to figure out how to get myself some health insurance. I didn't want to have my baby in a clinic. Even if I had to go down to the state and get state insurance, that would be better then nothing. I'd never been on the state before, but I had to do what I had to do. And today was the day I'd take care of all of this stuff, because I needed to see a doctor soon so I could find out how far along I really was and stop self-diagnosing myself.

I was getting ready to leave and catch the bus downtown when August finally called me back.

"Yes," I answered annoyed enough that he could hear it through the phone.

"What's up baby?" he said as if we'd been talking everyday.

"Nothing!"

"You wanna get some breakfast?" he continued.

I was tempted to say no, but then I thought I probably should eat something. I could get him to drop me off downtown, and if I found the courage, I'd tell him about the baby before he disappeared again.

"Sure, I'm ready now, so just call me when you're outside," I said hanging up the phone before he could respond.

Ten minutes later August pulled up. When I got in the car, he leaned over to give me a kiss, and I jerked away from him. He looked at me like something was wrong but I just ignored him.

"You OK?"

"Great!" I said sarcastically.

He stared at me a little longer. Then we drove to the diner in silence.

As I sat across from him in the booth at the diner, I couldn't stop thinking about how our baby would look. I wondered if it would have his beautiful dark brown skin and his smile. I started to feel myself get weak for him again. I hated that he had this control over me. I hated that he could just break me down just by showing his face. I hated him for making me love him.

After I ate, I was tired and decided I didn't feel like going downtown. Plus, I wanted to keep an eye on August, so I decided to hang out with him for the day, then stay the night with him tonight so I could have someone to cuddle up with.

We ended up at the restaurant in New Rochelle. I ate while he worked. I sat at the same table we ate at the first time he took me there. That view was breathtaking even in the middle of the day. We left the restaurant as the sun was going down. August packed up some food for us to take to his house for dinner and we were off.

When we pulled in the garage I noticed Aunt Georgia's car wasn't there.

"Where's your aunt?" I asked.

"She's in Maine. She went to visit my mother," August said, getting out the car and rushing to the door.

"Why are you in such a hurry?"

"I'm just tired and hungry. Let's go," He said, pushing me along.

August was acting really strange. In the car on the way to his aunt's, he kept looking over his shoulder. I wanted to tell him about the baby, but I decided to hold off since he seemed distracted.

Once he ate, I snuggled into the bed ready to cuddle but he turned out the light and laid down with his back to me. I tried to ignore his distance, but I couldn't hold it in.

"Are you mad at me?"

"No," he mumbled.

"I hope not, because let's not forget why I haven't been speaking to you!"

He just laid there in silence.

I was agitated. "So you're just going to ignore me?"

He turned around and planted a kiss on my forehead. "I love you. Now go to sleep. I'm tired," he said and rolled back over.

I was annoyed, but decided to leave it alone because I wasn't in the mood to argue and frankly I was tired too.

"AUGUST, I KNOW YOU'RE UP THERE WITH HER! AUGUST! AUGUST! AUGUST…"

I shot up in the bed. Screaming outside of August's window frightened me.

CRASH! I heard something hit the window. It sounded like a rock. August didn't budge. He lay there fast asleep. I shook him hard. "August wake up! I think Terren's outside."

It took August a minute to understand what I was saying, but as soon as he was able to comprehend, he grabbed me and held me down on the bed.

"Don't move!" he whispered.

"Why? Why is she here?" I questioned, trying to break loose from the strong hold he had me in.

"She's crazy! I don't know why she's here," he whispered.

"WHY DO YOU KEEP DOING THIS TO ME, AUGUST? AUGUST…AUGUST, I KNOW SHE'S UP THERE!" Terren screamed, then launched another rock up at the window.

"You need to go downstairs and stop this!" I protested.

August slapped his hand over my mouth.

"Shhh, I can't deal with her tonight! Remember what happened last time. I don't feel like fighting with her!" he pleaded.

"So you just want me to lay here while she stands outside screaming?"

"Please Casey. If she wants to be out there in the cold acting crazy, she can do it alone, that's on her."

RING, RING, RING, BANG, BANG, BANG, Terren made her way from screaming at the side window to ringing the bell and banging on the front door.

August wrapped his arms around me so tight, he almost cut off my circulation.

"This is crazy, August," I said, pushing him off me and pulling a pillow over my head.

"I know, I'm sorry Cay," he said, wrapping his arm back around me. "She'll leave soon. She won't stay out there all night."

He was wrong. Terren stayed outside all night long, throwing, screaming, banging and ringing the bell until the sun came up. August eventually fell asleep, but I was up all night long being tormented. All I could think about was how crazy I had to be to be bringing a baby into this. I needed to get my head checked.

TERREN

Terren woke up to the birds chirping. She looked around and realized she'd fallen asleep in her car sitting outside of Georgia's house. She looked at the clock: 6:15 a.m. She looked at the house and realized no one had come outside all night. She slammed her fist against the steering wheel, turned on the car, and took off down the street to pick her kids up from her sister's house.

She stormed into Melissa's house enraged.

"Where my kids at?" she yelled out.

"They're getting ready. Calm down! What is wrong with you?" Melissa asked.

"August had me outside all night and didn't have enough respect to come out and talk to me!" she shouted.

Melissa shook her head.

"He thinks he can just ignore me? I know he was up there with her! He's been staying at home for the last two weeks and all of a sudden he wants to stay at Georgia's house again? HE WAS WITH HER!"

"Terren! You have to stop screaming! First of all, my husband and my daughter are still asleep. Secondly, why are you just getting back if he never came outside?" Melissa asked confused.

"Because! Because I was gonna break down that door. I swear to God if I would've got in that house, I would have murdered both of them!"

"So you sat outside all night banging on the door?" Melissa clarified.

"Yes!"

"And that doesn't seem a little crazy to you?"

"Of course it's crazy! He's making me crazy! What is it about her that makes him keep going back? I give him everything, whatever he wants, and he still goes back to her! Why?" Terren plopped down on Melissa's couch, crying.

Melissa wrapped her arms around her sister trying to comfort her. "Terren it's not you. Whatever it is that August is looking for has nothing to do with you. Maybe the problem is that you give him everything. Maybe you need to take something away and for real this time. Change your locks, stop letting him come and go as he pleases. He is going to continue to treat you this way because you let him. He knows he always can come home to you no matter what he does."

"But he's my husband!" Terren sulked.

"Right now he's more concerned with being that girl's boyfriend then he is with being your husband. So let him. You have children that you're raising already. You don't need to be raising him too." Melissa patted her sister's head. "It's gonna be OK, Terren."

"But it's not!" Terren shouted, "I'm losing my mind and I might really hurt them. I'm emotional, I'm pregnant, I'm tired, overworked. I'm gonna explode! I swear Melissa, they're going to make me kill them!"

"Don't say that, Terren."

"I can't help it. Last night I'd never felt so much adrenaline. I tried to break down that door."

"Well it's good you didn't get in that house. Then what?" Melissa asked.

"I don't know what I would've done Mel, but I'd probably be in jail right now."

"Yea, and that would be great for your kids."

"I know it wouldn't have been good, but what I'm trying to explain to you is I wasn't even thinking about my kids, all I could see was red. All I felt was hate and I couldn't control it."

Terren stared at her sister with bloodshot eyes and a tear-stained face and wondered how much more could she take before she finally just snapped.

CASEY

Valentine's Day was coming up, and I was excited because I'd saved up some money August had given me so I could get him a gift. Although there'd been a lot of tension between us lately, especially after Terren showed up at his house screaming and banging at the door, I wanted to do something nice so we could possibly get back to how we were in the beginning.

I hit the mall next on the hunt for his gift. While I was there I decided to go to the salon. I needed a change, so I got my hair cut into a layered bob, and dyed it brown in the back and blonde on top. I loved it, it was a different look for me and easier to manage.

I had no idea what to get August. I mean after his wife tried to give him the ultimate threesome, I didn't know what could measure up to that. I searched the mall high and low. Finally I settled on this absolutely beautiful red lacy lingerie set from Victoria's Secret. I'd put on some weight, but not enough to notice my pregnancy. I planned on writing him a poem and reading it while wearing the lingerie. Then I would finally tell him about the baby. That would be the gift that kept on giving.

August had to go into work on Valentine's Day. When he got off, he came by my house to pick me up. I packed an overnight bag with my new lingerie and was excited about showing it off to him. He had a big smile on his face when I got in the car.

"I love your hair!" he said, running his fingers through it.

"Thank you." I smiled.

"It makes you look exotic."

I couldn't hide my smile as he drove away blasting slow music.

August had roses all over the room. There was a white teddy bear as big as me holding a heart that said *I love you* sitting on the bed along with a box of chocolates, a huge balloon, a bottle of champagne and a platter of fruit waiting for me.

I almost cried. He closed the door behind me and turned on the stereo.

I was elated. "Oh baby, this is so sweet!"

"This ain't it," he said, walking over to the closet and opening it up.

When he opened the closet, it was filled with new clothes and boxes of new shoes.

"For me?" I screeched, jumping inside the closet moving clothes from side to side. There were dresses and skirts, shirts, jumpsuits and jeans. I laughed when I looked at the shoes because he'd bought me a pair of Jordan's and a pair of classic red-bottom pumps, two totally different shoes. It was too bad I wasn't going to be able to fit half of those clothes in a few months. But it didn't matter. Everything was perfect, and I was about to top the night off with my gift.

After his surprise I made him leave the room so I could change into my lingerie. I slipped on my red lingerie, and lit some candles, then called him back into the room. I could tell by the look on his face he was pleased. I started reading the poem while he stood mesmerized by my body in red lace.

When I was done reading, August took my hand and pulled me close to him, and we started slow dancing. I thought that I should tell him about the baby while we danced, but since I wasn't sure how he would react, I decided to wait. I didn't want to ruin this perfect night.

He put his all into making love to me that night. He had me wide open, and I didn't know if I would ever be able to leave him. I was his forever.

I woke up in August's arms. I lay thinking about how everything was finally lining up. I loved August, I was about to have his baby, and I knew everything would be perfect once I told him about it. Maybe then he would finally divorce Terren and we could get married.

I made breakfast, and we ate downstairs at the kitchen table. I imagined us in our own place. As I watched him pour his coffee, I knew this was the perfect time to tell him about the baby. "August."

He took a sip of his coffee, "What's up baby?"

"I…I'm…"

BANG, BANG, BANG, BANG, BANG! August jumped out of his chair and ran to the window. He peaked out the curtain to see who was there.

"It's Terren," he said in a panic.

"What! What is she doing here?" I asked, heartbroken that our fairy-tale moment was interrupted.

He paced back and forth. "I don't know!"

Aunt Georgia ran down stairs. "What is going on August?" she shouted.

"Terren's at the door," he yelled.

BANG, BANG, BANG, BANG. Terren screamed, "I KNOW YOU'RE IN THERE AUGUST!"

"August, you need to get rid of her. This is crazy!" Aunt Georgia said running towards the door.

"Hold on!" August said, jumping in front of Aunt Georgia before she could reach the door.

He looked at me. "Baby, can you go upstairs for a minute please?"

I was dumbfounded. "Why do I have to go upstairs?" I asked, annoyed at his suggestion.

"I just need to get rid of her. Please, for me, just go

upstairs for a second."

I glared at August, and then stomped up the stairs like a little kid. When I reached the top step, I sat down so I could hear everything that was going on.

August opened the door and Terren burst in.

"Terren don't come in my house with this nonsense," Aunt Georgia screamed.

Terren ignored her. "Why are you playing with me August?"

"What are you talking about?"

"Why haven't you been home?"

"Terren, calm down in my house, please," Georgia interjected.

"You're wrong too, Georgia! You let August lay up in your house with another woman and you know he's married."

"Now Terren you need to relax. She's not the one coming by my house starting trouble, it's you," Georgia defended.

"That's besides the point."

I felt myself getting angrier by the second. I stood up and contemplated running down the stairs and punching her in the face, but I knew nothing good would come out of that. I decided to move. I didn't want to hear anything else from her.

I stomped past August's bedroom and decided to go to the family room at the end of the hall. I left the door open and sat on the couch facing the door so I could see down the hall. I was shaking. I crossed my legs and my arms to keep myself from exploding.

Terren must've heard me upstairs because I heard her yell, "SHE'S HERE?" Then I heard someone running up the stairs.

I wasn't hiding. When she got to the top of the steps, she could see into the family room where I was sitting. She wobbled her fully pregnant self down the hall to the back room and stood in front of me at the door.

"What are you doing here?" she asked.

"How about you ask August that?"

"Get out!" she ordered.

"If August tells me to leave then I will leave," I said, trying to keep my composure.

Terren's face turned white. "I said get out!"

I could feel my blood boiling. I tried to calm myself. I started repeating in my head, *she's pregnant, I'm pregnant, she's pregnant, I'm pregnant, she's pregnant, I'm pregnant…*

By my third chant, her scream broke my trance.

"I SAID GET OUT!"

It felt as if the ground under me shook. I'd reached my last ounce of patience. I took a deep breath and repeated, "If August asks me to…"

Before I could finish my sentence, Terren jumped at me and slapped me across my face. All of my reflexes kicked in, and I wasn't thinking about babies anymore. I stood up, pushing her with all my strength, and slammed her into the door.

Terren was strong. We started wrestling back and forth, slamming each other into wall after wall. She pinned me against a wall and punched me in the face. I pushed her up against the wall and punched her back. We both started throwing blows, catching each other in the face and the sides, and every so often we would hit a wall and punch right through it. All of a sudden Aunt Georgia came out of nowhere. She tried to get in between us, but we kept swinging at each other hitting her from time to time.

We fought for a while with Georgia in between trying to pull us apart. August finally found his way up the stairs. He grabbed Terren and wrestled her to the ground. We were now down the hall in front of August's room. Aunt Georgia pushed me into the room, trying to calm me down. I could hear Terren in the hall screaming at August.

"Why are you doing this to me? Why are you putting me through this August, why?"

I started crying. Aunt Georgia wrapped her arms around me. I could see August and Terren in the hall. They'd begun wrestling again.

"Let me go August," Terren pleaded.

"If I let you go you have to leave," he demanded.

"OK just let me go! You're hurting me."

August held her down for another moment, then slowly stood up, freeing her. He fell into the wall exhausted from their fight. Terren got up and looked August in the face.

"I hate you!" she said and spit at him.

August's eyes shot open and he started profusely wiping the spit off his face. Terren ran into the room where I was sitting on the bed, pushed Aunt Georgia out the way and tackled me. Aunt Georgia started screaming. We started tussling around on the bed. We were rolling around the bed kicking and punching until I felt a hard blow to my stomach. Woosh! Terren's kick knocked the wind out of me. I went crazy. I started kicking and screaming and punching until I found myself on top of her. I grabbed her by the neck and started choking her. She was struggling to breathe. I didn't care. I wanted her dead.

Someone grabbed me, trying to pull me off of her, but my grip was so tight around her neck that as I was being pulled up, so was she.

"CASEY, LET HER GO!" I heard August scream. I dug my nails into her neck one final time and pushed her head back into the bed. Her head hit the wall as she fell back on the bed. August flung me off her. I flew into the wall so hard my head bounced off of it, knocking me out. I dropped to my knees and then fell smack into the floor, face down. Everything went black.

When I came to, I was lying on the couch downstairs and Aunt Georgia was shaking me.

"Casey! Are you OK?" she cried out.

I was confused. I shook my head and blinked my eyes as I regained my consciousness.

"Are you OK?" Aunt Georgia asked again.

I moved my head up and down signaling *yes*. The memories of the fight came rushing back.

I jumped up. "Where's August?" I shouted.

"He's upstairs with Terren. We called a cab for you. She won't leave until you leave."

"So I have to leave?" I cried.

"It's for the best." Georgia said.

BEEP…BEEP. The cab was outside. She ran to the door.

"OK baby, let's go," she said, helping me to my feet.

I was so confused, but I didn't have the strength to fight it. Georgia shoved me into the cab, handed him some money, and sent me on my way.

Back in Harlem, I crawled out of the cab and inched my way up the stairs of the brownstone. I opened the door and Tate was sitting on the couch watching TV. I dropped down to my knees and fell flat on the floor in the doorway.

Tate ran over to me. "Oh my God, what happened to you?" she asked, shaking me.

I tried to speak, but I couldn't move my mouth. I closed my eyes and blacked out again.

I woke up in the hospital attached to an IV. I was groggy, and my vision was blurry, but I could see that Brooke, Tate, and Candice were sitting by my side. I was in a lot of pain. Tate saw me open my eyes first. She jumped out of her chair and hovered over me.

Her eyes were bloodshot red. "Casey, Casey are you OK?"

Brooke and Candice stood up. Candice squeezed my hand. "Who did this to you?" Candice asked.

I didn't know how to answer her question.

I turned my head away from them.

"The doctor is going to want to know what happened," Candice said with attitude.

"Why am I in the hospital?" I shouted.

"We brought you because you passed out and was bleeding," Brooke answered.

"Bleeding?" I repeated.

The doctor walked in the room.

He walked right up to me. "Good to see you awake."

"Can you please tell me what's going on? I got into a little fight. I don't know why I'm here," I spat.

"We need to speak in private," he explained.

Brooke looked over at Tate and Candice and signaled them to leave the room.

The doctor looked me in the eye. "Casey when you came in you were losing a lot of blood. We stopped the bleeding but we couldn't save the baby. Unfortunately, you had a miscarriage."

"A miscarriage?" I choked out.

"Yes, I am sorry to inform you, ma'am, but you lost your baby."

Chapter Ten

Death

CASEY

Numb. I lay in the bed curled up in a ball forcing myself to breathe. I didn't want to breathe. I didn't want to be alive. I wanted to be dead—like my baby! Why did I deserve to be alive? How did my baby deserve to be dead and I'm alive?

I was the dirty adulterer. Did my baby have to die for my sins? Was this my fault? When I first got pregnant, I'd wished death on my baby before it even had a chance. I remember wishing I could flush it down the toilet. Maybe it didn't want to be born to me. In some cultures, they say the babies pick their parents—maybe mine changed its mind.

The pillow was soaking wet from my tears. Tate, Candice and Brooke kept popping into the room checking on me, but I didn't understand why. The worst had already happened. There was nothing else that could go wrong.

I lay with my back facing the door. I heard it open again. Which one of them was it this time? I wanted them to leave me alone, but it was August. I didn't even flinch. He may as well have been transparent because I could see right through him. He reached out to touch me and for the first time since I got home from the hospital, I moved. I jerked away from him so hard a rush went through my already pounding head.

He put his head down. "I'm so sorry, Casey."

I had no idea what he was sorry for. There were a million possibilities. He'd done and was responsible for so much tragedy that I didn't know which one he was apologizing for. But I really didn't care. He was dead to me just like my baby—dead!

"I came over here as soon as you left. I came for you, but nobody was home. Brooke said ya'll were at the hospital. What did you go to the hospital for? Is it when you hit your head?" August seemed scared. He looked disgusting and weak to me.

I wasn't going to tell him about my miscarriage. It was my baby that died, and I wasn't going to give him the opportunity to pretend he gave a damn. He didn't deserve to know it even existed. I would suffer the joy and pain of that experience alone. It was mine and all mine and I wasn't ever going to tell him.

"Please talk to me. Casey, I'm so sorry."

I wanted him to shut up. The one thing I did want right now was something that could make me more numb than I already was: weed.

I got out the bed adjusting the over-sized pad I had to wear home from the hospital. I walked by August and searched for my shoes on the floor. When I found them, I slipped them on and started towards the door.

"Where are you going?" He asked.

"I need some weed."

"OK," he said, jumping up excited that I'd spoken to him.

When I got downstairs, Brooke and Tate were sitting on the couch. Brooke ran over to me.

"Where are you going?" She asked me, but she was looking at August.

"I'll be back tonight," I said, assuring her I wasn't staying the night with him.

"I'm coming with you!" Brooke slid her feet into her boots.

I shrugged my shoulders up, signaling that I didn't care if she came or not. By the look on her face, she was not taking *no* for an answer. I knew Brooke was making sure if anything else went down, she wasn't going to miss it.

When we got in the car, August searched around for some weed. He opened the glove compartment and then closed it. He opened the ash trey, and there was a nearly finished blunt sitting inside. He picked it up and handed it to me.

"This is all I got on me. I ran out the house so fast I didn't think to bring anymore."

I snatched the blunt from him, grabbed the lighter from the cup holder, and lit it. It was so small, I barely got two puffs out before I started to feel the heat on my fingers. I rolled down my window and tossed it out.

"This was a waste of my time," I said, grabbing for the door handle.

"I got more at home!" August blurted out, trying to keep me from getting out of the car.

I shot him the look of death.

"Terren is not there. I'll call Georgia to make sure she didn't come back."

Before I could agree, August had his phone out and called Georgia, putting her on speaker.

"Georgia, did Terren leave?"

"Yes, she's gone!" Georgia yelled through the phone. "August, Terren has disrespected my house for the last time. She can't come back to my house again! I mean it!"

"Fine with me!" He said before he hung up the phone and drove off.

August pulled into the garage and jumped out the car. "I'll be right back."

I felt myself tense up. I couldn't sit outside. It was as if I needed to revisit the fight scene to be sure I wasn't imagining the whole thing. So I got out the car. Brooke followed. Aunt Georgia was sitting on the couch looking frazzled when we walked in.

"August this has to stop!" Georgia yelled out to him before he could get all the way through the door.

"I know," he said and rushed up the stairs.

"How you doing?" she asked, looking up at me concerned. She wasn't her normal upbeat self. There were some red marks on her face from where she'd been hit.

I shrugged my shoulders.

"Stay here Brooke, I'll be right back," I said following August up the stairs.

When I hit the top step, I could see August standing in the doorway to his room. The hallway looked like a tornado had swept through it. All of the events of the morning rushed back to me as I glanced at each hole in the wall.

I walked over to August, who still hadn't moved from the doorway. As I approached him he turned to stop me.

"You don't want to go in there," he said, staring intensely.

My foot hit something. I looked down and there was an old Dutch Master box open on the floor. I almost choked when I saw my bible that I'd left there, stuffed in the box, covered with cigar filling, and wet from some sort of liquid. I bent down and picked it up. As I pulled the box closer to my face, I was able to identify the liquid—rubbing alcohol.

If I weren't convinced before, there was no longer any doubt about it—Terren was a psychopath. Who in their right mind would vandalize the word of God? She must be possessed. I was speechless, and that was just the beginning.

When I looked in the room I dropped the box on the floor.

The first thing I saw was the teddy bear August had given me for Valentine's Day. It was laying on the floor sideways, looking up at me with its face burned off. The sheets and pillows were ripped off the bed, and the mattress looked like someone attacked it with a knife. All of the clothes and shoes that August bought me were pulled out of the closet, thrown into a pile and soaked in bleach. The curtains were torn down, stereo broken. Everything was either smashed, cut up or knocked over. I couldn't believe it.

I turned and started heading back towards the steps.

"Casey," August called out to me.

"Get me out of here," I demanded without looking back at him. I ran down the stairs.

"What's wrong?" Brooked asked.

"I have to get out of here," I said, rushing out the house with Brooke following close behind me. I swore to myself that was the last time I would ever step foot in there again. Too much had happened. I would never look at August the same, and Terren was clearly never leaving him. I had to protect myself, because if I didn't, nobody else would.

TERREN

Terren lay in Melissa's bed, crying hysterically. This situation had spiraled out of control, and no matter how hard she tried to get a grasp on it, she couldn't.

As Terren lay sobbing she felt Melissa reach over and open the top drawer of her nightstand, Terren looked up as she watched Melissa pull out a joint. She knew Melissa only smoked on occasions, so for her to be smoking right now, she must be feeling Terren's pain.

Melissa lit the joint. She took a pull and blew it in the opposite direction of where Terren was lying. Terren sat up and looked at her cross-eyed.

"Don't judge me," Melissa said, taking another puff and rolling her eyes at Terren.

"I'm not. Let me hit that." Terren said holding out her hand for Melissa to pass her the joint.

"You're pregnant."

"Don't judge me." Terren mocked.

Melissa shrugged her shoulders took another pull of the joint and passed it to Terren. Terren grabbed the joint, inhaled as much smoke as her lungs could take, and slowly exhaled; then she smoked again before passing it back to Melissa.

Terren sat up, looking at the ceiling.

"I miss this feeling," Terren whispered. She and Melissa use to sneak and smoke all the time when they were teenagers. Terren quit when she made the volleyball team.

"Girl, sometimes you just need to get high," Melissa confessed.

"I feel defeated Mel," Terren said as tears started to fall

down her cheeks.

"I don't know how you're putting up with all this."

"Every night he's not home, I know he's with her. I wish I could just hate him, but I don't know how. Sometimes I get so angry at him … then when he walks through the door, all I can see is the August that I used to know. But I don't know him anymore. He's a stranger. It's even affecting my kids. They act different when he's around. I think they've seen me cry too much. I don't know what to do."

"I don't have any advice for you, Terren, because I've never been in that situation before. All I can suggest is taking it one day at a time. Everyone has a breaking point, and if he continues on like this, you will reach yours."

Terren started laughing. "I can't believe I fought that little girl today."

"I can't believe it either." Melissa laughed.

"I couldn't control myself. I told her to leave and she wouldn't listen. The sad part is, I can tell he has her brainwashed. I know August. You should've seen all the stuff he brought her for Valentine's Day." Terren sucked her teeth.

"Was it as expensive as the tennis bracelet he got you?" Melissa reminded her.

"No. I wish he would come home with some damn sneakers and a teddy bear for me. Been there, done that. I'm not fifteen years old anymore." She laughed. "But it wasn't what he brought her, it was the fact that he's spending my kids' money on stuff for her. That money belongs in my household; we have two kids to feed and one on the way. He's lost his mind. Girl, I got so mad that I bleached her clothes and lit the damn bear on fire. I wanted to burn the whole house down because it looked like she'd been living there."

"You're crazy."

Terren stopped laughing. "I'm going to get my husband back."

Melissa coughed. "Terren, I think you need to re-evaluate what's more important: you or him. You have so much to lose—your career, your children—do you really think he's worth all that?"

Terren looked Melissa in the eyes and said, "Yes, he is, Mel. He is, because he is half the creator of all that. He's my other half, the reason I have my children, and my career. So, yes, he's worth it, and I'm going to fight for him until I have nothing left."

Melissa shook her head. "Well Sis, do what you think is best for you, but I want you to know, he didn't give you those children or your career and certainly not your life—God did, and maybe if you focused a little more on God than on August, you'll get some real clarity on how you should handle this situation."

"Don't preach to me!" Terren rolled her eyes. "I'll deal with God later. Right now August is all the man I have time for, so God will have to wait."

Melissa's eyes widened in fear, "Girl … this is the last thing I'm gonna say, then I'm done. But that statement right there, that's your first mistake, and I'm afraid for you because you know better than to put any man before God!"

"OK Mel, I heard you. Now let's change the subject before your high, self-righteous self breaks out the bible, and Lord knows I'm not in the mood for that." Terren rolled over in the bed, turning her back to Melissa.

She closed her eyes and began thinking about what her next move would be against August and Casey.

CASEY

After I ran out of his Aunt's house, August dropped me and
Brooke back off. I snatched the weed he'd gotten me out of his
hand and jumped out of the car without saying a word. When
I got into the house, I ran up the stairs into the girls' room.
Brooke followed close behind me. We closed ourselves in the
bedroom and smoked. I took a puff of the weed and passed it to
Brooke. I lay down on the bed and curled up in a ball, pulling
my knees close to my chest and wrapping my arms around
them. Then I burst out crying. It felt like the weight of the
world came crashing down on me.

Brooke rubbed my back. She kept telling me to let it
out, just let it all out. I felt my body start to shake, my nose
was running, I was crying so hard I was gasping for air. I was
crying for my lost child, I was crying for my sister, I was
crying for everything that happened since I moved to Harlem.

"MOMMY…MOM…MMMY…MOMMY!" I hollered
out as if my mother would somehow hear me.

Candice came running in the room.

"What's going on?" she screamed in a panic.

I couldn't say anything. I just kept rocking myself back
and forth and crying. Candice bent down next to me and started
rubbing my head, then she burst into tears.

"It hurts me to see you like this, Casey. I swear I want
to kill August for making you feel like this! I COULD KILL
HIM!" she screamed.

Then she crawled in the bed with me and wrapped her
arms around me. Candice rocked me while Brooke rubbed my
back until I cried myself to sleep.

The next morning, I woke up at the crack of dawn with an unbelievable headache. Candice still had her arms wrapped tight around me, and Brooke was asleep on the floor next to the bed. I crawled from up under Candice's arm and dragged myself to the bathroom. When I looked in the mirror, the evidence of the day before was all over my face. There was a big lump on my head, and the right side of my tear-stained face was swollen.

I turned on the hot water and started to splash it on my face. I grabbed a washcloth, drenched it in the hot water, and placed it on the lump on my head.

I was surprised Candice was out of her room. She'd gone further downhill since Bruce took the girls. She wasn't even concerned with getting them back. All she did was lock herself up in her room and get high. And every now and then, she'd come out to eat or to go get more drugs.

I kept thinking about my mother. I needed her. She was the only person in the world that I could think of that might make me feel better. I didn't have anywhere else to turn.

I grabbed my cell phone and locked myself in the bathroom. It was early, but I knew my mom would be up having her coffee right about now. She picked up on the second ring.

"What's wrong?" she answered.

"Well good morning to you too. Why does something have to be wrong?" I asked.

"Because you don't get up this early in the morning, and even if you did you wouldn't be calling me unless something was wrong. So what's wrong?"

"I miss you," I said, prolonging the truth.

"I miss you too, baby. I wish you would call me more often."

"I'm sorry," I said, knowing I should check in with her

more.

"Uhm hum," she muttered. "So what have you been up too? How is school?"

"School…school's OK," I lied. I wasn't prepared to tell her I hadn't been going to school and had missed too many classes to go back until next term.

"Just OK? You've been dying to go to that acting school since you were a little girl, now you are there and it's just OK."

"Mom, it's OK. Look I didn't call you to talk about school. I have to tell you something."

"Are you OK?"

"Yes, I'm fine. I've been seeing somebody." I blurted out.

"Oh. OK." She hesitated. "Tell me about him."

That caught me off guard. I didn't have anything positive to say about August at the moment. So I had to be a big girl and tell her the truth.

"He's married." I felt the words slip out of my mouth like an untrained parrot who repeated a secret that he overheard. There was silence on the other end. I could imagine the look on my mother's face—I knew her so well I'd memorized that look of disappointment that I knew was plastered on her face right now. I was happy I wasn't there to see it.

I continued my confession before she could say anything to make me chicken out. "I didn't know he was married at first, but then his wife caught us together. She's pregnant, but he told her that he wanted to be with me. I was going to leave him, but I didn't … and I've been dating him and I fought his wife yesterday."

My mother remained silent on the other end. Her silence was killing me more than the disappointment I could feel oozing through the phone.

"Mom," I called out for her to respond.

"Casey, I can't believe what I'm hearing," she whispered like it was a secret she didn't want anyone else in the world to know about her daughter.

"Mom I know I'm—"

"You know better than this," she said, cutting me off mid sentence. "I didn't raise my child to mess with someone's husband."

Her words cut me. Whoever said *sticks and stones may break your bones but words will never hurt you* obviously had never disappointed their mother.

"How could you get involved with a married man, Casey?" she sneered.

"Mom, I just told you that I didn't know he was married when I first met him."

"But you know now and you're still dating him?"

"No, I'm not anymore," I lied.

"You just said you got in a fight with his wife yesterday."

"Yeah, but I'm not dealing with him anymore … now," I tried to convince her.

"Since yesterday?" she repeated.

"Yes, but—"

"And she's pregnant?" she asked, cutting me off again.

"Yes, but…"

"Casey, I am so disappointed in you."

I knew that. "Mom, you don't understand You're not even letting me explain what happened," I pleaded.

"What could you say to make this any better? Does Candice know about this?"

I couldn't even go there about Candice. I was not ready to discuss Candice with my mom.

"Not the whole story, she doesn't know he's married."

"Well, I need to talk to her. She is supposed to be looking out for you, and you're out there having affairs with married men and getting into fights with pregnant wives. Now I see why you said school is just OK—because it doesn't seem like you are focused on school at all."

My mother read me like a book. I wasn't even there and she could see right through me. Although I didn't expect my mother to be thrilled about what I told her, I did expect her to be a little understanding and compassionate—but she wasn't.

"You know what you have to do, don't you Casey?" she asked a question more like a statement.

"Yes moooom," I slurred out like a curse word.

"I cannot believe this. I am going to have to tell your father. There is no way I can keep this from him."

I gasped. I didn't even think about her having to tell my father. I wasn't ready for that.
"Mom, please don't tell him, let me tell him," I begged.

"If you think you're going to sweet talk this to him, you are wrong," she barked. "He is not going to approve of this at all, young lady. I wouldn't be surprised if he yanks you out of that school and makes you come back home."

"Mom, I know he'll be upset, but I'm begging you, please—just let me tell him."

"You have until the end of the day because you have just ruined my day and your father knows when I'm upset so I won't be able to hide it from him and if he asks me I will not lie to my HUSBAND!" She sliced the word *husband* at me like a sword.

"Fine!" I shot back, annoyed at how harsh she was being.

"I have to go. I need to pull myself together before your father gets up," she said.

"Goodbye," I said hanging up the phone before she could respond.

I didn't care, I wanted to get off the phone with her anyway. She'd made a bad situation worse. She went from being the only person I wanted to talk to, to the last person in the world I wanted to talk to.

Two weeks had gone by, and I hadn't gotten out of the bed except to go to the bathroom. I was barely showering or eating. The most I ate was a bag of chips here and there. I was smoking all day everyday. August would come by to do his daily check in and leave me some weed to ease my pain, but I wasn't really talking to him, just hi's and bye's.

After that conversation with my mother, my anger and sadness turned to depression. I called my father later that evening in tears. He'd already gotten the 411 from my mother because apparently she was so upset she couldn't hide it from him. He was way more understanding than she was. He let me cry and told me that everything would be OK. He told me that I was strong and could get through anything with God. I don't know if he was just being kind or if he just felt sorry for me. Either way, his reaction was way better than my mother's. That's why I was Daddy's little girl.

The numbness had overtaken me. No matter how hard I tried to feel, I couldn't. Brooke thought I should talk to someone, she said it could have a lot to do with the fact that I had a miscarriage. But I didn't think it was that because I'd blocked that out my mind altogether. Whenever a thought about the baby came into my head, I would immediately smoke. As far as I was concerned, that whole situation was just a nightmare. It never really happened, so there was no reason to dwell on it. There was no baby coming to prove me wrong, so it just didn't exist.

I hadn't heard from Terren at all since the fight. Maybe August had been staying at her house again because I'd been staying home. I didn't care though 'cause I wasn't in the mood to be bothered. I just wanted to be left alone.

It was Saturday night, and Brooke nagged me into

going out with her. She said I needed to get out of the house. As much as I didn't want to go anywhere, I decided it would be a good distraction so I agreed. After taking a quick shower, I pulled out a pair of my favorite jeans that hugged my curves and a sheer top and vest. When I pulled the pants up, I couldn't believe my eyes. They had somehow gotten bigger—way bigger. I looked down at them to make sure they were mine and that they hadn't been switched with an old pair of Candice's. But they hadn't. These pants didn't even seem like they belonged to me. I grabbed a belt out of the closet and looped it through the hoops. The belt made the pants buckle when I pulled it all the way through. The belt was even too big—I had to pull it so far that I had to poke another hole in it to close. I was confused. I looked in the mirror and noticed my hips were gone!

I unbuckled the belt and the pants dropped to the floor. I took a scan of the rest of my body and noticed my breasts had also deflated. Overall I looked sick. What happened to me? Who was this person staring back at me? I had dark circles around my eyes, my lips were black, my shoulders were boney – I'd become a mere ghost of myself.

I stripped everything off and started scavenging through the closet for something else. I found a pair of DKNY jeans that I'd just bought less than a month ago. I knew they should fit because I bought a size five and I'd been a size five since I graduated high school. I jumped into the jeans with ease, I didn't have to do the usual squat and tug to get into them. When I pulled them up they were sagging in my hips and baggy in the butt. I screamed.

I pulled the jeans off and threw them back in the closet. I flopped down on the bed, slapped my hands over my face, and started screaming into my palms. The louder I got, the more I squeezed my hands over my mouth to muffle the sound.

I jumped up and started pulling clothes out of the

closet, trying on everything, determined to find something that fit. But I had no luck. Everything I tried on sagged, drooped or hung off of me. The only thing that didn't fall off was a pair of stretch pants that used to look like they were painted on, which now fit like sweat pants. The adjustable elastic waist was the only reason they didn't fall. I gave up. I wasn't going out tonight or any night looking like this. I looked for my phone in the mess I created so I could call Brooke and let her know I wasn't going, but before I could locate it, the doorbell rang. I ran downstairs and opened the door ready to disappoint Brooke, but instead I was shocked to see Terren standing in the rain.

Terren noticed my disposition. "I don't want any trouble, I have my kids in the car." She gestured her hand towards the running vehicle. I could see her son and daughter peeking out at us. "I just want to talk to you."

I hadn't seen Terren since the fight, and all the emotions I'd been trying to keep pinned away came rushing back. All I could think was, my baby was dead because of her. I'd always blamed August for my miscarriage, but seeing her reminded me whose fault it really was.

I wanted to snap her neck. Her belly was growing bigger, while my baby was dead—I was furious! On top of that, her other two healthy kids sat staring and judging me. She'd won. Even if August and her never got back together, she still won. She'd always have a part of him: they were sitting in the car and growing in her belly.

I looked her in her eyes and was about to start cursing her out for having the nerve to show up at my house. But before I could say the first word she said, "I can't keep going through this with you."

How was I the one putting her through anything? She was the one who couldn't leave me alone. She is the one who killed my baby.

Her eyes were intense. "Didn't I tell you I wasn't going anywhere?"

I was frustrated, "Why are you telling me this? I don't care what you do anymore! I got the point. I promise to leave August alone, but can you please keep him away from me!"

Terren continued, "I know when he see's you. I know he gets up early so he can come see you before work, and he always checks on you before he goes home. I know my husband's routine whether he stays at home or not. But I want you to know he has been staying at home since our little fight and I'm assuming it's because you don't want to stay at his Aunt's house anymore."

Had she been following me? She must have, how else would she know where I lived? How had I not noticed her lurking around?

I took a deep breath. "Terren, I don't want to stay with him. I just want to be rid of both of you! Since you've obviously been stalking me, you'd know I've been keeping my distance from him." The truth is I knew deep down where he was staying anyway, I just didn't care.

"Do you know why I won't leave him?" Terren asked.

"Why?" I asked, waiting to be humored.

"Because I made a vow before God to stick by my husband through good times and bad, and I know this has to be the worst of times, but we will make it through this."

I rolled my eyes and thought about her throwing my bible in the Dutch box. Where did she think God was when she did that?

Terren started laughing. "You are so young."

I sucked my teeth. "I'm a grown woman."

"You're a kid." Terren laughed again. "You have so much to learn."

"So what, Terren, are you here to be my teacher?"

"I wish you would stop with your attitude. All I came

here to do is to talk to you. I really don't want to fight anymore. I've put myself in your shoes, and I understand why you love him. I know he has been really sweet to you and likes to help take care of you, but that is just who he is. He needs to feel needed."

"What do you mean *needed*?" I asked suddenly very interested.

"He likes to be in control. That's why he gives you money—it's a control method. He knows as long as you depend on him for something, he will have a way to keep you around. That is his method. And it doesn't help that the sex is mind-blowing!" Terren closed her eyes, thinking about sex between her and her husband. "He has a way of hypnotizing you in the bed. My man is very passionate and knows how to hit them spots."

I almost cracked a smile thinking about sex with August. I knew exactly what she was talking about. That was a major reason why I stayed around. August knew how to put it down.

"This is what you came here to talk about?" I said, holding back the smile that always seemed to emerge when I thought about our sexual chemistry.

"No! I came to ask you to be stronger." The rain started to come down harder, pitter-pattering all over our faces. "August loves his kids more that he loves you, more than he loves me even. He will never be able to stay away from them, and you better believe if he keeps this mess up too much longer, I will keep them away from him because they don't need to be subjected to all this craziness."

"You're confusing me. One minute you are telling me you're never going to leave him, and the next minute you are threatening to take his kids away. Which one is it, Terren?"

"See, you're not listening. If I threaten to take his kids away August will chose his kids. It's just a tactic."

"Did you ever think he is tired of playing games? Maybe that's why he doesn't want you anymore, because he's sick of your games!"

Terren took a step closer to me.

"Listen, I have been trying my hardest to be nice to you when all I really want to do is break your little neck. I love August, and I will do anything to protect my family. Regardless of whatever lies he is feeding you about me, he loves our family just as much. I will wear you down. I'm warning you, I will unleash a havoc that will destroy you!"

My jaw dropped. She seriously showed up here to threaten me, and I had no comeback. I was exhausted from all this drama. Terren didn't even know she'd already destroyed me. Everything good about me had died.

"August is my life, I will fight for him until the end. He is my love, my husband, my best friend! Do you understand me?"

All I could utter out was, "You can have him."

"No, honey, you're still confused. I already have him. You never had him. I've shared him long enough. Now it's time for him to come home."

"OK Terren, I'm fine with that. Let him come home please!"

"You have to play your part, Casey. You have to stay away from him, be strong, don't give in. Love yourself more than you love him."

"OK Terren. Whatever you say."

Candice came down the stairs. She opened the cracked door.

"Why are you standing outside in the rain?" she asked.

"I'll be in soon…"I started to say, but when I looked at her, she looked like she saw a ghost.

"Terren!" she screeched.

Terren squinted her eyes at Candice. "Candice! What

are you doing here?"

"I live here! What are you doing here?" Candice looked at me. "How do you know my boss—ex-boss?"

"Boss!" I choked. "Terren is your boss?"

"Yes, I am—was," Terren replied. "What's going on here?"

"This is my sister," I interjected.

"Sister," Terren repeated.

"This is insane! Candice, your boss is August's wife!" I explained.

Candice's mouth dropped. "AUGUST IS MARRIED?'

I couldn't answer her. I was all talked out. I felt the cold set into my bones as my wet clothes started to settle in on my body.

"This is so humiliating!" Terren yelled. "I can't believe you two are sisters!"

Candice looked to me. "I can't believe you're messing with a married man!"

I stood there mortified and angry at the same time. Terren and Candice were getting on my nerves. How dare Candice judge me! If she wasn't out getting high leaving me here to take care of her kids and putting responsibilities on me that I wasn't prepared for, I would've never gotten involved with August. And if Terren weren't a psycho, I wouldn't have lost my baby. Terren and Candice started exchanging words back and forth, their voices sounding like nails on a chalkboard. I couldn't take it anymore.

"EVERYBODY JUST SHUT UP!" I screamed. I pushed into the house and slammed the door in Terren's face. Candice fell into the banister.

"What the hell is wrong with you?" she screamed catching her balance.

"Get away from me!" I shouted as I pushed past her.

"Have you lost your damn mind?"

"No, but you have!"

"I'm the one who lost my mind?" Candice yelled. "You're the one running around here messing with a married man, and he's my boss's husband!"

"Your ex-boss! Remember you got fired! And don't you dare judge me, Candice! You don't even have custody of your own kids!"

Candice fell silent for a moment, then she ran up in my face so close to me, I could feel her breath on my cheeks.

"You don't know anything about me, little girl! You don't know what I've been through in my life, and you damn sure don't know anything about my marriage! You're running around here with somebody's husband while I'm going through a divorce. Who are you?" Tears started running down Candice's face.

"Who are *you*? I came here to be with my big sister who I've admired all my life, but then I get here and you're on drugs!"

"Oh, I guess my sin is greater than yours, huh, Casey? Precious little Casey with the perfect life, well I got news for you sweetheart, nobody's perfect. Not even Daddy's Little Girl."

"Sure Candice, my sin is greater because I ruined a family, it's OK though that you turned your house into a crackhouse regardless of your children and your little sister being here. All you do is lock yourself in your room and get high all day!"

Candice drew back her hand and slapped me so hard, I fell into the wall.

"YOU BETTER GET OUT OF MY FACE BEFORE I HURT YOU!" Candice shouted.

I couldn't believe she slapped me. "YOU WANT TO HURT ME CANDICE? WHY? BECAUSE I REVEALED YOUR TRUTH?"

"DON'T WORRY ABOUT MY TRUTH! WORRY ABOUT YOUR OWN TRUTH, HOW YOU'VE BECOME A LITTLE WHORE."

Candice's words tore right through me. My temperature was rising, and my fists were clinched together. I knew this feeling all too well, and if I stayed any longer I wouldn't be able to control it.

I jerked past Candice and ran up the stairs into the girls' room and started throwing all my stuff into a pile on the bed. I had to get out of this house. I'd made up my mind. I was moving back to Connecticut. There was no reason for me to stay in Harlem. I wasn't in school, my sister was crazy, Terren was threatening me, and August was too tempting. I had to go. I snatched up my cell phone and called my father.

CANDICE

Candice sat rocking back and forth trying to calm down, but she couldn't stop thinking about what Casey said. *Where are your kids, Candice?*

Her hands were shaking when she picked up the phone to call Bruce.

Bruce answered half asleep.

"Where are my girls?" Candice's voice poured through the phone.

"Candice?" Bruce questioned in a sleepy daze.

"YES!" she belted out, then regained her composure in fear of Bruce's reaction. "It's Candice!"

"Candice, it's three a.m." He yawned.

She ignored him. "I want my girls home now! You can't just take my children away from me."

"I took them because I don't want them being influenced by your erratic behavior!"

"Erratic behavior? I'LL SHOW YOU ERRATIC BEHAVIOR!" Candice screamed, ending the call.

Candice threw on a coat and ran to her car. Winter had settled on New York. The frost on Candice's window prevented her from throwing the car in drive and breaking all the traffic rules to get to Bruce's house. She turned the heat on blast and stuffed her hands into her pockets to warm them. She felt a cold tube in her pocket. She pulled it out, and it was a half full vile of coke. Without hesitation she opened up the vile, put some coke on her finger, and took two big snorts. The drugs made her forget about the cold. She put the car in drive and took off down the street.

Candice got to Hoboken in less then an hour. She ran through the lobby of Bruce's building, avoiding the doorman who she usually greets.

He tried to get her attention, but she jumped on the elevator before he could catch her.

When the doors opened to Bruce's floor, Candice practically fell out of the elevator. She was moving so fast that she bumped right into Bruce, who was waiting for her in the foyer.

Bruce pushed Candice off before the impact. "Get out of here, Candice!"

"No, I want to see my kids!" she demanded.

"I never keep you from seeing them, you choose not to come around. Now you want to see them at this hour?" He noticed how discombobulated she was. "Are you high?" he snapped.

Candice avoided his question. "I just want to see my kids, Bruce?"

"No! You're high! Just look at you! Look at your eyes and how wild you're acting!"

"GET OUT OF MY WAY, BRUCE!" Candice screamed, pushing Bruce aside. "I WANT TO SEE MY DAMN KIDS!"

Candice ran into Bruce's apartment screaming the girls' names. "Asia! Daisy! Come on girls, get up, you're coming home with Mommy tonight."

She burst into the girls' room, waking then out of their sleep, quickly scooping them into her arms and carrying them into the hall.

Daisy and Asia were so excited to see their mother.

"Mommy, mommy we missed you," they called out in unison.

Bruce ran back into the apartment after Candice, leaving the front door open. He grabbed Candice, trying to peel the girls off her.

"Girls, mommy is sick. You can't go home with her tonight."

They kept a tight hold on Candice.

Bruce tugged at them until he finally broke their hold. He got Daisy loose first. When he picked her up, she started kicking and screaming. He tried to calm her down while he ran her back into her room. Once in the room he put her down and grabbed her tightly by the shoulders and said, "Listen baby, Daddy is trying to protect you and your sister, your mommy is sick right now, and it will be very unsafe if you drive in a car with her. You're the oldest here I need you to trust me. Do you trust me?" Bruce asked, looking into Daisy's eyes.

Daisy pouted and shook her head yes so that he knew she believed him.

"OK I'm going to go get your sister, then I need you to keep her in the room with you while I call help for your mommy. Do you understand?" he asked her.

Daisy nodded yes.

Bruce ran back into the hallway in time to see Candice running with Asia towards the door. Bruce ran after Candice, catching her by her shirt and pulling her backwards.

Candice and Asia screamed as Candice fell backwards. Bruce tried to catch them, but it all happened so fast that he lost his balance, and they all fell with Candice and Asia landing on top of him.

Bruce scrambled to get from up under them and to get Asia while Candice's grip had loosened. Candice and Bruce tussled around, pulling Asia back and forth until finally Bruce snatched Asia hard enough to rip her out of Candice's arms. Once he had her, he ran her back to the room with Daisy.

He pushed Asia into to the room, slamming the door shut behind her.

Candice jumped on Bruce's back, punching and kicking him. Bruce slammed his back into the wall, banging Candice up against it. She continued to kick and punched him as he repeatedly rammed her into the wall, trying to get her off of him.

She fell down to the ground, grabbing his leg on her way to the floor. Bruce lost his balance and fell down beside her. Candice started punching him in his face and chest. Bruce tried to brace himself, but Candice was swinging so wildly he kept getting hit. Bruce let down his defense in attempt to restrain her, which left his face exposed long enough for Candice's to punch him in the eye and again in the nose.

Blood erupted from Bruce's nose. He flipped Candice over, and she kicked him in between the legs. Bruce slumped over in agony. Candice grabbed a vase and hit Bruce over the head with it. He fell face down on the floor.

Candice scrambled to make a run for the girls' room, but Bruce shook his daze off and lunged at her, pulling her legs from under her. She tumbled down, slamming face first into the floor. He pulled Candice by the leg, dragging her to him. He climbed on top of her and back slapped her across the face. Candice didn't give up her fight. She was bucking out of control until she hit Bruce in the face again. It dazed him, giving Candice a moment to try to sliver out of his grasp, but Bruce caught her and pulled her down so hard that her face smacked into the floor again. This time she landed on her nose. Blood gushed out, covering the floor. She grabbed the leg of an end table in an attempt to pull herself up, but it was too light and toppled over, sending everything on it crashing to the floor.

Daisy and Asia's cries echoed through the house. Candice and Bruce continued to fight. Anything that got in their way was destroyed or used as a weapon. The elevator in Bruce's foyer opened up, and a team of police ran into the house.

The first cop into the house grabbed Candice. As the cop pulled Candice up she continued to stomp Bruce, kicking him in the head while he was still down. The cop flung her around, forcing her into the hallway. Another cop ran to help Bruce. The elevator opened again and another set of cops rushed in.

It took six squad cars and twelve officers to get the brawl under control. By the time everything was said and done, both Candice and Bruce were arrested and Bruce's penthouse apartment looked like the crime scene of a murder.

CASEY

Five fifteen a.m., my phone rang waking me out of my sleep. Aunt Caroline's voice cried out.

"Casey, your sister is in the hospital and she's being held under arrest."

I shot up in the bed, "What? Why?"

"For breaking and entering, vandalism, domestic violence and being under the influence of narcotics." Aunt Caroline sobbed.

I couldn't believe it. What happened? She and I were just downstairs fighting.

Bang, bang, bang, bang. The knock at the door frightened me. I ran to answer it. My father pushed through the door.

"Daddy?" I shouted.

"WHERE IS YOUR SISTER?" he roared.

I looked down at the phone. I could hear Aunt Caroline crying. There was no lie I could tell to cover for Candice this time. Afraid of what my father's reaction might be, I handed him the phone, relying on Aunt Caroline to break the news.

The waiting room of the hospital was silent. The only noise came from my father rocking back and forth in his chair. I hadn't seen him in six months, and he looked like he'd aged quite a bit. He definitely had more grey in his hair than he did when I left home.

I was happy to see him. I couldn't believe he got there in a little less than two hours. He must've left as soon as he hung up with me after I called him venting about me and Candice's fight. My father must have done one hundred miles an hour the whole way to Harlem. He didn't play when it came to his girls!

The policeman told us Candice was in very bad shape and would need to stay overnight in the hospital. He informed my dad that she'd been in a domestic altercation with her husband, and they were both pretty beat up. Both of them were also under arrest until further investigation could be done. The officer also dropped the bomb that they'd brought the girls to child protective services for the night.

Around ten-fifteen in the morning, a doctor came to speak with us.

"We had to remove shards of glass out of your daughter's head and face," the doctor explained. "Her nose was broken, and there are some cuts on her eyes that we had to stitch up. We gave her medication that should help the swelling go down. She should have a full recovery, but she will have some permanent scaring."

"When can I see my daughter?" my father asked.

"You can go in now, but she is just waking up from sedation, so try to let her rest as much as possible."

"OK." My father trembled.

"Because she is under police protection, only immediate family can be admitted in, and only two at a time," The doctor explained.

"I don't want to go in," Tate whined.

"I can wait," I said. "You and Auntie can go in," I said, sitting back down.

My father and Aunt Caroline followed the doctor down the hall and through the swinging double doors. Not even a minute later, Aunt Caroline came rushing back through the swinging doors with her hands over her face, crying.

"I can't go in there," she cried.

I grabbed her and hugged her. I squeezed her tight and took a deep breath. I knew I would have to suck it up and go comfort my father.

I let go of Aunt Caroline and walked towards the double doors of doom. I inched my way down the hall until I saw the back of my father's head standing in one of the rooms. I almost fainted when I saw my sister. She looked like the elephant man. If the doctor hadn't told us that was Candice, I wouldn't have known it was her. She was unrecognizable. There were staples running across her forehead holding together a long cut. Her eyes were swollen shut, her lips were busted, and her nose was bandaged. I burst into tears. My father grabbed me and held me in his arms. He took Candice's hand that was strapped to the hospital bed into his and began to pray.

The next few days were a madhouse. My father finally got the girls and had agreed with the courts that he and my mother would take care of them until Candice and/or Bruce was in a position to do so.

Bruce had been just as badly beaten up. He was going to be in the hospital for a few days. Then he would need to get things at his house taken care of before he could even attempt to get the girls back.

Once Candice and Bruce were in a condition to be questioned by the police, they both took responsibility for the fight and decided not to press charges. So Bruce's handcuffs were taken off, and as soon as he was medically cleared, he would be able to go home.

Candice, on the other hand, still was being charged for the narcotics, so she would either have to go to rehab, serve jail time or both, depending on the judge.

As soon as my father got the girls from the social worker, he packed us all up and brought us to Connecticut with my mother. He didn't stay ten minutes. He used the bathroom, kissed my mother, and rushed back to New York to my sister's side. Since Tate had to go to school, she stayed behind with Aunt Caroline until the end of the year. Then she would move back to my parents' house in the summer.

When I walked through the door, my mother stared at me like she'd seen a ghost. She wrapped her arms around me. "What happened to my baby?" she cried out.

For the first time in a long time, I felt safe. I needed my mother like never before. After a long cry in her arms, I ran myself a bath and soaked my entire body in the water. I wanted every inch of me cleaned, inside and out.

When I got out the tub, I took my time and massaged lotion and cocoa butter into every crease in my skin. I laid face-up on my bed and examined my room; it was exactly as I left it. I was so happy to be home. I was so comfortable I dozed off. I was awakened by the sound of my cell phone ringing.

"Hello."

"Casey!" Brooke shouted through the phone. "August is on his way to your house."

"Brooke, I'm in Connecticut."

"I know! He's on his way to Connecticut."

I shot up in the bed. "How does he know I'm here?"

"Long story short, he came to the hospital looking for you. Kayden told him you moved back home. He looked really sad and said he wanted to send you something, and Kayden gave him your address."

"Why would he do that?" I cried out.

"I don't know, but a few minutes later he pulls me to the side and asks me *why didn't you tell him you were leaving? I said I don't know.* Then he said, *well you can let her know I am on my way to Connecticut to see her since she won't answer my calls.*" Brooke exhaled after vomiting all that information out.

"Oh my God! When did he leave? How much time do I

have to stop him?" I asked in a panic.

"I've been calling you for like two hours, so if he drove there straight from the hospital he could be there soon."

I hung up the phone and called August. It went to voicemail, I called again, and it went to voicemail. I called him three more times, and they all went to voicemail. I decided to be proactive. I threw on some clothes and figured I'd sit on the porch so I could avoid him having to meet my mother.

When I got to the bottom of the stairs, I was stopped in my tracks. I stood frozen, staring at my mother with a gun pointed in August's face. I wanted to say something to stop her, but I couldn't move my mouth. I was numb to the fact that my mother could pull the trigger and kill August right there in front of me—I didn't care. My life had gone so far off track after I met August. He was the main culprit that sent me on this downward spiral. All his lies and deceit derailed all my plans. Then, I thought about how much better my life could be if August weren't here, if my mother would pull that trigger and shoot him dead, like my baby…just dead.

Chapter Eleven
Life

CASEY

My mother didn't shoot August. She did, however, have something on her mind that she made sure she shared with him. She told him, "I will kill you if you come back around my baby."

Then she cocked back the barrel of the .45 revolver, keeping it pointed straight in his face, and said, "Now, get the hell off of my property."

August saw me standing in the stairway. He looked at me as if he wanted me to rescue him, but I couldn't. I was tapped out of heroism, tired of fighting and getting hit. I was the one in need of a rescue, and my mother came along and did it.

She knew that he was the reason behind my pain and the one who'd changed her once vibrant, ambitious daughter into a vaguely familiar shadow of herself. He was the married man having an affair with her only child. He was the one.

August held a strong face as long as he could, then he backed away, keeping his eyes on the gun. She kept it pointed at him until he drove away. After that, I thought I'd never hear

239

from him again, but less then an hour later he called my phone. I let it go to voicemail.

He called for three days before I answered. I should've never listened to his messages. Each message broke me down a little more. I couldn't resist all his *I miss you*'s, *I'm sorry*'s and *I love you*'s.

When I finally spoke to him my heart skipped a beat, I knew I was in trouble. I shouldn't have given him three days to prepare his defense because he was ready and coming strong.

"I filed for divorce. I went down to the courthouse yesterday morning and filed the papers. I can't lose you," August pleaded.

I'd been waiting to hear him say that since the moment I found out about Terren.

"How long is it going to take for it to be official?" I asked to see how airtight his story was.

"It shouldn't be long, because I'm going to give her whatever she wants, and I am going to take care of my kids," August explained. "There will be nothing to fight about.

It seemed too simple, and from what I knew about Terren, it would never go that smoothly.

"What made you do this now after all this time?" I asked.

"It was your mother."

"My mother!" I screeched.

"Yeah, she really made me see how much I've hurt you, and I don't want you to hurt. I love you."

Did my mom help me get my happy ending?

"Baby, I know you don't believe me, but I can show you better than I can tell you."

"How August? I'm in Connecticut, and I don't plan on coming back anytime soon."

"Good, you stay there for a while and let me get all

this divorce stuff straight. I don't want you coming back until I have all my business in order so we can be together for real. I want to marry you."

I stopped breathing. "What?"

"You heard me. I'm going to marry you, Casey. Just let me take care of this divorce first. Then I'm coming to get you, OK?"

"OK," I said, and just like that I was tangled back up in his web.

Connecticut was home. I was comfortable, safe, and my mommy was there to nurse me back to life. In less than two months, I was looking and feeling more like myself. I'd gained some weight back and re-dyed my hair black. I got a job waitressing in the mall and was saving up my money to put towards my classes in the fall. I was enjoying being young again, something I'd forgotten to do in Harlem.

For the most part, it was just my mother and I at the house because my father was in Harlem helping Candice. She was going away to rehab for a while and renting out the brownstone while she was gone. Rehab was a part of her probation for her narcotics charge. The court gave her until May first to check in. My father kept a close eye on her—he was with her every second of every day.

Bruce got temporary custody of the girls until Candice's probation was up. Then she would be able to petition for joint custody again. Bruce didn't waste any time after he got out of the hospital to get Daisy and Asia. They were back in Hoboken within days.

My mother was catering to me like I was one of her patients. Every morning she made me breakfast; she even let me request my favorite meals. She let me use her car to get back and forth to work while she drove my old bucket. She said she'd rather me be in the safer car. It was like she was building her case for me to stay in Connecticut. And she was doing a very thorough job.

I felt August slipping back into his old ways. He would only call me in the mornings on his way to work. I might hear from him once during the day, and then he'd call me when he was leaving work. But at night he was unavailable. His excuses were he'd fallen asleep early or his phone was dead. I had a feeling in my gut he was lying, but being in Connecticut there was no way I could prove it. Unfortunately, being upset with August didn't stop me from missing him, especially at night. I missed cuddling up with him.

In three days, Candice would be checking into rehab. My father still hadn't found a tenant for the brownstone, and it was beginning to stress him out. He'd decided he would take on the mortgage if they couldn't find a renter, but I knew he really couldn't afford that. There was also still so much work to do there before it would be ready for someone else to move in. So, he asked me to come and help him finish packing up to move things along faster. He also wanted me to accompany him bringing Candice to the rehab for her check-in. As much as I didn't want to go back to Harlem, I couldn't tell my father no, he already had enough on his plate.

Harlem felt like a different world compared to when I first moved here. I remember feeling like Harlem was heaven—now my feelings were polar opposite. I looked out the window into the busy New York streets and it depressed me. I missed the peace and quiet of Connecticut.

I called August to let him know I was coming, but he hadn't answered any of my calls since yesterday morning. I felt anxious about seeing him. As much as I'd tried to get over him, it just seemed like I wanted him more. My father was looking weary. I could tell me and my sister's drama was stressing him out.

As I walked up the steps to the brownstone, so many bad memories came flooding into my mind. I thought I was strong enough to come back, but now I wasn't so sure.

The house was a mess. Candice came running down the stairs, jumping, and shouting my name. She threw her arms around me squeezing me tight.

"I'm so happy you're here," she said in a deep exhale.

I hugged her back. My father was shocked to see her in such high spirits because she'd been moping around since she got out of the hospital.

"You seem chipper," I blurted out.

"I'm feeling good," she said, picking up a box and rushing into the kitchen.

She did look a lot better. Guess that's what a few months of sobriety will do for you. You could still see some of the scars from the fight, but overall she looked healthy.

I really didn't want to do anything. I started pushing things on the floor around with my feet. Everywhere I looked I was reminded of something bad that happened in that house. Right in front of the door is where I passed out the night I had my miscarriage. Candice and I got into our fight in the living room. Tate even lost her virginity while living in this house. This house was cursed!

Just as I was about to plop down on the couch, August walked through the front door. I jumped up.

"What's up baby?" he said, grinning at me.

I couldn't resist smiling. When August was around, I understood what it meant to have butterflies. I wanted to reach out and grab him, but I didn't want him to know how happy I was to see him, so instead, I took a deep breath in an attempt to contain my excitement. I kept thinking, *I'm mad at him…I'm mad at him.* He hasn't been answering my calls, but him showing up let me know he was getting my messages.

"You just gonna stand there and stare at me?" he asked smugly.

I looked around the room to make sure Candice or my father hadn't stuck their heads into the living room. I know neither of them would be pleased to see August.

I pushed him outside before falling into his arms and allowing him to bear-hug me. He lifted me off my feet. It felt good being in his arms again, too good. I could feel myself being sucked back in, and the last thing I needed was to be swept away in his web of lies. I needed a clear head to talk to him.

"OK, that's enough," I said, pulling myself out of his grasp.

"Don't be like that. I missed you," he said.

"You have a funny way of showing it."

"Baby you wouldn't believe what's been going on here. Terren went crazy when I brought her the divorce papers. She threw my phone out the window. I still don't have a phone. I only knew you were here because I've been checking my messages. I've been sleeping in my car because Terren keeps showing up to my aunt's house. I can't deal with it anymore. I wish she'd give me my divorce and leave me alone."

I wanted to believe August, but his story was too convenient. Even if he couldn't answer my calls, he knew my phone number. Why couldn't he call me back on another phone? I wasn't buying it; it just didn't feel real.

I rolled my eyes. "August, you are a ball of excuses."

"Baby, I'm not making excuses, I'm serious. When I got your message that you where coming back, that was the best news I've had in months. I missed you so much."

Even though I knew there was a possibility August was lying through his teeth, it sure sounded good coming out of his mouth. I knew I shouldn't believe him, but in this case I had to give him the benefit of the doubt. What girl didn't want to hear her man tell her how much he loved and missed her? His charm was working, but I still wasn't ready to back down.

"Well, I guess you're still going to miss me, because I'm only here for the day. My dad and I are taking Candice to rehab, then I'm going back home."

"WHAT?" August let out.

I snapped around to look at the door, to make sure no one heard him. I wasn't ready to deal with my father's reaction to August being there.

"Listen, you should go before my father comes outside and catches you here. You think my mother was bad. My father shoots when his gun comes out."

I heard some rumbling around that got me nervous.

"You have to go," I instructed, rushing him along.

August stopped me. He put his big hands on my shoulders and looked into my eyes.

"Baby, don't leave me again," he pleaded.

"August, I can't deal with all the drama that you come with. I've finally started feeling alive again. Why would I stay here to go right back into the same drama that I left behind?"

"It won't be the same, I promise."

"How do I know that when you just told me that she was upset about the divorce and threw your phone out the window? That lets me know right there that nothing has changed. For all I know, you've been staying the night at her house, which is why I can't catch up with you at night." I blurted out the accusation before I lost the courage to say it.

August wrapped his hands around my face. "Baby, please believe me. I love you! I have not been staying at the house with Terren. All I've been doing is trying to figure out a way to get you back. You mean everything to me. You are my future and she is my past."

I tried to ignore how fast my heart was beating; August knew all the right things to say. "I only love you," he said, staring into my eyes. "I wasn't playing when I said I wanted to marry you." August pulled a small box out of his pocket and opened it. My mouth dropped when I saw the diamond band blinging at me.

"What is that?" I choked.

"It's a promise ring," he smirked. "I promise we are going to get through all this. And when all is said and done, I'm going to marry you."

For the first time in a long time, I believed him. He couldn't be lying. Why would he buy me this ring? Why would he look me in my eyes like that and lie? Why would he do that? He had to be telling the truth. That was it. I broke.

"I love you too!" I confessed, snatching the ring out the box and stuffing into my pocket.

August's eyes widened. "You don't know how long I've been waiting to hear you say that."

The war was over and August had won, again.

TERREN

Terren lay in her hospital bed staring at the ceiling. She'd been in the hospital for three days after being admitted for exhaustion and dehydration. She'd also started spotting, and at almost nine months, the doctors insisted they keep her on bed rest to avoid complications with the delivery. Even though she would have rather been at home, Terren knew that the doctors were right, especially since there was way more to the story than exhaustion and dehydration. The part of the story she didn't tell the doctor was she was stressed out because of her husband's indiscretions and involved in multiple physical fights while pregnant with her child.

The latest fight, which most likely led to her spotting, was with August. He'd moved back into the house about two months ago, swearing he'd changed and he wanted to be there and take care of his family. Since she needed August now more than ever, being so far along in her pregnancy, she let him back in—no questions asked.

At first everything was great. He was taking care of the kids, and making love to Terren again. Their lives were finally getting back to normal.

There was only one thing that was bothering her; she didn't know what happened between him and Casey. Terren was happy Casey had miraculously disappeared, but she couldn't help but be curious to where.

Unfortunately, her curiosity was short lived. One day as she was searching for her son's baseball cleats in August's car, she stumbled on a second phone and half-filled-out divorce papers tucked away in his trunk. She picked up the phone and saw that there were voice messages on it. She called into the voicemail but it was passcode protected. She typed in their son's birthday because she knew that August used that code for everything, he just didn't know that she knew. Just as suspected, it worked. She played the voicemails and there she was—Casey.

Six voicemails later, Casey had answered all Terren's questions. Casey was ranting on and on about August not answering her calls at night. She said, she'd never believe he was going to leave his wife if he couldn't even be trusted to return her phone calls. Then she dropped the bomb and asked how long the divorce was going to take because she wasn't moving back to Harlem unless it was finalized. Terren was so furious, she ran upstairs as fast as her pregnant body would allow her.

August was sitting on the couch when she nearly broke the door down. She launched the cell phone, and it hit him right across his head. August grabbed his face where he'd been struck in horror.

"YOU WANT A DIVORCE?" Terren screamed.

August played dumb. "What are you talking about?"

"Don't you dare lie to me!" Terren yelled, waving the divorce papers and storming towards August. She swung at him. August tried to restrain her, but Terren's punches were quick and precise. They wrestled to the floor. Kiarra and August Jr. were crying, but Terren couldn't stop beating on August. She picked up anything she could get her hands on to strike August with.

August knew he wouldn't be able to win this fight without hurting his unborn child, so he struggled his way out of Terren's wrath and ran out of the door. Terren ran into their room and started packing all of August's stuff. She threw his clothes into garbage bags, dragged them over to the nearest window, and dumped them down to the ground.

Terren got chills just thinking about that night. Since she'd been in the hospital, August had been in to see her everyday. He told her that he'd gotten those divorce papers a long time ago when he thought she was going to leave him. He promised her that Casey had been calling him and he was not returning any of her calls—that is why she'd been leaving him all of those messages. Terren wanted to believe him, but she knew him too well for his lies to get past her. In her heart, she knew he was still in communication with Casey, but right now there was nothing she could do about it.

Thinking about it all made her cry. She tried to hold it together, but she was due for a breakdown. She knew she was coming to her end with August and Casey. She didn't know how much more she could take before she ended up really hurting one of them.

She decided she would take this time in the hospital to really evaluate her marriage and come up with a plan of action. As much as she didn't want to, she knew one option would have to be considering divorcing August. Even though she felt like she was losing if she divorced him, she knew that might have been the only peaceful resolution to this problem. One thing was for sure, this was her last time ending up in the hospital. If anyone else got hurt because of August and Casey's mess, it wasn't going to be her.

CASEY

Admitting Candice into rehab was a lot harder than I ever anticipated. My father broke down, which was a complete shock because he was always so strong. It was so emotional, we all started crying. Even though Candice's stay at rehab would be no longer than six months, depending on her recovery process, for some reason, it seemed like we'd never see her again. Stress was all over my father's face. I could tell this situation was taking a toll on him. I wanted to take his pain away, but with all my baggage I was dealing with, I couldn't find comforting words.

August was miraculously available when I called him in the middle of the night. Luckily he answered, because I was feeling vulnerable, and if he didn't, I may have changed my mind. I decided to stay in Harlem. My father needed someone to stay at the brownstone and show the place to interested renters. I came up with the brilliant idea that I could be that person. This would give me a chance to help my parents out and give my relationship with August one last shot since he'd promised to marry me now.

I had two suitcases full of clothes that I'd left at the brownstone, so I would be fine for a few weeks. My dad was thrilled when I told him I'd stay in Harlem to help. He didn't show any concern for the problems I had there. I think he was just exhausted from everything that had been going on and wanted to be back at home with my mother. My mother was hesitant, however, she figured it would only be a week or two before I was back home under her care, so she agreed. What my parents didn't know was that I was secretly looking for a job so that I could stay in Harlem and get a place with August. I figured if I could find a job in two weeks, then that would be my excuse to stay in Harlem once the brownstone was rented.

August pulled up minutes after my father pulled off. We both decided it would be safer if he stayed in the big empty brownstone with me instead of me staying by myself. It felt good to be in his arms again. It felt even better having sex with him again—old habits die hard. After everything that had happened between August and I, our sex was still mind-blowing.

I started looking for jobs right away. I needed to get a job so I could get a place. Even though I knew August would insist on paying the bills, I still wanted to get a place that I could afford on my own, just in case he decided to go back to his old tricks.

There were a lot of interesting positions open, but the one that caught my eye the most was a marketing assistant at the museum where Brooke worked. It paid more than my minimum requirements and had benefits. I called Brooke right away to see if I could use her as a reference. She was so excited to hear I was moving back that she called HR and got me an interview for the next day.

The interview took about thirty minutes. I moped back to the parking lot where August was waiting for me. As soon as I opened the door he asked, "Did you get it?"

I smiled, no longer able to hide my excitement. "Yes! I got the job!" I said, giving him a big hug.

I felt good. Things were turning around in Harlem. I went from being jobless, stressed out, dealing with a married man, and recovering from a miscarriage to now having a good job, with benefits, and getting my confidence back. Everything seemed to be going my way; August was finally going to be all mine. We were moving in together, he was finalizing his divorce, and Candice was in rehab. I was happier than I'd been in a long time. There was only one place for me to go from here—and that was up.

Chapter Twelve
May

CASEY

Life in Harlem was once again nothing I could've ever planned. I was doing well at my job. It was perfect for me because I was able to be creative. On a daily basis I was thinking of new ways to promote the museum. If I wasn't doing that, I was assisting with putting on an event. I also got to work closely with Brooke. I loved it.

August and I were on cloud nine. He stayed with me at the brownstone until it got rented last week. My parents were not pleased when I told them that I would be staying in Harlem. My mother didn't even care about me having a job. She knew me staying there really had everything to do with August and work was just my excuse.

My father was happy I had a job because he was being drained with everything that was going on with Candice. He acted as if he'd hit the lotto when I told him we found a renter. Once the brownstone was rented, I packed my suitcases up and loaded them into the back of August's car, and that's where they stayed. I was living out of his car. August wanted me to stay with him at his aunt's house, but I didn't feel comfortable staying there after everything that happened with Terren. I hadn't heard anything from her since I returned to Harlem, but the memories of the craziness were too recent for me to forget. So I avoided his aunt's house until late at night when I would sneak in to sleep, then I'd wake up first thing in the morning, shower, and be gone before anyone even knew I was there.

The good thing about living out of the car was there were no bills. I was saving every penny I made so that when I found a place, I'd have the deposit ready. Looking for places in Harlem was not easy. Everything was so expensive or in the projects, neither one of which I wanted. I had to stay within my budget, and it had to be in a decent area. As much as August insisted, I couldn't bring myself to include him in my budget. I'd been so traumatized from everything we'd been through that I still wasn't sure how long this moment of peace would last, so I remained cautious, especially since his divorce was still not final.

I didn't have a problem including him in everything else though. We went apartment hunting together, we picked out furniture together, and I let him pay for all of it. I didn't want him to feel like I didn't need him.

I used my lunch breaks to walk around Harlem looking for apartments. I walked past a man selling fresh fruit pops. I purchased a mango pop. It was so sweet and juicy. I closed my eyes so that all of my senses could experience this mango's yummy goodness. As I swallowed the final piece of mango I had to stop and stand still to let the soft fruit ease through my body. It was incredible!

I opened my eyes and staring back at me was a *for rent* sign stuck into the window of a quaint little building. I'd walked past this building a few times and never really noticed it. It had character. I was eager to get inside. There was a man sweeping the steps. I figured I'd see if I could get some information out of him.

"Excuse me," I called to him.

When he looked up at me, his dirty blonde, overgrown hair swept across his eyes. He pushed the hair away and smiled at me. His decaying teeth and rugged attire made me nervous.

"How can I help you?" he asked politely.

"I noticed the *for rent* sign in the window. I know it's spur of the moment, but I'm on my way back to work and was wondering if I could see the apartment really quick."

"Sure dear, come on in. You're in luck because I just put that sign out," the man said as he stuck his key into the building door, motioning for me to follow him.

I walked up four cement steps that led to the outside doors of the building, then the man used another key to open the inside doors. I was already feeling good because the building was secure.

"Let me warn you the apartment is not ready yet. The last tenants just moved out and they left the place a mess."

"That's fine. I just want to see its potential."

The inside of the building was immaculate. The floors looked like they were newly waxed, and there was a fresh clean smell that lingered in the air. The building had antique light fixtures mounted to the walls that looked like they could have held candles before the invention of electricity. Harlem was known for having very old historical sites.

I followed him to the third floor. As soon as he opened the door, I was horrified. The first thing I saw was the bright yellow kitchen walls, and black scratched chalkboard floors. The bathroom would've been decent if the bathtub wasn't filled with scum and dirt. However, as I walked around the apartment examining each room, I could see potential beyond the filth. The rooms were very big, which was different from all of the other places I've seen. Other than the color on the walls in the kitchen, it was spacious and had a built-in china cabinet that was gorgeous. The appliances looked fairly new, and there was plenty room for me to put a decent sized table. There were also floor-to-ceiling windows in all the rooms that let in great light. I just wasn't excited about the one in the kitchen that led out to a fire escape.

I looked around the living room and had a vision of what it would look like with carpet on the floors and a fresh coat of paint. I could make it work. Actually it would be perfect!

"When can move in?" I blurted out.

"Well, I can have it cleaned by next week …"

I cut him off, "I'll clean it myself." Honestly I preferred to do it myself to make sure it was done right.

"OK, it's a month security and the first month's rent. If you move in anytime this month the rent will be prorated from the day of move in."

I felt a surge of excitement run through me. It was already the second week in May. Doing the math in my head, I needed $1,000 to get my keys, and I already had that saved, and I wasn't even calculating the money I would be getting from August.

"Great! I'll bring it to you in the morning."

I had to get back to work, but I would be back in the morning with the money. I got the renters application that I'd fill out and return with the deposit. I couldn't believe it; just like that I wasn't homeless anymore.

When August picked me up from work, I could not wait to tell him about the apartment. I tried to describe it to him, but my description wasn't doing it any justice. He would have to see it himself, so I had him drive by. When we pulled up in front of the building, August's mood completely changed.

"What's wrong? I asked.

He kept his eyes on the building while talking to me. "Nothing. I'm good."

"Isn't this a nice building? It's really clean on the inside, and the rooms in the apartment are so big," I said getting excited all over again.

August stared blankly, but didn't say anything.

"Do you want me to see if the super is still around so he can show you?"

"No. I'm good," he said and pulled off without any explanation.

A week later, I moved in and transformed the apartment. I scrubbed it clean from top to bottom, painted the walls, put down tile in the hallway and bought carpet for the bedroom and living room. I sat watching August as he installed carpet. He was so meticulous about his work. I wondered how he could be so particular about somewhere he didn't even want to live.

August's mood about moving in together had changed overnight. The day I got the keys, he didn't even want to come upstairs. I asked him flat out why the change of heart, and he told me he wasn't ready. He said he wanted to wait until his divorce was finalized before we moved in together. It made sense, but it also broke my heart. But God had already prepared me for this disappointment, which is why I was looking for places I could afford on my own.

The first night in the apartment we got into a big fight. August wanted me to stay with him at his aunt's house. He said I shouldn't stay in an empty apartment. Although I understood his concern, it was mine, empty and all. I was staying in my own place and I didn't want to wait. I'd worked too hard for this, and with or without him I was going to live there.

August claimed he wasn't living with me, but he stayed there every night. He had a toothbrush, a bunch of clothes, sneakers, and many other miscellaneous little things lying around. He also gave me money to furnish the place. We purchased a new living room and bedroom set, big TVs for each room, every kitchen appliance you could think of, and a cozy bar table that fit perfectly in front of the built-in china cabinet. We turned the filthy, trashed apartment I first walked in, into my cozy little piece of heaven.

The weekends were my favorite since I was off work. I really got a chance to enjoy my place and explore New York. I wanted a good book to cozy up with in front of my window, so I decided to go to the library. I loved walking into a library. The smell of old books was intoxicating. I searched for a book that I've had my eye on for a while, *The 48 Laws of Power.* When I found it I headed to the desk to check it out.

As I was exiting the library, I bumped into Umaja looking cheerful as always. His smile widened when he saw me.

"Hi, gorgeous, how are you?" he said, holding his arms out for a hug. "I haven't seen you in a while. You lost weight."

I disregarded his weight comment. "Hi Umaja! How have you been?" I said settling into his embrace.

"Girl, I have been running around like a chicken with his head cut off. I finally finished my script, and I wrote a whole new play that I am about to have produced in Manhattan. God is good all the time," Umaja said, throwing his arms into the air in a praising motion.

I frowned my face up in envy. "Wow congratulations! That's wonderful."

"Yes girl, I've been working, working, working. You disappeared for a while. I missed our talks."

I laughed, not thinking he really wanted the details of my crazy life. Besides, compared to his, my life was just embarrassing. "Oh, it's a long story."

"I'm free for the rest of the day. Let's go grab some coffee and catch up."

"Oh, no, I can't."

"Come on. It's on me, and I will throw in a chocolate éclair."

A part of me wanted to make up an excuse as to why I couldn't go, but another part of me really did miss our talks.

"OK."

We walked a couple blocks down the street to a little coffee shop. Umaja ordered coffee and éclairs for us.

"Oh, I'm actually fine," I interrupted.

"Oh no, girl, I don't eat sweets alone," he said, turning to the girl at the counter and completing his order.

After we got our food, we found a quiet table in the back of the shop and settled ourselves in.

Umaja leaned in towards me like a reporter. "So tell me, honey, what in the world have you been up too?"

My story was embarrassing, but Umaja had the type of personality that put you right at ease. I opened my mouth and started telling him everything that had been going on over the last couple months, and I didn't stop until he knew every single detail. I even told him the biggest secret of them all—the miscarriage. He was the only person in the world I'd said it out loud to.

I found myself crying when I was talking to him about the baby. I thought that I'd buried those feelings, but I guess they were a lot closer to the surface than I'd known. I would've been about six months pregnant. I was sad, but after talking it all through with Umaja, I believed God spared me by not giving me a child by August.

Umaja sat in silence and listened to every word. Not once did he me make me feel like he was judging me. He showed genuine concern of my well-being. He made me feel safe.

"Casey, let me tell you something. You get yourself down to the school and you register for the new semester. You have to do that for you. Do you see how much better you feel about yourself because you got a job and your own place? Sweetheart, you need to do what you came here to do! Don't let no man, woman, or child stop you from your dreams! Do you understand me?"

"Yes," I whispered.

Umaja's words rang in my head as if someone flipped a switch on. He was right. I was working now—I could save up my own money and pay for my classes. I didn't need anyone to do that for me.

"You're right," I yelled out.

"If you want, I will go with you to register. I'm always in the city," Umaja volunteered.

"That would be great," I said, excited to have someone who shared my love for the arts.

"Perfect, I'll take you into the city and show you a good time. You need some positive energy in your life."

"I really do." I smiled.

"There is one thing that I want you to do for me."

"Yes."

"Know your worth. A man will only do to you what you allow him to do. So if you think you're worth more, than you need to demand more or show him the door! You hear me?"

I sat for a moment and let Umaja's words process. He was absolutely right. It was time that I started looking out for me and figuring out what I was doing with August. He and I were in a pretty good place right now, aside from the fact that he reneged on moving in with me but he was still married. I needed to get to the bottom of what it was that we were doing, because my patience was wearing thin. It was time for me to make a decision—was I going to continue committing adultery, or was it time for me to reassess my worth and shut it all down until his divorce was final? I mean what good is a promise ring without the opportunity of the promise being realized.

Umaja and I talked for three hours. For those few of hours, our spirits had connected. Something in my heart told me God sent him to me, because what we shared in that coffee shop was spiritual and I needed it. I was so happy to have him in my life. As far as I'm concerned, Umaja would always hold a special place in my heart for helping renew my faith in myself, in my God, and helping me to trust men again.

TERREN

"Push, *push*," the nurse instructed Terren.

She'd been in labor for sixteen hours, and the baby was finally on its way out. Melissa held on to Terren's hand—she'd been by her side since her water broke. Terren gave one final push, and she felt her baby slide out of her body. The baby came out screaming. She took a deep breath and let her head relax into the pillow.

A moment later, the doctor looked over to Melissa and asked her if she wanted to cut the umbilical cord. Melissa looked at Terren for approval, and Terren nodded yes to her before Melissa proudly cut the cord. The doctor handed the baby to Terren announcing *it's a girl*. Holding her baby in her arms, Terren was filled with joy that was immediately followed by pain because her husband was not there.

After Terren was cleaned up and the doctors had dispersed, she lay in the hospital bed using every ounce of strength she had not to cry. Melissa entered her room carrying food she'd bought from a vendor; she hadn't eaten anything since she got to the hospital yesterday. Terren had Melissa call August back to back to let him know she was in labor, but he never answered the phone.

August hadn't been up to the hospital to see Terren in almost a week. He'd call her every morning, always with a new excuse on why he hadn't been to see her. When Terren would call him, he only answered during the day, never at night.

The nurse pushed the baby into the room in a bassinet.

"Do you want to hold your baby girl?"

Terren shook her head yes and reached her arms out.

The nurse placed the baby in Terren's arms, and Terren pulled her in close to her chest. She looked down at her newborn that was the spitting image of August, and she burst into tears. "Why would he do this to me?"

"He's with that girl," Melissa blurted out.

Terren's tears stopped. She looked over at Melissa like she was a stranger.

"What did you say?" Terren asked, needing to hear it one more time.

"August is with his mistress … he's living with her. They live across the street from me." Melissa exhaled as if coming up for air.

"What do you mean *they live across the street from you*?" Terren asked, pulling her baby closer to her for comfort.

"About a week ago I saw them moving a carpet into the building across the street. I wasn't sure what was going on at first, so I started watching, and he has been staying there every night. They have been buying furniture and TVs and groceries. He goes to work from there and he sleeps there."

Terren's jaw dropped.

"I wanted to tell you sooner, but I didn't want to put any more stress on you with the baby," Melissa confessed. "When I saw them the first time, I was on my way to cross that street and cuss them out, but Josiah told me to mind my business."

Terren's blood was boiling. August had gone too far. It was one thing that he'd cheated on her over and over again, but he'd taken this fling to a whole new level now. Not only had he moved in with her, but he continued to take money out of her household and putting it into someone else's house. That was it. She was fed up! She was going to make him suffer for everything he put her through. And Casey—Casey's life lines had run out. Terren wasn't doing any more talking to her. This was a clear violation, a declaration of war. Terren had poured her heart out, cried, threatened, fought, even begged her to leave August alone, but she still hadn't gotten the message. All Casey ever did was lie. *I don't want him Terren. He's always chasing me Terren. He won't leave me alone Terren.* Casey was no longer a pathetic little girl; she was a manipulative, liar with two faces. She knew exactly what she was doing, she was the enemy—and now it was time for war.

Terren's eyes dried up. She didn't have any more tears left. All she could feel now was hatred and rage. She looked down at her child and realized she didn't feel the joy that mothers feel when they first bring a baby into the world; she felt betrayal and disrespect. All she could think about was August laid up with Casey as she gave birth to their child.

Every time she'd look at her daughter, she would be reminded of how much turmoil August put her through for her entire pregnancy. Right then she decided if she had to be reminded of it every time she looked at her child, he would have to live with it everyday of his life too. She looked into her baby's eyes and said, "Casey. I'm gonna name you Casey, after your daddy's whore, so he will never forget what he did to me, to us, to our family, for as long as he lives."

CASEY

August was in a bad mood. He was stomping around the house pouting, slamming doors, and looking for any reason to argue with me. The problem was, I was in such a good mood from my conversation with Umaja that nothing he did or said could change that. I just ignored him. I wished that coffee shop was open twenty-four hours because Umaja and I would still be there talking. I couldn't wait to hang out with him again.

August stomped into the room and threw a bag of weed and a dutch at me. "Roll this." He frowned, and then he went into the bathroom and slammed the door. I laughed, picked up the bag of weed, and opened it up. I definitely didn't care about his attitude now. I was about to roll up this blunt, smoke it, take me a shower, and go to bed. August would have to deal with whatever he was going through alone tonight. I wasn't in the mood, especially once I smoked.

Shortly after I was finished rolling the weed, the bathroom door swung open and August came out holding a freshly rolled blunt in his hand. I squinted my eyes at him, realizing it was going to be that type of night. I knew August, and if we were rolling up two blunts just between the two of us, he was really stressed.

August came in the room and laid beside me. He propped his head up on a pillow and lit the blunt he had in his mouth, then passed me the lighter.

"You want me to light this one now?" I asked.

He shook his head yes. So I did.

"Where were you today?" he asked catching me off guard.

"I went to the library then I had coffee with a friend."

"A friend? What friend?"

"This guy I met when I first moved to Harlem. He's a writer like me. We have a lot in common."

August sat up and stared at me funny.

"Why are you looking at me like that?" I asked.

"What you mean you had coffee with a *friend*?"

"First of all, calm down," I said feeling my high about to be blown.

"Don't tell me to calm down!"

"Wait, what? I said I had coffee with a friend. This man is like fifty-something years old. I'm not the least bit interested in him. He's just a nice person that shares similar interest with me and has good conversation. What? I'm not allowed to have friends now? You're still *married* and you refuse to commit to even living with me."

"Are you outta your mind?" August barked. "You don't have a clue what I gave up for you. My wife is in the hospital right now having a baby, and I'm here with you!"

His words slapped me in the face. "Excuse me? Terren's having the baby!" I gasped.

Emotions I didn't even know were there started flooding in. Terren was having the baby, a baby I would never have.

We just stood there staring at each other until he stormed out of the room.

I slowly eased back onto my pillow. I couldn't get August's announcement out of my head, *my wife is in the hospital having my baby right now...* it played over and over in my head until I fell asleep.

When I woke up the next morning, August was stretched out on the living room floor sleeping. I stood staring at him, I had a burning desire to start kicking him. I was distracted by a crumpled up piece of paper next to his hand on the floor. I crept over and picked it up, then tippy-toed into the bathroom. I pulled the piece of paper apart and rubbed my hand over it to flatten it out. It read:

> *Your wife is having your baby. It would be nice if you get off your back and meet her at the hospital. I shouldn't have to tell you, she really needs you right now. If there is even a small piece of a real man inside of you, come take care of your responsibility instead of laying up there with your whore. —M*

I couldn't believe my eyes. Who was M? How did she know about me? Who was she to Terren? Where did August get this note? Is this what had him all unhinged last night? I could understand him being upset because he wasn't there for the birth of his baby, but why didn't he just go? It's not like I don't know about the child. I wouldn't have gotten upset, at least I don't think I would've. Terren's baby was finally here and August's mood has changed overnight. Is this a sign of what life is going to be like with him now that they have a new baby? Terren warned me how much he loved his kids.

August may have been able to stay away from his child, but I wasn't that strong. I needed to see this baby. I told August I had some errands to run so I could drop him off to work and use his car. What he didn't know is I called every hospital in Manhattan to find out which one Terren was at. I didn't have a solid plan, but I needed to see her, I needed to see the baby. Somewhere beyond my fury and my jealously, I was concerned for them and I wanted to see that they were OK.

I stepped onto the hall of the maternity ward carrying a teddy bear and some balloons that said *Congratulations*. My plan was to see the baby first. In my heart, I believed seeing their baby would give me a glimpse of what my baby would've looked like.

As I approached the nursery, one of the nurses was coming out from behind the glass encased room with all the newborn babies inside.

I stopped her before I could think about what I was doing. "Hi, um … I came up here to visit my…sister, but she's asleep and I really want to see the new addition to our family. Can you please point to which one is my sister's baby? Her name is Terren Mitchell, she is in room 702."

"Oh sure," she answered pleasantly with a big smile on her face. Then she walked back into the room of babies.

I stood on the other side of the glass waiting for the nurse to point out which baby belonged to Terren. The nurse stopped beside one of the baby beds that read, *I'm a girl* and picked up a brown-skinned baby draped in a pink blanket with a pink little hat on her head. She walked over closer to the window so I could see the baby. As soon as I laid my eyes on that child, my knees gave out. Her little face made me melt. She looked exactly like August, the way her nostrils flared up like his and her perfect oval eyes sank into her face just like his. I wondered, *would my baby have had his eyes?* I watched as the nurse rocked her a little before placing her back down in the bed. The nurse's face lit up as she walked back out the room.

"Your niece is beautiful Auntie … um, sorry, what's your name?"

Without thinking I whispered, "Casey."

"Aww, how sweet. Your sister named her after you." She smiled.

"What!" I shrieked.

"She named her Casey. You two must be really close," the nurse stated, looking back through the window at the babies again. Then she smiled at me once more and walked away.

I froze in terror. Did the nurse really just say that Terren named her daughter Casey? No, she couldn't have. That's insane! Why would she name her daughter after me? That didn't make any sense. In what universe was it OK to name your child after your husband's mistress? I dropped the teddy bear on the ground and let the balloons float up to the ceiling. I ran out of that hospital as fast as I could, because if I stayed there any longer, I could pretty much guarantee they would be admitting me, and it wouldn't be for physical pain, it would be for mental illness, because I'd never felt more crazy than I did right now.

I ran into the restaurant to confront August. "DID YOU KNOW YOUR CHILD IS NAMED AFTER ME?" I screamed as he came out from the kitchen.

"Casey, not here!" he said grabbing my arm and pulling me outside.

August shoved me into the car, then jumped in and sped away.

"YOU'RE A LUNATIC!" I screamed.

"Casey! What are you talking about?"

"Your precious wife named your daughter after me! You didn't know?"

August didn't respond.

"DID YOU KNOW?"

"I just found out this morning. I called her when I got to work. I'm sorry," he whispered.

"DON'T YOU THINK THAT'S CRAZY?"

"I said *I'm sorry*," he said a little louder.

"You're … sorry?"

"Yes."

"What is it that you're sorry for August? Please let me know?"

August took a deep breath. "I'm sorry for falling in love with you." His voice cracked.

"SHUT UP!" I screamed. "You think I want to hear that? You're not in love with me. You're in love with yourself. I wish I never met you!"

August's whole body tensed up. "I'M SORRY I DIDN'T TELL YOU I WAS MARRIED! I'M SORRY I DIDN'T TELL YOU MY WIFE WAS PREGNANT! I'M SORRY TERREN NAMED OUR DAUGHTER AFTER YOU CASEY! I'M SORRY CASEY, WHAT ELSE DO YOU WANT ME TO SAY? I'M SORRY!"

I could hear August speaking, I could hear him apologizing, but all I could see was red. When we pulled up in front of my building, I jumped out the car and ran upstairs. August followed close behind me.

"Casey, talk to me," August said as we walked through the door.

I turned and looked him in the eyes. "I want you out of my house, August!"

I was about to lose my religion cussing him out, but I was stopped by a knock at the door. Both August and I turned our heads around looking down the hall at the front door. No one knew where I lived. I wondered if it was M.

There was another knock, this time louder. I thought. I rolled my eyes and pushed past August, who looked strangely frightened.

He grabbed my arm. "Don't answer it," he whispered.

"What!" I said, snatching my arm away from him. I stomped to the door and swung it open without even asking who it was. And there she was, August's greatest fear, Terren holding a car seat with baby Casey bundled up inside.

She gritted her teeth. "Where is my husband?"

I looked down the hall at August, who now looked like a deer stuck in headlights. "It's for you," I said, opening the door wider to be sure he could see Terren.

August stood silent.

"What's wrong August? You surprised to see me? You know my sister lives across the street. Did you think my sister wouldn't tell me you were shacking up while I was in the hospital on bed rest?" Terren ranted.

My eyes widened. Everything made sense. M was Terren's sister, and she lived across the street, and August knew that, which is why he changed his mind on moving in with me as soon as I found this apartment. He knew the whole time, and instead of being honest with me, he decided to make me feel like I did something wrong. Now his wife was standing at my door with their child.

"What are … you doing … here?" August stuttered. "You should still be in the hospital."

"Don't you want to see your child?" Terren taunted him. "I checked myself out. I was sick of being in there, plus I thought we could all celebrate baby Casey together!" She glared.

I watched August's eyes look down from Terren to the car seat, but he didn't move.

"August! Don't you want to see your child?" Terren cried out. I could hear the frustration in her voice.

She looked over to me. "This is what you wanted, right? Now you get it. You're a part of our lives forever, CASEY!"

I was over this drama. I was not going to stand here in my house and deal with them. This was my peaceful place. As far as I was concerned, she could help him collect his things, and they could be on their merry way.

"Both of ya'll can get out!" I said pointing to the door, but nobody moved.

"AUGUST!" Terren screamed.

When he still didn't move, Terren pushed her way into

my house, knocking me into the door as she shoved her way in with the baby.

The back of my head slammed into the door.

"Are you crazy!" I yelled, grabbing her by the arm to stop her.

She snatched her arm away from me and charged towards August, dropping the car seat on the floor. She jumped on August and they began to tussle.

"GET OUT OF MY HOUSE!" I screamed.

Terren and August were wrestling. I tripped over the car seat trying to push them out of my apartment, but I was no competition for both of them. I tumbled over them hitting the floor again.

August had Terren pinned down on the floor, I ran over to August and kicked him in the back. He let out a loud cry as he flew into the wall, letting Terren free. She jumped up and started wailing on him. I started kicking him and punching him too. At first August was trying to brace himself from all the blows. Then the next thing you know he jumped up like a wild animal caught both of us by the arms and slung us across the hallway into the living room. I landed on top of Terren, and in her rage, she started swinging at me. One of her punches landed in my face, and I went ballistic. We were in a full out brawl. Out the corner of my eye I could see August grab the car seat and hurry out the door, leaving Terren and I rolling around on my living room floor. Not even a minute later two cops burst into my apartment, pulling Terren and me apart, slamming us up against the wall and throwing handcuffs on us.

I sat in the holding cell furious. I could not believe that I'd been arrested. I could hear Terren weeping in the cell next to mine. I wanted to yell at her to shut up, but a part of me felt sympathetic. How were we the ones locked up and August was out there free?

The absolute worse part of this was I had no one to call. My sister was in rehab; I couldn't call my parents, not to mention they wouldn't be here for another couple of hours. The only person I could think to call was Brooke, and I had her number stored in my cell phone and I didn't know it by heart. I burst out laughing. I just laughed and laughed and laughed until I was hunched over in pain with tears streaming down my face. Sometimes you just have to laugh at yourself.

An officer opened my cell and looked at me like I was crazy. "You're free to go."

I stopped laughing, afraid of who'd come to bail me out. I was escorted to the front desk, I signed some papers, and was given a summons to appear in court. I looked around the lobby, trying to figure out who came for me. There was a woman holding the car seat with baby Casey in it staring at me with the most judgmental disdain I'd ever seen. I assumed that was the infamous M there to get Terren. I rolled my eyes at her and walked out of the police station.

August was parked out front. I ignored him and started walking down the street. He jumped out the car and ran up to me.

"Where you going?" he asked.

I didn't respond.

"I told them that she came to your house and assaulted us," he announced.

The sound of his voice made me hate him more. I was done with him. I stopped and looked him in his big brown eyes, the same eyes that used to make me melt, now they just made me sick. I was done. There was nothing that August could say to me to anymore. It was over.

I pulled his promise ring off my finger and handed it to him,   "Your stuff will be on the curb," I said calmly.

"Casey…just let me take you home."

I just tuned him out and walked away. I would've

walked home to Connecticut before I got in the car with August. I felt like Carrie from *Sex and the City* when Natasha caught her and Big together and Natasha ended up in the hospital: *We were so over we needed a new word for over*!

Chapter Thirteen
Summer

CASEY

Summer had finally come to Harlem. With all the turmoil that the winter brought, I was excited for a change. I was keeping myself busy with work, and I'd taken Umaja's advice and enrolled in some summer classes at my school. Being in class reminded me of why I was in New York in the first place. I was focused, I had a plan, and I was finally taking control of my life.

Umaja was such an awesome person. He had to be at least twenty-five years my senior, but he was one of the easiest people to talk to. He was also incredibly talented and very connected in the New York theater community. He took me to celebrity parties, exclusive events, and all kinds of shows in the city. Finally, I was a real New Yorker.

Everyone Umaja knew was an actor, singer, writer, painter, producer, or somehow involved in the arts. Being around him lit a creative spark in me that had fizzled out. I believed Umaja was sent from God to encourage me to focus on my goals. I loved our pure innocent, non-sexual love.

We had a routine; we'd meet up after my classes, walk

around the city, go window-shopping in Chelsea, and drink wine down at the Hudson. We'd always find something to do. This Friday night he was taking me to a party in the city. I rushed around my apartment trying to find something to wear because this was not a typical party, it was a wrap party for the actress Ella Joyce, who was best known for playing the role of Eleanor in the 90s TV show, *Roc*. Umaja's friend Floyd was having the wrap party for her in his Manhattan high rise.

Umaja was on his way, and I was running late as usual. I threw on a short white dress with a lace overlay that used to fit perfectly, but now my cleavage fought with the crossover v-neck. Then I put on these amazing blue strappy Chloe sandals I was excited to wear every since I'd found them at this awesome consignment shop one day.

As soon as I got downstairs, Umaja was coming around the corner. I fiddled around with the top of my dress, trying to readjust my breasts so that Umaja's eyes wouldn't pop out of his head.

"What an honor it's going to be to show up with you on my arm," Umaja complimented as we strolled down the street.

"The feeling is very mutual." I smiled, appreciating the extra effort he made tonight, breaking out his Gucci loafers.

"How about we stop and get a drink before we go?" Umaja suggested.

"Sounds good to me," I agreed, knowing that one good drink would make me feel extra sexy in my too-tight dress.

Umaja hailed a cab. We ended up in Chelsea near these shops that he and I frequented. At the corner I could see a bouncer standing outside of a bar that looked pretty packed judging by the groups of men that were standing outside smoking.

We headed straight to the bar. There was only one empty stool, and Umaja insisted that I sit on it. Umaja ordered us drinks, then leaned in close to me and told me he was going to run to the bathroom. As I sat there waiting for our drinks, I scanned the dimly lit bar. There were so many men in there. All of them exquisitely dressed, laughing and leaning in close to each other. I took another look around and noticed that I was the only female there.

"Here you go," the bartender said, handing me our drinks.

I picked mine up and took a big sip. I glanced around the club at all the men, *was this a gay bar? Was Umaja gay?* In all the time that Umaja and I had spent together, he'd never given me any indication of him being gay. He'd even talked to me in depth about his past and how his last relationship tore him apart, however never one word about the gender of the person who did the heartbreaking. I guess I just assumed that he was talking about a woman.

I took another huge gulp of my drink, almost clearing the cup. Umaja came out of the bathroom and began walking back to me. Everything about him said straight man—except for the fact that he'd never made any advances towards me.

Umaja wrapped his arm around my waist. "How's your drink?" he yelled over the music.

"It's yummy."

He picked his drink up and I watched him take a sip. "This is good," he said raising his glass.

The more we drank, the more comfortable Umaja got in his element. He was introducing me to his friends, some of whom were very flamboyant. We laughed and drank and danced for almost an hour. By the time Umaja mentioned to me that we should get going, I was disappointed because I was having so much fun.

When we exited the bar, Umaja wrapped his arm around my shoulder and kissed me on the cheek.

"You looked like you didn't want to leave," he pointed out.

"I didn't."

"I had to practically pull you out of there."

I stopped walking and looked at him. "I didn't know you were gay."

He chuckled. "Oh, honey, what is there to know? At the end of the day we all end up in and out of love. Both men and women will smash your heart into pieces and love you back to life if you let them."

I smiled and he guided me down the street on to our next adventure.

Floyd's apartment was unbelievable, and the view…the view was breathtaking! We could see all of Manhattan from up there. The place had to be professionally decorated. There were imported drapes and rugs, porcelain vases, marble counters and one-of-a-kind portraits lavishly dressing the walls.

Floyd danced over to us as we walked through the door, with two glasses of champagne in his hands and a welcoming smile on his face.

"Hello," Floyd sung, pushing the champagne glasses into our hands.

Umaja leaned towards Floyd, and they gave each other quick smooches on their cheeks.

"Thank you," Umaja and I said in unison as Floyd leaned into me, repeating the kissing greeting.

"Don't you look smashing," Floyd complemented me while motioning for me to turn around.

I gracefully spun around, feeling even sexier now.

"Hot!" Floyd declared, tapping his hand across my butt. "Come on in and make yourself at home. We have plenty of food and alcohol, so don't be shy," he said, waving his arms around.

Umaja pulled me through the crowd, introducing me to everyone. When we finally made it over to Ella Joyce,

Umaja gave her a big hug like he'd known her for years. I was so impressed by Umaja's charisma. He knew how to talk to people.

He pulled my arm, shoving me towards Ella.

"This is my friend Casey. She's an aspiring actress going to film school here in the city. What advice would you give her, Ella?" Umaja pressed.

Ella Joyce flashed her bright smile at me, took my hands into hers and muttered three simple words: "Never give up."

She allowed her words to resonate with me before she let go and was pulled into another conversation.

I held on to that moment for as long as I could before Umaja dragged me back into the crowd, introducing me to someone else.

The introductions went on for about forty-five minutes before we ended up on the balcony. The lights were shining so bright it looked like a hand-painted portrait.

"Look at that, our glasses are empty," Umaja noticed, sliding my glass from between my fingers. "Let me get us a refill," he said as he walked through the sliding glass doors.

I continued to admire the city, and thought about how blessed I was to have Umaja in my life.

A warm hand rested on my shoulder. I turned around assuming Umaja had returned with my champagne.

"Casey?" I heard the vaguely familiar voice say.

When my eyes landed on the tall, dark, handsome man, I felt my knees buckle a little. "You're Casey, from Grand Central. Remember me? Ty."

"Ty." I repeated his name to him like a child who was just learning to speak.

"Yeah, you remember me?" he asked again.

I placed my hand over my heart. "Of course I do."

"I can't believe I found you." Ty's voice rang with

excitement.

I was flattered. "You were looking for me?"

"Well, I wasn't running around the city looking into windows," he joked. "But every time I was out, I hoped to run into you."

"Really?"

"Yes, really. You cut your hair."

"I needed a change."

Umaja returned with our champagne. He smiled when he saw Ty.

"Hello," Umaja said, handing a glass to me, yet keeping his eyes locked on Ty.

"Hi, how you doing?" Ty smiled.

Umaja looked at me for an introduction.

"Umaja, this is Ty. I met him the day I moved to the city. Ty, this is my friend Umaja."

"Pleasure." Umaja smirked.

There was an awkward silence as we shifted eye contact from one another. I thought Umaja would get the hint and find his way back into the party, but he didn't—he just swayed back and forth between me and Ty until Ty decided to end the confusion.

"Well, I'm gonna go back inside," Ty said turning back towards the balcony doors.

I almost jumped out of my skin, afraid to watch Ty leave me again without a way to reach him.

"How do I get in touch with you?" I spit out.

"Take my number."

I pulled out my cell phone and punched in the digits.

"Got it. I'll call you."

"I'll look forward to it," Ty said before heading back into the party.

As Ty walked away, Umaja shot me a disappointing look.

"Casey, this is supposed to be your time of healing. No distractions, remember?"

"I agree, but you know what they say, the quickest way to get over someone is to get under someone else." I laughed.

Umaja couldn't help but laugh with me. "You're crazy girl, you know that?"

"Yeah, I know."

We clicked our glasses together, then strolled back into the party to dance the rest of the night away.

It took me a few days to work up the courage to call Ty, but I was very pleased when I finally did. Ty was a perfect gentleman. We started out slow. I was so nervous about getting involved with someone new since I was fresh out of my situation with August, but I needed a distraction because I was starting to feel lonely. It had been almost a month since I'd spoken to August, and as much as I hated to admit it, I did miss him. In his absence all I could remember were the good times. I knew at any moment I could break down and call him, and I didn't want to do that, so I figured at the very least Ty could be the distraction I needed.

Talking on the phone was all either of us had time for. During the day Ty worked for a media firm in the city, and at night he DJ'd. So most nights he would leave work and go straight to a gig. Between my work schedule and Ty's, phone calls were enough for me.

Ty called me all the time. We spoke in the mornings, throughout the day we'd find moments to chat during lunch, or on our breaks; he'd call me when he was in transition from work to his gigs and when he was on his way home from his gigs.

Our late night conversations were the best. We talked about our families, work, friends, foods that we loved, music and movies. There were no limitations on our conversations.

Getting to know him had become my favorite pastime. We were the same age, had the same favorite foods, we were both ambitious and both into the arts … Ty was a breath of fresh air.

The absolute best thing about Ty was he was drama free. He wasn't married, he had no children, and he hadn't even had a girlfriend in years. All his focus was on becoming a full-time DJ. He had a dream that he was chasing, and I understood that. He was an inspiration to me.

After weeks of phone calls, Ty finally found an excuse for us to spend some time together. He got us tickets to the Kanye West and Jay Z concert at Madison Square Garden, so I got out of work early on Friday to get ready.

I hadn't been on a real date since August took me to Times Square last year, and that was more of a spontaneous thing than a date. Ty made me feel alive again. I didn't know what would come out of this, but I did believe God was showing me that there were other options out there for me, and I was excited to explore them all.

The concert lived up to its expectations. Ty got us floor seats. We were so close to the stage, I could have reached out and touched Kanye. I sat at my desk thinking about how much fun I'd been having with Ty. Even though we were both busy, we always found ways to sneak in a moment or two. It helped that he didn't work far from my school, so we would sometimes meet for lunch or dinner. We synced our times up to travel back home together, take walks down by the water or just explore the streets of New York. No matter what we did, both of us had smiles on our faces, laughter coming out of our mouths and intrigue in our eyes.

I wanted to do something special for Ty. He'd mentioned once or twice that he wanted to taste my cooking one day, so I thought making him dinner would be the perfect way to show him how much I was appreciating his company.

There was only one thing that was making me feel nervous about cooking for Ty—August.

Although I hadn't had any communication with August, for some reason I still had a strong sense of loyalty to him. He was the only man that I ever had in my apartment, and he still had some of his stuff there. His spirit filled that apartment, and as much and as I didn't want to admit it, my heart would still speed up a little when I would brush across his sweater in the closet. I could still smell his scent on my mattress no matter how many times I changed the sheets. Deep down I felt like my apartment was our apartment, and I didn't know if I was ready to let anyone else into our space.

I had to push past those feelings if I was ever going to truly move on. I reminded myself that August was married! Not only was he married, but the only loyalty August had was to himself. I decided to rip off the bandage. I picked up my desk phone and dialed Ty's number. He answered on the first ring.

"Good day, Lovely."

The sound of his voice reassured me that I was doing the right thing.

"Do you have any gigs Friday night?"

"No ma'am. I'm all yours," Ty replied. I could hear him smiling.

"You just assume that I'm going to ask you to do something?"

"No, just hoping."

My smile widened. "Well, if you're interested, I would like to cook you dinner Friday."

"Oh yes, I'm interested."

"Good. Then it's a date."

"It's a date," Ty confirmed.

"Perfect. Well, let me get back to work. I will talk to you later."

"OK. Have a good day."

"You too," I said and hung up the phone.

I stood up from my desk in an attempt to shake off my excitement. I shook my legs, stretched my arms up in the air and rolled my neck. As I began to sit back down, a deliveryman walked around the corner carrying a large bouquet of long-stem red roses. I looked around the office to see who he could be delivering them to.

All the women's eyes were following the flowers.

"I'm looking for Casey," the deliveryman said.

Did he really just say my name? I could feel everyone's eyes on me.

"That's … me," I stuttered.

He handed me the vase of roses. "Please sign here," he said, handing me a clipboard and pen.

I reached out my hands, allowing him to pass me the roses.

I placed the roses on my desk and signed the paper. Then he disappeared back through the doors.

I couldn't believe Ty sent me this gorgeous bouquet.

I reached for the phone to call Ty and thank him. As I was about to dial his number, I noticed there was a card sticking out from the bouquet. I took the card from the little holster and opened it up. And there they were, three simple little words, *I love you.*

I could feel my breath leave my body. As I stared at the words on the card, I knew Ty couldn't have possibly said *I love you* this quick.

The flowers weren't from Ty, they were from August.

I eased myself back into my chair, keeping my eyes glued to the roses. My mind was racing. Why would August pick now to send me flowers? Since the arrest, he hadn't made any attempts to reach out to me. I hadn't even heard anything from Terren, so I thought that maybe they were back together. The only reason Terren ever crossed my mind these days was because our court date was this Thursday. I wondered if that had anything to do with these suspicious flowers.

I had to admit they were fabulous. Each rose was perfectly bloomed with the brightest shade of candy apple red shinning off each petal. The long stems were reminiscent of an exotic world-famous supermodel. Everything about these roses said *love*. They said the sender loved me, and as much as I didn't want to admit it, the feeling overtaking my body at this moment was telling me that I loved him too. My heart was racing the way only August could make it run.

I contemplated my next move. Should I just accept the roses as a nice gesture and ignore the feelings they brought with them, or should I give in to my heart and call August and say *thank you*? I rationalized that saying thank you would be the right thing to do. *I mean, he had to dish out a few hundred dollars on these flowers. The least I could do was let him know that I got them. I mean what harm could come from a simple thank you? It was the right thing to do...right?*

I stared at the phone, hoping that it would ring and my boss or a customer would be on the other end to distract me. But it didn't ring. So, I picked it up and dialed August's number. As soon as I heard his voice I melted. This was a mistake!

"August," I whispered.

"I knew you would call."

I could hear his arrogance through the phone. "I just wanted to say, thank you for the flowers." My voice was shaking.

"I miss you."

I paused, and then quickly lost control of my own mouth. "I miss you too."

"Can I see you tonight?"

I thought, *ABSOLUTELY NOT!* "Yes" rolled off of my tongue faster than my brain could send it the NO signal.

"I'll meet you at the house after I leave work."

I was a slave to my own voice. "O … K."

"Love you," August said, sealing the deal.

I felt the words slip through my lips. "I love you too." And just like that, it was over. I had given up my power in less than thirty seconds.

I raced home after work. I didn't want August to get there before me. I wanted to straighten up and take a shower. I had no intentions on doing anything with him, but since I hadn't seen him in a while, I wanted to at least smell good.

I kept going over in my head how I wanted this night to play out. I wondered if he'd been thinking about me the entire time. I wondered where he'd been and why he stayed away so long. I wondered if maybe his divorce had gone through now, maybe that's why he stayed away because he wanted to be divorced by the time he came back to me.

When I got out of the shower, I put on this pretty flowing maxi dress. It was nice enough to wear outside, but subtle enough to pass for a housedress. Worst-case scenario, August would think I wore it to work today instead of putting it on just for him.

My apartment was pretty clean already. All I had to do was fluff the pillows on my couch, open up the windows for the breeze, and spray some air freshener. To complete the scene, I placed the flowers that August sent me in the living room window. I figured he'd appreciate that.

The knock on the door made me anxious. I took a few deep breaths and ran my hands over my hair to ensure it was in place.

I opened the door wide enough to offer a non-verbal invitation inside. August looked as good as I remembered. I closed the door behind him and locked it. When I turned around, August and I were standing face to face. Everything about us was in sync, our eyes were locked, and we were breathing at the same pace.

August reached his hand out and placed it on my cheek. I allowed my face to surrender to his palm. I exhaled. He pulled me closer to his face, our lips to meet. I lost control. We opened our mouths at the same time. The same breath of air to ran through both of our bodies before we kissed.

My body gave into his every demand. His hands guided my movements. He backed me up against the wall, moving my dress to the side, exposing my legs. The breeze from the window swept in, caressing our bodies enough to stop the sweat that was peeking through our pores.

August's touch was a familiar sin. As his kisses grazed my neck, those body tremors that he somehow was capable of giving me resurfaced. He removed my dress so fast I didn't even realize it was off until I felt his manhood run against my thigh. Then time stopped.

I got lost in his strokes. My eyes rolled back as my head massaged the wall. He lifted me up off the ground and wrapped my legs around his waist. I cried out in ecstasy as that familiar tension burst out of me. August dug deeper with every moan. I was gone. He sucked me back into his web, and this time I didn't know if I would ever become untangled again.

We lay facing each other, our naked bodies sprawled across the living room floor. The moon's light streamed through the window like laser rays, landing softly across our frames, highlighting our body's sensual curves.

Even in the darkness, I could feel August's eyes burning into mine. As wonderful as the lovemaking we just shared was, it was followed by a consuming guilt that I couldn't ignore. I knew that it would be a risk seeing him, but I had no idea I would plummet back into the abyss. I thought that I would slip slow enough that I would be able to catch myself before falling. I guess I underestimated the power that he had over me. Or was it the power that I *surrendered* to him? Whatever it was, it all added up to the same thing. He rendered me powerless.

"What are you thinking about?" August whispered.

"Nothing," I lied.

He ran his hand across my back. "I missed this."

I smiled, not wanting to admit I missed it too. I'd already given him my body tonight. There was no reason for me to make myself vulnerable to an emotional tsunami too.

I really wanted to ask him if he was finally divorced. I just couldn't muster up the courage. I figured, *why ruin the night? I may as well enjoy the fantasy before the morning comes and reality sets back in.*

I turned my back to August and inched my body close to his. He pulled me in until our bodies interlocked. I forgot how good it felt to cuddle with him. I closed my eyes and rationalized, *if he is still married at least tonight he's all mine.*

In the morning my body's natural alarm clock sounded right on time. The moon's rays had swapped with the morning sun landing on my face. August was still sound asleep. I wiggled myself from his embrace and crept into the bathroom. I took a quick shower, brushed my teeth, and slipped into my bedroom.

I grabbed for my lotion and noticed my cell phone for the first time since yesterday. There were two missed calls on it, both from Ty. I gasped, pulling the phone into my chest as if to shield my heart. What had I done? How did I forget about Ty? Guilt rushed through me. I knew Ty and I weren't exclusive, but we had an unspoken trust between one another, and now I had broken that trust. I knew once I spoke to him, he would remind me of his calls he made to me last night, and I would have to be dishonest with him and say something like I fell asleep early.

I needed to call him back and now. I didn't want to wait

until I got to work. I had to get August out of the house before Ty called again. I went back in the living room and nudged August to wake him up. He didn't budge, so I pushed him a little harder. He looked up at me in a panic.

"Sorry to wake you up like this, but I have to go into work early. I'm already running late."

"And?" August said, shrugging his shoulders.

"What do you mean *and?* I have to go, so I need you to go too."

"I'm not going to work till ten, so I'll take a shower and lock up before I leave."

I was beyond frustrated. I didn't want August staying in my house while I wasn't there. On the other hand, I didn't have time to debate with him because I knew Ty's phone call would be coming in a matter of seconds.

"OK, just make sure you lock the door behind you," I huffed.

He smiled at me and rolled back over. I snatched up my bags and hurried out the door.

I called Ty as soon as I got outside. I knew if I went the entire day without speaking to him it would just increase my paranoia.

Hearing Ty's voice answer the phone put a smile on my face. "Hi."

"Good morning," Ty greeted me.

"I'm sorry I missed your call last night," I said before he mentioned it.

"No worries."

"What time did you get out of the club?" I asked, trying to navigate the questions.

"I got out around twelve. My boy finished up for me. I got in the house a little before one. What did you end up doing?"

"Oh a friend of mine came by with some drinks, I drank

a little too much and passed out early." I decided if I told a half-truth, it wouldn't be as bad as a complete lie.

"I missed talking to you last night."

"I missed talking to you too."

"I guess I'm getting used to our little routine," Ty admitted.

"I am too."

"You sure?"

His question caught me off guard. "Of course I am. Why would you ask me that?" I felt a lump form in my chest.

"Just making sure. The last thing I want to do is be a nuisance by calling you all hours of the night. I know my schedule is crazy."

"Oh please. I'm a nighthawk. I really don't mind the late night calls. I look forward to them. I was so sad this morning when I realized I missed your calls," I said, finally being completely honest.

I heard him exhale. "Good."

"So do you still have Friday night open for me?" I asked.

"I'm all yours."

"Trust me, it will be worth it. Not to brag, but I am a pretty good cook."

"I'll see," Ty laughed.

TERREN

Terren bundled baby Casey up and tucked her into her car seat. Then she lifted the seat off the couch and headed out the door. When she got outside, Melissa was waiting. Terren hoisted the baby into the back seat, and then slid into the passenger side next to her sister.

Terren gazed out the window as they drove. She didn't want Melissa to see that she'd been crying. Originally, August was going to drive her to court, but he'd stayed out for the last two days, and she didn't have the energy to go chasing him down.

Melissa broke the silence. "So is he gone again?"

Terren nodded her head *yes*.

"Why do you allow him to keep doing this to you?" Melissa blurted out.

Terren didn't respond.

Melissa took a deep breath. "I thought that you two had an agreement that he would be there to support you today. Wasn't that a stipulation to you letting him move back in?"

"Melissa, leave it alone," Terren whispered.

"I would love to leave it alone Terren, but you keep dragging me in. Do you know how hard it is for me to have to sit back and watch how he treats you? Do you have any idea how angry it makes me to see you crying all the time? Do you?"

"I'm sorry to inconvenience you, Melissa. I apologize for thinking that I could turn to my sister when I need her."

"I never said you couldn't turn to me, but how many times are you going to turn to me about the same thing? August has shown you time and time again that he only cares about himself."

"OK!" Terren yelled.

"No. It's not OK. Didn't he say that he was done after you got arrested? He's been home, so-called doing well for over a month and now, right before you are about to go to court, he disappears again. I wonder why? It's because he's still dealing with that girl. I'm sure she probably took him back too. He obviously likes weak women."

"Really, Melissa, I'm weak? That's how you feel about me?" Terren whined.

"That's what you're showing me, Terren. It's like you're not even trying to be strong. Don't you even wonder how this is affecting your kids? Do you think this is a good example for your daughters?"

"You don't think I think about that? It's on my mind all the time!"

"Well you don't act like it. To me it looks like you like this craziness."

"What are you talking about?"

"What else makes sense? You must get off on the drama now. Maybe in your mind this is some twisted way of showing him how much you love him."

"That's crazy."

"Tell me about it! This entire situation is crazy. He's been going back and forth between you and her for almost a year, he didn't even show up to the delivery of your baby, now you're going to court after being arrested with his mistress, and even after all that you take him back. Then he promises he will change and be there to support you. But where is he? Where is he, Terren?"

Terren continued to stare out the window.

"WHERE IS HE TERREN?" Melissa screamed so loud Terren jumped out of her seat.

"I don't need you to remind me of everything that's happened, Melissa. At the end of the day, August is my husband, and I'm going to fight for him. I love him, and no matter what he's putting me through right now, I know he loves me. I don't know how much more I can take, but I know I'm not ready to give up yet. I don't need you to judge me for that, just be my sister and support me—please."

"I'm not judging you. I've been nothing but supportive to you. However, it's very hard to sit around and watch him hurt you. I can't support that, because I don't understand it."

"Some things are just not for you to understand."

"I guess not." Melissa said rolling her eyes.

They drove the rest of the way in silence. Terren hated having to defend her marriage. She hated fighting with her sister even more, but even though Melissa was annoying her to no end, Terren knew she was right, because if the situation were reversed, Terren would be giving Melissa the same speech. But the truth was, unless Melissa was actually in her shoes, she would never understand. No one could predict how they would behave in her position, fighting in a ring with no rules. Terren never thought in a million years that she would be here, that her marriage would be a catastrophe. Here she was, carting around a newborn to a courthouse to go in front of a judge with her husband's mistress. Her world was turned upside down, and she had no idea what to do to rotate it back, but that was all she wanted. She wanted her family back, she wanted some normalcy, she wanted her children to grow up with both parents in their home. She'd worked to hard for it, and she refused to let some little manipulative girl come in and take it away.

CASEY

I sat in the hallway of the courthouse, tapping my foot against the shiny linoleum floor waiting for the recess to end. I had to take the entire day off to be here. This process was stressing me out. But nothing topped the fact that Terren and her sister were there together with the baby.

She and I sat in court while August was sound asleep in my apartment. I wasn't going to let him in last night, but he insisted he wanted to be there for me in the morning as support before I went to court. If he really wanted to be supportive, then he would've came to court with me so I wouldn't be sitting here by myself while Terren and her sister shot me evil looks.

When the recess was over, I hurried into the courtroom and got a seat close to the front. The judge entered the courtroom, the bailiff did his thing, and we all sat down in unison like the trained robots that we were.

There had to be at least twenty more cases called before they finally got to us. I could feel sweat beads forming on my forehead. I was hoping the judge would treat us like the rest of the people who'd approached the bench by barking some orders at us and sending us on our way. My game plan was to just nod and agree to whatever terms he administered.

Terren approached the bench like she was on a mission. The judge stated both of our names and read our case out loud.

"Mrs. Mitchell, you showed up at Ms. Gardener's apartment and assaulted her?"

"I didn't assault her, your honor. I was trying to speak to my husband, who was at her house," she defended.

I dropped my head in shame, wondering if the lady with the traffic violation was judging me like I was judging the arsonist.

"Nevertheless, you showed up to her house and assaulted her?" the judge repeated.

"It was not my intention to assault her. My husband has been staying at her house and hadn't been around to help take care of his children. He moved across the street from my sister's house with her and didn't even show up to the hospital when I gave birth to our daughter," she explained.

"I understand that made you upset, Mrs. Mitchell, but that still does not justify you assaulting her," the judge asserted.

"Well, what was I supposed to do? I needed to talk to him about taking care of his children," Terren pleaded.

"That's what child support is for," the judge explained.

"But he's my husband—I can't file for child support if we're still married," Terren whined.

"If he's not living in the house with you, then you can file for a legal separation and enforce child support while he is not living in the home."

"Legal separation?" Terren repeated like the judge was speaking a foreign language.

"Yes, that is an avenue you can take."

"We're not separated!" Terren declared.

"You just told me that he's living with Ms. Gardner."

I felt the need to interject; I couldn't let all these people think I was as stupid as Terren was making me out to be. "Um, your honor? He's not living with me."

The judge stopped and looked over at me. "Well, he was at your house the night of the incident, correct?"

"Yes, he was, but he doesn't live with me. My name is the only name on my lease."

Terren jumped back in. "Yeah, but you let him stay there even though you know he is *my* husband."

"Listen, I didn't know he was married when I first met him…"

"But you know now, and you still sleep with him!" Terren shouted.

"Mrs. Mitchell, you're out of order," the judge interjected.

I felt like every woman in the courtroom was looking at me.

"But he is my husband," Terren cried out again.

"I understand he's your husband, Mrs. Mitchell. Is Mr. Mitchell here in the courtroom?" the judge asked.

Terren shook her head. "No, he's not here," she whispered.

I was so embarrassed to be in this situation. Even though we were here because of Terren showing up at my house, it still felt like the only guilty party in this case was me.

"Unfortunately, Mrs. Mitchell, regardless or not if your husband was at Ms. Gardner's house, you're still responsible for trespassing and assault. Ms. Gardner, do you want to press charges against Mrs. Mitchell?"

Terren looked at me in agony. I didn't want Terren to be sent to jail or anything, I just wanted her to stay away from me. This was the second time she and I had been in an altercation, and I didn't want it to happen again.

"What will happen if I press charges?" I asked.

"She will be fined and could do up to thirty days in jail," the judge explained.

Me and Terren's mouth dropped. I never thought that it could go that far. I was sympathetic to the fact that she just had a baby. I didn't want to see her go to jail.

"No. Your honor, all I want is for her to leave me alone. Whatever problems she has with her husband, I want her to deal with him and not me."

The judge nodded. "You can drop the charges against

her and enforce a restraining order that says she cannot be within a thousand feet of you."

I took a minute to think about it. A restraining order seemed so ridiculous.

"Your honor, my sister lives across the street from her. It's impossible for me to stay a thousand feet away from her," Terren explained.

"Mrs. Mitchell, I'm sorry, your sister will have to visit you."

"I don't want a restraining order your honor," I interrupted.

I could feel Terren look over at me, but I kept my eyes locked on the judge.

"Are you sure?"

"Yes," I said looking over at Terren. "Please don't make me regret this," I said to her.

"You're not doing me any favors, Casey!" Terren snapped.

The judge mumbled some other instructions to us and then dismissed our case. I walked out of the court before Terren. I didn't want to be caught in the hallway with her.

When I got back to my apartment, August was sprawled out on the couch watching TV like he didn't have a care in the world. I couldn't believe how at peace he looked. Meanwhile, his wife and I just came out of an emotional inferno. I wanted to throw something at his head so he could have a little taste of the grief we experienced.

"Hey baby, how did everything go?" August asked like I'd just come back from a job interview or something.

"It was court, with your wife, how do you think it went?" I was aggravated.

"Yeah well, you ain't in jail so it went OK," he joked.

How could he joke about this? I just spent the whole day in court being ridiculed by his wife and to him it's all fun and games. I walked over to the window to get some air. I closed my eyes and took a deep breath.

"THIS ONE RIGHT HERE! I CAN'T BELIEVE HE IS AT HER HOUSE RIGHT NOW!"

My eyes shot open to the familiar voice screaming outside. There she was. Terren and M were instructing a tow-truck driver to hitch up August's car. My mouth dropped.

"HE MUST BE OUT OF HIS MIND IF HE THINK HE JUST GONNA KEEP PLAYING WITH ME!" Terren yelled as the tow-truck driver finished locking up the car up.

I couldn't move. I wanted to tell August, but all I could do was watch like it was a movie. The tow-truck driver handed Terren a clipboard and she signed her name. As she continued yelling profanities, she started crying and pointing in my direction.

"What's that?" August asked.

"Terren is towing your car," I answered just as cool and collected as he sounded when he greeted me from my court appearance.

"WHAT?" he shouted, jumping up off the couch. He got to the window just in time to see the tow truck pulling his car away.

August scrambled around my apartment, throwing his clothes on. He barely got his shoes on before he was out the door. I stood at the window watching as August ran across the street to catch up with Terren. As soon as she saw him, she exploded, screaming and hitting him. He was yelling things back. People on the street were stopping and looking. Melissa took the baby into the building. I watched and listened long enough to find out his car was registered in Terren's name, so there was nothing August could do about the towing.

I giggled, shut my window and closed my curtain. I walked over to the door, locked it and put on the chain. I'd seen enough. I grabbed a garbage bag and walked through my apartment throwing anything that belonged to August in it. I didn't know how I'd found myself mixed back up in this craziness, but I knew I had to get him out before I got too far tangled up again. After I got all of his things into the bag, I sat it by the door and waited for him to show up so I could give it to him. But he didn't come back. I thought maybe he went to go get his car out of the tow yard, but he didn't show up for the rest of the night. I really didn't care. I had a dinner to prepare for with Ty and I didn't need the worry of August showing up on my mind. I looked at the last two days as a sign; I needed all that to happen with August for closure. Ty was my future now and August was my past.

The next night I prepared chicken Alfredo for my dinner with Ty. I set the mood with candles that I'd placed on the kitchen table. Ty knocked on the door just as I was putting the garlic bread in the oven.

Ty was so damn fine. He held up a bottle of merlot with a bow around the neck.

"Thank you." I smiled, taking the bottle from him and gesturing for him to come in.

He entered slowly. "You don't know how long I've imagined what it looked like inside your world," he said.

"Well I hope it's not a disappointment."

"No, not at all," he assured.

"Come in, have a seat." I guided him to the living room.

"It smells great in here. Let me find out you know how to burn."

"I told you I have skills."

"I can't wait to see for myself."

"You're in luck, because dinner is pretty much ready. I'm just waiting for the garlic bread to finish, and then we can eat. I'm going to open up this bottle of wine," I said heading towards the kitchen.

"I'll just have water or juice if you have it. I don't drink, I just brought it for you."

I turned to face Ty. "Excuse me. So you just want to get me all liquored up so you can take advantage of me?" I joked.

Ty laughed. "No, I just didn't know what else to bring to dinner and you told me you liked wine."

"It was very thoughtful, thank you," I said as I entered the kitchen.

Dinner was perfect. I couldn't remember the last time I'd laughed so much. And even though I'd drank half the bottle, Ty didn't try to make a pass at me once. He was a complete gentleman.

I took the last sip of wine that was in my glass and realized Ty's glass of lemonade was empty.

"Would you like some more to drink?"

"Yes, please," he answered.

I grabbed up both glasses and sashayed towards the kitchen. I reached in the refrigerator, pulled out the pitcher of lemonade and began to refill Ty's glass when I heard a knock at the door. I stopped pouring. I wasn't expecting anyone, but I knew in my heart who it was. I hoped Ty didn't hear the knock. I tried not to move, praying if I were quiet long enough, August would go away. Just when I thought it was safe to put the pitcher down, there was another knock this time louder.

I tippy-toed into the living room where Ty was. He looked up at me so sweetly and was about to open his mouth to say something, but I put my finger up over my mouth signaling to him to be quiet. His eyes widened in confusion. I crept to the door, secured the chain, then turned the lock and inched it open.

August stood looking at me through the chained door.

"What are you doing? Let me in," he demanded.

"What are you doing here, August?"

"I need to talk to you," August said, pushing at the door.

"I don't want to talk to you right now! Why would you just show up to my house unannounced?" I asked so Ty could hear.

"What do you mean? I want to talk to you about…"

I cut him off. I didn't want him to mention yesterday with Ty listening. "Look I don't want to talk to you right now."

"Open the door girl!" August said, pushing at the door again.

"Go away August!" I said, closing the door in his face and locking it. I took a deep breath and stood in the hallway for a moment to collect my thoughts before I faced Ty again.

Bang, bang, bang. August began pounding on the door. I hurried into the living room where Ty was now standing up.

"I'm guessing that's your ex," he said, sounding disappointed.

"*Shhh* … I'm so sorry, but I really don't want him to hear you. He is crazy!"

Ty frowned at me, then whispered, "So what do you want me to do Casey?"

I had to think fast.

Bang, bang, bang. August's banging was rattling the chain. I had to get Ty out because August was not going to leave. I started scanning the room trying to figure a way out. I saw the fire escape at the kitchen window.

I walked up to Ty and whispered to him, "I am so sorry for asking you to do this, but I need you to go down the fire escape."

"What?" Ty looked disgusted.

"Please, I have to get rid of him, and he is not going to go anywhere until I open the door. I really hate to put you in this situation, but this is the only peaceful way out. Trust me."

Ty shook his head at me. I took that as an OK and quickly walked to the kitchen, pulling Ty along. I opened the window. Ty looked at me shamefully before he dunked out onto the fire escape. No sooner than he could get his foot through the window I was shutting it and locking it behind him.

August was now calling out my name and banging on the door. I waited until Ty was clear out of sight and ran through my house trying to dispose of any evidence of Ty being there. I dumped the glass of lemonade down the drain and put the glass in the sink with the rest of the dishes. Once I felt comfortable enough to deal with August, I removed the chain and opened the door. As soon as the door cracked open, August pushed through, knocking me over.

"Are you crazy?" I shouted.

"You got somebody in here?" he yelled, storming through each room, opening up closet doors and looking behind furniture.

"Have you lost your mind?"

"I know you had somebody in here."

"What are you talking about?" I pretended.

He pushed by me into the kitchen and looked out the window down the fire escape. "He jumped out the window?"

"I don't know what you are talking about," I lied.

He looked around the kitchen, noticing the dinner plates in the sink.

"You cooked him dinner Casey?" His voice cracked.

"August, I don't have time for you right now. You come to my house banging on my door after disappearing with your wife yesterday, and now you think you can just pop up here questioning me?"

"Don't turn this around. You know I had to get my car. Who was up in here?" August said, grabbing my arm.

"Get off of me!"

"Tell me who was in here!"

"August, let go of me right now!" I said through gritted teeth.

August shoved me into the wall hard before letting me go.

"GET OUT OF MY HOUSE!"

"YOU WANT ME OUT SO YOU CAN CALL HIM BACK!"

"You know what? I don't care what you think, August! I'm single. I can do whatever I want! You're married, remember? Go home and question your wife!"

"You're right! I don't have time for this!" August said as he stomped towards the door, punching his fist through the wall before storming out.

I hurried over to the door and locked it. I placed my back against the door and slowly slid down to the floor. I sat there trying to sort out in my head why I let that happen. How would I ever explain this to Ty? Would he even talk to me again?

Just as the thought crossed my mind, I heard my cell phone ringing. I jumped up and ran to follow the sound. When I found Ty's name flashing across the screen, I picked it up.

"Ty."

"Casey, are you OK?" he asked concerned.

"I'm fine. Where are you?"

"I'm outside your building. I didn't want to leave until I knew you were OK."

"Stay right there, I'm coming down."

I ran down the stairs. Ty was sitting inside of his green Ford Explorer. I jumped in the passenger seat.

"I'm so sorry, Ty!"

"Why did I just jump out of your window, Casey?" Ty asked.

"I am so sorry. There's no excuse for what just happened."

"Are you still dealing with him?"

"No! Absolutely not!" I lied.

"Then why did he come here tonight?"

I couldn't tell Ty that I'd been seeing August for the last couple days. If he wasn't running away yet, he would be if I told him the truth. I had to come up with a good excuse and quick.

"He came to get his stuff that he left at my house. He called me the other day and said he was going to come pick it up, but he never said when. I wasn't expecting him to just show up unannounced like that."

"Casey, I really want to believe you, but I think I'm going to need some time to process everything that just happened. That didn't seem like a relationship that was over. It seems like there is some unfinished business there."

"Ty, please believe me. There is…" Before I could get the sentence out of my mouth I saw August walking back up to my building. I wanted to hide but I knew I wouldn't be able to explain any other antics to Ty tonight. I figured I would just act like I didn't see him, but by some sick twist of fate August looked right into Ty's car. I knew there was no way I was going to get myself out of this one, so I decided to just follow through on my lie to Ty.

"That's him," I said to Ty.

"He's back. What does he want now?"

"He was so upset that I didn't open the door for him that we got in an argument and forgot his stuff. Stay here and wait for me, please. I'm just going to go give him his stuff."

Ty looked at me like I had three heads.

"I'll be right back. I promise," I said, opening the door and walking up to August with an attitude.

"I hope you came to get your stuff," I said to him, rolling my eyes.

He looked hurt. "You serious?"

"I'm dead serious," I said, turning away from him and walking to the door.

He followed me upstairs. When I got to my apartment, I walked in and went straight to the closet where I had thrown the garbage bags with his stuff. I pushed them over to him.

"You really packed my stuff?"

I sucked my teeth. Then I walked over to the door and held it open for him to leave. "Sure did!"

He shook his head, picked up his bags and walked out. I followed him downstairs to finish my apology to Ty. I felt like I was free and clear. Ty would see August leaving with his bags and believe me.

I wanted for August to disappear down the street before I got back in the care with Ty, but as I approached Ty's car, I heard something hit the ground. I turned around and August had slammed his bags down.

"Of all the years I was with my wife, she ain't never put me through nothing like this." August sulked.

I was stunned that he had the audacity to compare me to Terren. But I chose to save face and shot back at him, "Well lucky for me, I'm not your wife."

August eyes turned bright red. I couldn't take his stare, so I turned away from him.

As soon as I turned around, August grabbed the back of my shirt, yanking me back to him. He spun me around and grabbed my neck, throwing me down onto the hood of Ty's car.

I could feel his nails digging into my skin. He lifted me up, then slammed me back down into the hood. I tried to pry his hands off of me, but I couldn't. I started to black out.

Suddenly, he let go of me. I fell off the car and hit the ground. I could hear some commotion going on, but I was too dazed. I felt someone's arms wrap around me, helping me to my feet. When I was able to focus I realized Ty was trying to get me back into his car.

"Come on let's get out of here," Ty urged.

I looked around to see where August had gone, but I

couldn't find him.

"Where's August?" I asked Ty.

"He's out. Let's go before he wakes up," he said, trying to push me into the car.

"What do you mean before he wakes up?" I asked.

I shook myself out of Ty's grasp and started looking for August. Then I saw him laid out on the sidewalk with blood pouring out of his head.

"Oh my God! What did you do to him?" I screamed running over to check on August.

"I hit him over the head. I had to get him off of you!" Ty yelled.

"What did you hit him with?" I said in a panic.

"Does it matter? He was choking you!"

I ran to August's side and started shaking him trying to get him to regain consciousness.

"August, August wake up!" I was pissed at August, but I didn't want him to die. I didn't know what Ty hit him with, but whatever it was, it split August's head open.

I kept calling his name and shaking him, trying to get him to wake up. His eyes slowly opened.

"Oh my God! Thank you God." I ripped the bag open with August's stuff in it and pulled out a T-shirt and wrapped it around his bleeding head.

"YOU HAVE TO BE KIDDING ME!" Ty screamed. "YOU'RE REALLY GONNA HELP HIM AFTER HE JUST CHOKED YOU?"

"YOU COULD HAVE KILLED HIM!" I cried.

"YOU'RE CRAZY! IF YOU'RE WILLING TO PUT UP WITH THAT THEN YOU DESERVE EACH OTHER!" Ty barked before jumping in his car and speeding away.

I sat in the middle of the sidewalk rocking August in my arms, holding the shirt around his head trying to stop the bleeding. I reached in my pocket, pulled out my cell phone and called 911.

It took about ten minutes for the ambulance to arrive. When they finally got there, it looked like a murder scene, there was so much blood on the ground, on me and the T-shirt. The paramedics hoisted August up into the ambulance, and I insisted that I ride with him.

I was terrified on the way to the hospital. August lay there going in and out of consciousness. Finally he looked up at me and said, "Casey please don't leave me." Then he closed his eyes and passed back out.

Chapter Fourteen
Heat Wave

CASEY

The Fourth of July was our non-official family reunion. For years, family members would come from near and far and gather at Aunt Caroline's house to celebrate. I was really nervous to be around my family, especially my folks and Candice who had just gotten out of rehab. I'd been a horrible sister; I hadn't reached out to her since we dropped her off. I just didn't know what to say to her. And since August was still in my life, I didn't want to bring him up in fear that would interfere with her healing process.

Because of the sensitivity of our relationship, I didn't invite August to the cookout. That was a hard decision to make since we'd been joined at the hip since that night Ty bust him upside the head with a lug wrench. I found out what the weapon was once August woke up in the hospital with twelve stitches in his head. Seeing August with blood gushing out of his head did something to me. Once he was released from the hospital, I allowed him to come back to my house so that I could keep an eye on him while he slept. The doctors said the first twenty-four hours were crucial to make sure he didn't have a concussion. I had all intentions of sending him on his way once he was in the clear, but he turned into this needy little boy, and I couldn't put him out on the street like that.

I made a fool of myself defending August when Ty was trying to help me. I called Ty a few days later and to my surprise he answered. I apologized for everything, and he listened but the only words he had for me were, "You deserve better. I hope you realize that one day," then he hung up the phone, and that was the last I'd heard from him.

I was disappointed about losing Ty, but the timing wasn't right. I was in way too deep with August to get involved with anyone else. I couldn't help but think *What if I'd taken Ty's number when I first met him? We would've been so good together;* nothing like August and I. Loving August was like being addicted to toxic waste. I knew it was dangerous and could kill me, but I drank it anyway.

My parents picked me up from my apartment before we headed to Jersey. My mother wanted to see my place. I made sure August wasn't there and did a good job of hiding all evidence of him. My mom gave her approval after checking every room, and then we drove to Aunt Caroline's.

Candice ran up to the car when we pulled up. I almost didn't recognize her. She'd gained a lot of her weight back, but it looked good on her. When she wrapped her arms around me, I knew all that happened before had been forgiven.

Bruce pulled up right after us. It seemed like everyone at the cookout got quiet. The girls broke the silence when they jumped out of the car and started running to Candice and screaming *Mommy.* They collided into Candice's arms so overwhelmed with joy that they all broke into tears. Once the girls let go of Candice long enough for her to stand up and acknowledge Bruce. He didn't say one word, he just wrapped his arms around her. She melted into him. It was a magical moment.

I looked around the cookout at all the happy faces and realized I was the only one there who was pretending. I'd been boasting to everyone about how well I was doing at work and bragging about my classes, but I hadn't mentioned August. We all pretended he didn't exist. Or maybe they were all just wishing that I'd finally wised up and left him alone.

I snuck inside the house. I knew this feeling in the pit of my stomach and soon I wouldn't be able to hold back the tears, I didn't want to ruin everyone else's day so I slid into the bathroom and let it out. As I cried, I had flashes of everything I'd been through in the last year. I thought about when I found out about Candice's drug addiction, all the fighting with Terren, having a miscarriage, getting arrested, and finally the latest— August choking me. My life was a total mess!

"Casey, baby, are you OK?" I heard Aunt Caroline's voice call through the door.

I wiped my hands across my face, trying to get rid of the evidence of tears.

"Yes, Auntie I'm fine. I'll be out in a minute," I said trying to mask the hurt in my voice.

I flushed the toilet as if I was using the bathroom, then turned on the faucet and splashed some water on my face. When I looked at myself in the mirror, I knew there would be no way I'd be able to lie my way out of this one.

When I opened the bathroom door, I was startled to see Aunt Caroline still waiting for me. She grabbed my hand, guided me into her room and closed the door. We sat next to each other on her bed. She held my hands in hers, looked into my eyes and said, "Baby, you have to stop seeing that married man."

My eyes widened. How did she know that I was still seeing August? She ignored the look of shock on my face. I didn't bother trying to pretend I didn't know what she was talking about. I was dying to talk to someone about this, and who better than one of the wisest women I knew?

Tears started falling out of my eyes again. Aunt Caroline grabbed my head and placed it on her shoulder. She rubbed my back and whispered in my ear, "It's going to be alright. I promise. You will get through this."

"Auntie, I didn't know he was married. His wife just came out of nowhere."

"She didn't come out of nowhere, baby, she was there before you. You came out of nowhere. That is her husband and the father of her children. She's not going anywhere," Aunt Caroline said without breaking her embrace.

"I know Auntie, but I love him."

"Oh baby. I know you love him."

"I've never loved anyone like this before."

She let loose her embrace and wiped the tears from my eyes.

"You only get one love like that. You'll never love anyone that way again."

Aunt Caroline's words cut me deep. The thought of me wasting my one true love on August made me sick to my stomach.

"Listen to me carefully. I know it feels like this man has a hold on you. I know you feel all alone, but you're not, you have God. You have to get down on your knees and pray to God to get you out of this relationship. It is not good for you or anyone else in it. The love you have for that man is too strong for you to fight on your own. Lord knows I am praying for you, but you have to pray for yourself if you really want to be delivered from this. You hear me? That is the only way."

Then Aunt Caroline took my hands and we got down on our knees and she prayed for me. She prayed for my deliverance. She prayed for my life.

After the cookout I couldn't get Aunt Caroline's prayer out of my head. Everyday I was with August, I felt more and more convicted, but I couldn't get rid of him that easy because August was currently on his best behavior. He was coming home early, taking me on surprise dates, cooking me dinner, and I hadn't heard one peep out of Terren. He'd become all the man I wanted him to be.

My best attempt to argue with him was when I decided to finally bring up what happened the night he choked me. But to my surprise, he apologized profusely, claiming that he was so hurt to have seen me with another man that he lost it. Then the next day he showed up at home with my promise ring and two diamond bracelets, promising he'd never put his hands on me again.

Even with all of his romantics, I still couldn't shake the seed that Aunt Caroline planted in me. I knew she was right. I knew that this new Prince Charming side of August wouldn't last for long—it never did. This was the game that we played with each other, we'd been through it time and time again and this was just round twelve.

I knew I had to take Aunt Caroline's advice and go to church. Umaja invited me to his church a couple of times, but I kept coming up with excuses to not go. If there was ever a time to accept his offer, this was it. When I called him and told him I would be going to church with him on Sunday, in true Umaja fashion, he got excited and set up a detailed schedule of where and when we would meet before service and where we would go to lunch after. I didn't want to be rude and make August feel like I was leaving him out, so I invited him to come along. I figured he would just say no anyway. To my surprise he agreed. He said he'd been thinking about going to church for a while and he would love to go with me. When he agreed to go to church it was the first time in a long time I thought maybe, just maybe we had a real chance. Maybe we would be the one out of a million couples that overcame all adversity and ended up together … maybe.

Sunday morning I woke up early. I was so excited that August and I were going to church together and that he'd finally meet Umaja that I decided to make breakfast. If this was going to be the first day of the rest of our lives, I wanted everything to be perfect. I brought August his breakfast in bed. His eyes lit up when he saw the mound of pancakes, bacon, and eggs.

"You spoil me," he said, leaning in and kissing me on the cheek.

"I just wanted us to share a good meal before church. I don't want you in there getting antsy because you're hungry," I joked.

August face turned to stone.

"Oh baby, I forgot to tell you—my mom and sister came in town last night and we're all meeting up at my aunt's house today, so I'm not going to be able to make it to church."

My heart sank. "What? Why are you just now telling me this?"

"Well I just found out last night that they were here, and I forgot all about church. What's the big deal? We can hang out with my family today and go to church next Sunday."

I was so disappointed. I'd been looking forward to today all week.

"August, can't we still go to church this morning and meet up with them after we get out?"

"They're only going to be here until tomorrow. I don't want to waste half the day at church when I can be spending that time with them. You should stop being selfish because I never treat you like that when you want to be with your family."

I couldn't believe he was calling me selfish for wanting

him to honor his word and go to church with me. I let my body
sink down into the bed. I wanted to put the covers over my
head and cry.

"Don't worry baby, I promise we'll go next week,"
August said. Then he put down the plate of food that he barely
touched and picked up a blunt that was lying in the ashtray
next to the bed. He lit the weed, took a couple of puffs and then
passed it to me.

I hesitated before taking it from him, but gave in
because I wasn't going to church anyway. I was upset that
August was disappointing me again. The least I could do was
take a few puffs to calm me down. I took a deep long inhale
of the weed and held it in my lungs as long as I could, then I
exhaled.

We passed the blunt back and forth until it was done.
I let myself nestle back into the bed, letting the idea of going
to church escape my mind. Just as I felt myself about to drift
off into a nap, my phone rang. I jumped up out of the bed and
scrambled around in search of my phone. I got to it just before
it went to voicemail.

When I answered, Umaja's voice came booming
through. "What a gorgeous Sunday morning it is."

"Oh, hey Umaja."

"Oh, hey to you. You sound like you're still in the
bed. You better be getting ready because I ain't gon' be late to
church for nobody honey, not even your cute self."

"I'm sorry Umaja, I was just about to call you and tell
you I'm not going to be able to make it today."

"Mmhmm, I bet it has something to do with that man."

I could here him sucking his teeth through the phone.
"No, it's just…"

"Listen honey, you don't have to apologize to me. It's
your salvation that you have to worry about. I have my own
sins to repent for. Now, I'm gon' get off this phone and get

myself to church. I will make sure to say a special prayer for you. Love you, bye," he said, hanging up before I could get another word in.

I sank back down in the bed and closed my eyes, but I couldn't get Umaja's voice out of my head. *It's your salvation that you have to worry about ... I bet it has something to do with that man ...*

I grabbed the pillow and put it over my head, trying to block his voice out, but I couldn't shake it. Then Aunt Caroline's sweet low voice whispered in my mind. *You need to get on your knees and pray to God to deliver you from that man ...*

Her words struck a nerve. I jumped up and ran to the shower.

When I got out of the shower, August looked confused.

"What are you doing?" he asked.

"I'm going to church!"

"So you not gonna go see my family with me?" he asked like a spoiled child.

"I can come over after, but I really had my heart set on going to church, so I'm going to go."

"You know what, don't even worry about it. You go to church and I will go be with my family. There ain't no need for you to show up later. Don't do me any favors."

"You're really mad that I'm going to church?"

"Hell yeah I'm mad. We already said we were going to see my family then you get a phone call from your little friend and all of a sudden you running around here all in a hurry to go to church."

"My little friend?" I repeated. "First of all, I don't know why you said it like Umaja is anything more than a friend to me. If you were to go with me, you would meet him and you would see that, but you're choosing to break your word to me and do something else, so that's on you."

"Yo just go to church. I don't feel like arguing wit' yo stupid ass today."

My mouth dropped. "Have you lost your mind …" As I was about to start cursing him out, something said *Stop.* "You know what, you're right! I'm not arguing with you today!"

I was so frustrated I snatched my clothes and got dressed in the living room. I left the house without saying a word to him.

By the time I got to the church, the pastor had already started preaching. I snuck in and found a seat in the back by the door. Once I settled in, I realized I was high. I felt the heaviness in my eyes, and my body was very relaxed. I started sniffing myself hoping that I didn't smell like weed. I scooted over as far as I could from the other people sitting in the aisle with me. I was so embarrassed. The lady in front of me turned around and looked at me. I could've sworn that she frowned her face up. I wondered if she knew I was high.

August was right. I was stupid. I don't know what made me think that going to church would be the answer to all of my problems when *I* was my biggest problem. Aunt Caroline would be so disappointed if she knew I was sitting up in church high. I wanted to sneak out, but I was too afraid to draw any more attention to myself. So I just sat there hoping no one would catch a whiff of marijuana seething from my pores.

In the middle of my mental panic, something the pastor said caught my attention. He said, "Whatever situation you're going through right now, it's only temporary." My eyes shot open as if he'd walked down from the pulpit and pointed me out. Those words resonated deep into my heart. Then he told the church to repeat after him.

"Say, it's temporary!" he instructed.

Everyone repeated after him, but I couldn't open my mouth. He instructed everyone to say it again and again and again until finally I couldn't hold back. I opened my mouth and let the words roll off my tongue. "It's temporary!" I whispered. "It's only temporary." Then I felt the tears slowly roll down my cheeks, washing away my pain and confirming this was all temporary, I would get through this just as Aunt Caroline assured me. It was temporary.

TERREN

Terren's heart started pounding when she saw August walk through the door at his aunt's house. She hadn't seen him since the day after she got his car towed. She wasn't going to come to his aunt's house today for fear of him showing up with Casey. He'd already brought her to Maine to meet everyone, it wasn't like he was afraid to parade his mistress around. The only reason Terren showed up was because his mother called her and said she wanted to see her grandchildren. She felt a little bit of superiority in the fact that she did have his kids. She figured why should she be the one who was left out, so she decided to go and face whatever challenges the day might bring.

She exhaled when August walked through the door alone. Terren watched her children's faces light up as they ran up to their father, jumping on him and squeezing their little arms around his neck. They were always so happy to see him. It didn't matter how long his absence or how much they went through, they always loved him unconditionally, the way she did.

"Come here boy and give your mother a hug," August's mother said to him, stretching out her arms in his direction.

He gave his mother a big hug, picking her up off the ground and swinging her around.

"Stop playing boy, now put me down." She laughed.

August lowered his mother back down to the ground and kissed her on the cheek. "Lookin' good, old lady." He smiled at her.

"You the one lookin' old," she joked. "What happened to the back of your head?" she asked, noticing the still-healing cut where the stitches were just removed.

"Oh nothing, I took a fall in the restaurant the other day after someone spilled grease on the floor." He laughed.

"Oh Lord. You have to be more careful son," she said, rubbing her hand over his cut.

"I'm OK ma. I'm just happy it was me and not someone else."

"Yes, I know. But you're my baby and I don't want anything happening to you."

"I know mom," he said, leaving her embrace and walking towards Terren. He greeted her by kissing her on her forehead.

"Hi baby," he said to her like everything was great between them.

Terren frowned.

"Don't be like that, baby, it's family time," August reminded her.

Terren knew he was right. His family was in from out of town, their kids were there. She didn't want to ruin that. She made a decision to go with the flow and pretend that they were one big happy family.

She smiled and laughed and flirted with him. When the food was ready, she got up like a good wife and fixed his plate, brought him something to drink when he was thirsty, and even made him seconds when he asked for them. She did all this knowing that it would all be over in a couple of hours. But she couldn't resist the feeling of happiness that she felt as she watched him hold baby Casey in his arms. She wanted that feeling to last forever. But every time his phone rang, her heart was filled with dread that, that was the call that was going to take him away. Her heart nearly jumped out of her chest when he went outside to take a phone call. She tried as hard as she could to keep herself planted in her seat, but she couldn't resist the urge to follow him.

Terren opened the back door and crept up behind August so not to startle him. She wanted to catch some of his conversation, but she was too late. He was hanging up right as she got close enough to eavesdrop. He turned around and looked at her like he didn't have anything to hide.

"What's up baby?" August said flashing his big smile.

"Who were you on the phone with?"

"Just someone from the restaurant."

"So you're about to leave?"

"Nah baby, I'm not going nowhere. Unless you start cussing me out and telling me to get away from you again." He laughed.

"Does it seem like I want you to get away from me?" she asked.

"Nope. Thankfully, 'cause I don't want to be anywhere else right now than here with you and our family."

Terren smiled. She waited so long to hear those words. It didn't even matter if he was telling the truth or not, it was her truth.

They went back into the house and kept up appearances for the rest of the night. When it was time to leave, August helped Terren pack the kids up in her car and kissed her on the cheek.

"You mind if I come home tonight?" he asked sweetly.

Terren moved in close to his ear and whispered, "It's your home, isn't it?"

"Damn right it is." He smiled.

As August started to move away from Terren to close her door, she grabbed him, pulled him close to her and kissed him. She kissed him the way they used to kiss when they were teenagers. She kissed him in a way that gave him permission to do as he wished with her. August returned her affections, letting her know he planned on fulfilling her wishes. And just like that he had her, again.

CASEY

I was so excited to tell August about what happened at church, I called him as soon as I got home, but he didn't answer. Once midnight struck and I still hadn't heard from him, I knew there was more to the story than him being upset with me for going to church. My gut told me that he was with Terren. I stayed up all night running to the window, calling him and crying. I was exhausted by the time the sun came up. The preacher's voice was in my head all night saying, *this is temporary*. Was August not showing up God's ways of telling me something? I replaced *this* with *August is temporary*.

As crappy as I felt, I still dragged myself to work. I sat at my desk staring at the computer. I could've stayed like that all day, but my boss broke my trace when he marched up to me.

"Casey, I need to see you in my office."

"Oh, OK," I said, jumping up and following him.

He shut the door behind me. "Please have a seat," he instructed.

I nervously sat down in the chair across from him.

"Unfortunately the company is doing some cutbacks, and we will be getting rid of your position effective immediately. We ask that you clean out your desk and pick up your unemployment package at HR before you leave."

My mouth dropped. "I'm fired?" I blurted out.

"No, not fired, laid off. But again you can collect unemployment, so be sure to pick up the paperwork at HR."

I sat silent.

"Well, if you don't have any questions. I thank you for your hard work and wish you the best of luck," he said walking to the door and opening it.

I was in shock! I couldn't believe I lost my job. I wondered if I was being punished for showing up to church high. I needed to get out of the building. I looked around my desk, trying to figure out what was mine to take and what belonged to the company. It didn't take me long. Everything I owned there fit easily into my purse.

When I got home, I rolled a fat blunt, ran a hot bath, poured what was left of the wine Ty brought over, turned on Erykah Badu and zoned out.

I lay in the bathtub until my skin started to wrinkle. After dragging myself out, I allowed my body to collapse face down into the mattress. Even though I'd smoked two blunts and drank a quarter bottle of wine, I didn't feel any better. I didn't have a buzz, and my high didn't feel the same. I felt more nauseous than anything.

My mind was racing in a million different directions. How was I going to pay my rent? I had no idea how unemployment worked. How much were they going to pay me? Was there even a guarantee that I'd even be granted unemployment? What was I going to do if I didn't get it?

I was at a loss, and to add insult to injury, I still hadn't heard from August. I'd planned on kicking him to the curb once and for all since he didn't show up last night, but now I thought I may have to keep him around so he could help me pay my bills. My back was against the wall. I just wanted to hit something, so I did. I picked up my pillow and threw it. When that didn't make me feel better, I threw another pillow, then I ripped the comforter off the bed and then the sheets, then I pushed the mattress onto the floor and the stereo off the dresser and threw the ashtray at the window and ripped the curtains down. I pushed, threw, and ripped everything I could get my hands on until I wore myself out. When all that still wasn't enough, I finally broke down crying. I fell on the floor, in the middle of my disaster, kicking and screaming until I got my tantrum out of my system.

Around seven o'clock that evening, I was awoken by a knock at the door. I grabbed a sheet that was laying on the floor and wrapped it around my naked body and went to answer the door. August stood there looking like the dirt bag that he was wearing yesterday's clothes. I let the door swing open and turned and walked away from him.

"Why are you wrapped in a sheet?" he asked.

I ignored his question, walked back into my room, slammed the door shut and locked it. I didn't want to be bothered with August or his lies. I didn't even care if he stayed at my house or not. All I knew was he wasn't going to be laying a hand on me. I lay back on the floor, curled up in my sheet, and went back to sleep.

I was granted unemployment and it was a Godsend. Although it wasn't as much as I was making while working, at least it covered my rent. I was happier than I'd been in a long time. I'd embraced my inner insomniac and was staying up to watch the sunrise every morning. I was sleeping during the day, exercising, cooking, writing, reading, exploring the city, doing all the things I'd been depriving myself of while I was working.

Umaja loved my newfound freedom. We had these writing lunch dates a couple times a week, and we'd even joined this writer's workshop that helped me start developing a new script. We were going to plays and museums, we even did yoga in the park when I could get him out of bed early enough.

The best thing I'd done was join his church. I'd been back every Sunday since the day I showed up high. I started off just going on Sundays, then I started going to bible study, and that's when I knew I wanted to join. I was starting to understand the bible much more. What I liked most about bible study was that I could ask questions and the pastor would break it down to me in a way that made sense. Going to bible study was making me see my life more clearly.

Although I was still letting August stay in my house, things between us were different. We were barely speaking. I would come in and out without telling him where I was going or when I was coming back. I would make dinner and only fix enough for myself. Sometimes when he would try to talk to me, I would pretend I was so into my writing that I didn't hear him. That really annoyed him when I did that. Even though I continued to mistreat him, he kept coming back.

The one thing that I hadn't totally purged was sex. August knew how to get me open. His ability to make my knees shake with just one touch was a talent of his that I couldn't resist. I could walk around all day without saying a word to him, then at the end of the night he'd crawl into bed and all that anger turned into anticipation. The angrier I was, the more orgasms he delivered.

Saturday afternoon, Umaja and I were headed to our favorite coffee shop. We were half a block away when I realized I didn't have my phone. I told Umaja to go ahead and get a table for us and I'd be right behind him. I wasn't ten feet away from my building when I ran right into Terren.

We both froze when we saw each other. I decided to keep walking to avoid confrontation.

"Casey," Terren called out behind me.

I stopped, took a deep breath, and turned around to face her. "Listen, I really don't want any problems, Terren."

"I don't want any problems either. I just want my husband back."

"Oh my God!" I said throwing my arms in the air in surrender. "How many times are we going to do this song and dance?" I shouted.

"I'm tired Casey! My kids are tired! Do you have any idea what this has done to our family?"

"Terren, why do you think I have so much power over August? I'm not holding him hostage."

"Casey, you are the woman in the relationship, you have all the power. He can only do what you allow him to do."

"Terren, I don't have the power. I am powerless when it comes to August. Please tell me how to stay away from him, please."

"Just tell him to go home," she said casually.

"If it were that simple, girl, then he would've been back a long time ago." I laughed.

"No, you have to say it and mean it."

"Say it and mean it. I got it," I said sarcastically. "Let me go and do that right now."

"Casey, this is not a joke. My children need their father to come home, I'm begging you, because I'm desperate now. I've run out of ideas on how to keep him, and frankly, I'm beginning to think I'm going crazy. I'm losing it Casey, please help me, please."

I shook my head. "Fine, Terren. I don't know how, but I'll take care of it."

"Casey, I understand the hold he has on you. He has it on me too, but we have to help each other. If we both stand together on the same team, we can get him to do the right thing. Can we be a team now instead of fighting each other?"

I was completely caught off guard and all out of clever remarks so I agreed, "Sure Terren, we can be a team."

She looked defeated. "Thank you," she said then continued towards her car. When she got in, I noticed her kids were inside. As she drove off, her son turned around and looked out the window at me. The sadness on his face destroyed me. I knew that Terren's plea was out of pure desperation. She didn't want to beg me to leave her husband alone, she didn't even want to ask me to help her, but she had to, for her children.

The next few nights were hell. I couldn't get Terren out of my mind. Every time I closed my eyes, I could see that little boy's face pressed against the window of the car staring at me with his big tear-filled eyes. I lay in bed thinking about them. I wondered how the baby was doing. I thought about how hard it must be taking care of a new baby without the father around. I felt horrible. It's not like I ever felt good about being involved with a married man, but I was different now that I'd been studying the bible.

My anticipation for August's touch had turned to dread. When I looked at him, I didn't see the man I loved anymore, I saw a deadbeat. I wondered why he chose to be there with me and not with his family. All Terren wanted was to keep her family together. She was pretty and definitely loved him. Every time I saw her kids, they looked well taken care of, so she must've been a good mother. I started to question August's character. I didn't understand why he was putting her and his beautiful children through this. I was losing respect for him.

Coincidently, we were talking about marriage in bible study. We were studying Ephesians, and in Ephesians 5, it talks about how God honors marriage and how married people should behave. Through our studies I began to see Terren in a different light. I no longer saw her as crazy for fighting for her husband but instead I saw her as loyal and God fearing. Ephesians 5:22-29 clearly states, "Wives, submit yourselves unto your own husbands, as unto the Lord. For the husband is the head of the wife, even as Christ is the head of the church: and he is the savior of the body. Therefore as the church is subject unto Christ, so let the wives be to their own husbands in every thing." Terren was doing as she was supposed to do as a wife. However, when I kept reading, August's character also became clear. The scripture goes on to say, "Husbands, love your wives, even as Christ also loved the church, and gave himself for it; That he might sanctify and cleanse it with the washing of water by the word, that he might present it to himself a glorious church, not having spot, or wrinkle, or any such thing; but that it should be holy and without blemish. So ought men to love their wives as their own bodies. He that loveth his wife loveth himself. For no man ever yet hated his own flesh; but nourisheth and cherisheth it, even as the Lord the church:"

I realized, August must hate himself, why else would he be treating his wife the way he does? And furthermore, if his hatred were for himself, why would I ever want him to leave her and marry me? The change wouldn't come from me being his new wife, the change has to come from within him. There was absolutely no good that I could offer August, except prayer. I made up my mind. August had to go! I had to be totally transparent and let him know that I'd changed. God had opened my eyes, and I couldn't erase what I'd seen.

When August walked through the door from work, all my confidence went right out the window. His mere presence made me weak. I didn't understand how a man could have so much power over me. He went straight into the bathroom and got in the shower. I started pacing around the room. I knew I wasn't going to be able to put him out tonight, but I had to do something. I didn't want to have sex with him. I started panicking. All I could think to do was pray. So I dropped down to my knees and started praying. I begged God, *Please don't let him touch me tonight, Please God give me the strength to say no to his touch. God please don't let him touch me, please don't let him touch me, please don't let him touch me.*

I prayed that prayer until I heard the shower turn off, then I jumped in the bed and pretended to be asleep.

"Casey," August called me.

I squeezed my eyes together trying not to make a peep. "Casey," he called again.

I lay as still as possible. I felt August sit on the edge of the bed. I heard him fumbling around with something, then I smelled the smoke from the blunt. He stayed up and smoked for a while, then he laid down and passed out. I was safe, at least for the night. My prayer worked. Now, I just had to pray him out of my life completely.

After about a week I'd gotten pretty good at avoiding August's advances. I would pray before he came home and then make myself busy. I'd write until he fell asleep or lay in bed with my headphones on and zone out. I made sure I listened to men-bashing songs and I would sing the hooks out loud so he knew I wasn't in the mood. I would also lie close to the edge of the bed to make sure my body language was clear that I didn't want him touching me.

I could tell he was getting frustrated. He kept trying to talk to me, but I kept my conversation to a minimum. Being silent made me feel powerful. Day five I was forced to break my vow of silence. My period came on, and I'd run out of pads. To make matters worse I didn't have any money until my unemployment came in, so I had to call August and ask him to pick me up some pads on his way home.

It took everything out of me to make that phone call. I took a deep breath, counted to ten, picked up the phone and called him. When he answered, the sound of his voice made me nauseous.

"August I need you to pick me up some pads on your way home."

"Pads?"

"Yes, pads. I wear Always with wings."

"Yeah, aight."

"Thanks," I said and hung up the phone.

I ran in the bathroom and dug up under the sink in hopes of finding at least a panty liner. When I didn't find anything, I started searching through all my purses and I was in luck: I found two pads and four tampons.

I started watching a movie on Lifetime. By the time it was over, I noticed it was an hour after the time August usually got home. I wasn't going to call him again. I hoped he just had to work late, but for some reason I had a bad feeling about his tardiness. I told myself if he chose tonight to pull one of his all-nighters, that would be the perfect opportunity to get rid of him for good. I was so ready for him to mess up.

Twenty minutes later he was at my door. When I opened it August walked past me like he was upset. As much as I'm sure he wanted me to care about whatever he was upset about, I didn't. All I wanted was my pads.

I followed him into the bedroom. I got straight to the point.

"Can I have my pads please?"

He looked at me out of the corner of his eye. "I didn't get them."

I thought I heard him wrong. "You said you didn't get them?" I repeated.

"Yeah man I ain't get them," he snapped at me.

I bit down on my lip in fury, "Why didn't you get them, August?"

"Because I wasn't goin' into no store to buy pads! I don't even do that for my wife!"

I'd been wondering all this time what it would take for him to push me to my breaking point, and just like that I found out what it was. Pads!

"Get out of my house," I whispered.

"What?" He looked up at me like he heard me wrong.

"I said, get out of my house!"

"I'M NOT GOIN NOWHERE!"

My eyes darted around the room, searching for anything that belonged to him. I saw some of his jeans lying across the laundry bin. I ran over to the bin, picked up the jeans and threw them at him. "GET OUT OF MY HOUSE! I WANT YOU OUT!"

August jumped in my face. "You got a lot of mouth. I couldn't get you to open your mouth for a whole week. Now you're ready to let out your feelings? Let it all out, Casey, let's here it."

"You think this is a game, August? I'm not playing with you! I want you out!" I picked up more of his clothes and started throwing them out of my room and into the hallway.

"You act like this is a palace or something. I don't have to be here. You don't have to put me out, I'll leave."

"GOOD! TAKE ALL YOUR STUFF WITH YOU THIS TIME BECAUSE YOU DON'T NEED ANY EXCUSES TO COME BACK."

I started throwing everything I could get my hands on at him. I threw his lighter at him, and it hit him on the side of his face.

"Keep playin' wit' me little girl! Hit me with something else!" he spat.

"OH I'M A LITTLE GIRL NOW. THEN WHY ARE YOU ALWAYS WORRIED ABOUT WHAT I'M DOIN? HOW ABOUT YOU WORRY ABOUT YOU'RE LITTLE GIRLS…OH, NO, YOU LEAVE THAT BURDEN TO YOUR WIFE! YOU DON'T EVEN TAKE CARE OF YOUR CHILDREN! YOU'RE A SORRY EXCUSE…"

Before I could get the rest of the sentence out of my mouth August charged me, grabbed me by my neck, and slammed my face into the wall. I felt my head bounce back, but before I could react to the first hit, he slammed me into the wall again, this time letting me go so once I bounced off of the wall, my whole body gave out and collapsed onto the floor. I was stunned. August's voice broke my daze.

"WHERE ALL THAT MOUTH AT NOW?" August yelled.

I jumped up so fast, I got dizzy. I gathered enough strength to punch him in his face one good time before he grabbed me up again and slammed me down onto the floor like a rag doll. I felt something in my body snap when I hit the floor. I was kicking and screaming and swinging trying to get August off of me, but he was too heavy for me to put up a real fight. "GET OFF OF ME YOU…"

WAP, WAP… August's hand went across my face slapping me back and forth.

"SHUT THE HELL UP!" he said pressing his big hands into my throat. Then he slapped me again. *WAP, WAP*… this time I saw stars.

August took his hands off my neck and then put his knee into my throat. The weight of his body began to suffocate me. I kept wiggling, trying to break free from him, but the more I moved around, the deeper his knee sunk into my neck. I blacked out, then came to. My eyes were rolling into the back of my head. I heard him rattling something, but I couldn't make out what it was.

I saw his belt hit the floor next to my head. I looked up at him long enough to see he was unbuckling his pants. The pressure on my neck released when he stood up to take down his pants. That was my chance to get away. I scrambled myself from under him and tried to pull myself up, but August grabbed my leg and yanked me back down. He started ripping my clothes off. He couldn't get my T-shirt over my head, so he wrapped it around my neck and held on to one end like a noose. Once he was done with that, he ripped off my underwear so hard that the fabric sliced the skin on my inner thigh.

He yanked my head back with the shirt noose so that

my chin was pointing straight up in the air. Then he whispered in my ear, "This is what you wanted all along!"

I tried to scream, hoping someone would hear me, but every time I did he'd tighten the shirt around my neck. I tried to fight him, but my hits weren't phasing him at all. I stretched my arms out, trying to find anything on the floor that I could hit him with. I felt a shoe. I grabbed the shoe and smacked him in the head with it. He shook the hit off like a man possessed. Then he forced himself into me, slamming in and out. The friction was burning. I was crying and hitting him over and over with the shoe, but he was on a mission, and he was not going to stop until he finished.

The sounds of my screams seemed like they were tuning him on, so finally I just lay there like a corpse, and when I stopped responding, he let go of the shirt noose, wrapped his hands around my neck again and started chocking me. It wasn't until I started gasping for air that he looked like he was enjoying it again. Finally, I felt him get rock hard inside me. He rammed himself into me over and over until he came … inside me.

When he was done, he let his dead weight fall down on top of my limp body. I gasped out for air. All the muscles in my body tightened up. My pelvic walls spit him out, I pushed him off of me, and curled up into a ball. He rolled over on his back, breathing like a gorilla. Then he stood up, put on his pants, and walked out the door leaving me lying in blood, his sweat, and cum.

As soon as he left, I crawled into the bathroom. I used the toilet to pull myself up. When I was able to position myself on the toilet, peeing was a challenge. The pee hit all the open cuts in and around my vagina as well as ones on my inner thigh, sending burning sensations through me.

After my battle with the toilet I turned on the shower

and crawled into the bathtub. I sat on the bathtub floor, letting the water wash over me. The water stung almost as bad as using the bathroom did. I watched the water running off my body and down the drain. It was streaming with shades of pink and red. I grabbed my washcloth and soap and started scrubbing my body. The only water not contaminated with blood was the water falling from my eyes.

After about an hour in the shower, I limped out of the tub and wrapped myself in a towel. On my way out the bathroom, I caught a glimpse of my face in the mirror and my heart stopped. I didn't even recognize myself. The left side of my face resembled an inflated balloon, my nose was two times its normal size, my lips were busted, and my right eye was almost completely swollen shut.

I needed something to stop the pain. I opened up my medicine cabinet and all I had was Aleve and Aspirin. I grabbed both of them. I opened the bottles and took two of each, washing them down with water from the bathroom sink. When I looked at myself again, I decided I needed to stop the swelling, so I took two more aspirin. I put the pills back in the cabinet and started to walk into my room. Realizing how much pain I was in just trying to walk, I opened the cabinet back up and grabbed the Aleve and took three more. As I was about to replace the cap on the Aleve, I stared at the bottle, then poured the remainder of the pills into my hand. I stared at the pills contemplating what would happen if I just took all of them. I could just end all the pain right now.

My life had gone into this downward spiral, and it seemed no matter how hard I fought to get out, I couldn't. I'd allowed myself to fall head-over-heels in love with a married man who turned out to be the devil. I'd sacrificed my career plans, isolated myself from my family, compromised my salvation, and become someone I not only didn't recognize, but someone I didn't even respect. And when that wasn't enough, he took my power. He beat me and raped me. I had nothing left. I didn't know how I could recover from this. I stared at the pills and thought; I could just end it all right now.

I lifted the pills to my mouth and as soon as my jaw dropped, I heard a small voice in my head that said, *it's only temporary*…

I balled the pills up in my hand and shot them at the wall.

I went into my room and crawled into bed. I curled up in fetal position and started rocking myself back and forth. There was a bible sitting on my night stand that Aunt Caroline had given me. I reached over and grabbed it, pulling it close to my chest I started whispering, *Jesus, Jesus, Jesus* over and over again.

I lay hanging onto the bible my Aunt Caroline gave me and suddenly I had a flashback to when I was twelve years old, sitting in the church calling on Jesus. I remembered the spirit of the Holy Ghost falling down on me, and how he comforted me. I needed that comfort right now. I started whispering His name, *Jesus, Jesus, Jesus, Jesus,* until I fell into a deep sleep.

While asleep, I had a dream. In the dream I was lying in the middle of the street, with my Aunt's bible in my hand, covered in blood. I tried to get up but I was too weak. All of a sudden I felt my spirit leave my body. It floated up into the sky until I was looking down at myself. I watched my breathing get slower and slower. Then I heard myself let out a deep gasp, and my aunt's bible fell out of my hands into the street.

I wanted to rush over to my body lying there lifeless and give myself CPR, but I couldn't come down. I started screaming and crying, begging for someone to come and help me. When no one came, out of desperation I started hollering, *Lord help me! Please help me oh God, save my life. Please don't let me die here in the middle of the street. Father forgive me for my wrongdoings. Lord I need your help right now, please God help me. I'm dying, God I'm dying, please don't let me die God.*

Then I started shouting the name of Jesus. *In the name of Jesus, I call on you, I call on your blood, the blood of Jesus.* As I was shouting I saw a white light beam out of the sky. It shined directly on my body. Out of the light, an angel descended down with wings so big, they reached from one side of the street to the other. The angel lay down next to me and wrapped me in his wings. Then he got up and started trying to revive me. He was pumping on my chest, but I wasn't responding. When he couldn't wake me up, the angel started praying. The angel started calling on Jesus, shouting to the Lord to save my life.

When the angel was finished praying, he grabbed my body and pushed me up onto my knees. Then he let go of my limp body and I watched as my body fall forward, a loud thunder sounded from the light, followed by a gust of wind that pushed me back up on my knees. My body gasped out for air. I was coughing and choking, trying to catch my breath. I started screaming *Jesus, Jesus, Jesus.*

I shot up in the bed out of my sleep still shouting *Jesus, Jesus, Jesus, Jesus.* I rolled off the bed and onto the floor, got on my knees and kept calling on Jesus. I remembered my dream as clear as day. It didn't feel like a dream, it felt like I was dead and God opened up the gates of Heaven and sent the Holy Ghost to come and save my life.

Chapter Fifteen

August is the Fall

AUGUST

August drove to Liberty Park in Jersey City. He parked his car where he had a clear view of the Statue of Liberty. He sat back and allowed his mind to drift off. He thought back to his childhood and how this park played a significant role in he and his father's relationship. It was their getaway from the women in the house. Every Saturday, his father would take him along to run errands. Typically they went and had breakfast, then they'd go to the bank, sometimes have the car serviced, and end up either shooting a few rounds of twenty one or at Liberty Park talking about life.

Those were his favorite moments. They'd sit and talk about sports, women, cars, and August's favorite—his dad's stories about when he was growing up. His father was always honest with him and didn't romanticize how important the man's role was in this world. He would always say, "The man is the foundation of the family, and it's his job to make sure that his family always has somewhere safe to live and food on the table." He had a quote that August never let go of: "The man's check is a must and the wife's check is a plus."

His father maintained that role until the day he died. His mother only worked when she wanted to, and when she did, her money was used for her pleasure. It never went towards bills, because his father handled it all. Even in his death, August's father left his wife with enough money to maintain her lifestyle, and she'd never had to work if she didn't want to. So she built their dream home in Maine where they'd planned to retire and fulfilled her husband's wishes in their home on the lake.

August aspired to be just like his father. He always knew he'd be married with children. His father taught him having a family was a man's greatest accomplishment. When he met Terren, even though they were young, he knew she had all the qualities that he wanted in a wife. She was beautiful, smart, athletic, and sassy. She reminded him of the women in his family. Her father's no-dating-until-sixteen rule turned a high school crush into his first love. A year's worth of conversations made their friendship unbreakable. By the time they were able to date, nothing could come between them.

The first years of their marriage were pure bliss. They were young, ambitious, and in love. They seemed to have the world at their disposal. No matter what challenges life threw at them, they'd overcome. Everything changed when August's father died. He found himself in a really dark place. That's when he started making bad business decisions. He started gambling, he lost his club, and all of their savings. Terren was pregnant, and they couldn't afford their apartment anymore, so they had to move in with his mother-in-law. When he needed his father's voice of reason the most, he wasn't there.

Terren had just finished her master's and was hired at an accounting firm in the city. When she stepped into the role of the provider, her attitude changed towards him. She was very irritable and argumentative. She'd pointed out on more than one occasion that she was the one keeping their family together. She even blamed him for her miscarriages, saying if she didn't have to work so hard, it would've never happened.

The shift in their roles made him look at her differently, even worse, he hated the man he'd become—he hated himself.

Georgia's Pearl was his lifeboat. Aunt Georgia's investment in him got him back on track. The restaurant's success helped him rebuild his self-confidence. He was so excited to be the provider again that he told Terren she could quit her job and stay home with the kids. He thought that everything would go back to normal once they were back in their proper roles. But instead, Terren refused to quit her job. She continued to question his ability to keep the restaurants in profit mode. She questioned every decision he made about expanding. She cursed the restaurant and said it wasn't stable and things could change at any moment. She didn't even get along with Aunt Georgia. He started to hate being around her. He stayed because he loved his family, he couldn't imagine his children growing up in a home without their father, and deep down, he wished one day the Terren he fell in love with would resurface.

Casey came out of nowhere. He never planned to cheat on Terren, but Casey was hard to resist, she was a gift and a curse. She reminded him of what it felt like to be needed again. She was ambitious, full of life, kind, and she looked at him the way Terren did when they first met; more importantly she believed in him. She made him feel like a man again.

He tried his best to keep their relationship platonic. He made sure he didn't pursue her sexually at all in the beginning. It was nice to just have a woman to talk to who believed in him. He was able to be the man he always wanted to be without the suit of flaws that Terren kept him in. He was successful, powerful, and generous and caring, that was the way Casey looked at him—and he loved it. He loved her.

Now, he was stuck loving two women. There was Terren, a woman who knew him inside out and loved and hated him to the same degree. Plus she was the mother of his children. And there was Casey, who loved the man he'd become, the man he always wanted to be. But did she feel that way anymore?

He never thought he'd be the type of man that would put his hands on a woman; he never thought he'd be the type of man who'd be in love with two women—but he'd become that man. He didn't want to be this monster. He was sure his father was rolling over in his grave. His father would never have cheated on his mother. But he wasn't his father. He was a different man with different circumstances. Of course he could've done things differently, but he couldn't change it. All he could do was find a way to make it right. He loved Terren, but he loved Casey too, and if he had to choose, he wanted a fresh start with Casey. He'd already tried to reconcile the mess he'd made of he and Terren's marriage, but it always failed. His love with Casey was spotless—well, it was until recently. He loved Casey too much to lose her over one lapse in character. He needed her to look at him the way she did when they first met. She was his key to being the man he always wanted to be. The man his father raised.

He'd made up his mind. It was time to let Terren go. He'd always be in his children's lives, but he couldn't be married to Terren anymore. He loved the possibilities of a life with Casey. He and Terren had come to the end of their story together. He wanted to be with Casey. First, he had to bring Terren the divorce papers. Then, by any means necessary, he had to get Casey to forgive him. He was determined to get her back.

TERREN

August had called and said they needed to talk, and Terren knew he'd finally come to his senses. Casey must've held up her end of the bargain. She watched August as he sat on the couch watching a movie with the kids. Terren thought back to when she first fell in love with him. She believed that the August she fell in love with was still in there somewhere, and she wasn't ready to give up on him. She still had fight left in her. It wasn't much, but she was going to give it everything she had.

She started using reverse psychology on August. She'd been giving him the space he'd been begging for, all in hopes that Casey was doing her job. She stopped calling him and begging him to come home, she stopped showing up at his aunt's house, she let him wonder what was going on with her for a while. She figured August needed to see what losing her would be like. She thought that would make him wake up and be with his family.

After two weeks of Terren giving August the silent treatment, August finally called wanting to talk. Terren was ecstatic! Even though she was excited that he was there, she knew that she had to keep up appearances and act like she wasn't impressed with his efforts. So she kept herself busy. She cleaned up the kitchen, washed the clothes, stayed attentive to the baby, doing anything around the house that kept her out of his view. If her plan went right, he would ask to stay the night or pretend to fall asleep on the couch with the kids so that he wouldn't have to leave. She had it all figured out.

Around midnight, they were all passed out on the

couch as suspected. Terren's heart melted looking at them all sprawled out together. She took a mental picture, knowing that this was a memory she would treasure forever. She was going to wake the kids up to go get in their beds, but they all looked so peaceful she decided not to bother them. She tucked her baby into her crib and went to take a shower.

After her long hot, blissful shower, Terren wrapped herself in a big fluffy towel and went into her room. She was pleasantly surprised when she saw August sitting on her bed waiting for her. She kept her cool and continued to get herself ready for bed. She had to walk in front of August to get to her dresser. As she reached her hand out to grab the bottle of lotion, she felt August's hand touch her waist.

"Terren, can we talk?" August said softly.

Terren was smiling in her head, but she knew not to show August how happy she was.

"Sure, what's up?" she asked turning to face him.

"Sit down," he said grabbing her hand.

Terren took a seat next to August on the bed.

"What's going on?" Terren asked, trying her hardest to mask the joy she was feeling. She knew her plan had finally worked and he wanted to come home.

"I've been thinking a lot about everything we've been going through, and I've realized that I'm the one to blame for where we went wrong."

Terren's mouth dropped. She wasn't expecting to ever hear him admit to his wrongs.

"After losing my father, I lost a piece of myself that I was never able to get back. Then losing the club and you having to support us made me feel like I failed you."

"You didn't fail us," Terren said sincerely.

"Just listen to me, because I want you to understand. I always wanted to give you the best. You trusted me to take care of you; to be a good father to our children, to be loyal to you, and all I did was mess that up over and over again. No matter how hard I tried, I couldn't live up to your expectations." August put his head down in shame.

Terren wrapped her arm around August to console him.

"August baby, we all make mistakes, I'm not perfect either."

"I just want to be a good father to my kids."

"You are. Those kids love you," Terren reassured him.

August sat up, removing Terren's arm off his shoulder, and held her hand.

"I love my kids. They are the most important things in my life. I know that I haven't been the best father, but I'm going to make it all up to them. I'll never neglect them again. I promise you Terren, I won't."

"I know you won't, baby. I know."

"That's why I think we're going to have to work extra hard now to let them know that they're our number one priority."

"We will. We will be better for them," Terren agreed.

"I'm happy we're on the same page, because they're going to need us working together through this divorce. The last thing they need is to see us fighting anymore."

Terren's face twisted up in confusion. She wasn't sure she heard him correctly. "Did you just say divorce?"

"Yes. We can't keep living like this," August said bluntly.

"You want a divorce?" Terren asked again in disbelief.

"Don't you?" August asked.

"No, I don't want a divorce!" Terren cried out. "Why would I want a divorce?"

"Why wouldn't you want a divorce? All we do is argue and fight. We haven't been the same in years."

"No, we haven't been the same since you started sleeping with that child!" Terren protested.

"We were broken way before I met her."

Terren jumped off the bed and started pacing back and forth.

"I can't believe this … I can't believe this."

"What is there not to believe? If we're not fighting, we're not talking at all. We haven't spoken in weeks. You have me afraid to come see my kids because I don't want to fight with you."

August's voice was starting to screech in Terren's head.

"Are you out of your mind?" she yelled.

August stood up. "Here we go!"

"No! You want to pretend the reason you haven't come to see your kids is because you were afraid to argue with me. What about all year long when I was begging you to be home with your kids, but you were laid up over there with your mistress. What was your excuse then?"

"I just told you, I apologized, and I was going to do better."

"Oh, you're going to do better by splitting up our family?"

"Terren, we haven't been a family in a long time. I can't be the man you want me to be anymore."

"Why August? Why are you doing this?" she cried.

"I'm not doing anything, Terren. It's just over. You stopped needing me a long time ago."

"Oh, so your mistress needs you?"

"Don't worry about her. This is about us."

"Oh, about us! Now it's about us. Was it about us when you were with her?"

"Forget it! I don't even know why I tried to talk to you," August said, heading towards the door.

Terren jumped in front of him. "Where are you going?"

"I'm leaving. I didn't come here to argue with you."

"No, we have to talk about this. You can't tell me you

want to break up our family and then just leave."

"Move, Terren. We can talk about this when you calm down," August said, moving her to the side.

Terren grabbed August and pulled him close to her. She tried to hug him and kiss on him, but he pushed her away, shoving her onto the bed.

"Stop!" he shouted.

"What? You don't even want to touch me anymore?" Terren cried out.

"Get yourself together, Terren," August said as he walked out the door, leaving Terren sprawled out, half exposed on the bed.

Terren didn't have the strength to run behind him and fight back. All she could do was scream, *come back.*

"Come back," she called out to him until she heard the front door shut. She lay there devastated that her plan had backfired. She had given August everything she had, and he rejected her time and time again, and now she didn't have any fight left in her.

CASEY

It took two weeks for my face to start to resemble characteristics of a human and not a deflating hot air balloon. It was perfect timing, because Tate was coming to stay with me for the rest of the summer. I was nervous that she would bring me more grief like she did while I was staying with Candice, but I was excited because I'd fallen into a deep depression, and having someone familiar around that I loved might just do the trick.

Just as I'd hoped, having Tate around was helping me heal. It was just like old times, I had my little sister back. Even though she really liked August because he was always nice to her, she believed that I deserved better, someone *not married.*

August hadn't gotten the picture that it was over. He was still calling me everyday, and even though he'd stopped popping up at my house, I had a feeling he was lurking around. I don't know why he thought I'd ever be able to be with him again after what happened. Although as I was getting more involved in church, and reading my bible more, I understood it was very important for me to forgive him, but for *me,* not for him. Going to church was teaching me a lot about forgiveness and how forgiving someone was more about healing and being able to move on. Then of course the whole *God forgives so you should too,* so I really needed to forgive him for my own salvation. It was the only way I could be closer to God. The only thing that August didn't understand was it didn't matter if I forgave him or not, I would never forget what he did. That was why I could never go back to him, or to the person I was with him. That person died that night, and it was only because of God's mercy and His grace that I was given a second chance. I'd never jeopardize my life again for any man.

Sunday night I was waiting for Tate to get back home. After church, she asked me if she could go hang out with some of her old friends. As much as I wanted to say no, I wanted Tate to know that I trusted her, so I let her go as long as she promised to be back by ten.

Nine forty-five p.m., I was watching the clock. I really didn't want Tate to come back after curfew, because I didn't want to have to play the disciplinary role with her. I was enjoying just being her sister again, so I sent a little prayer up to God to have her come back on time.

Five minutes later I was getting anxious. I walked over to the window to see if I saw her walking up the street, but I didn't see her. Then my phone rang. I ran to go answer it.

"Casey." Tate's voice rang through.

"Yes, where are you? Is everything OK?" I asked in a panic.

"Yes, I was on my way home and August saw me walking, so he offered me a ride, and we stopped to get ice cream. He wanted to know if you wanted anything."

I felt my blood pressure rise.

"What do you mean, you're with August?" I asked through clenched teeth.

"I told you he saw me walking home," she answered nonchalantly.

I took a deep breath before responding because I could feel myself about to explode. "I don't want anything! Just get back here right now!"

"Um, OK. We are only around the corner. I will be right there."

"Hurry up!" I spit out before hanging up the phone.

I threw on my shoes and ran downstairs to wait for Tate

outside. I was so angry, I didn't know what to do with myself. I didn't want August anywhere near me. Just thinking of him alone with Tate was driving me nuts.

A few minutes later, his car came around the corner. I could hear them laughing all the way down the street. The sound of August's voice was making me more furious. When they stopped in front of my building, I ran over to the car, yanked the door open, and dragged Tate out.

"Oww… Oh my God, Casey what's wrong?" she screeched.

"Get in the house!" I said, pushing Tate onto the sidewalk.

She scrambled to stay on her feet, and then ran into the building.

August jumped out of the car and ran over to me. "Casey, can I talk to you?" he said grabbing my arm.

I yanked my arm out of his grasp. "DON'T TOUCH ME!" I screamed.

August backed away from me. "I just want to talk to you," he pled.

"I don't have anything to talk to you about! What don't you understand? There is nothing you can say to me ever again. Get that through your head. I HATE YOU!"

August's mouth dropped.

I stood up straight, and looked him in his eyes. "Stay away from me and my family, you *rapist*!" I screamed. Then I ran back into the building.

When I got upstairs, Tate was standing at the door looking at me in horror. She overheard me call August a rapist, and she demanded to know what happened. So I told her every gory detail. It was painful to open up about it, but it was also therapeutic. I did need to tell someone, because holding it in was killing me. Tate was devastated when I finished telling her what happened. She wrapped her arms around me, squeezed me tight, and we cried together. She didn't know it, but she helped me lift a huge burden off of my heart. By the time I fell asleep that night, I felt a thousands pounds lighter.

The end of the summer was approaching fast, and everyday that passed, I was feeling more depressed. I didn't want Tate to leave. She'd become the person that I could lean on. I didn't know what I was going to do without her.

To make matters worse, she and Candice were moving all the way to Atlanta. Bruce got offered a position to open a new office for his law firm in Atlanta and suggested that Candice move with him so that she could be close to the girls and help them through the transition. Candice was thrilled she'd been doing great and jumped at the opportunity, not only because she wanted to stay close the girls, but she also felt that it would provide her with the fresh start she had been praying for.

Tate ran into the room jumping up and down holding a CD in her hand.

"Oh my God, Casey, I got a song for you," she said, running over to the stereo and pushing the CD into the tray.

As soon as she hit play, bass started blaring out of the stereo with Mariah Carey and Jermaine Dupri's voice over the music.

My face lit up when I heard the lyrics, *I gotta shake it off.* We both started jumping up and down and dancing around the room like we'd just found the winning lottery ticket.

"Girl, this is your theme song!" Tate yelled over the music.

"YESSS IT IS!" I screamed while twirling her around.

We must've listened to that song twenty times before we fell out on the bed in hysterical laughter. I looked over at Tate and thought about how happy she'd made me, and I got sad thinking about her leaving again.

"I'm gonna miss you when you move to Atlanta," I said, breaking her laughter.

She looked over at me with her big eyes and smiled. "Oh, don't go getting all emotional on me now." She laughed.

I over-exaggerated a frown and poked my lips out.

"Anyway, I decided I'm not going to Atlanta with my mother. I want to move back to Connecticut. I told Grandpa, and he convinced my mother that she doesn't need to take on too much since she just got out of rehab, and she agreed to let me move back with them."

"What? When were you going to tell me?" I screeched.

"I was, I just forgot," she said nonchalantly.

"You forgot?"

"I mean I literally just found out this morning that everything was set."

I thought about Tate being back home with my parents, and about how good that would be for her. We were all so happy together when we were there. Then it hit me, I wanted to go back too. I needed my family right now.

"I'm going home too," I blurted out.

"What? What do you mean you're going home?" Tate asked.

"I'm moving back to Connecticut with you."

"Stop playing," Tate said, getting excited.

"I'm serious! I'm not in school right now, I got laid off from my job, and my unemployment will be up in a couple of months. I don't have a reason to be here."

"We're going to be a family again." Tate smiled.

"Yes, we are!"

I'd been through so much in the last year that I hadn't properly healed from. I knew moving back home wouldn't be the answer to all of my problems, but it would be a solid foundation to begin the healing process. I was so excited. This was the best decision I've made since I moved to Harlem.

Two weeks later, I was on my way out of Harlem and back home to Connecticut. My father would be here with the moving truck in the morning, and I still had a million things to do. Tate and I had already packed up most of the big stuff, but there were still some small things I had to pack, and I had to clean the entire apartment before I left. Tate had gone to stay the night at Aunt Caroline's. She wanted to spend some time with her before we headed back to Connecticut because the next time we'd see her again would be at Thanksgiving. So everything else that needed to be done I'd be doing alone.

I looked around my apartment, and although it was filled with boxes, it looked so empty. I thought about the first time I walked into that place and how excited I was that it was going to be mine. Leaving was a bittersweet moment.

I turned the stereo on and started to tackle some of the cleaning. I filled up a bucket with hot water, soap, and a bleach mixture. Just as I was about to stick my hand in the bucket, there was a knock at the door.

I froze. I knew it wasn't Tate, because she would've called if she left Aunt Caroline's early, so there was only two other people that would be knocking on my door—August or Terren.

I stood still. I don't know why I thought if I didn't move that they would think I wasn't home and leave. Never mind the fact that the music blasting was a dead giveaway that someone was home.

Knock, knock, knock…

I stood looking at the door, trying to will them away with my mind. Then I thought, *What if it isn't them?* Maybe I was just being paranoid.

Knock, knock, knock…

I took a deep breath, walked over to the door, looked through the peephole, and sure enough it was him—August was sitting on the floor with his back against my door.

My fear turned into anger.

"Casey," he called out.

I jumped away from the door like I'd been caught.

"Casey, I hear you," he said softly.

I couldn't believe he was sitting outside my door. I didn't understand why he wouldn't just leave me alone.

"What do you want?" I screeched.

"I just want to talk to you," he said so low that I could barely hear him over the music.

I felt a pain shoot through my chest. Suddenly, I felt bad for him. He seemed pathetic sitting on the floor in the hall. I turned down the music, walked back over to the door and sat down on the floor with my back against the door. If the door had been removed, we would've been sitting back to back.

"Talk," I answered.

There was a brief silence. Then I heard the words come out of his mouth that I didn't even know I'd been waiting to hear until I actually heard them.

"I'm sorry," August whispered.

Tears started to roll down my face.

"How can I make it right with you?" he asked.

Deep down in my heart, after everything that happened, I still had a soft spot for August, and I really wanted to give him an answer on what it was he could do to make it right, but I didn't have one. I couldn't think of one thing to say to him.

"Casey, please tell me how I can make it right. I'll do anything."

I was at a loss for words.

"I told Terren I want a divorce. I know I've said that before, but it's for real this time. I don't want to be with anyone but you. It's over!"

"I'm moving," I heard myself blurt out. I wasn't even planning on telling him that, but for some reason I felt like he needed to know.

"What? When? Where?" he asked sounding a little frantic.

"Back home to Connecticut."

"Are you serious?"

"Yes. Tomorrow."

"Tomorrow!" he shouted. "Why would you do that?"

"It's over August," I said defeated. "Go home to your wife."

We sat there back to back for a few more minutes. Then I heard him get up and walk away. I stood up and looked out the peephole to see if he was really gone, and he was. Just like that, it was over. August and I had ended our rollercoaster of a relationship sitting on the floor with a door between us. Suddenly I felt sick and full of regret.

TERREN

Terren rushed into Melissa's house, pushing her kids through the door and lugging a car seat with baby Casey strapped inside. Melissa strolled in after them, pushing her kids along. The kids ran through the house into the their rooms. Terren sat down in a chair in the kitchen and rested the car seat next to her. "Thank you again for picking us up and letting us stay here tonight, I just couldn't stay in that house." Terren gasped.

"It's not a problem. Like I said, Josiah is on nights this week anyway, so it will be good to have the company while he's at work." Melissa puckered her lips up into a kiss and blew it towards baby Casey.

"She'll love sleeping in the bed, because when she's at home she sleeps in her crib."

"Well, when she's at Auntie's house, she sleeps in the bed." Melissa smiled. "I'd rather you be here with me than over there sulking anyway."

"Yeah, that house just has too many reminders of him. I'm never going to get over him living in a shrine of our life. And it's not like I can just throw all our pictures away, because most of them have our kids in them."

"I know this has to be tough."

"It's the hardest thing I've ever been through. I still can't wrap my head around it. I'm … getting … a … divorce." She pouted.

Melissa shook her head. "Terren, I'm not going to pretend I know what you're going through, but I have to believe it is for the best. There is no reason anyone should ever have to go through everything that you went through with

August. He doesn't deserve you."

"That's what I keep telling myself, but right now its just words that I say to get through the day."

"Well, it's the truth. You're beautiful, smart, successful. Any man would be lucky to have you."

Terren took a deep breath then let out a loud exhale. "Well, I don't know about successful, now that I've been turned down for my promotion."

"Terren, you have been under a lot of stress, maybe it's best that you didn't take on more work right now."

"Mel, do you know I've never been turned down for a promotion? Work was always the one thing I had under control. Now I'm holding on to my job by a thread. I never understood how women would let their personal lives interfere with their work, but after all this, I totally understand."

"This is just going to make you stronger. There will be another promotion, and you will be in a better head space to take it on," Melissa encouraged.

"Yeah, maybe, as long as I can get through this divorce without having to fight Casey over my husband again."

"Girl, I told you he hasn't been over there. I haven't seen his car in weeks. Maybe something clicked for her after your last conversation."

"Who knows with that girl. I hope so, though, because I don't know what I would do if I saw her and August together again. I think I'd lose my mind."

"Well, let's not do that please, because then I'll be inheriting three more kids, and my apartment is just not big enough," Melissa joked.

A crash came from the back room. Terren and Melissa rushed into the kid's room to check on them. When they entered the room the boys were wrestling on the floor and Kiarra was dancing around on top of the bed.

"Are ya'll crazy?" Melissa screamed.

Everyone froze.

"Kiarra get off the bed right now!" Terren instructed to her daughter.

Josiah rushed into the room. "What's going on in here?" he asked in a panic.

"Daddy, daddy." Melissa's kids rushed over to him hugging him.

"What are you doing here?" Terren asked.

"He comes home on his breaks to check on us when he works at night." Melissa answered. "Jo, you have your gun on," she pointed out.

"Oh, wait kids," he said removing the holster. "I heard screaming when I walked in the house, so I ran straight back here to see what was going on," he explained.

"Here give it to me, I'll put it up," Terren volunteered. "You two can put the kids to bed and have a few minutes alone. I'll be in the living room," she explained while grabbing the holster with the gun in it from Josiah.

When Terren went back into the living room, she was headed to the cabinet where Josiah keeps his gun locked up but was distracted when she heard some noise outside, so she walked over to the window to see what it was. She almost fainted when she saw what was going on.

AUGUST

August stood in the middle of the street holding a bouquet of roses yelling up to Casey's window. "Casey! Casey!"

He was in love with Casey, and she was leaving, and there was a chance that he would never see her again. After the conversation he had with her earlier, he realized he never told her how much he loved her. He'd said sorry for what he did, but he hadn't told her he was in love with her.

August couldn't stand the thought of Casey leaving without telling her how he felt. He decided he was going to go over there one more time, look her in her eyes, and tell her how he felt. This time he wasn't going to show up empty-handed. He picked up some flowers first, so that if all else failed, he could write *I love you* on a card and leave the card and flowers at her door. He had to try everything he could, because he feared if he didn't, he would regret it for the rest of his life.

Casey opened the window and yelled down to him, "What is wrong with you? Get out of the street."

"Only if you promise to let me see you," he yelled back.

"Can't you see me right now? Now get out of the street," she demanded.

"No, I need to see you closer. I have to talk to you."

"August, please get out of the street," Casey begged.

"Only if you promise to talk to me."

Casey stared at August standing in the middle of the street holding up the flowers like he was an actor in some low budget 80s movie and couldn't help but laugh. She felt sorry for him because all he had to do was knock on the door again and she would've let him in. After he left earlier, she felt so bad that she didn't get the proper closure with him that she was actually going to call him in the morning so she could say goodbye.

Casey threw on her shoes and went downstairs to get the closure she needed so that she could go home with a clear conscious and a clean slate to begin her healing process.

As soon as August saw her step out the door, his face lit up. He walked up to her and handed her the roses.

"Thank you," he said sweetly.

"You're welcome," Casey said, not able to hold back a smile. She didn't understand how he still had the power to bring butterflies to her stomach.

"Are you really leaving?" he asked.

Casey shook her head. "Yes."

August looked deep into her eyes. "Don't leave me."

Casey stood quiet.

He took her hand in his. He had to tell her how much he loved her. He had to let her know if she stayed, this time would be different. It would be them against the world. Not only was he getting a divorce, he wanted to get married again—to her.

August stared into Casey's eyes. "I—"

"AUGUSSSTTTT!" A woman's voice came ringing from behind him.

He turned around and saw Terren running at them, pointing something towards them.

She was running so fast, it took August a moment to see she was holding a gun. As soon as August realized what it was, he moved as fast as he could to shield Casey.

POWWW

August couldn't get to Casey fast enough. The bullet seemed to move in slow motion as he watched it penetrate Casey's chest. He ran towards her to try and brace her as he watched her knees buckle and drop to the ground. He panicked. He slapped his hand over the hole in her chest, trying to stop the blood from flowing out, but as soon as he covered her, he felt the gun smash into the side of his head.

The impact dazed him. Before he could regain his composure, Terren was wrestling him. He instinctively grabbed her hand that she was holding the gun in, trying to get it away from her. They were tussling around, falling into cars, until he tripped falling backwards towards the ground, pulling Terren down with him.

POWWW

Screaming came from everywhere. August froze. Terren's body lay limp on top of him.

"Terren!" he shouted as he lifted her body off of him. Her eyes had rolled into the back of her head. She'd been shot. August laid her flat on her back in the street. He shook her, trying to get her to regain consciousness, but she was not responding. He looked over at Casey, who was also laying lifeless across from he and Terren. He crawled over to Casey to see if she was still breathing. He pulled her up and wrapped his arms around her, trying to get her to open her eyes. "Casey, Casey! Wake up!"

When Casey didn't respond, he scrambled back over to Terren, grabbed her in his arms, and tried to revive her. "Terren, Terren! Wake up!"

Terren didn't move.

August felt desperate. People were running towards them. Melissa came out of nowhere, shouting at him and pushing him.

"GET AWAY FROM MY SISTER!" she screamed, pushing him off Terren as she grabbed her into her arms.

August was in shock. He sat on his knees in the middle of the street, covered in the blood of the two loves of his life. He looked up into the sky, and started screaming.

He looked over at Terren and Melissa. He looked over at Casey who was laying there by herself. He crawled over to her and cupped her in his arms. He shook her again. "Casey, please wake up. Don't leave me. I … love … you …" he cried.

He continued rocking her. He could hear the ambulance humming towards them. "Hang on, baby. Everything is going to be OK. Just hang on." He softly slapped her face to try to wake her. She slightly opened her eyes.

"Casey, oh my God. I love you. It's going to be OK. Just stay awake. Talk to me. Say something."

Casey opened her eyes a little wider. Looked up at him and said, "Jesus."

Chapter Sixteen
Delivered

Three months later…

CASEY

I was dead. The doctor told me my heart stopped. If the ambulance had shown up one minute later, I wouldn't have made it. The bullet missed my heart by three centimeters. It got lodged into my back, so they had to rush me into surgery to remove it for chance that it could have moved towards my spine and possibly paralyzed me. They said I was in the operating room for six hours.

I woke up in ICU, attached to so many machines I couldn't move. As horrible as all that was, when I opened my eyes, my family was there. My mom, dad, Candice, Tate, and Aunt Caroline were all at my bedside praying for me. Their prayers worked, because three weeks later I was released from the hospital with the promise of a full recovery.

By the time I got out of the hospital, my parents had already cleared out my apartment and moved all my stuff back home. I never got to say goodbye to my place. After we left the hospital, we all went and got something to eat, and Bruce brought Daisy and Asia along. We had our last family dinner for a while, because they were moving to Atlanta by the end of the month, and we wouldn't see them again until Christmas. Candice looked great. She and Bruce were getting along so well. Half way through dinner, Candice got everyone's attention.

"I have an announcement to make," she said tapping her fork against her glass. "We didn't want to say anything until we knew Casey was going to be OK. But now that she is headed towards a full recovery we wanted you all to know, I'm pregnant! Bruce and I are having another baby and getting back together."

After all the turmoil that our family had gone through, this was the best news that we could have gotten. I was overwhelmed with joy. Not only had God saved my life, but he also saved Candice, and now he was giving our family another life. *God is so good.*

I sat in my room looking out the window. The last days of fall were here, and the trees had turned many shades of orange, red, and yellow to confirm it. I thought about how lucky I was to be alive to see another fall. I felt a tremendous amount of guilt that I couldn't say the same for Terren. She died on the operating table.

Her death hit me hard. It took me a long time to understand why God had taken her and not me. She was a mother of three, she had a new baby to raise, and now she was gone. I blamed myself. All she ever wanted was her family together. She'd asked me over and over to stay away from her family, and I didn't have enough self-control to give her that courtesy. Every night before I go to sleep, I say a prayer for her children. I pray that God sends them comfort and that they live a full happy life.

I believe God chose to deliver me, regardless of me being promiscuous, an adulteress, a chronic marijuana smoker,

a liar, and a cheat all because of my encounter with the Holy
Ghost when I was a child. We are taught in church that once
you have the Holy Ghost, he never leaves you. I believe the
moment I asked to be saved, God put purpose on my life,
and the Holy Ghost was there with me helping me through
my darkest moments. That's why I kept being called back
to church. God saved my life and made Terren a part of it.
Terren's life is a constant reminder to me to make the best of
this second chance that God has given me.

Tate poked her head through my room door. "Can I
come in?" she whispered.

I waved her in and smiled, happy to see her face. She
sat down on my bed, holding an envelope in her hand.

"I've had this letter for three months. I didn't know if
I should give it to you or not, but now I feel like it's not my
decision to make for you."

I looked at the letter strangely. She handed it to me.

"It's from August. He tried to come see you in the
hospital, but Grandpa went crazy and told him to never come
around you again. A couple days later, he waited in the parking
lot until he saw me alone and asked me to give this to you."

I took the envelope from her and stared at it. Tate stood
up. "I'll leave you alone," she said as she walked out the room.

I didn't know what to do. All these months went by and
I hadn't heard anything from August, and no one in my family
told me he came to see me. I didn't know what to think about
him. I slowly opened the letter. It was only one page. It said,

Dear Casey,

*I didn't mean to fall in love with you. We never had
a chance. Because of my choices, my children will
have to grow up without their mother. I'm not going
to insult you and lie and tell you I'm not hurting
over my wife's death. I am, and I wish it had been
me instead. I did love Terren. She was my first love.*

I didn't know how much I loved her until she was gone. I'm sick inside knowing that I drove her to her death. I'm writing you to let you know that I don't blame you, and I don't want you to blame yourself. I am the reason Terren is dead and you were shot. It's all my fault. I do love you, Casey. You were a breath of fresh air in my life at a time when I felt like I was suffocating. If we'd met at a different place and time, you would have been the one I married. But that was not in our cards. I'm sorry for not figuring that out before anyone got hurt. I'm taking my kids and moving to Maine with my mother. Hopefully they will be able to heal there, although I probably never will. I wish you a happy life and I hope that you find a man that can love you and only you. You deserve it. I love you Cay and
    I'm sorry.
    August

I stared at the letter and thought about his words, *I never meant to fall in love with you. We never had a chance.* He was right, but it was too late. All I could do now was forgive myself for the horrible choices that I made while I was with August and make sure that I never make those same mistakes again. One thing is for sure, I will never mess with a married man again. Too many people get hurt in the backlash. Adultery has to be the worst sin in the bible because it has the potential to lead to all the other sins: lying, stealing, coveting your neighbor's belongings—it's not showing honor to your parents, you're not honoring God, and it can lead to murder. I vow to God that I will never commit adultery again!

I looked at the letter from August once more, then I ripped it to shreds and threw it out the window. As I watched the small pieces of paper float slowly to the ground, I was ridding myself of August, of the past, and of all my shortcomings. God had delivered me from my wicked ways. He rebuilt me to have strength and wisdom like I've never known, and I was going to use this new power to be the best me that I could be. Not only for me, but for my friend, Terren.

* 9 7 8 0 9 8 5 4 6 6 4 2 8 *